T0370356

THE SIXTH COMING

RICHARD DONAHUE

authorHOUSE®

AuthorHouse™
1663 Liberty Drive
Bloomington, IN 47403
www.authorhouse.com
Phone: 1-800-839-8640

©2010 Richard Donahue. All rights reserved.

No part of this book may be reproduced, stored in a retrieval system, or transmitted by any means without the written permission of the author.

First published by AuthorHouse 7/23/2010

ISBN: 978-1-4520-2818-7 (e)
ISBN: 978-1-4520-2816-3 (sc)

Library of Congress Control Number: 2010910010

Printed in the United States of America
Bloomington, Indiana

This book is printed on acid-free paper.

CONTENTS

v

ACKNOWLEDGMENT

I would like to give thanks to the following folks – for having "hung tough" with me on my six – almost – seven year journey: First of all – my loving wife – Ischa - who never doubted me; Secondly – my dearest friend – Maxine – who patiently endured countless proof readings of my text; Thirdly – my great friend – Fred – without whom I would have been sorely tested to resolve the more complex political, religious and spiritual issues of my book. Lastly – I would like to thank my faithful four footed friends – Tessie and Corky – a Jack Russell Terrier and a Chow mix – who will forever live on in the embodiment of Gho'a and Cinnamon.

& THE TURQUOISE KINGDOM &

&& SUN DAGGER &&

The Golden Dagger sliced through the pale blue dawn – to pierce the silver whorls through to their cold stone heart.

The Stone Hauer awoke from his half dream - - - half muse - - - and - - - smiled.

It was the summer solstice and his work - - - the toil of forty long years - - - was close to perfection. Once the golden dagger of the solstice sunrise precisely pierced each of the nineteen silver stone spirals he would be free to return to his family and beloved land to the south.

He half-turned and gazed down from his vantage point atop the turquoise palace - - - deeply inhaling the sweet cool intoxicating darkness.

Vast forests of giant oak and chestnut - - - abounding with game for the taking - - - stood invisible in the grey dawn to the east - - - as did the wild inland waters - - teaming with the fruits of the sea - - - lay hidden to the west - - - taunting - - - mocking this proverbial bird in its golden cage.

As the Stone Hauer slowly cast his gaze around the close confines of his tower prison - - - his mind's eye caught a glimpse of the soft wisp of a fleeting shadow below. Slowly - - - but - - - oh-so-slowly - - - the faint silhouette of a shrouded form softly emerged from the swirling mists - - - to stand proud and motionless - - - in a direct line with the rising sun to the east.

In his mind - - - the Stone Hauer knew that he couldn't see her - - - but in his heart - - - he knew that she was there - - - the "Sun Maiden" - - - the eldest daughter of the "Emperor of the Celestial Blue Mountain" - - - and - - - royal heir of the "Empress of the Turquoise Waters."

Toward the west - - - Stone Hauer could hear the sounds of men stirring as they made ready for the day. They would be readying their boats for their daily foray into the rich fishing grounds of the ancient Glacial Sea.

The Stone Hauer savagely broke from his musings and became dead earnest.

It was time for action - - - action as fierce as the sun dagger searing its way through the flesh of the sleeping dawn. His race was against the speed of fleeting shadows - - - torn apart by a majestic sunrise.

He would not have another chance for another nineteen years.

He now had only seconds - - - not minutes - - - to fine tune the sun dagger - - - and - - - to bring the sun and moon calendars once again into perfect alignment.

As the sun slipped over the horizon - - - Stone Hauer's subconscious registered the wafting melodic chanting of the shrouded form far below - - - but - - - his muscles and mind were burning with the task of the moment before him - - - as - - - sinewy arms set his silver steel hammer ringing against the cold lifeless stone.

&& THE MORNING SONG &&

The Sun Maiden steadfastly gazed skyward - - - her gaze riveted toward the east and toward her mistress - - - the rising morning sun.

Her royal duty - - - as Sun Maiden - - - was to welcome her majesty from her long nocturnal slumber and to give thanks to her warming and healing rays.

As the infant dawn slowly stirred - - - the - - - Sun Maiden slowly turned and solemnly walked toward the sacred stairs leading upward to the sacred garden - - - as her guardian shadow burst through its renegade brothers and sisters - - - wayward vanguards of the night - - - with a vengeance.

Slowly and then explosively - - - the blue black sky burst asunder with a kaleidoscope of reds and purples as her majesty the sun shook off her shroud of darkness and stepped forward into the infant dawn.

The Sun Maiden was barely aware of the frenzied voices breaking their silence far above her - - - and - - - the shattering of stone against the unrelenting blows of the silver steel hammer driven by the Stone Hauer's sinewy arms.

She turned - - - as if in a trance - - - and - - - gazed upward - - - her long golden bronze hair slowly - - - shyly - - - lithely - - - following the arch of her graceful body.   The long dark archway seductively beckoned her - - - as her senses quivered at the fear of the shadows still so deep and void of light that nothing living could survive them.

Slowly and timidly - - - driven as much by feel as by sight - - - she reached the stairwell and hesitantly paused and let slip her Waiting Shroud from her shoulders:

Her bare back - - - free of the restraint of the silken fabric of her Waiting Shroud - - - warmed with the first caressing rays of the awakening sun - - - as her footsteps - - - dull - - - from the cold of the night - - - steadily warmed the cold stone - - - with each measured step.

The sun - - - kissed her daughter - - - and - - - threw her sun shadow into the abyss of the portal where it waged battle with the demons of the dark - and smote them down - - - with a fiery sword of light.

Chup-Kamui - - - she - - - who had once cherished the night - - - but - - - who now worshiped the dawn - - - gently quickened her pace as she trod the once - - - rough hewn steps - - - now - - - worn smooth by generations of silken slippers - - - slowly chasing her guardian shadow - - - as - - - she ascended to the Garden Level of the terraced palace - - -

Veiled hand maidens - - - still - - - in the warm embrace of their colorful waiting shrouds - - - held the flickering candles by which they had fended off the impetuous advances of the night.

One-by-one they embraced Chup-Kamui - - - and - - - then in unison followed her solemn steps to the great silver fountain - - - already - - - half encircled by a waiting assembly of the "other races."

The Sun Maiden paused - - - and - - - breathed in the fragrance of red roses and purple lilacs - - - as she tasted of the sweet early morning dew on her lips. As one - - - her hand maidens lifted their veils from their faces.

Chup-Kamui - - - first - - - with the handmaidens following suit - - - generously partook of soothing draughts from the silver fountain - - - as - - - the other races followed - - -

Southing Draughts - - - served in goblets of the most precious of stones: red rubies, green emeralds and blue sapphires and the most precious of metals: platinum and gold.

With the morning sky - - - now - - - in full celestial raiment - - - the solemnity of the moment - - - and - - - the dread of the night - - - was broken - - - with mirthful outbursts of joy and pleasure at the rebirth of creation.

We stand before thee once again - - -
   Alone in the cold dark dawn - - -
Patiently awaiting thine guiding light - - -
   To lead us from the deep dark places - - -
To thine Garden Door - - -

At thine beckoning we stir again - - -
   With footsteps timid as a fawn's - - -
Mortal senses quivering - poised for flight - - -
   Darting - - - pausing - - - leaving no traces - - -
Of the path we've wore - - -

We haltingly ascend once again - - -
   That secret staircase that spawns - - -
Placid pathways of pleasure and delight - - -
Unite us with thine garden graces - - -
   Of this - we thee implore - - -

Celestial light once again - - -
   From this wellspring have we drawn - - -
All are we equal of birthright - - -
   As we trod equal steps of equal paces - - -
As our forbearers of legend hoar - - -

We drink deep draughts once again - - -
   As night's shadowy veil is withdrawn - - -
We bid gleeful farewell to celestial twilight - - -
   And welcome in its stead smiling faces - - -
With this nectar have we all nightly oaths foreswore - - -

&& THE GLACIAL SEA &&
(THE WELTERING WATERS)

The Stone Hauer sat lazily in the sun - - - enjoying the bustling closeness of men - - - and - - - women.

He had crossed over to the mouth of the canal - - - which formed a harbor to a massive inland sea - - - born of the broken marriage of ice and cold eons ago - - - as - - - miles high ice dams far to the north - - - burst asunder - - - by - - - the - - - pent up passions of the retreating icen glaciers - - - explosively spewed forth a torrent of water so terrible and merciless that it slashed its way through rock and sky - - - until its passion spent - - - it lay exhausted and dying - - - at the foot of this very mountain.

Now - - - although now nothing more than a glacial pool - - - these ancient waters still fought to gain purchase on the unyielding rocks - - - only - - - to fall - - - time-and-time again - - - exhausted - - - back into the icy depths - - - to lay gasping and roiling in agony - - - until their strength - - - once again renewed - - - they attempted one more futile onslaught.

The Stone Hauer - - - seated - - - eyes fixed on the icy blue expanse before him - - - slowly drew several deep breaths - - - each breath - - - slowly - - - rhythmically - - - matching - - - the eternal lapping of the waves upon the shore.

Slowly - - - deliberately - - - purposely - - - The Stone Hauer - - - closed his eyes - - -

Eyes closed - - - The Stone Hauer listed to sounds - - - sounds - - - long forgotten - - - painfully - - - searching - - - searching his memory for their source and their meaning.

The constant chattering of maidens off to the market - - - was a sound not so easy to forget - - - even for one as old as he - - - but - - - other sounds were much more pervasive - - -

Pervasive - - - Ancient - - - Sounds - - -

   The quick rapid sniffing of a stray dog on the scent - - - searching for scraps of bait and fish hastily discarded from the returning fishing vessels - - -

   The creaking sound of a wooden winch - - - transferring cargo from a deep drafted sea-going vessel to a shallow horse-drawn river barge - - -

The almost too faint rhythmical sound of a mechanical chain-pump hoisting captive river waters to the uppermost terrace of the turquoise palace - - -

Captive River Waters - - - captive - - - being hoisted to the uppermost terrace of the Turquoise Palace - - -where - - - at the whim of a palace gardener - - - they would be set free to cascade down as miniature waterfalls - - - to shower mounds of flowering vines which chose to lazily overhang the palace walls - - - rather than to strive for the sun.

The Stone Hauer took a deep breath - - - holding it for a long slow count of ten - - - and - - - then - - - breathed it forcefully out through his nostrils - - -

The Stone Hauer - - - blowing memories forcefully out through his nostrils - - - purging - - - his mind of years - - - no of lifetimes - - - of forced labor and mental stagnation.

As the Stone Hauer forcibly exhaled the years of imprisonment from his body and soul - - - ancestral memories flooded his being - - - primordial memories of a time long before even his forbearers had been born.

Then slowly - - - subconsciously - - - childhood memories began to form and to rise to the level of his consciousness - - - warm gentle memories of the sun - - - and of the sea - - - and of his mother's smile.

Although still not fully yet registered in his consciousness - - - his longing spirit began to search this vast glacial sea for men of his own kind - - - and - - - for the massive sailing ships that would board him passage to the south and to his home and family.

As he slowly scanned the sea - - - searching for familiar silhouettes - - - he recognized at a glance the low slung silhouettes of the long ships from the north and the high top-heavy silhouettes of the swift boats from the south.

The long ships - - - long narrow austere ships from the north - - - sturdily built to withstand the harsh river ice and to navigate the sharply turning and twisting rivers - - - crudely and harshly fashioned from rough hewn planks of oak - - - quickly lashed together with a thick coarse hemp rope - - - then hammered fast to timbers with massive wooden dowel pins and finally sealed with a coarse black oakum - - - hemp rope heavily impregnated with tar - - -served as sturdy barriers against wave and storm.

The swift ships - - - brightly colored sailing ships - - - loosely fashioned of bound bundles of reed and rush so that not only might the sea might find easy passage through the hull but that the ship might also better find an easy passage through the sea - - - by brashly riding the crest of monstrous waves without fear of ever being swamped.

But strangely - - - he noticed - - - that the great and the small remained almost invisible.

There were the behemoths - - - giant lumbering barnacle encrusted barges - - - moving so slowly as to appear as great motionless islands of this inland sea - - - moving forests of lumber and mountains of stone to fuel the sometimes monstrous acts of manmade creation: towers and temples and tombs.

And there were the bobbing gnat-sized - - - coracles - - - circular skin boats of the hunters of water fowl - - - detected more by the exuberant sound of a successful hunt than by sight - - - loaded - - - to overflowing with geese and duck and swan - - - and - - - all manner and sort of water fowl save for the majestic blue heron - - -

For - - -

The Blue Heron alone was the sacred bird of the king.

But The Stone Hauer's searching eye - - - could not find that for which he was longing.

As the Stone Hauer stood and stretched - - - snapping his tendons back into place after too much inactivity - - - he returned his gaze and his thoughts to the docks - - - and - - - to the present - - - seeking to read the thoughts of those around him.

There was no doubt - - - that to the casual early morning market goers - - - on this calm and sunny day - - - the long ships - - - with a single sail and five oars to a side - - - seemed not crudely constructed - - but bespoke of a gentle life of sea breezes and favorable winds - - - begot of a lifetime of gentle sailing on a gentle glacial sea. But the Stone Hauer was enough of the world to know that while these ships boasted a crisp canvas sail with which to catch the morning breeze and a romantic notion of a market go-er or two - - - these long ships were for the most part blatantly austere.

But austereness like beauty - - - is in the eye of the beholder - - - for the Stone Hauer knew that for the old grizzled seafarers - - - long since reduced to repairing torn fishing nets - - - these long sailing ships were an object of scorn - - - for these men of steel - - - who had had their ancient spirits tempered in a baptism of blood and fire long before memory - - - were of a time and place where a man battled his way through life with courage and wit and did not have to depend upon a whimsical breeze to blow him to shore at a day and time of its own choosing - - - for these men - - - whose wayward lives had become as turned and twisted as the rivers that they loved - - - vehemently eschewed the sail for the oar and the cabin for the elements - - - showing an open and profound distain for those younger and softer than they - - - who had greedily and foolishly forsaken strength for comfort and had become emasculated in the process.

But enough of these long ships and men of twisted steel!!!

The Stone Hauer - - - once again - - - hopefully cast his gaze westward in the direction of his memories - - - searching for a mast and sail of a more gentle and enduring nature - - - that of a great sailing ship - - - which sought not to barricade its children from their mother sea and father sky with heavy planks and coarse black oakum - - - but sought - - - with reed and rush - - - to coax mother sea to gently rock her boat cradle and gently lull her children to sleep - - - where once asleep father sky could bear them away on soft warm breezes to the here-to-for unforetold lands of discovery and compassion.

As the soft lullaby of the gentle waves softly lulled his mind's eye to sleep - - - the Stone Hauer found himself as the happy boy-child he once was - - - wandering these self-same lands of compassion and discovery - - - innocently hand-in-hand with a girl-child - - - and as one with these children of the warm gentle seas.

The Stone Hauer slightly awakened at some distant sound - - - but - - - soon closed his eyes as he felt his worn spirit meld with the splintered memories of this ancient glacial sea - - - for he too was ancient - - - and - - - he too could remember the passions of his youth - - - and - - - the time when he had the power to grind rock into sand.

Again - - - in a half-dream - - - the Stone Hauer heard the distant and faint whirling of the chain-pump - - - and saw the glacial sea's one more futile attempt to escape the confines of its valley - - - willingly becoming the slave to gain the top of the mountain where perchance it might slip away unnoticed - - - as a gentle mist - - - to rain down amidst unknown adventures.

He opened his eyes - - - and - - - gazed back across the canal - - - at the palace prison from which he had just this morning - - - in all haste - - - departed - - - magnificent in its splendor - - - but terrible in its confinement - - - turquoise belvedere pinnacle against an early morning magenta sky.

Soft wisps of clouds serendipitously wafted in the sky - - - forming fleeting images of loved ones and childhood scenes - - - merging into faces and places - - - only to drift away again as with his fleeting thoughts.

Slowly inexorably cloud fragments coalesced - - - taking more of a solid form as faces - - - sweet maiden faces - - - took shape before his mind's eye - - - slowly coming to life - - - teasing at first by softly blowing into his ear as a warm summer sea breeze - - - then once lulled by promises of paradise on earth - - - shaking his entire being with a bone-numbing chill as a slight gale danced among the waves. As the sun burned once again through the clouds the maidens spoke with a burning command: "Free us mighty one - - - for - - - as your reward - - - you will be reborn and with your rebirth will come our freedom."

The Stone Hauer started - - - almost falling off of his perch - - - but - - - it was not the warm blue sky at which he was staring - - - but - - - rather the ice cold ancient glacial sea - - - and - - - not the magnificent palace bedecked with its over-hanging gardens of climbing vines - - - but - - - a piece of driftwood draped with seaweed.

Enough of this - - - snorted the Stone Hauer - - - I'm HUNGRY!!!

&& SOYALA &&

But let us now turn back from the Stone Hauer - - - and - - the bustling market place - - - to a time a few hours earlier - - - and - - - to a place - - - much more quiet and serene.

Let us turn back from the bustling harbor of the Great Glacial Sea - - - and - - - return to the Silver Gray Fountain - - - and - - - the Palace Gardens.

Chup-Kamui - - - the - - - Sun Maiden - - - paused - - - and - - - breathed in the fragrance of red roses as she tasted of the sweet early morning dew upon her lips. As one - - - her hand maidens lifted their veils from their faces. Chup-Kamui - - - and - - - then - - - the hand maidens - - - and - - - finally - - - the host of other races all partook of soothing quieting draughts from the silver fountain - - - served in goblets of the most precious of stones: red rubies, green emeralds and blue sapphires and the most precious of metals: platinum and gold.

> We drink deep draughts once again -
> As night's shadowy veil is withdrawn -
> We bid gleeful farewell to celestial twilight -
> And welcome in its stead smiling faces -
> With this nectar do we all nightly oaths foreswore -

With the morning sky - - - now in full celestial raiment - - - the solemnity of the moment was broken - - - with mirthful outbursts of joy and pleasure at the rebirth of creation.

As the revelry of the rebirth of creation escaped the closed circle - - - and wafted over the palace gardens - - - Soyala - - - the second and youngest daughter of the "Emperor of the Celestial Blue Mountain" - - - nestled cozily against the trunk of a great mossy oak - - - as she day-dreamingly munched on a golden fruit.

"Ah – Soyala - - I've found you" - - - chirped a pleasant voice. "Are you still chasing the stars at this early hour - - - or - - - are you spying on your sister???"

A slight smile coyly curled Soyala's lips as she imperceptibly turned and gazed at her brother - - - the Builder - - - bedecked in his usual finery - - - complete with plumed hat and velvet cape.

"Sister?" - - - - Soyala replied - - - "Oh - - I hadn't really noticed - - - after all - - - why spoil such a beautiful morning?"

"Come - - - sister - - - I'm hungry and breakfast is impatiently waiting for us!"

"You are impatient for breakfast - - - you mean! Come brother - - - I'll race you to our table below!"

Before her brother could reply - - - Soyala stood up and lazily stretched - - - nonchalantly balancing herself on the great gnarled bough upon which she had been laying - - - and - - - peered down to the terraced gardens fifty feet below.

"Come - - - brother" - - - she said mocking her brother - - - "our breakfast is getting cold!"

With that - - - she leaped - - - sensually paused in time and space and thought - - - before - - - knifing sharply downward towards garden pool - - - long raven black hair streaming behind her - - - as - - - her brother scrambled for the stairway leading to the lower terrace and then the path leading to their special breakfast nook.

Soyala cleaved the deep blue water with barely a froth of spray and dived deep into this man-made pool - - - enjoying its serene cool clarity. She arched gracefully upwards and broke the surface - - - with a rain-bowed spray showering her head like a great jeweled crown.

With a few quick strokes Soyala reached the edge of this azure pool and with one fluid motion - - - was on her feet - - - - crystal clear droplets magnifying each individual muscle fiber of her striated golden brown body - - - as she shook the water from the long lustrous hair - - - which proudly reached to her mid-back.

As - - -

Soyala - - - pulled her soft emerald green kirtle over her head - - - to let its folds fall gently to her ankles - - - she smiled - - - for the day was indeed beautiful - - -

Emerald Green - - - and - - - fashioned from a soft cotton fabric - - - her soft cotton dress was tastefully trimmed with a rich red fur - - - and - - - embroidered with the delicate form of a wistful hummingbird - - -

Even as Soyala turned into the morning - - - her snood - - - an exquisitely fashioned jeweled hair net - - - glistened in the morning sun - - - dew drop sized amethysts vying for brilliance and sparkle with the tiny jeweled water droplets still nestled amongst the strands of her silken black hair - - -

As - - -

Her bother - - - stumbled along beside her - - - panting from his mad dash down the palace stairs - - - he - - - as was his habit - - - sought to divert attention from the fact that she had - - - once again - - - beaten him to the lower level: "Ah little sister - - - the day bodes well for your sister - - - for with this year's summer solstice she shall come of age to become our High Priestess!!!"

Soyala blushed slightly and whirled to face her giant of a brother: "Ah little brother" - - - a shared joke between the two twins - - - for - - - she was the older of the two - - - "what brings you here at such an early hour to talk of YOUR sister? Should you not be now resting and dreaming of all those hearts you have broken with your smile and soft blue eyes?"

The Builder feigned a scowl - - - and - - - lifted his twin off her feet so that he could stare her in the eyes: "But sister" - - - he said with mock pain and embarrassment - - -"How can I think of - - - let alone dream of - - - anyone but you? Besides" - - - he said - - - as he gently lowered her to the green grass carpet beneath her feet - - - "I have a very fine surprise for you - - - this especially fine morning!"

&& THE GROTTO &&

Soyala twirled with feigned shyness - - - then fixed his laughing eyes with a piercing gaze: "Surprise? A gift - - - perhaps?? Perhaps a mountain palace - - - far to the north - - - to be shared with Khangard - - - King of the Birds!"

"To the north? FAR to the north?? A feathered nest in the sky???" - - - The builder astounded - - - "but if I were to send you away to a northern palace I should die of loneliness - - for I should but scarce see you anymore." At this thought - - - he was genuinely sad - - - but he soon regained his mirth. "But come - - - try harder - - - my gift must be somewhere close - - - for - - - I do intend to see your smile each and every day. Come little sister - - - please try and guess my gift to you - - - for unless you guess soon - - - you shall already be upon it!"

Brother and sister had begun to slowly walk along the foot stoned path - - - to the breakfast area - - - where they have spent their mornings together since childhood - - - the builder chirping as merrily - - - over bridges and escarpments - - - as the indigo and scarlet tanagers - - - just awakening from their nighttime slumber - - - chirped over their sweet repast of golden nectars. Soyala lost in thought - - - startled slightly as she rounded a shrub veiled bend - - - her broken thoughts stumbling into a grotto - - - beautifully sculptured from the living stone.

"Wh - - - wha - - - what is this?" she stuttered. "This is beautiful - - - no - - - this is impossible - - - no - - - no - - - this is impossibly beautiful!!! But - - - But - - - How?" - - - the words trailed off never to leave the tip of her tongue.

"Surprised little sister?   The builder beamed with amusement and pleasure at his twin's stammering and sputtering - - - for until now he had NEVER seen her at a loss for words! "Come let us breakfast - - - I'm hungry!" - - - he teased.

"Hungry? Breakfast? You're ALWAYS hungry and you're ALWAYS eating! Besides - - - who can think of food at a time like this? At times - - - you're impossible!"

"Yes - - - impossible - - - it is indeed impossible to do the impossible - - - unless one is truly impossible - - - don't you agree - - - Sister?"

Soyala - - - mouth agape - - - just stared at the magnificence before her. What had been a cozy sheltered nook the day before - - - shielded from curious eyes by its cloak of mountain mosses and creeping vines - - - had - - - overnight - - - magically transformed itself into a splendor of sculpted stone and polished gems. Hanging ferns and flowers had seeming sprouted by moon glow to grow out of sculpted nooks & crannies - - - some cleverly fashioned as a dancing maiden's hand basket - - - others mimicking velvet carpets of delicate ruby reds and moss greens.

"But how? When?? There was no time. . Just yesterday - - -" stammered Soyala to her bemused twin. "How could you have - - - or - - - am I still dreaming???"

The Builder reveled in this moment - - - and - - - savored his twin's - - - for sure - - - all too brief loss for words.

"Little sister - - - you are both dreaming and awake - - - for - - - your dreams ARE my command. But look closer - - - a little bit closer and tell me what you see - - - for - - - we are still shielded from the sun and the shadows are many."

Soyala peered first into one shadow - - - then another - - - and then yet another - - - and audibly gasped: "But - - - no - - - this is truly impossible. That which I thought impossible was but child's play for one as clever as you - - - but what is now before my eyes is truly impossible - - - for all save a Shaman!"

There - - - hidden - - - by the last of the fleeing shadows was an archway - - - flanked by two turquoise maidens with baskets bursting to overflowing with bite sized burgundy grapes and fist sized purple plums - - - was an entrance to a grotto - - - or - - - were her eyes deceiving her in that it was it still only a teasing shadow masquerading as a door to unknown pleasures?

But no - - - it was no shadow - - - for as the shadows softened and wore thin with the advent of day - - - they slowly shredded into thin taters of blue velvet fragments only to be whisked away in the soft morning breeze.

Soyala stood transfixed - - - as if one of the stone maidens - - - mouth agape - - - eyes flitting from one disappearing shadow to another. Broken - - - shattered - pieces of stone - - - slowly assembled themselves into a ruby red half moon - - - which quickly waxed into orbs of gold and gemstones. Shimmering slivers of gold grew downward from the shadows to firmly root themselves in the polished stone floor - - - where once having gained purchase - - - they quickly sprouted upward as intricately molded golden legs to gently cradle a fiery gemstone seat - - - burnished to a rich red luster by tireless hands. Giant pillows as white and fluffy as billowing clouds - - - cushioned the back of this ethereal couch - - - to bridge the golden earth to an azure sky - - - which slowly - - - almost coyly - - - slipped out of the shadows - - - to lay itself down as a watery reflection of the earthly fire.

Still further retreated the shadows - - - retreating to a point where Soyala thought there afforded no more sanctuary - - - when - - - the sun – annoyed with the shadows' grudging pace of retreat - - - burst forth to seize her realm from the obstinate night - - - and - - - in one blinding flash revealed the true magnificence of the Builder's gift.

For as quickly as disbelieve evaporated - - - curiosity grew to overwhelming proportions as Soyala darted to the archway of the vaulted room.

"May the ring which was sundered yet become one" - - - she amazed.

&& The Gift &&

The builder smiled and sat down on one of the polished turquoise benches - - - and - - - eagerly attacked the mounds of scrambled eggs, roasted bacons and toasted breads set down before him by one of Soyala's hand maidens. His view of food was that of the god's second most precious gift to man – the first being a maiden's smile.

He was happy.

The sun was shinning - - - the food was beyond his wildest dreams - - - and his sister was the happiest he had ever seen her. Yes - - - nothing could spoil this eternal moment.

All was peacefully silent - - - save for the tempestuous tanagers and the soft mummer of the garden waterfall. Soyala was serene with her inner song and the Builder was deeply immersed in his thoughts - - - quietly struggling to decide whether to next attack the hams or the sausages - - - when - - - much to his surprise - - - and - - - later regret - - - he blurted out in between mouthfuls of sausages and eggs: "I really think that our sister will truly enjoy this place - - - don't you agree - - - Soyala?"

Soyala flashed red - - - and - - - whirled around to face her brother - - - pounding the table with her fist with such force as to make the jars of honey madly dance out of her way:

"What? She'll enjoy?? What do you mean - - - 'She'll enjoy?' placing her face but inches away from her brother's - - - as she continued: "You mean - - - that - - - you have built - - - this - - - this - - - place - - - for Chup-Kamui to enjoy??? You have taken MY garden - - - away from me - - - to - - - to - - - give to YOUR sister?!"

The Builder - - - who - - - although dimly aware of his own words - - - most certainly heard those of his sister. As her words slowly transmuted into thoughts - - - the burden of searching for words of salvation and redemption while trying to swallow a mouthful of melted cheeses and scrambled egg became overwhelming.

As he began to sputter forth both broken words and broken yolk - - - and - - - then to hem and haw - - - desperately searching for one word then another to string together into a coherent sentence - - - he - - - stammered: "Happy? No. Your Garden?? No - - - I mean - - - yes - - - I mean - - -

"Yes - - I mean no - - no - - - I mean - - - yes - - -

14

"What I mean - - - he sputtered and stammered - - - "What I mean is that if she were here she would most certainly like this garden - - - but - - - she isn't here - - - is she - - - I mean that if she isn't here - - - she can't like this garden - - - because - - - she hasn't seen it - - - and - - - if - - - she hasn't seen it - - - she can't like it - - - can she?

"Yes - - - that is what I mean - - -

"Understand? - - -

"No - - - I don't know what you mean - - BROTHER! The question is: Do you know what YOU mean - - - BROTHER?

"Do you wish you were having breakfast with YOUR sister - - - here - - - now - - - rather than having breakfast with me? Do you rather that SHE have this garden as her own - - - rather - - - than me? Soyala asked frostily - - -

"Explain yourself - - - brother - - -

"No - - - -no" stammered the Builder - - - wondering which was worse - - - the fiery inferno of rage - - - or - - - the icy cold of scorn - - -

 He cautiously continued - - - having forcibly cleared the last remnant of scrambled egg from his throat: "Slowly sister - - - slowly" the builder responded - - - one question at a time - - - or else you'll give me indigestion!!!" sputtered the Builder gasping for breath and grasping for words.

"You'll not live long enough to ever have a chance to develop indigestion - - - for I'll give you no peace with which to dab your fork into your smoked meats and cheeses until you answer my questions!" - - - retorted Soyala.

A look of true anguish flashed across the builder's face - - - as he pitifully looked at the tables piled high with his most favorite of favorite breakfasts - - - quickly followed by a cringe of pain as he looked at his much smaller - - - but - - - fiercely determined sister.

"My simple gift to you - - - is - - - this grotto - - - for - - - it is yours.

"Your most beautiful gift to me - - - is - - - simply - - - your being my beautiful sister.

"Our gift to each other - - - is our breakfast table - - - together - - - the - - - bounty of nature laid before us - - the - - - meats - - - and - - - the - - - cheeses - - - and" - - - as - - - his voice began to trail off with a hint of melancholy - - - and - - - desperation - - - "the - - - breakfast wines" - - -

Deflated of ego and mirth - - - the Builder shrugged his shoulders and sighed: "Sister - - - I mislead you - - - but not by intent - - - but - - - by misword."

As - - - he hastily added. "I had meant to say that I - - - as you - - - find this place - - - this moment - - - beautiful - - - and - - - that I wish to share it with no one - - - but - - - you - - -

"That is all - - -

"Continue" - - - coolly replied Soyala - - - somewhere in between fiery inferno and frigid scorn - - - still not entirely buying his logic.

"Sister" - - - continued the builder - - - no longer sagging so visibly - - - but still casting wanton glances at the banquet table - - - "have you not forgotten that with your sister's having come of age - - - each of her brothers must give to her that which becomes his craft and which his craft commands?

"Likewise have you not forgotten that just as our sister will become the Sun Goddess of the Summer Solstice - - - you - - - will become our Maiden of the Winter Solstice in but naught six month's time?"

"I'll have nothing to do with the ancient superstitions" replied Soyala.

"But none-the-less sister" said the Builder - - - frantically eyeing the hot steaming mounds of food - - - which were quickly becoming as ice cold as the ardor of his sister - - - "I simply obey our father the Emperor."

"So – brother - - - you build a gift - - not for me - - - but for my father?"

"No - - - no - - - I meant to say that this Grotto is not for our sister - - - built at the order of our father - - - but that what you see here - - - I have built for you - - - for - - - I did not desire that you to be wanting of a gift - - - when - - - your - - - I mean - - - my sister - - - was to receive so many."

"Yes - - - that is it" - - - The Builder smiled - - - as the words began to flow more freely - - - and - - - the hope of salvation of his breakfast appeared near - - - very near - - - at hand.

"Yes - - - I did not want you to be wanting of a gift - - - upon - - - your sister's receiving so many gifts from all of us - - - so - - - upon reflection - - - I came upon the happy thought of building this gift especially just for you - - - for - - - this - - - gift - - - my - - - gift - - - has been commanded of me by no one - - - save by your smile.

"You do remember how to smile - - - don't you - - - sweet sister?"

The Builder sensed a softening in Soyala's eyes and chanced a smile - - -

Smiling - - - even the more - - - as - - - he - - - sensed a renewed salvation - - -

Salvation - - - not only of his honor - - - but - - - also - - - salvation - - - salvation of that magnificent specimen of a smoked pork sausage - - - rescued from the smoke house just this morning - - -

Smoked Pork Sausage - - - smoked - - - finely - - - exquisitely - - - smoked - - - to a deep dark savory red - - - for weeks on end - - - with - - - cord upon cord - - - of - - - sweet aromatic cherry wood - - -

&& The Minstrel &&

"How sweetly he sings! If only I could turn his song into verse!!!" - - - burst forth a voice as melodious as the sweetest warbler. "Look - - - he is singing to his nest mate - - - I think - - - or - - - perhaps singing to the flowers so that he might entice them to share their sweet nectar blossoms with him.

If I could but find one as lovely and kind as you dear sister - - - I too would have my nest mate and sing to her all the day long."

"Dreamer!" teased Soyala - - - "You would sing and forget to eat - - - until you were but the wisp of wind to be blown this way and that by the flutter of a butterfly's wings. Come with me and I'll show you a nest of butterflies - - - all waiting to sing sweetly to you!!!!!"

"Dreamer indeed!" - - - Echoed the Builder - - - not in the kindest of fashion. "If we all were to dream as you - - - we would still be living in hollows in the ground - - - ringed by but a few stray rocks rather than reaching into the sky and enjoying the magnificence and splendor you see here before you! Why - - - you are so short that your legs barely reach the ground - - - no wonder that you cannot see into the sky!"

The Minstrel turned on his short dwarf legs - - - feigning a quizzical look - - - with a wit far from being short: "Ah - - - The Smasher of Stone has awakened?" - - - Queried the minstrel as he plucked a plum from a turquoise maiden's basket. "He leaves behind crumbs on the table as easily as he leaves behind mountains smashed into shards. His belly is as full as his head is empty. What knows the Maker of Shards of the delicacy of a blossom - - - let alone the affairs of the heart?"

"Sister" - - - flustered the Builder - - - "pay no heed to him. What I have built here - - - I have built here for you and no other. As a child - - - you had such sweet dreams here - - - that I thought that it would serve you well - - - as - - - our Priestess - - - to dream sweet dreams of our peoples' destiny. Smile dear sister - - - as we smiled as children - - - so that our people will smile at the sight of you. As the Three become One - - - may your smile and laughter become one with our destiny. What say you my sister - - - let me see you smile a smile and let me hear you dream your dreams."

Soyala turned to her twin and was about to speak when the Minstrel's words stabbed to the heart: "How can she sleep - - - my dear brother - - - let alone dream for you have torn away her bed of sweet soft mosses upon which she lay her dreams - - - and - - - pillow of gentle green grasses upon which she lay her smiles - - - and - - - cast in their place the assassin of dreams - - - cold dead stone! It would do us well to keep our feet firmly planted upon this sweet gentle earth - - - before we dared to reach to the unforgiving sky!"

"Sister - - - pay no heed to him - - - for he flits this way and that - - - (and) - - - (is as irritating as a gnat) - - - - he mumbled under his breath.

"Come - - - Let me show you one last delight - - - one last - - - impossibility - - - that - - - which I have had carved into the LIVING stone - - - Our chronicle as a people - - -

"Our Chronicle - - - dating back into our earliest beginnings - - - dating back into the time before the one ring was sundered.

"May these stations - - - Stations of Remembrance - - - help you to remember - - - remembering our history - - - as a people - - -

For - - - by remembering our history as a people - - - you - - - will be better able to divine our future - - - and - - - to lead and guide us - - -

"Come - - - Let me show you - - -

With these words - - - the Builder took his sister softly by her hand and gently guided her to the entrance of the grotto: "Sister - - - please - - - gaze upon our history - - -

"The Grotto is my gift to you - - - sweetest sister - - - for - - - The Stations of Remembrance are the inheritance of our people.

Soyala gently took her brother's hand - - - and - - - spoke: "Little brother - - - being here - - - with - - - you - - - now - - - being with you - - - here and now - - - has made me very - - - very - - - happy. My only wish is that all of my days could be as happy as this one."

She was about to speak further when both were startled by the blast of a hunting horn.

&& THE FISHTAKER &&

The Stone Hauer paused - - - and - - - inhaled deeply - - - filling his lungs with the brackish air. Yes indeed - - - it was good to have escaped the confines of the turquoise prison - - - and - - - to venture back into the world of men again.

The market place - - - bounded on the north by the vast inland sea - - - stretched between the harbor canal and the broad shallow river to the east.

All was alive - - - for the market - - - fresh and vibrant - - - echoing with the calls of the vendors hawking their wares - - - for this was the hub of commerce for all lands north and south - - - east and west.

There were the fishtakers - - gaunt and lean - - - from the east - - - hauling giant sturgeon to the smoking sheds - - - great gray wooden monoliths standing stark against the magenta morning sky.

There were the Mammoth hunters - - - hulking smelly beasts of men - - - from the north - - - with their stores of ivories and gargantuan woolly pelts.

There were the seed and nut gatherers - - - lithe and nimble - - - from the west - - - roasting giant chestnuts as big as one's fist - - - along side the smaller and more delicately delicious pinion nuts.

Then there were the weavers - - - so colorfully clad as if to taunt indecisive bazaar goers to not choose between fabrics and patterns at all but to buy all that they see.

Finally there were the tent dwellers - - - selling all what may be sold - - - whether it be flesh - - - fiber - - - or - - - fantasy. Around their wagons there was scarce order or calm. All sought their wares - - - The Fishtakers sought their hooks & nets - - - The Hunters bartered for bows & arrows and dried fruits - - - The Seed & Nut Gatherers dealt grains for baskets & flasks and smoked meats - - - The Weavers - - - swapped the stuff of dyes: the red madder - - - blue woad - - - and - - - yellow weld. Yes indeed - - - the tent dwellers were the sellers of the ordinary and the purveyors of the extraordinary: the much sought after red carmine dye - - - colorfully hawked as "The Blood of the Dragon - - - but - - - in actuality made from the ground remains of the diminutive female cochineal beetle - - - Karaku Pelts of unborn lambs - - - torn from the bodies of mothers in their death throes - - - silky and with a luminous sheen - - - by which to make the hats and furs of the vain and beautiful - - - silky albino pearls whitened in the breast milk of a virgin (or so they say) - - - all made all the more desirable after a drink or two of the bubbly wines served with a kiss and the sparkling laughter of their raven haired dancing beauties - - - long lustrous hair beckoning festive merry makers to partake of but one more sweet drink and to share in one more even sweeter smile.

And then again - - - there was the Stone Hauer - - - rippling with muscle and sinew as if carved from granite - - - towering above all save the tallest of the mammoth hunters - - - but yet moving with a grace second - - - (perhaps) - - - only to the trio of tumblers skillfully somersaulting their way through the crowd - - - his taut skin bronzed and with his jet black hair flowing down beyond his shoulders.

"Hey Great One!" a voice boomed in the Stone Hauer's ear - - - "You look as if you could eat a whole red sturgeon by yourself - - - so - - - you can surely pleasure yourself with but a few of my grilled delicacy here!"

The Stone Hauer wrenched himself from his daydream musings and turned to see a pleasant smaller man - - - one of the tent dwellers - - - proffering several smelts - - - grilled to crisp golden perfection - - - skewered on a stick.

"Come Great One! Try several of these - - - they'll be but a mouthful for one as mighty as you!!!"

The Stone Hauer smiled. Yes - - - he was hungry. "Great One" - - - he mused. In the turquoise tower - - - he was the "Worker of the Stone" or the "Hammer who Sings" - - - but never the Great One!

"Purveyor of the Fishes - - - I have met many such as you - - - with silver tongues - - - who in the twinkling of an eye and a slight of hand - - - can coax a weary traveler's gold from his purse to yours - - but - - - their manner of speech is but base metal as compared to your golden verse."

The little man beamed at the compliment.

"Okay - - - Persistent One of the Golden Tongue!" he roared. "I'll try several of your tasty morsels - - - if you can point me in the direction of the Grain Grinder and the Butter Churner - - - so that I might exchange my gold for all that is golden: your golden fish and the golden grain of the grain grinder and golden butter of the butter churner!!!"

The smaller man - - - eagerly handed over the fish and snatched at the gold. Here in the land of barter gold was scarce to see.

"Great One - - - many thanks. You can find your golden grain - - - finely baked into glorious golden loaves not but two hundred paces in the direction of that copse of trees - - - and - - - your golden butter lies not another five paces further - - - for indeed - - - the grain and the butter are as lovers and should not stray too far from one another - - - is that not true?" The merchant smiled - - - and - - - with a mischievous twinkle in his eye added: "And if you stride but some one hundred paces further still - - - in the direction of that great purple rock - - - you'll find the distiller of the golden grain - - - for his gift to us is the gift of the golden sun - - - a pure golden amber that will warm your bones as well as any maiden on a cold winter's night."

As he intently listened - - - the Stone Hauer - - - inhaled the seven golden fishes in the twinkling of an eye. "Oh - - - Golden Tongue of the golden fishes - - - might you tell me where I might find some golden lodging on this golden day?"

The little man smiled and proffered yet another seven fishes to the Stone Hauer - - - who waved them aside.

"Yes - - - The Inn of the Sky Maidens - - - a most curious name since the maidens one finds there today are - - - thankfully - - - very much down to earth!" he said as he playfully jabbed the Stone Hauer in the ribs and gave him a wink. "But this is but a name of old and many folks today may not remember her proper name - - - since both local and wanders hereabouts call her "The Widow's Walk" - - - so - - - you must ask for The Widow's Walk."

"The Widow's Walk - - - the Stone Hauer mused. How came The Inn of the Sky Maidens to be called The Widow's Walk might I ask?"

The merchant shrugged his shoulders: "Legend has it - - - she became her name after the occasional poor fishtaker's wife - - - who had thrown herself from its lofty heights upon learning that she has become widowed by the mistress sea - - - who - - - through lies and promises had seductively lured her fishtaker husband to her bed and claimed him for her own."

His face grew somewhat melancholy at some distant thought - - - but - - - then radiated mirth as he turned to the Stone Hauer: "Yes - - - the Widow's Walk will be a fine place for you to spend the night - - - because if I guess right - - - your passion is for more than heaping mounds of food - - - or - - - soft cotton cushions - - - but rather all that is golden. Yes - - - all that is golden - - - albeit that the gold be that of the finest golden STRAW of the stables - - - dancing amidst the glistening golden tresses of a sweet stable maid!!! He laughed at his own joke - - - and - - - then seconds later suddenly remembered the immensity of the giant standing next to him.

The Stone Hauer's face darkened - - - as the merchant cringed and took a step backwards - - - and then burst into laughter at the blanched face of the merchant: "Ha - - - mirthful one - - - two can joke as well as one!"

The Stone Hauer then turned - - - and - - - amicably ambled off in the direction of the copse of trees pointed out to him by the seller of the seven golden fishes.

&& BATTLE OF THE RODENTS &&

"Ah - - - there you are sister!"

The speaker was a lithe muscular fellow - - - bedecked in a dark loden green tunic – hunting horn in hand.

He moved quickly - - - but - - - silently - - - from the shadows and blew once again on his horn.

"Brother - - - Why such a racket? You would as if you were waking the dead!" asked Soyala.

"I must inform my charges that I have found you - - - and - - - that they have but moments to make all ready for we are already on our way to the forest. Come - - - hurry - - - for the day is half gone - - - and - - - we have a long ride ahead of us - - - or have you forgotten?"

"No - - - I haven't forgotten" - - - said Soyala as she continued to move toward her breakfast table - - for in the excitement - - she still had not eaten a bite - - - "but the day is still young - - - we still have time - - - and - - - I still haven't eaten a bite of breakfast! Besides - - - our brother is waiting."

"Let him wait!" - - - Impatiently replied the Hunter - - - "For he has let many a maid waiting for him at HIS pleasure."

At the sound of voices - - - The Builder rose from his table - - - sausage skewered on his fork - - - and - - - peered through the tangle of morning glory vines - - - and - - - in the direction of the voices as if to seek its source. As the Hunter quickly moved toward his sister - - - his keen eye espied his brother builder first: "Ah – Brother Razer of Mountains and Leveler of Forests - - - how do you do this fine morning?"

"I am here to enjoy MY breakfast with MY beloved sister - - - at OUR leisure - - - of course!" - - - replied the Builder. What brings you here - - - you moss coated scarecrow? Aren't you a little bit out of place - - - here - - - among civilized people - - - among those of us with manners - - - and - - - among those of us who have bathed in pools scented with rose petals - - - and - - - not taken mud baths in the swamps?"

"Not at all - - - not at all" smiled the hunter - - - skewering a juicy sausage - - - this one lightly smoked with pear wood - - - the next intended victim of the Builder - - - hoisting it on the tip of his dagger - - - and - - - waving it before the Builder's pleading eyes: "Not at all dear brother - - - for Soyala and I intend to breakfast on nature's bounty and in the presence of an intelligent squirrel or two and not a gibbering chipmunk!"

With these words - - - the Minstrel - - - "He-who-was-too-short-for-his-legs-to-reach-the-Ground" - - - danced into the middle of the group: "Ah - - - I see that I've disturbed the battle of the rodents - - - the chipmunk and the squirrel - - - how refreshing - - - for I was much afraid that I might disturb some boring battle between two lovers - - - each extolling the virtue of his favorite flower - - - a wild swamp orchid or a cultivated perfumed rose perhaps?"

 "Ah sister" continued the Minstrel - - - not waiting for any reply from either of his two brothers - - - "it is always a joy to see you - - - although I can't understand why you always seem to surround yourself with these two."

"Chipmunk?" - - - roared the Builder - - - "why you green moss-covered scarecrow . . . "

"Now brother" - - - replied the Hunter - - - you know that you steal from everyone. You steal the farmer's fields - - - and - - - drain the fowler's march - - - and . . ."

With this - - - The Minstrel - - - who had been silently sitting cross-legged on the morning banquet table - - - strategically placed halfway between the smoked meats and the toasts and jams - - - spoke - - - his mouth stuffed full of a mixture of blackberry preserve and toast: "Ah - - - self-righteousness is always refreshing to see at dawn's light - - - for we know not what shadows move by the dark of night. All claim to have been wronged by the other when the simple fact of the matter is that Nature loses to the Nature Lover. The Nature Lover loses to the Hunter. The Hunter loses to the Grower of Crops - - - and - - - the Grower of Crops loses to you dear brother - - - the Builder.

"It seems to my simple mind at least - - that you lose to no one - - so you should complain the least! In fact – you should rejoice!"

With this the Builder turned angrily toward the Minstrel and charged the table - - - only to find himself indignantly sprawled in the middle of assorted breads and pastries - - - for the minstrel - - - being as quick of body as of mind - - - had nimbly jumped aside. As the Builder lunged once again - - - for his cat-like brother - - - he slipped and sprawled on his back. As he grasped the table top - - - to pull himself to his feet - - - he succeeded only in catching the lip of a large pot of jam - - - which obligingly showered him with the most delicate of mixtures - - strawberry jam flavored with a hint of rose petals.

This was too much for the Hunter - - - who quipped: "Ah - - - so this is how you - - - dear brother - - - keep your skin so soft and silky - - - by bathing daily in rose petal jams!!!"

Then the Minstrel - - - never to be outdone - - - quickly - - - but from as great and as safe a distance as he could manage - - - sprinkled crumbs of breads upon his hapless brother: "Brother – would you like some bread with your jam?" He then quickly disappeared before his bravery got the better of his common sense and before his giant of a brother regained his feet.

Amidst the commotion the Hunter gently grasped his sister's wrist and began to lead her off - - - with her not protesting too greatly: "Come sister - - - we are off - - - the day awaits us."

The Builder - - brushing jams and breads from his cloths stammered and stuttered: "But - - - but - - -"

"No 'butts' - - - dear brother - - unless you'd like to 'lend' me that butt of a smoked ham I saw earlier on your table - - - besides - - - you won't mind if I kidnap our dear sister for an hour or two?"

"I know your hour or two - - - more like a day or two - - - or - - - more probably - - - even a week or two - - - if I'm not careful!" - - - stammered the builder as he searched in vain for his smoked ham. But his words were lost as the hunter hustled Soyala off through the pathways to the stairs leading to the lower terrace - - - where sheltered in an archway their two mounts - - - one jet black and the other snow white - - - stood stamping their feet and impatiently waiting.

"I've already saddled Silver Cloud for you - - - since she is your favorite. Besides - - - she is as anxious to be underway as you should be. Your riding cloths are here - - - safely tucked away in the corner. Come - - - let's hurry - - - because there is something that I would like to show to you. The great herds are underway - - - and - - - if we hurry - - - we'll be able to spot them - - - before they ford the river. I know that they're your favorites."

"With the quickness of a cat - - - he took bridle in hand and sprang into the saddle. Not to be outdone - - - Soyala ducked behind a wall and donned a sleekly fitted - - - dark loden green top and bottom riding outfit - - - smartly accented with burgundy cloth trim - - - her long brunette hair flowing - - - carefully tied into a pony tail with a strip of burgundy cloth."

"Well - - - brother. How did you manage to "conjure" up so pretty of a riding outfit - - that fits my body and spirits so perfectly - - - Soyala beamed?

"Ah - - - Sister - - - We must all have our secrets" smiled the Hunter - - - as he eased his mount into a walk down the winding path to the lower levels.

Soyala - - - not to be outdone by her older brother - - - facing frontward and swinging her leg for momentum - - - vaulted sideways into the saddle - - - without touching a stirrup - - - and - - - was soon following the hunter down the winding path - - - across the courtyard - - - and - - - through the massive stone archway.

The Hunter turned slightly - - - as he called over his shoulder: "Come sister - - - hurry- - - we have a fair day's ride ahead of us - - - if we wish to reach the bluffs by nightfall - - - for we have had a late start. If all goes well - - - we should reach our garden glen the day after tomorrow - - - and - - - be able to return in two weeks hence.

"But would I ride with you the whole day long - - - every day - - - and spend every night in our secret sanctuary - - - gazing at the three rings and traveling to our evening star - - - as we did as children. I wish that we could live these moments again – dear brother."

"I too - - - sister - - - I too - - - were it not for duty. Sadly we all have our duty."

Brother and sister slowly rode down the winding path leading from the terraced gardens thru the back gate of the palace and set their mounts at a comfortable gait - - - as the sun slowly rose higher in the sky and the hours gently passed.

It was early afternoon when the Hunter and Soyala came to a gentle rise on the bluffs overlooking the Great Plains: "Look sister - - - spoke The Hunter - - - "Indeed - - - the great herds are beginning their migration. Tomorrow we will ride among them!"

There - - - stretched before them - - - covering the vast plain like a massive shaggy blanket - - - as far as the eye could see - - - were the herds - - - grazing as they went - - - great rust colored males forward and to the flanks - - - guarding the much smaller females - - - which in turn guarded their young with their living bodies.

"But brother" - - - spoke Soyala - - - "We cannot ride among them - - - for - - - the beasts all know you and run from you."

"They run not from me - - - laughed the Hunter - - - but - - - from the tip of my spear - - - for they know it well!

"Then it is as I feared - - - I would not that they see me with you - - - for - - - they are as my children - - - and - - - I would not that they fear me for fear of you"- - - replied Soyala.

"I will do as you command - - - dear sister - - - laughed the Hunter.

"Well - - - dear brother - - - if you are at my command - - - I wish with dawn's awakening to ride straight forth to our island - - - so that we might spend our precious moments - - in the present - - - embraced with sweet memories of the past."

"Done!

"But - - - let us tarry in this spot for but a few moments longer - - - for our camp site is just on the other side of this bluff. Besides - - - we pose no threat to them from this distance. We are downwind and are specks to them - - - for although their sense of smell is keen - - - their eyesight is weak."

As they again rejoiced at the sight of the great herd - - - Soyala spoke: "You have made me most curious dear brother - - - for - - - what sort of gift might a Hunter give to me - - - especially what gift takes another two - - - or - - - three day's ride to reach?"

"Ah - - - sister - - - patience - - - for - - - you will soon see. You will soon see."

Quiet in thought - - - brother and sister spurred their mounts into a canter - - - and - - - soon crested the ridge of a small hill. As they journeyed further along the plain toward more rugged country - - - gently sloping plains gave way to intermittent geographical irregularities such as an occasional small canyon ringed with jagged cliffs. After a short while - - - brother and sister paused their mounts - - - as an excuse to give them breath - - - but - - - in reality to give themselves pause - - - once more - - - to drink in the spectacular panorama laying before them.

It was not long before the hunter espied - - - in the distance - - - a flock of wild peacocks - - - with a male in full plumage vainly strutting before his hens.

"Look sister - - - we are about to see a lesson that should serve us well. Cast your gaze toward that clump of brush to see what will soon arouse our feathered friend's interest."

No sooner had he spoken - - - when - - - abruptly - - - from that very same clump of brush - - - arose a challenge - - - a second plume - - - not as spectacular as the first - - - either in size or color - - - but a challenge none-the-less. The cock was not to be intimidated - - - especially by a supposedly younger and decidedly much smaller rival - - - so he let loose a series of guttural clucks as warning and placed himself between his hens and his rival.

Still the rival did not budge from his clump of brush - - - but - - - curiously and slowly moved forward - - - only tail showing - - - for - - - so short was he that his head did not even clear the grass.

Still the cock stood his ground - - - for if his rival wished a battle - - - there would most assuredly be one - - - and a royal one at that!!!

With a series of threat displays - - - he ran quickly and menacingly toward his rival - - - in a staccato series of clucks and a showering display of iridescent greens and purples and reds.

There was scant two meters between the cock and his rival when - - - grass and leaf exploded as a snake-like blur grasped the cock in razor sharp jaws and two clawed arms and quickly ended his life.

As the mime briefly paused to quickly survey his surroundings before dragging his prey into the safety and security of the brush - - - by which to enjoy his meal in leisure - - - he folded in his feathered tail and raised himself to his full height. He was indeed two legged and as tall as the peacock - - - but in his hunting crouch - - - had been bent over - - - head almost touching the ground - - - almost invisible in the tall grasses.

"Ah - - - sister - - - see? Our strutting friend has met his match - - - for all that seems smaller and insignificant is not necessarily so. If only our Brother Builder Peacock were here to see this - - - perhaps we would be more careful before whom he clucks and before whom he struts!!!"

It was but a short distance when they crested yet another hill along the bluffs - - which afforded both a panoramic view to them - - -of the jagged country stretching out in every direction as far as the eye could see - - - and - - - a leeward shelter for the night.

"Ah - - - look sister - - - how beautiful - - - how peaceful. Would our brother Builder to have his way - - - he would tear down the mountains and in their place build cold lifeless stone towers, temples and finally tombs - -- surrounded by funeral fires for the living - - - fueled by oak and ash slashed from the living body of our great green forests. I would not want to live to see such a day."

"Brother - - - See?" Soyala excitedly exclaimed - - - "Off in the far distance just to the other side of these canyons - - - where those mists rise? There lies our secret forest. Would I that we were already bedded down there for the night."

 "My heart is with you sister. I too wish that at this moment we were laying our weary heads upon beds of soft green moss rather than an outcropping of rock - - - but come sister - - - follow me - - - for but a few paces further we shall find our camp for the night. We'll have a spring for water - - - and dine royally on some pilfered treats - - - courtesy of our brother" - - - as he spoke he drew the roasted ham from his saddle bag - - - "and whatever Nature's bounty chooses to provide for us!"

Soyala - - - not to be outdone - - - laughed: "While not from Nature's bounty - - - I have likewise a small tidbit or two - - - courtesy of MY breakfast table!" With that Soyala – pulled two small baked breads - - - one rye - - - and the other - - - a heavy dark bread - - - from her saddle bags.

Sister – we have the makings of a feast! Let us not waste any time.

As the Hunter finished hobbling the two mounts - - - so that they could forage on their own - - - he busily began gathering goat chips for fuel and heat - - - as Soyala prepared their camp site in the lee of an outcropping of rock - - - facing the east - - - under a blanket of stars. Their pillows were small flat stones - - - padded with their saddle blankets.

As they divided the meats and breads between them - - - and soothed their throats and spirits with sips of cool clear spring water - - - the Hunter leaned back and inhaled deeply: "Freedom" - - - sister - - - "Freedom!" How many of our brethren cover their heads nightly with their blankets and have never yet seen a star singing across in the sky? Freedom sister - - - that is what I crave! Freedom."

With these words - - - he was sound asleep - - - not even having had time to draw his blanket around him.

As Soyala gently kissed his sleeping eyes and drew his blanket up around him - - shooting stars flashed overhead - - - dancing among the luminescence of the three celestial rings - - - a fiery display as if the heavens were rejoicing at the return of their children.

&& THE WIDOW'S WALK &&

The Stone Hauer paused and glanced over his shoulder at the turquoise palace - - - now so distant that it could nestle in the palm of his hand - - - and - - - felt a slight shudder rack his whole being. He clenched his fist crushing the fading visage - - - and - - - shook himself as one breaking the shackles of forty years imprisonment.

He turned and tugged at the wrought iron ring to the massive oaken door of the Widow's Walk.

The sound of music and mirth greeted his ears long before his eyes accustomed themselves to the darker enclaves of a vast room. Roughhew oaken timbers - - - which - - - no six men together could embrace - - - firmly rooted in the floor - - - grew dizzyingly skyward to branch out into the heavy paneled sky ceiling.

Smaller columns - - - supporting several lofts and sleeping rooms - - - and a massive stairwell - - - were decorated with delicately carved vines - - - heavily laden with grapes. Maidens - - - each more beautiful than the other - - - danced among the spreading spiraling vines - - - baskets overflowing with the round red fruit of the harvest - - - simple barter for the strong red wines - - - dark crusty breads - - - and - - - sweet cheeses they had left behind.

Lines of fishermen - - - home from the long day's adventures - - - jostled at the bar as each tried to outdo the other with tales of the monster fish that got away.

The Stone Hauer sought out a small enclave - - - and - - - wearily sunk down into its shadows - - - to quietly study the world of men - - - and - - - women - - - to which he now belonged.   He inhaled deeply - - - savoring the sweet pungent smell of tobacco and the soft pine wood shavings which covered the floor.

"Hello sir" a soft sparkling voice danced into his ear.   "What is your pleasure tonight? We have roasted mutton swimming in its own juices - - - and - - - sweet sea bass - - - poached in the juice of limes - - - gently cradled in a bed of steamed sea greens. "

The Stone Hauer started - - - unaccustomed as he was to the company of others.

He looked up into the most beautiful sparkling eyes he had ever seen.

"Sea greens? Sea Bass?? Poached sea bass you say???" He stammered - - - not quite sure how he should answer. He hadn't had to choose his meals for so long - - - that - - - he had forgotten how. And sea greens - - - such a commoner dish as to be shunned by the lords of the turquoise mountain - - - but such a long forgotten delicacy that he had almost forgotten the word. "Sea greens - - - yes - - - sea greens and poached sea bass! And a great loaf of black bread. I should like that very much. And a beer. No two beers!!! Two great dark beers and a flask of your house specialty. Yes - - - that is what I'd like. Mounds of sea greens and one great fish - - - flesh flaking from the bone - - - one big enough to cover this table! And - - - and - - - reds - - - if you have them - - - a great heaping pile of sea reds!!! "

The bar maiden smiled at the voracity of the giant sitting before her - - - and - - - in a twinkling she was gone.

The Stone Hauer was hungry - - - hungry for food and drink - - - music - - - and - - - merriment - - - and - - - most of all - - - freedom.

The Stone Hauer drew a deep breath and closed his eyes. To him - - - it was still a half dream that he would not have to spend the night imprisoned on the turquoise mountain. He savored the sensations now flooding his body - - - the pungent smells of strong tobacco and roasted mutton - - - the clamor and jostling of this strange admixture of peoples and languages - - - the colors: Ragtag Travelers simply clad with sun bleached remnants of clothing now devoid of any color - - - Merchants gaudily displaying their wares & wealth - - - and - - - Simple Seamen wearing their telltale seaman's hat and vest. Then there was the satin smooth sensation of the once rough hewn bench and table at which he now found himself seated - - - now polished to a mirrored patina from countless years of use. No more days and nights of velvet cushions and silken sheets plying their wiles to seductively rob a man of his strength and his wit!!! This was the life to which he was born.

He had no sooner begun to study the varied figures around him - - - to his left - - - a slip of a maiden serving great mugs of frothing beer to boisterous sailors - - - to his right - - - a stout fellow - - - no doubt an adventurer from the north - - - judging from the sinewy rippling muscles seeking to bust their way through his taut bronze skin - - - when the Stone Hauer found himself enveloped in a whirlwind of activity.

Two knaves appeared - - - struggling under the weight of a great wooden platter heaped high with steaming sea greens - - - softly cradling a giant of a sea bass.

Hands appeared from nowhere - - - piling his table high with mountains of black breads - - - pouring frothing flagons of dark beers - - - and - - - tapping miniature flasks of clear spirits distilled from all sorts of delicious exotic fruits.

And last - - - almost forgotten in the mounds of food and drink before him - - - was a bowl of steaming sea reds swimming in a delicate broth - - - beckoning him to partake but a little before he delved into the main course.

But the Stone Hauer was not to be denied or dissuaded. Even before the food had been laid upon the table - - - the Stone Hauer attacked. Loaves of dark breads were torn in two - - - and - - - mounds of sweet succulent fish were crammed into a cavernous maul - - - to be washed down with deep draughts of dark beer. Giggling bar maidens scurrying for the shelter of the distant enclaves quipped that they had been lucky to have escaped with their lives.

The clear spirits - - - while subtly hinting at their earthly origins - - - the soft amber of the pear spirits and the mellow burgundy of the plum spirits - - - were indeed heavenly divine. Indeed it was not too long before the Stone Hauer's spirits too began to soar heavenwards.

As he contemplated the large toothed head and white glistening bones laid out before him - - - he spoke: "Well fish - - - it seems that you and I have fed on the same worm - - - you on the worm and I on you who fed on the worm. But I was luckier than you - - - I was able to wriggle off MY hook!"

"What say you fish???!!!" As the Stone Hauer intently mused what response the fish would properly give - - - he was dimly aware of a brawl in a distant corner - - - or - - - perhaps it was a simple exchange of ideas - - - such as occur daily at the communal table of simple folk who live and die in the same house in which they are born. A burly dark bearded man - - - veins throbbing in his neck - - - shook his fist at a small thin twisted man - - - whose broken body bore the scars of a lifetime of labor.

"Woman?! That is no woman! It can't be - - - no one - - - man or woman - - - could sing that sweetly - - - it is the goddess herself - - - I know not which one - - - but - - - Goddess She must be - - - either of the Moon - - - or - - - of the trees - - - but - - - a goddess for sure - - - for - - - no mortal could sing that sweetly!"

The Stone Hauer smiled - - - the world of men. How simple were they - - - down here on the hard clay earth - - - far removed from the cloud towers of the turquoise mountain. Far enough removed from the heavens to believe that the stars were singing to them - - - sometimes in the morning and sometimes in the evening - - - not knowing or even imagining that it was a human voice they were hearing - - - and - - - not only a human voice but the same voice - - - Soyala's sweet voice - - - when on rare occasion - - - she thought no one could hear - - - she took it upon herself to sing of the ancient songs of praise to the morning and evening stars - - - to the Goddess of the Trees and of the Streams and Rivers - - - for - - - these were ancient loving god/desses - - - not the indifferent vain gods worshiped today.

The Stone Hauer leaned back - - - the food and drink warming his veins - - - and - - - quieting his spirit - - - gently coaxing his fluttering eyelids to close but for a moment - - - a long moment.

He was content. Tomorrow he was going home.

He lazily cast his gaze upwards toward the Sky Panels.

His eyes - - - now accustomed to the soft glow of the great room - - - could now easily discern what his light blinded eyes upon entering couldn't. Hmmmm - - - he thought - - - Sometimes one needs to move in the shadows to see more clearly by the light of the day. "Yes - - - yes - - - beautiful - - - very - - - very beautiful indeed."

The Sky Panels. Each individual panel - - - exquisite in detail unto itself - - - formed but a part of a complex whole - - - synergistic in its effect - - - growing from the deep rooted oaken columns to gently arch into the canopy of a vast vaulted ceiling - - - oaken columns that were more than columns. The Stone Hauer could now see that the massive oaken columns - - - which had appeared rough hewn to his light blinded eyes when he first entered - - - were anything but crude. They were sculpted in the forms of beasts and beings which were strange to the Stone Hauer. Great twisting winged serpents - - - with heads like fanged horses - - - half-risen from the sea - - - glided among the massive vines of a jungle canopy climbing into the sky. Small painted faces - - - eyes wide open in fear - - - peered through the scant shelter of giant leaves at the awesome toothed beasts. Others searched frantically skyward in the faint hope of celestial salvation - - - thin arms stretched heavenward. The Stone Hauer leaned back - - - his eyes and soul searching for the same salvation. Then he saw - - - what at first appeared to be thin wisps of clouds - - - slowly take human form - - - as puffs of cumulus clouds on a warm summer day slowly take the shape of loved ones before the searching eyes of a weary traveler. The delicate faces above were gentle - - - full of love - - - wispy garments concealed helping hands which reached lovingly out to the canopy top. The Sky Maidens. The Stone Hauer had heard of the legend of the Sky Maidens - - - they who gave birth to the very soul and being of the first ones - - but - - - until this very moment had never visualized their being.

Some ancient artist's trick — no doubt. The Stone Hauer shrugged his shoulders and shook his massive head as if to awaken from a dream. "Sky maidens. First ones." The Stone Hauer grunted and shook himself again - - - and - - - turned to that delicacy which he had been saving for last. The sea reds - - - swimming in a burgundy broth. The Stone Hauer grabbed the silver bowl with his two massive hands and slowly - - - deliberately - - - lifted the great bowl to savor its delicate aroma - - - inhaling deeply. He then gently lifted the bowl to his lips and ever so slowly - - - and - - - then methodically - - - began demolishing the last remaining remnants of his great feast. This sight - - - of the Stone Hauer at work - - - was not for the faint of heart - - - and - - - would cause all but the most hardened adventurers - - - to quickly lose their appetites and to bolt for the door!

As the Stone Hauer wiped his mouth with the back of his hand - - - he studied his face in the great silver bowl: "Not bad. Not bad at all - - - a little older - - - but - - -not old. More character I'd say - - - Handsomer - - - yes - - - to be sure - - - handsomer - - - a fine handsome character!!!"

As the Stone Hauer tilted the bowl - - - to catch the reflection of his face from every angle imaginable - - - he started. A face of exquisite beauty flashed and then burned into his consciousness. He was as one transfixed. His mind and body were on fire. He couldn't move - - - speak - - - think. A woman's face - - - a sky maiden's face - - - reflected in the great silver mirror of the great bowl - - - began to speak - - - to - - - entice - - - to - - - beckon - - - not in words - - - but - - - in thoughts - - an eternity of thoughts and pleadings in the passing of moments.

Then another face - - - then - - - yet another - - - and - - - a second voice - - - then - - - a third - - - then - - -

A firestorm of swirling faces - - - chased round and round the room by a chaotic choir of voices - - - burst as a whirlwind into the Stone Hauer's consciousness - - -

All - - - merging into one searing command - - - one passionate plea: "You must never leave this place - - - nor - - - your son - - - nor - - - your son's sons - - - until the coming of the sky burst and the arrival of the white stone canoes.

You must save us!!!"

The next words - - - if there were any - - - were lost in eternal blackness.

&& BREAK OF DAWN &&

The dawn lazily awoke - - - still snuggled warmly in its thick fleecy comforter of burnt orange clouds - - - as the Hunter shrugging off the shivers of a brisk mountain night - - busied himself kindling a fire to first warm his spirits and then his breakfast - - - as his sister still slept soundly.

His Fire Piston - - - made of a rich lustrous red-maroon wood - - - streaked with yellow - - - soon yielded a glowing ember which soon brought life to the slivers of aromatic spice woods he had gathered from the mountain top.

His oven was rudimentary - - - but effective - - - two holes - - - each two-hands-breadth - - - burrowed into the ground - - - connected by an underground passage. One hole to allow both fuel to feed the flame - - - and - - - the air with which to fan it - - - and the other sheltering the flickering flames over which to prepare a mouth-watering mountain feast!

Soon - - - two spitted mountain quail - - - rubbed with mountain sage - - - slowly roasted - - - as a pan of bannock - - - a thick rich unleavened bread - - - slowly baked - - - top side before the flames - - - on its flat stone serving platter.

As the hunter laid down his fire piston - - - he marveled - - - once again - - - at the simplicity of its construction - - - and - - - the efficiency of its mechanism. Simple in design it was made of two cylindrical pieces of wood - - - one a solid wooden piston - - - the other a closed end hollow wooden tube. To make it work was simple enough. Tinder - - - in this case - - - dried moss - - - was placed on the hollowed end of the piston. All one had to do was to force the piston into the hollow tube as hard and fast as possible - - - and trust in the packing wrapped tightly around the end of the piston to compress and thereby heat the air trapped inside the cylinder. If all went well - the air thus heated would instantly ignite the moss tinder to a red glowing ember and in a few scant moments thereafter one could soon enjoy the delicate aromas of roasted meats and baked breads.

Long before he had obtained this mechanical marvel from a distant and lonely traveler - - - through a simple barter of ermine skins - - - he had had on more than one occasion to make use of his wit and skill and stubbornness to simply survive until the morning - - - even having resorted - - - on occasion - - - to fashioning lake ice into a lens by which to focus the warming rays of the sun onto a pile of life sustaining twigs and mosses. Would he have had this simple tool long ago - - - he could have been at least assured of a bit more of a comfortable stay in the distant and frozen wastelands he had traversed in his youth.

Without a doubt - - - this fire piston was - - - next to his bow - - - his most cherished possession - - - for if one had food and shelter - - - and warmth - - - with but nothing more than a flick of the wrist - - - one could do anything!

Soyala began to stir as the smells of breakfast wafted in her direction - - - first opening one eye - - - then closing it and opening the other - - - for the effort of opening both at once - - - seemed to be a bit overwhelming.

"Tea - - - sister?" queried the Hunter - - - "brewed fresh from the most gentle and succulent buds of the wild roses which abound thickly here."

Soyala inhaled deeply of the aroma - - - as her half dream imagined her for a moment to be buried deep within the palace gardens - - - smothered by prison walls of climbing roses. "Yes - - - yes indeed! I need something to rid myself of this night chill."

"Nothing better than a Rose Tea - - - on a rosy morn!" - quipped the Hunter.

As Soyala sipped her tea - - - the hunter busied himself portioning the breakfast between himself and his sister - - - and - - - serving the sumptuous repast on stone platters - - - setting his creation proudly upon wind blown polished granite tables - - - as - - - the rising sun gently kissed the majestic splendors of nature awake - - - to softly lay crevice and canyon and creature in an unbroken panoramic view at their feet.

The breakfast was enjoyed in silence - - - for neither dared to speak for fear of breaking the magical spell of this eternal moment.

As the shadows grew shorter and threatened to disappear - - - the hunter stirred: "Soyala - - - it is time that we break camp if we wish to make our river crossing before nightfall."

&& THE GREAT HERD &&

Brother and sister slowly rode down the bluffs - - - not wishing to hasten their departure from this mountain paradise.

As the ground slowly leveled - - - they could hear the pebbles - - - kicked loose by their steeds' feet - - - slowly come to a rolling stop.

The Hunter spoke: "Soyala - - - we will skirt the herd - - - so as not to startle them and then strike north to our island."

"Very well brother - - - very well."

As brother and sister spurred their two steeds forward - - - one as dark as the darkest thunder cloud - - - and - - - the other as white as the purest snow blanketing a mountain top - - - they slowly moved into a living sea of flowing grass. Soyala had but to reach out her hand to stroke it - - - so high was it - - - as she dreamed its sweet fragrance of prairie flowers and golden grasses - - - and felt the mother sun kiss her willing cheek.

Sweet childhood memories of golden seas of grasses filled her being with a bliss long forgotten - - - as pungent smells and course grains gracefully gave way to sweeter perfumes and gentle flowers.

Lost in time and thought - - - Soyala startled as a piercing screech split the air.

From seemingly nowhere - - - a giant eagle - - - wings flashing golden in the sun - - - dived at the herd below.   Again and again - - - he dived - - - until the herd scattered in panic. The great males attempted to form a circle around the females and young - - - but the terror of the young was too great and some broke ranks to flee for their lives - - - or - - - so they thought - - - but in actuality - - - they fled straight to their deaths - - - as - - - talons pierced hide and sinew and crushed bone and skull.

The mother cried in agony at the loss of its young - - - but - - - the great herd - - - knowing the hunter eagle to be ready to gorge - - - and - - - to be soon satiated - - - serenely continued their eternal march toward the river crossing.

As the eagle began to tear flesh from its victim - - - The Hunter spurred his mount to a trot in the direction of the kill - - - with his sister following hesitantly behind.

"Sister - - - if I'm not mistaken - - - that is Golden Arrow. I raised him from a nestling. Let's see if he'll share his breakfast with us!!!"

The Hunter slowed his mount - - - as he neared the giant eagle - - - and hailed him: "Hail Golden Arrow - - - it is I - - - Kajika - - - your father. Remember me? Will you share your breakfast with us?"

As Thunder Cloud screeched his challenge - - - it passed by the Giant Eagle virtually unnoticed - - -

As The Hunter dismounted and gave his reins to Soyala - - - both steeds snorted their mistrust of the giant eagle. "Hold tight sister - - - for we do not want predator to meet predator - - - at least not so early in the morning. I'll go see what Golden Arrow is willing to share with us - - - for my hunger is great - - - and hopefully his hunger is not a great as mine!"

With these words - - - he moved forward toward Golden Arrow - - - who was jealously guarding his kill - - - a giant flightless bird which although still a chick - - - was easily twice as tall as a man - - - wingless - - - and covered with great shaggy feathers.

"Golden Arrow would you like some help with your kill - - - for - - - he is indeed as large as you - - - so - - - that you might take a great share back to your mate and your children?" With that the Hunter drew his dagger - - - and - - - with Golden Eagle's taciturn approval - - - deftly sliced through hide and sinew - - - and - - - severed a giant leg - - - alone as large as a grown man - - - loose from the carcass - - - nimbly moving out of harms way as it thudded heavily to the ground. The giant eagle screeched his approval and thanks - - - grasped his bounty in his mighty talons and happily flew towards his nest and his mate.

Come sister - - - before Golden Arrow returns - - - we must quickly care for our mounts and take a small prize for ourselves - - - for he might favor feeding his children over our feeding our bellies. With that the Hunter began slicing off fist sized chunks of flesh - - - which he tossed to Silver Cloud and Thunder Cloud - - - both of which snatched the proffered pieces in the air and quickly swallowed these tidbits whole.

Soyala gently stroked the feathers of these two giant birds - - - his jet black and hers snow white - - - and - - - checked the fastenings for the saddle and bridals - - - and cinched all firmly.

Meanwhile - - - the Hunter was busily securing delicate breakfast morsels from the great flightless bird for himself and his sister - - - slices of liver - - - and - - - of heart - - - and - - - of the breast and thigh flesh. These he carefully rubbed with salt and preserving spices - - - wrapping each morsel separately in dried moss - - - which he then rolled carefully in a soft piece of supple leather - - - which he then carefully stuffed neatly into his leather saddle bag.

As The Hunter began to mount Thunder Cloud - - - he stopped abruptly - - - and - - - with an afterthought and a smile quickly dismounted. As he deftly drew his hunting knife - - - he spoke to a distant speck in the eastern sky: "Ah - - - Golden Arrow - - - my friend - - - would that I could visit - - - for just a while - - with your nest mate and your children - - - so that you and I together could teach your children hunting - - - as I had taught you. I miss you my friend."

With these words - - - and - - - a few deft strokes of his razor sharp blade - - - he severed the second massive leg of the chick as a gift for his giant friend and then quickly mounted Thunder Cloud - - - for he knew - - - that although his friend Golden Arrow was but a returning dot in the eastern sky - - - it would be but a few more moments before he would return to reclaim his prize from Thunder Cloud and Silver Cloud with a vengeance - - - for - - - although he was but a speck to the human eye - - - his eagle eye was easily already able to discern each minute movement of these two predator birds and their two human masters - - - and - - - the prize was his - - - not theirs!!!

With one last soulful glance at Golden Arrow - - - Kajika sprang astride Thunder Cloud - - - and - - - without a word to his sister - - - soon set his mount at a trot in the direction of the more rugged terrain more than a day's ride ahead.

&& DANCE OF THE LION KILLERS &&

As gently sloping plains gave way to intermittent geographical irregularities such as an occasional small canyon ringed with jagged cliffs - - - Thunder Cloud - - - and - - - then his smaller nest mate - - - began to revert to their wild nature by gliding over the smaller crevices which were becoming more and more frequent as the vast plains reluctantly yielded to deep fissures running across the landscape.

As the landscape continued to become more and more savage and broken - - - Thunder Cloud and Silver Cloud began to likewise yield to more primitive urges - - not entirely broken by bridle or stirrup - - - as their motion became fluid and relentless.

The hours passed as the sun climbed high in the sky - - - as both riders reached the crest of a hill - - - which afforded a most spectacular view of their goal on the distant horizon - - - a vast plateau - - - shielded by fog and mist - - - held prisoner by the two forks of a raging canyon river.

Soyala had turned toward her brother and was about speak - - - when the still of the moment was broken by the sound of a deep booming rat-a-tat rat-a-tat-tat answered by a lighter triller rat-a-tat rat-a-tat-tat - - - as Thunder Cloud became rigid and froze.

As both riders simultaneously turned - - - they saw before them - - - not a hundred yards distant - - - two magnificent male Crested Lion Killers in full plumage - - - each strutting before a covey of drab colored hens.

"Brother - - - they are beautiful. They are as of our Silver Cloud and Thunder Cloud - - - but more magnificently plumed. I have never seen them in the wild - - - or ever imagined them to be of such beautiful plumage - - - although I have heard stories told by travelers."

Their plumage rivals even the iridescent ruby reds and sapphire blues of our most precious gemstones - - - and their rising and falling emerald crests are simply beyond description! See how they sway their heads in time to their own music! How beautiful. Are they dancing for their wives?"

"Soyala - - - these are the wild ancestors of our mounts - - - and not many survive in the wilds these days. They have not yet learned the civilized ways of the dance. They are fierce and of an uncontrollable nature. Even our Thunder Cloud - - - with his fierce nature - - - would not last but seconds against either one of these fiery champions - - - for - - - their wills and senses have not been weakened by generations of pampering at our hands. Sister - - - be prepared - - - for what you are about to witness is anything but a chivalrous dance for their ladies' pleasure."

Soyala stared transfixed as both cocks slowly circled each other - - - heads gently swaying in time to their rat-a-tat rat-a-tat-tat display calls. It was almost as if in a slow motion fist fight between two human champions – who having been exhausted by too many blows - - - wearily lean into each other's arms seeking a moment's rest. However – this lull was all too brief and all too deceiving - - - for as the intensity of their display calls increased in frequency the pitch fell from a high staccato rat-a-tat rat-a-tat-tat to a deeper and more menacing rat-a-boom rat-a-boom-boom.

Their combs - - - which has risen and fallen with each display - - - were now flushed full of blood and passion - - - and burned bright emerald green against the barren yellow landscape.

The displays were over - - - now it was dead earnest. The older cock - - - winner of such battles past - - - was careful and methodical.

However - the younger cock - - brazen in his contempt for the older of the two had his sights fixed only on the waiting hens - - a prize not yet won.

As he brazenly strutted his utter contempt for his aged opponent - - - and - - - raised his head in one more brazen display of full plumage and cresting - - - for what he presumed to be his harem already won - - - the older cock - - - blood surging - - - locked his crest in full display and with one great arching movement of his massive head - - - driven with the power of his muscular legs - - - in a movement almost too swift for the Soyala's eye to follow - - - sliced off his opponent's head.

As his headless body continued to kick up small clouds of dust - - - the reality that death had severed head from body and had forever silenced his mating call - - - had not yet penetrated the dim brain of the suitor - - - for - - - he still continued to mouth his rat-a-tat rat-a-tat-tat as his eyes rolled in the direction of the hens - - - vainly searching for the harem which had already departed with the victor.

Brother and sister - - - each absorbed by the violence and beauty of what they had both seen - - - spurred their mounts forward - - - and rode in silence toward the still more rugged country lying before them.

Hours passed as they finally crested the last and highest of the hills - - - which afforded yet another panoramic view to them of the landscape they had just left behind - - - and even more spectacular and more magnificent than the last - - - of the jagged country laying before them - - - stretching out in every direction as far as the eye could see.

"See - - - off in the distance - - - where those mists rise - - - lies our secret forest - - - just to the other side of these canyons. It is best that we make camp here for the night - - - because although not far - - - we still have the most dangerous part of our journey before us."

As the morning mists slowly began to rise - - - Kajika and Soyala were already mounted.

"Ah - - - look sister - - - how beautiful - - - how peaceful."

"I feel as one with these mountains - - - old - - - somehow ancient - - - and - - - enduring."

"It always pains me sister - - - to think - - - that would our brother Builder to have his way - - - he would tear down these mountains and raze these forests - - - for - - - he would in their place have naught but cold lifeless stone towers, temples and finally tombs fueled by fires of oak and ash slashed from the living body of our great green forests."

"Even as I speak - - - it feels to me as if he were - - - bit-by-bit - - - tearing flesh from my living body - - - and - - - slashing great gaping wounds in my eternal spirit."

I would not want to live to see such a day - - - sister - - - when our mountains and forests are reduced to rubble and bare naked earth."

"Nor would I - - - brother - - - nor would I!"

"Come sister - - - follow me - - - we have not far to ride."

With that - - - Kajika gently spurred Thunder Cloud and was soon off at a quick trot toward the canyons separating the rugged terrain from the river plateau - and the vast forests toward the east.

The morning was cool - - - and the ride was pleasant.

It was not long before both Kajika and Soyala took pleasure in soaring their mounts over the broad deep canyons which crisscrossed the end of the plains and the beginning of the river forest - - - impassable for any horse or creature less sure footed than a mountain goat.

Soyala - - - who had been able to ride almost as soon as she could walk - - - was one with her mount which was one with her namesake - - the silver clouds above - - - as Soyala's long lustrous raven-hair streamed out behind her.

It was not long in the making before both noble creatures could sense a great race was in the making - - - as they made their crest feathers flat and fought each other for the lead. Soon - - - Silver Cloud - - - slightly smaller - - - but much quicker took the lead toward the siblings' secret forest glen - - - with Thunder Cloud running and gliding as a dark shadow of his smaller but more determined and fierce nest mate.

With Kajika laying low on Thundercloud's massive neck - - - the landscape blurred into the sky and back again - - - as Thundercloud - - - determined to catch and surpass his nest mate - - - launching himself blindly into space with a spring of his massive thighs and then kept barely aloft by the short staccato beats of his stubby wings - - - wound an undulating and hairbreadth glide over the lesser canyons - - - crisscrossing the landscape.

The race was short - - - with the preordained outcome known to all - - - save Thunder Cloud.

As Thundercloud - - - with Kajika astride - - - gently glided to Soyala's side - - - Kajika - - - eyes aglow and skin flush with the excitement of the chase - - - laughingly dismounted - - - for it was an established fact that defeat is only in the mind of the vanquished and it was assuredly Thunder Cloud - - - and not he - - - which had lost the race.

43

Likewise - - - defeat is only a state of mind - - - whether it be for man or bird - - - for Thundercloud - - - as he glided to Silver Cloud's side - - - gave the most perplexed of all human emotions - - - refusing to acknowledge that she could have possibly beaten him

Soyala stood quietly on the precipice of the Great Riverside Cliff - - - as hundreds of feet below - - - frenzied frothing waters waged eternal battle with the Great Gorge - - - violently seeking to escape the prison of these great rock walls.

Just to the other side of the Great Gorge rose the Red Rock Plateau - - - likewise held prisoner for an eternity between the two forks of the seething angry waters. Locked in mortal combat - - - the Red Rock Plateau at first vied to escape - - - by burrowing its head into the clouds - - - but thrice failing and in total desperation - - - began - - - surreptitiously disguised as red mud waters - - - to throw itself grain by grain over the precipice of the falls - - - where it might - - - perchance - - - transcend this existence and reincarnate itself as a quite river shoal - - - far beyond the destructive madness of these ranting and raving waters.

Soyala turned - - as a slight breeze shyly kissed her cheek.

As Thunder Cloud began to preen his nest mate - - - Kajika laughed aloud again: "It appears as if your Silver Cloud has won the day once more - - and - - - that Thunder Cloud has already forgotten his loss and is doing his best to make Silver Cloud to forget her win!!!"

Soyala smiled a half-smile - - - and - - - once again turned toward the Great Gorge - - - eyes misting at the sight of the frothing depths below - - - for a great uneasiness was beginning to awaken within her.

She raised her eyes and studied the Red Rock Plateau - - - perhaps twenty miles in breadth and one hundred or more miles in length - - - solidly built upon layers upon layers of stratified rock - - each tens of feet high - - - purples - - - whites - - - reds - - - greens - - - laid down over the eons. Beautiful! Magnificent!! Stunning!!!

She too had felt like this giant island - - - isolated - - - as frothing and frenzied royal patrons swirled endlessly around her - - - greedily gobbling up - - - piece by piece - - - her parents dignity and her freedom.

"Come - - - Soyala" - - - as a joyous voice broke her out of her musings: "We'll stable our two feathered friends here in this box canyon - - - with a supply of fresh game - - - and - - - then quickly make our way down to the falls. It has been quite a while since I've been here - - - so I hope that

I still remember the way. This should not take long - - - for - - - game is plenty where the foot of man has rarely trod!!!"

Prattling merrily - - - mouthing words that Soyala could only partially hear - - - for her own inner voices - - - Kajika blocked the entrance of the box canyon with brush and rock - - - forming a neat corral for the two nest mates. It was not long before he had procured two brace of mountain deer and one brace of mountain goat for his hungry traveling companions - - - and - - - brother and sister were soon on their way down the rubble strew path leading to the Thundering Falls.

The path was most narrow and ideally suited for the sure footed mountain goats which called this rugged place their home - - - but Kajika and Soyala were most nimble of foot and after about a two hour's descent succeeded in reaching the falls - - - and - - - little time thereafter in reaching a short out-cropping of rock hidden underneath the falls - - - behind which was hidden a small cave entrance.

Here they paused briefly to leave some of their heavier sleeping and traveling items behind - - - to drag in by ropes behind them - - - and - - - proceeded to the back of the cave where they had to lay face down to squeeze through a small muddy hole in the back of the cave wall. This in turn lead to a pitch dark rock tunnel - - - perhaps twenty feet long but not much larger than themselves. Pushing their items ahead of themselves - - - they soon worked their way - - - by feel - - - into a small chamber twice a man's height - - - which allowed them to stand and stretch.

Kajika - - - with the help of his fire piston - - - soon had the soft glow of a candle to light their way - - - as they began a slow gradual climb upwards.

Although the climb was slow - - - it was not tedious - - - as brother and sister relived this selfsame journey - - - of primordial dark and damp and dream - - - they had made as children. Where once fearsome rock giants - - - wielding club and sword had once dwelt - - - now stood shoulder high boulders and glistening stalactites.

Their eyes - - - already accustomed as they were to the dark - - - were soon able to discern a soft patch of golden daylight above to the right seeping slowly through a crevice far above them.

Soyala - - - once again took the lead - - - and was soon climbing a rock chimney to the surface - - - left hand and left foot on one side of the chimney - - - and - - - right hand and right foot on the other side - - - muscles rippling and taut - - - eyes focused and simmering with emotions which had not yet burst into flame.

45

As Soyala climbed out of the cave entrance into the paradise world of the Red Rock Plateau - - - Kajika - - - not to be outdone - - - was soon standing at her side - - - breathing in the unspoiled beauty of this sacred place "Ah - - - peaceful - - - is it not - - - sister?"

No sooner were these words out of his mouth - - - when - - - suddenly and without any warning - - - a crashing of brush accompanied by a trumpeting roar - - - caused brother and sister to jump aside for life and limb as a shaggy bull elephant - - - all of three feet tall - - - charged straight past them - - - fleeing for his life!

Close on his heels - - - nearly as tall as he and nipping at his tail - - - was an irate gander - - - apparently defending his nest and his mate.

As brother and sister laughingly extricated themselves from the brush and thorns into which they had thrown themselves - - - Kajika spoke - - - his anger slowly rising: "Ah - - - it is truly sad sister. Once - - - not long ago - - - still within the memory of our grandfathers - - - great herds of mammoths roamed these lands - - - giant cousins of these little beasts.

Now they have all been but exterminated and reduced to what you see here on this island plateau - - - and - - - this island plateau alone. Victims of the basest beast of all - - the mammoth hunters who satiate their blood lust by savaging whole herds for nothing but their skins and tongues and tusks - - - and - - - exterminating all else just for the sheer joy of killing."

As his breathing became labored and heavy - - - he continued: "I beg of you sister - - - as our Priestess Initiate - - - in six month's hence - - - to call upon whatever gods and goddesses you pray to - - - to deliver us and our world from this madness."

Soyala gently reached for his burning flesh - - - with a soothing hand - - and both slowly walked - - - each deep in his and her own thoughts - - - toward the rise where short green grasses slowly yielded to meadows and then a tree line which hinted of forest glades within.

&& Two Old Friends &&

Soon they came to the edge of the forest - - - thick with fruit and nut trees - - - and the most joyous of sounds - - - the gurgling of a bashful brook - - - the soothing lulling melody of cooing ring necked doves and the rustling of foraging fowl.

As they slowly weaved their way through forest meadows of red poppies and blue butterflies - - - to their hidden forest glade - - - they were silent in their thoughts.

"Ahhhh" - - - sighed Kajika - - - "this hidden glade is my favorite spot in the whole world!"

"What do you know of the whole world?" rejoined his sister - - - in fact - - - you've never ridden beyond the mark. You know nothing of the North - - - or - - - South - - - or - - - anywhere in fact!"

"But sister - - - this is paradise - - - and - - - if I am in paradise - - - why do I need to know anything else?"

Not wishing to engage in a conversation already lost before it had begun - - - Soyala breathed in the fresh air and magic of this place - - - while the Kajika busied himself with preparing breakfast.

"Sister - - - do you remember this place - - - really remember this place? Here we used to play as children."

Soyala stopped - - - paused - - - and - - - began to remember. Yes - - - the scent of the flowers was the same - - - the gurgling of the brook was the same - - - the kiss of the summer breeze against her cheek was the same. Yes - - - yes - - - here was the giant chestnut tree - - - that she used to climb - - - her Stairway to the Stars. Her mind's eye flashed back to a time long gone - - - but still somehow a part of her being - - - running – playing and doing her best to hide from the strict eye of her royal nursemaid. Stealing her brother's bow and arrows and stealing away to secret hiding places among the great roots of this giant tree to play at song and dance - - - drawing and tapping an arrow against the taut string of the bow - - - and - - - then plucking its string with her fingers.

Abruptly and noisily - - - her idyll was interrupted by the clanging of metal pots. Metal pots? She turned and saw the Kajika assembling a weird assortment of all sorts of utensils. From secret nooks and crannies he pulled forth clay crocks filled to overflowing with bread doughs and jams - - - and - - - a metal kettle with which to brew a tea of forest herbs and spices.

Soyala amused asked: "Well dear brother - - - is this how a hunter survives in the wilderness? By knowing the growing places of clay jugs and brass pots - - - which magically sprout from the ground - - - like mushrooms - - - at his command?"

Kajika's face flushed with a moment of embarrassment - - - then he laughed. "Well dear sister - - - I must confess that I might have better hidden the crocks and pots - - - and pulled forth from the ground already backed breads, ladles of honey and roasted meats - - - all the better to impress you - - - but I was in too much of a hurry! Besides - - - it would have been useless - - - for - - - what man's cunning could hide itself from a woman's wit?"

As Kajika made ready the kindling for the stone oven - - - evidently crafted from the skill of a child's hand from the outcropping of a massive boulder - - - Soyala kneaded the dough into biscuits and laid out an assortment of sweet stuffs - - - honeys and jams. With the fire now started in the simple stone oven - - - and - - - while Kajika and Soyala waited for the fire to die down to its embers - - - Soyala busied herself with searching for her favorite spices - - - with which to flavor the breakfast sausages - - - and - - - herbs - - - with which to brew the tea. Meanwhile Kajika searched out a quiet pool in the dancing brook in which to wash the heavy layers of salt and preserving spices from the sausage casings and meats taken from the huge bird - - - and - - - to mince the meats - - - which he then flavored with the herbs and spices brought to him by Soyala.

"Ah - - - I see that you've found the wild mountain berry - - - and - - - the green bristle grass. Excellent! We'll soon have a feast to top all feasts!!!"

As the sausages sizzled and the biscuits baked - - - Kajika readied his childhood smokehouse - - - a rustic but highly functional stone box with which to smoke the remainder of the sausages and meats for the long ride home.

"We must make due with a few days of smoking time - - - with heat of course - - - so that we might have a treat or two on our ride back home. Ah sister - - - this is the life - - - is it not? How can you live in that stone prison of yours - - - and - - - shut yourself away from the sky and the trees?"

Soyala mused - - - but - - - did not answer - - - her thoughts were elsewhere as she studied the massive trunk of a gnarled and broken forest giant: "Brother - - - Look! See? Here is OUR tree - - - Our Forest Uncle - - - here where we used to play as children in our nightly climb to the stars. Do you remember? He lives still - - - gnarled and broken - - - but rejoicing in his great age."

"Yes - - - rejoicing - - - as I rejoice too in seeing him once again" - - - responded Kajika - - - "and I imagine too - - - that he too rejoices in having attained such a great age."

As Kajika paused - - - studying the massive gnarled trunk he continued as with an afterthought: "However I'm sure that our practical brother Builder Brother would not rejoice for he would consider him worthless - - - since his limbs are too gnarled and broken to provide lumber - - - and - - - he no longer bears fruit - - - or - - - has enough of a leaf to provide any shade. Yes - - - I'm quite sure that our brother would consider him useless and would sooner see him struck down that to have lived at all!!!"

"Not to have lived at all?" Soyala astounded - - - than paused and continued - - - "Yes - - - sadly you are right in that our brother builder would perceive him as being useless - - - but - - - he is a priceless living treasure to me - - - and - - - one which I would gladly die for - - - for within him - - - and - - - nowhere else - - - lives our memories as children together - - - and - - - our journeys - - - whether to the stars - - - or to other secret places. Yes - - - back to that time when we knew no bounds - - - to a time when it was not strange for us to see the clouds smile down upon us or for the evening stars to invite us to dance or for the celestial rings to be our shimmering sliding board. How much have we lost with time - - - dear brother? Are our lives really all the richer with our years? Or have we lost that innocence and boundless energy we once had? Have we indeed imprisoned our minds in great steel cages - - - only free to roam within the confines of the prison bars of our duties?"

Kajika sighed: "Yes - - - dear sister - - - you are right. Our duties have become our prison bars. Here - - - with you - - - I know no duties - - - but - - - to love the forest with all of my heart and with all of my passion - - - and - - - to love you my most dear sister - - - as - - - the wonderful gift any devoted brother could ever hope for."

"Here - - - deep in the forest - - - in - - - solitude - - - is the only place I feel truly free. Here - - - I can let my mind roam - - - unfettered - - - once again - - - as a child - - - laughing and singing with the girl-child I once knew.

"Yes - - - solitude - - - and - - - freedom - - - climbing into the gnarled boughs of our Forest Uncle - - - to be closer to the stars - - - to ride the winds of dreams high into the midnight sky - - - to dance - - - amongst the stars - - -

"Yes - - - dear Soyala - - - I find our Forest Uncle priceless - - -

"Although he is gnarled and broken - - - having fended off the ravages of time and the relentless onslaughts of storm and wrack - - - Our Forest Uncle - - - is - - - indeed - - - priceless - - -

"Priceless? Yes - - - it is strange that someone - - - someone who both you and I know - - - someone whose name will soon come to me - - - used that very same word - - - 'priceless' - - - recently too.

"I remember - - - said Kajika - - - slapping his thigh - - - "Our Gadfly Minstrel of a Brother was prattling to me - - - as he is wont to do - - - about the value of being useless - - - yes - - - useless - - - now - - - what was it? Ah - - - I remember.

I never really understood what he meant until this very moment.

Useless.

How would he have said this? If our uncle of the forest had grown tall and straight - - - he would long ago have been felled for his lumber. If he had given fruit - - - his limbs would have been plucked bare - - - so that he would have died of loneliness. Had he given shade and sanctuary - - -

49

his roots would have been starved of the nurturing rain and sweet air - - - for - - - the countless feet of every wayfarer seeking his shade and solitude would have pounded this very ground into impenetrable stone. But here he stands in great age - - - all because he was useless.

Yes - - - he stands here today - - - because he was useless.

Strangely - the Gadfly was right - - - but - - - please don't ever tell him I said so."

"Your secret is safe with me - - - dear brother" - - - laughed Soyala - - - "but please - - let us be children once again - - - for an eternal moment if need be - - - for - - - if we could but travel to the stars as we once did as children - - - but - - - only one more eternal moment together."

Soyala was suddenly interrupted in her thoughts - - - by a crashing of brush. She jumped - - - looked wildly around and dived behind a rock - - - with naught to be seen except for her big round eyes - - - both as large as a saucers - - - fearing for another irate goose nipping at the heals of a frantic shaggy elephant running for its life.

Kajika - - - laughing so hard - - - that he had to hold his sides - - - could barely stand.

"Sister - - - sister - - - you should not wish so loud for your wish might come true!!! You wished that we be children again - - - and indeed your wish has come true!!! Our playmate has come to join us. Surely you remember our shaggy cinnamon colored playmate?!"

With that - - - Soyala searched her memory - - - confused - - - and - - - then suddenly burst into a smile then laughter as she danced from behind the rock. Cinnamon? He is here?   Oh - - - I would love to see him again - - - and - - - cuddle him once again. Will he come? Will he remember me?"

"Soyala - - - a Giant Ground Sloth never forgets!" He chided his sister. "Besides - - - I have made sure that he would not - - - could not - - - forget - - - for - - - see - - - see what I have here! His favorite snacks!!!" As he opened yet another saddle bag - - - he brought forth strange looking fruits - - - and - - - other delicacies only appetizing to a Sloth.

"Yes - - - sister - - - he'll be here soon - - - for - - - his nose is very keen - - - and - - - his stomach is never full! Yes - - - I would very much would like to see you cuddle him as you did when he was a baby!!! In fact - - - here he is now!"

Soyala followed the direction of her brother's gesture - - and - - - her smile slowly transformed itself into a gaping speechless mouth - - - which had dropped wide open at what she saw. There he was - - - towering above both of them - - - Cinnamon.

Should Soyala have stood on Kajika's shoulders - - - she still would not have been able to reach the giant sloth's shoulder - - - so tall was he. But as he was tall - - - he was even more gentle - - - as he slowly lowered himself to all fours and then rolled over - - - begging Soyala to rub his chest. If delight could but be measured by a creature's content - - - his closed eyes - - - rhythmic breathing - - - and - - - blissful smile would have defined that moment of perfect happiness for all time to come.

The three spent many happy hours together - - - almost as if obstinate time had obligingly taken a leap backwards into their childhoods - - - and - - - paused for a blissful eternal moment from her relentless march forward.

They rolled on the grass together laughing and playing together. When they tired of that Cinnamon took the two siblings for a loping gait around the forest glade - - - before his stomach brought him once again to his senses and Kajika was obliged to dig deeply into one more of his secret forest stashes to provide a bag full of fist-sized tidbits to the gentle giant.

Although it may have been hours - - - it seemed but seconds before a stern command echoed through the forest - - - as Cinnamon's jealous mate demanded his return to her affections - - so with a sheepish look - - - the gentle giant rolled to his feet and amicably ambled off in her direction.

& Back Home &

&& Slough Boy &&

The Slough Boy's thoughts nestled comfortably atop the golden haystack of a river barge lazily being drawn along the river's inlet - - - as he dreamed once again - - - his fantasy of fantasies of being gently cradled in the loving arms of two long-haired maidens from the south.

As the rhythmic clop-clop-clop of the two great horses' hooves softly lulled him to sleep - - - his mind's eye swiftly and deftly wrote a litany of seductive verse - - - with which to captivate the two straw haired maidens.

"Hey Slough Boy! Wake up and get your lazy butt over here!!!" A voice exploded his dreams into a thousand fragments as his eyes shot wide open. "We don't pay you to sleep. Earn your pay - - - or we'll find someone else - - - we've got another barge to walk through. You can sleep on your own time."

The Slough Boy sprang to his feet - - stumbling - - momentarily dazed and confused - - - as his eyes and mind fought to focus.

A barge stood at the end of the tunnel - - - its horse already unhitched - - - with its channel master impatiently waiting for the walk through.

The Slough Boy half ran - - - half stumbled toward the barge - - - his eyes wide with a mixture of fright of the channel master - - - and - - - anxiety at meeting - - - although it would only be but for a fleeting second or two - - - the two straw haired maidens.

"Come on you lazy toad - - - we don't have all day to wait for you!" screamed the channel master.

The Slough Boy - - - shot past the channel master and the mocking eyes of the two long haired beauties and scrambled to the top of the barge - - - bracing himself to start legging the barge through the horse-barge tunnel - - - which formed the land bridge crossing between the Widow's Walk to the southern forest beyond.

As he lay on his back atop the barge housing - - - he stared at the cold damp moss grown brick forming the bottom of the bridge above - - - wondering what traveler and what adventure might be passing over his head at this very moment. He could hear the clop-clop-clop of horses' hooves and half-wondered half-mused whether these were the barge horses - - - or the horse hooves of some weary adventurer - - - momentarily paused between two great adventures.

The Slough Boy fancied himself to be as one of the lean light barge horses - - which leaning slowly into his harness and trusting to the elasticity of the rope to break the initial inertia of a heavy load - - - could handily out pull one of his more heavily muscled cousins. In fact he had won many a wager from big muscular fellows - - who were more bravado than deed.

"Hey Slough Boy - - - are you asleep again???" He heard the maidens giggling. "Start moving! We're all waiting on you - - - and we don't have all day!!!"

The Slough Boy began to push with his legs - - - feeling the blood surge into his massive thighs - - - as he slowly began to move the barge forward.

The horses - - - already unhitched and lead from their cobble stoned tow-path over the hill to the other side of the great wide bridge - - - were already impatiently snorting and stomping at the other end - - - eager to reach their stable and a bucket of oats.

"Move – move!" the channel master cried. "We must make the edge of the river forest by nightfall."

The Slough Boy picked up the momentum - - - as the barge slowly began to move the 300 yards to the end of the tunnel. He had done this a many thousands of times - - - almost since the time when he could walk - - - at the beginning - - - laying next to his father - - - and then alone. So many times - - - in fact - - - that he knew the exact number of steps he would need to reach the other end - - - and his copper coin.

As the Slough Boy pocketed his copper coin he doffed his cap and ran off in the direction of the Widow's Walk - - - and to its cellars - - - for a cup of stale ale - - - some dry bread - - - and - - - if he was lucky - - a bit of hard cheese.

As he burst through the door - - - he almost ran head-on into the Crazy One - - - with his great shaggy head of hair and wild eyes - - - just finished from unloading an entire wagon load of salted hams and smoked sausages for those with silver and gold jingling in their pockets.   His daily charge was to roll out the empty beer and wine flasks - - - and to roll in the new. His pay was his keep and his home was this cellar.

"Hey Great One" the Slough Boy chimed - - - "Do you have a flagon of ale for me - - - from one of those barrel bottoms?"

The Great One grunted - - - and shook the empty barrels around him - - - until he found one that sloshed a flagon or two around on its bottom - - - and - - - then effortlessly lifted the massive barrel to pour two flagons of beer - - - one into the Slough Boy's waiting mug - - - and the second for himself.

"Ah - - - a bit of foam - - - so not TOO old and stale this time!" Cheered the Slough Boy.

With another grunt - - - The Great One slowly unwrapped a greasy cloth - - - from a nice thick section of hard salami - - - salvaged from the banquet hall above the night before - - - and offered half to the Slough Boy - - - along with a sizable piece of crusty stale bread - - - an oak barrel turned on end being their rustic but totally functional table.

With that the Slough Boy emptied his inside pockets of a pair of giant white radishes - - - each about a foot long - - - and an onion - - - "borrowed" from a farmer's barge on the way to market - - - and offered one of the radishes and half of the onion to the Great One. "Ah - - - we're to have a real feast today! Nothing is better than ale - - - salami and a great white radish with a bit of salt." With that he reached for a piece of rock salt carefully hidden away in a niche in the wall and ground it against his stone seat until there was a small pile of power. When the powder was of a size and consistency to his liking - - - he carefully replaced the rock salt in its niche - - - divided the small pile of salt into two - - - and swept the grains of his pile into his hand to sprinkle onto his radish with the flair of the most accomplished chef.

Without any further ado - - - they both delved into their modest repast - - - while the Slough Boy chattered away about the beauty of the long-haired maidens of the south - - - and the clopping of horses' hooves - - - on their way to untold adventures - - - over his head.

The two had no sooner finished their sumptuous repast - - - and - - - their tales of untold adventures - - - before the door at the head of the stairway swung open and a barmaid peered in. "Hey Old Man - - - have you moved all of those empty barrels yet? We have a delivery from the brewery coming this afternoon." As she descended the stairs - - - her critical eye searched not for the empty barrels - - - but rather scanned the cellar walls for further signs of "mischief" - - - as the Crazy One was wont to scroll strange and evil symbols on the walls - - - sometimes deeply etching the walls with an old horse shoe - - - or whatever other piece of metal he could find.

"Humph - - - I see that you too are lollygagging about with not much to do. Idle hands are the evil one's plaything. I don't know why the mistress keeps you." With that huff - - she ascended the stairs - - slammed shut the door - - - and left the two friends in peace.

"Well Great One - - - how has your day gone? Mine has gone reasonably well - - - since I have a pocket full of copper coins to show for it!!!" With that the Slough Boy emptied his pockets and counted out ten copper coins - - - which he admired - - - and then carefully put back into his pocket.

"How are your drawings? Have you any new ones with which to entice me?"

The Great One grunted once again - - - picked up a lighted candle - - - and - - - moved back into an enclave in the far reaches of the cellar - - -

Moving back - - - into - - - an - - - enclave - - - carefully hidden by massive barrels and carefully stacked beams - - - The Crazy One - - - paused - - - and - - - gestured.

"Here" - - - come here - - - over here - - -

As the Slough Boy's Eyes - - - slowly adjusted to the light of the candles - - - he could see - - - half hidden amongst the ripples and curves of the hand hewn rock - - - paintings - - -

Paintings - - -

    Paintings - - -

        Rock Paintings - - -

            Petroglyphs - - -

Petroglyphs - - -

Hidden behind piles of broken beer flasks and scraps of wood - - -

Rudimentary - - - Fashioned from the most basic of tools - - -

Genius - - - Scratched & Plastered onto bare rock walls - - -

Artistic Genius - - -

Scratched into granite blocks with a rusty horseshoe stylus - - -

Boldly stroked with tufts and tussocks of white hog bristles - - -

Emblazoned with the perfumed rouge of Drunken Dandies - - -

Artistic Genius - - -

Scavenged from the Hog's Banquet Table - - -

Salvaged from the broken promises of love and lust - - -

Savored from the memories of times past and future - - -

Artistic Genius - - -

Fusing - - -

Oil - - -

Pigments - - -

Memories - - -

As the Slough Boy - - - looked - - - and - - - gazed - - - and - - - wondered - - -

He could see - - - shapes - - - forming - - - melding - - - moving - - - beneath the flickering light of the torches - - -

Myths - - -

Creation Myths Solemnly Carved in Stone

Salvation Myths Brightly Colored with each Telling

Legends - - -

Crannogs on the Sea

Whale-Wolfs and Riders

As the Slough Boy - - - looked - - - and - - - wondered - - - and - - - nodded - - - The Crazy One grunted in satisfaction - - -

Nodding in satisfaction - - - The Crazy One - - - carefully closed - - - the opening to the enclave - - -

Closing the enclave - - - The Crazy One nodded his head - - -

Nodding his head - - - The Slough Boy - - - could see - - - in one brief burst of Flickering Candle Light - - - the - - - visage - - - of - - - he - - - who - - - but one year earlier was - - -

The Smasher of Stone - - -

The Silver Hammer - - -

The Stone Hauer - - -

Soyala sat quietly - - - cross-legged - - - palms upturned - - - in a meditative pose.

Before her - - - stretched like a silver blue carpet - - - lay the reflecting pool - - - cradling within its polished blue-stone walls - - - Marimo Lake Balls - - - fluffy plant balls of reds - - - blue-greens - - - and - - - orange-yellows - - - dancing - - - as one - - - with the almost imperceptible wind kissed ripples of the reflecting pool - - - and hence - - - melding as one with the ebbs and flows of their universe.

Far beyond her - - - Soyala could hear - - - as if in a dream - - - her sister's calling upon the sleeping sun to wake - - - but to Soyala - - - the dream-time was the wake-time - - - for only then could her spirit soar high above these palace gardens to dance as one with the three celestial rings and to be in full communion with the spirits of her ancestors and those spirits of the generations not yet born.

As her majesty the sun shook off her cloak of darkness - - - and - - - as the infant dawn crept along the secret garden pathways - - - the palace gardens became alive with the joyous sounds of rebirth - - - as - - - bird and butterfly - - - and - - - even beast - - - eagerly tasted of the sweet nectar of the trumpet vines.

Soyala stood - - - with one fluid languid motion - - - stretching her arms upwards toward the magenta morning sky - - - as if to embrace her sky mother and to invite her on an early morning stroll through the secret garden pathways.

As Soyala moved along these selfsame pathways - - - in quiet meditation - - - she slowly - - - and - - - sometimes a bit more quickly then she would have wished - - - accumulated a worshiping entourage of friends - - - some new - - - but for the most part mostly old and trusted friends.

As she approached a sheltered nook - - - she spoke: "Ahhh - - - my friends - - - you're letting me know that I've neglected you in the last few days. Yes - - - you're right - - - and I'm sorry. Come here and I'll make you feel better. Look what I have here for you - - - your favorite treats!!!"

Long-haired handmaidens - - with flower garlands in their hair - - - and - - - baskets overflowing with fruits and green leafy treats - - - patiently waited - - - as Soyala carefully made her way to a bench next to a small fountain. In this far corner of her favorite garden spot - - - Soyala began to welcome all of her friends. However - - - trying to say hello to all and not neglect any proved to be an impossible task - - - as she was soon buried under dozens upon dozens of assorted creatures - - - of all sizes and shapes - - - each seeking its favorite place of comfort:

Humming birds buzzing about her head - - - closely scrutinized all that was red - - -

Butterflies fluttering with the gentle breezes - - - sipped nectar from the silver chalices of the trumpet vines - - -

White winged doves nestling comfortably upon Soyala's head and shoulders - - - cooed softly as proof of their contentment - - -

Meanwhile her more adventurous furry playmates - - - stripped ground squirrels and fluffy red tree squirrels - - jostled for position in her lap - - - as one after the other tumbled to the ground to scamper once again up the bench in an animated attempt to jostle a less rambunctious competitor and cause him to come tumbling - unharmed - to the ground.

All-the-while - - - a miniature tree sloth - - - hanging upside down from a tree branch - - - watched the commotion in quiet anxiety as he tried to decide whether a two foot journey to creature comfort was indeed possible before the morning had long faded into twilight.

However - - - it was not long - - - when much to his relief - - - his motionless form was soon discovered by one of Soyala's hand maidens - - - and he was soon munching contently on his favorite fruit.

As much as the air around Soyala's head was awhirl with frenzied activity - - - the ground around her feet was awash with even more commotion - - - buried under the swirling blur of fur and feather and lizard scale.

As a covey of ground quail impatiently clamored around her feet - - - a gentle green iguana graciously took a mixed proffering of exotic fruits from her hand - - - as a giant tortoise patiently and politely waited for his favorite leafy green treat.

A miniature fox curiously eyed a giant iguana - - - wondering whether it might prove to be a tasty treat some day - - - but a sharp slap across his nose from a leathery tail - - - left a red welt across his nose to remind him that the offerings of scraps from the breakfast table were perhaps not as tasty but a whole lot safer.

Soon all were contently munching on their favorite treats and were being stroked in their favorite spots - - - when Soyala's favorite feathered acrobats - - - impatient at the wait for her to ascend to the next higher level of the terraced canopy - - - gently glided to her side.

Likewise - - -

Magnificent scarlet and orange tanagers - - - flanked by black-red orioles glided to branches above her head as if to crown her glory with spectacular rainbow colors - - - as they patiently took their turn gently sipping nectar from giant indigo-blue chalice vines - - - which - - - heavily hung with purple-red flowers - - - appeared to form a regal garland 'round her head.

Meanwhile - - -

Soyala's favorite feathered companion - - - Gho'a - - - her pastel plumage making her almost invisible against the Rosa - - - Aqua - - - and - - - Lilac petals and stamens of the enclave wall - - - gently glided to Soyala's side to take a morsel of meat from Soyala's fingers with her toothed beak - - - and - - - then - - - turned - - - and - - - resolutely climbed back to her favorite perch where she could enjoy her repast in peace and quiet - - - above the commotion of her less dignified companions.

Even as - - -

Some of her younger and somewhat more impatient cousins - - - clawed-winged scissor-tailed flycatchers - - - brilliant in their lemon yellow and lime green plumage - - - quickly glided toward the handmaidens - - - who were busily handing out hand-over-fist - - - their favorite treats as quickly as supplies would allow.

However - - -

It was not long in the making before the hand maidens' baskets of treats became empty - - - and - - - just quickly as they had appeared - - - they were gone - - - fur and feather and lizard scale - - - some darting off to secluded sleeping shelters - - - with others choosing to lounge lazily in the sun upon some large flat rock - - - while last - - - but - - - not least - - - the giant box-tortoise chose to simply close the door to his house right where he lay.

Only one - - - Gho'a - - - "The Beautiful Lady" - - - remained - - - watching - - - for she was the truest of the true.

As Gho'a glided to Soyala's shoulder and playfully nibbled on her ear - - - impatient for her ride to the next higher terrace of the Overhanging Gardens - - - Soyala handed one last treat to her friend - - - and serenely began making her way along the garden pathways to the polished stone stairway leading to the terrace above.

&& THE TESSEN &&

Soyala's garden path led her upwards - - - from the Pool of All Beginnings and All Ends - - - to the second terrace and the Silver Fountain of the palace gardens.

As Soyala - - - marveled at the stark contrast of the eternal beauty of the three celestial rings above her - - - and - - - the transient beauty of the palace gardens which surrounded her - - - Gho'a's focus was much more practical and focused.

Perched comfortably on Soyala's shoulder - - - Gho'a snapped at the occasional flying insect - - - screeching her pleasure as she craned her neck forward - - - resolute in her determination to be the first to espy any new movement or chance motion around each and every bend.

As Soyala rounded the last bend of the garden pathway leading to the silver fountain - - - Gho'a - - - beside herself with excitement - - - at receiving her second treat of the day - - - half fell - - - half glided - - - from her comfortable perch on Soyala's shoulder - - - to the feet of her favorite long-haired handmaiden and her basket of treats.

As the handmaiden surreptitiously removed Gho'a's treat from the deep folds of her scarlet garment - - - for it was not easy to hide such a treat from so many prying eyes - - - and bottomless stomachs - - - Gho'a puffed up her feathers in pleasure and gently took the offering from the fingers of the handmaiden with toothed beak and blissful spirit - - - and resolutely climbed a Flowering Vine - - - using her clawed wings to gain purchase - - - to a favorite tree perch to enjoy her repast in leisure.

It was not long before all of the baskets were empty - - - and Soyala's entourage was busy salvaging crumbs from the garden grasses - - - when as if with one thought - - feather and fur and scale disappeared - - - save for the tortoise - - - which quickly pulled itself into its castle fortress.

As Gho'a shrieked an alarm cry - - - fearful for Soyala's safety - - - shrieking handmaidens scrambled down the garden path - - - disappearing in every which direction.

Soyala smiled - - - then - - - half turned and glanced over her shoulder - - - as a hulking shadow - - - closely followed by a scowling bearded warrior - - - rounded the corner. Close at his heels was a giant spotted hyena - - - the object of Gho'a's frantic alarm cries.

Burilgi - - - "The Destroyer" - - - roared a greeting to his sister - - - and - - - then callously swept a turquoise bench clean of young creatures - - - two squirrels and quail - - - frozen in fright - - - with no more an aforethought than had he swept away bacon bits and cake crumbs after a messy and ill gotten breakfast.

His spotted companion - - - meanwhile - - - lay his massive toothed head at his master's feet - - - nonchalantly sniffing the hidden smells on the ground around him - - - ignoring the crashing of brush and alarm cries - - - as if the hastily departed entourage were beneath his dignity.

"And how do you fare - - - fair sister?"

(Burilgi chuckled to himself - - - at his exceedingly clever play on words.)

"Well, brother - - - very well - - - but as you saw - - - I was faring a bit too well!!! At least until you showed up. But I see that you're not alone - - - and that you've brought the Bone Crusher along with you."

Soyala smiled as she reached out to stroke the massive head - - - as Crusher whined in recognition of his name.

"Hello - - - Crushy - - - how are you doing today? Are you keeping your master out of trouble?"
- - - Soyala smiled.

 "So - - - Burilgi - - you appear to be in good spirits - - - but what brings you here?"

"Humph" - - - grunted the giant - - - "What brings ME here?! - - - Why your birthday of course!
Today is your birthday - - - and I am here as your birthday present!!!" - - - he roared.

"Burilgi - - - my birthday isn't today."

"It isn't?"

"No - - - it isn't even this month."

"It isn't? Not today? Not even this month?? Impossible!!!"

"YOU must be wrong! But - no matter - - - I'm here - - - which is all that is important - - - and
- - - cause enough for celebration!!!"

The giant turned and barked an order at a group of several young servant boys - - - fearfully
huddled further down the garden pathway: "Come here - - - you lazy tadpoles! Come here and
be quick about it!!!"

Four lads scurried along the path - - - struggling under the weight of a massive silver serving
platter - - - while a fifth - - - waged battle with a great creaking wooden wheelbarrow - - - holding
a sloshing keg of ale.

"Yes - - - I'm here - - - and if my being here isn't enough for YOU to ENJOY your birthday - - -
I've brought MY favorite breakfast cake for you to enjoy!"

Amidst the bluster - - - and frightfully tiptoeing around the Crusher - - - the servant lads hurriedly
set up a serving table - - - and laid a massive chocolate cake - - - topped with a thick creamy icing
- - - upon it - - - as Gho'a - - - peering safely through a space in the thick foliage of the flowing
vines - - - critically surveyed the scene.

As the cake was laid out - - - and as the servant lads gingerly placed the keg of ale and a pair of
flagons on a companion table - - - a sixth youngster - - - slight of build and not quite as large as
Burilgi's muscular thigh - - - struggled up the pathway - - half carrying - - half dragging a massive
meaty bone - - - almost as large as he - - - as Crusher whined his anticipation.

63

"Ah yes" - - - grunted Burilgi in satisfaction - - - "Nothing like a heavy dark ale first thing in the morning - - -

(Unless it is a heavy dark ale served by a heavy dark lass – he thought to himself)

"To fortify oneself for the long day ahead - - - and - - - come night - - - it is most fitting that one should have a light blond ale - - - (he chuckled) - - - to settle the stomach - - - for - - - a sound night's sleep - - - I always say!!!"

Burilgi snatched for the bone - - - as the youngster ran for his life - - - not wishing to be mistaken for the selfsame bone - - - tore a piece of juicy red flesh from it with his flashing white teeth - - - and tossed it to Crusher - - - who - - - soon lived up to his name - - - for almost instantly conversation could hardly be heard for the sound of the massive jaws crushing the thigh bone of some giant beast into one raw meaty pulp.

"Come sister - - enjoy your cake - - - and have an ale!" - - - roared Burilgi as he sloshed some ale into one of the two flagons - - - and - - - handed one of the flagons to his sister.

"Burilgi – thank you - - but I will save my ale for later" - - -

(Much later" – Soyala muttered under her breath).

"Besides - - - don't you think that I would much better enjoy my cake if it were cut into pieces which were a little bit smaller?" half queried Soyala.

As Burilgi grunted confusion - - - for the thought had never entered his head - - - Soyala continued: "Unfortunately I'm afraid that it must remain uneaten - - - for we have nothing with which to cut the cake."

With that Burilgi slammed his sword onto the table - - - causing the remaining servant lads to jump two paces in fright: "Here sister - - - cut your cake!" - - - he roared.

"Burilgi - - - I can't use a sword to cut a cake - - - besides" - - - she said glancing at the blade - - - "it isn't even sharp."

"How right you are sister! My sword is for crushing men's bones - - - and - - - not for slicing one of your dainty cakes!!! Besides - - - I have something much better in mind!" - - - smiled Burilgi as he pulled a decorative fan from deep beneath the folds of his warrior's tunic - - - poising it aloft in real admiration - - - allowing it to shimmer and shine in the early morning sun - - - before - - - fanning himself and taking another deep drink from his flagon.

The design was stunning - - - and at the same time delicate - - - long-tailed orange-red flycatchers perched amidst the peach-colored blossoms of a fruit tree.

Knowing her brother full-well - - - to say that Soyala was shocked - - - in that her brother would own a fan - - - let alone use one - - - was an understatement.

As Soyala sat perplexed at the sight of her giant of a brother sitting before her fanning himself - - - and as she pondered how she might best escape this giant of a brother - - - a voice unexpectedly sang out: "Enjoying your morning libation - - - Great Gurgling One?"

At the annoying sound of the Minstrel - - - Burilgi abruptly turned - - - spilling a half flagon of ale - - - all over himself.

"Well - - - if it isn't the gnat - - - hovering around us with an annoying buzz - - - hovering dear sister - - - for- - - if he were but a little bit taller - - - his legs might almost reach the ground!"

"My - - - my - - - for he seeks to cut me with his wit" - - - quipped the Minstrel - - - "but do not fear dear Soyala - - - for no matter how sharp his wit - - - it cannot match even the sharpness of his dull - - - dull - - - sword!"

Burilgi's face reddened dangerously.

"Burilgi - - - the cake" - - - Soyala interjected - - - attempting to divert her brother's attention from his much smaller nemesis - - - "how are we supposed to cut the cake?"

Without moving his eyes from the Minstrel - - - Burilgi's hand - - - holding the fan - - - moved with a speed too fast for the eye to follow - - - and - - - slashed the cake neatly in two - - - and - - - then into four pieces.

"THERE - - - sister! - - - HERE - - - is your cake!!!"

The Minstrel - - - rooted in his spot - - - whether frozen in fright or arrogant in his defiance one cannot say - - - continued his taunt: "That was an accident - - - Oh Master of the Breeze - - - there no way that you can do that again!"

Burilgi's hand flashed two more times - - - dividing the cake neatly into eight equal pieces.

In a flash - - - the Minstrel grabbed two pieces and then bowing - - - handed one to his sister: "Here sister - - - a piece of cake?"

As Burilgi's face flashed an even darker shade of red - - - the Minstrel - - - having obtained his objective of breakfast cakes and not wishing to press his luck - - - beat a hasty and dignified retreat.

Soyala - - mouth agape - - - surveyed - - - first the cake - - - then - - - the fan - - - then - - - once again - - - the cake - - - "Burilgi - - - how? How did you slice that cake with a fan?"

"Ah" - - - Burilgi smiled - - - "but it is NOT a fan - - - dear sister - - - but a cast bronze blade from the North - - - disguised as a fan. It is my gift to you - - - designed for your defense or pleasure as you choose.

"It is an excellent weapon for a shield maiden - - - since it does not appear to be a weapon at all!"

"Amazing" - - - marveled Soyala - - - as - - - Burilgi handed the Tessen to her - - - how light and how beautiful - - - but also deadly. But how did you get the idea?"

From a pouch at his side - - - Burilgi withdrew a bloody comb from a giant bird - - - and tossed it on the table - - - as the Crusher whined in hopeful anticipation: "I thought that you'd ask - - - from this - - - the comb of a Lion Killer!!"

As - - -

Burilgi once again pocketed the bloody comb - - - much to Crusher's confusion - - - he continued: "Dear sister - - - I hope that you never have need of this - - - but if you should - - - use it wisely."

With these words - - - he ambled on down the path - - - with Crusher following closely at his heels.

Soyala followed a few moments latter on her way to the uppermost terrace - - - with the beautiful lady - - - Gho'a perched contently on her shoulder - - - leaving only the tiniest of creatures behind to scavenge the crumbs from Soyala's breakfast cake.

&& KAJIKA'S DREAM &&

Of Myths & Troodons

"I was in a Troodon Cage with Two Troodon Masters - - -

Seven Troodons were whirling around me - - - eyeing me - - -

Eying me - - - and - - - one small toothed bird - - - all the while moving about me - - -

I looked closer - - - at the small helpless bird - - - and - - - saw that it was Gho'a - - -

I wasn't afraid for myself - - - but - - - I was worried that the Troodons would kill and eat Gho'a
- - -

But - - - Gho'a was unafraid - - -

Because the Troodons were milling around - - - The Troodon Masters began tossing chunks of fish
to them - - - to quiet them - - - which - - - they - - - and - - - your loyal Gho'a gobbled up - - -

The Troodon Masters then took a stiff piece of paper - - - an - - - exceptionally - - - stiff piece
of paper - - - and - - - laid it against an opening to a second upper cage - - - to - - - use - - - as a
ramp for the Troodons to enter into the upper level - - -

I lay under this ramp - - - and - - - could see the Troodons - - - through a tiny crack above me
- - - as they passed over me - - -

Although - - - each - - - would glance down at me - - - sometimes menacingly - - - as they passed
overhead - - - none stopped to eye me closer - - -

None stopped - - -

Until - - -

The sixth Troodon - - - which - - - stopped - - - and - - - snapped at me - - -

But - - -

I blocked the snapping Troodon with my naked arm - - - since it appeared to be playful and not intent on hurting me - - -

However - - -

The last Troodon began snapping in earnest - - -

Snapping at me so fiercely that I had to use both arms to cover my face - - -

Covering both arms - - - out of concern - - - that - - - it would bite me - - -

All the while I knew that I could show no fear - - -

For - - -

If I were to show fear - - the Troodon would eat me - - -

Therefore - - -

I was not afraid - - -

After considerable snapping - - - the Troodon Masters moved The Troodon on its way - - -

Once all of the Troodons had entered the second level - - - The Troodon Masters - - - removed the ramp and introduced me to the applause of an Emperor - - -

Introduced me - - - to an Emperor - - -

An Emperor - - - Who - - - I could not see - - for - - - lights were blinding me - - -

The Emperor then rewarded me for my bravery with a Golden Arrow fletched with Troodon Feathers - - -

&& The Overhanging Gardens &&

As - - -

Soyala continued her slow climb upwards - - - she thought of the three tiers of this palace complex - - -

The lowest level being the Reflecting Pool - - - symbolic of all beginnings - -

The second level being the Overhanging Gardens - - - symbolic of life and rebirth - - -

The third and uppermost level being The Royal Residence - - - symbolic of spirituality - - - and - - - self actualization - - - atop which sat a tiny belvedere - - - housing both the sun and moon calendars of these learned and knowledgeable peoples - - -

Great Cavities had been dug into the solid rock - - -

Some - - - filled with crystal clear waters - - -

Others - - - filled with deep dark dank earth - - -

Water Filled Cisterns - - - to serve as pools and lakes for the palace grounds - - - providing refreshment and sport - - -

Earthen Filled Planters - - - to provide anchor and support for the mighty trees which decorated the palace grounds - - -

However - - -

As magnificent as were the palace grounds - - - the palace was even more so - - -

For - - -

It was not a simple residence - - - but - - - a masterful three story complex - - -

Three Stories - - -

One - - - Royal Residence & Sleeping Chambers - - -

Two - - - Royal Reception & Banquet and Feasting Halls - - -

Three Stories - - -

One - - - Above Ground - - -

Two - - - Buried Deep within the Roots of the Mountain - - -

Above Ground - - -

The Royal Residence - - - sitting atop a great banquet and reception hall - - - was not the best place for those wishing to sleep during the time of festivities - - - but - - - when feasting and drinking - - - who has time for sleep?

Below Ground - - -

The Two Great Halls - - - buried deep within the mountain - - - were a place of Royal Receptions and Merriment Making - - -

One - - - used daily - - -

Another - - - rarely seen - - -

One Hall - - - Rarely seen - - - seldom talked about - - - not so much secret - - - as - - - forgotten - - -

Built to house the forbearers of these noble people - - -

Built to honor the forbearers of these noble people - - -

Built to hallow the forbearers of these noble people - - -

Built to honor and comfort the dead - - - and - - - to remember the living - - -

City of the Dead - - - a - - - Necropolis - - - seldom remembered - - - spoken of only in whispers - - -

&& CHILDHOOD MEMORIES &&

Soyala continued her climb to the uppermost terrace - - again accompanied by Gho'a - - - going over and over - - - Kajika's Dream - - -

Kajika's Dream - -

An innocent dream - - - or - - - a portent of something dark and sinister - - -

But - - -

The Day was Young - - - and - - - certainly most beautiful - - -

But - - -

Nothing more beautiful than The Beautiful Lady - - - Gho'a - - - perched on Soyala's shoulder - - -

Beautiful Day - - -

     Beautiful Sky - - -

          Most - - - Beautiful and Loyal Companion - - -

It were as if Soyala could stretch and touch the sky - - -

And - - -

As if - - - her Sky Mother - - - could reach out - - -

     Caressing her daughter - - - with - - - soft sea breezes - - -

          Snuggling with her in a soft thick comforter of white fluffy clouds - - -

          Basking in warm radiant smiles of golden yellow sunshine - - -

Mother Sky - - -

Caressing her daughter with soft gentle breezes - - - kissing her cheeks - - - one-by-one - - - tenderly - - -

Love - - -

Carefree Love - - -

      Unrequited Love - - -

Unrequited Love - - -

      Wafting across the turquoise mountain top - - -

        Melding and dancing with the blue-green sea - - -

Showering Love upon the emerald green forest canopy - - -

Love - - -

This was the Sky Island - - - high above the clouds - - -

High Above the Clouds - - - out of sight and sound - - - of - - - Fisher - - - and - - - Farrier - - - and - - - Draughtsman - - -

Out of sight and sound - - - but - - - one with the mountain - - - and - - - the sky - - - and - - - the silent lapping waves of the great glacial sea so far below - - -

Almost - - -

      Almost - - -

        As If - - -

As If - - -

Soyala were yielding so some primeval force - - - some - - - enchantment - - - of - - - peoples - - - and - - - places - - -

Some Racial Memory were awakening to the sight and sounds of carefree clouds and streaming sunshine - - -

Some Atavistic Memory of Mountain Top Sky Islands - - - far above the clouds - - - were steaming forth from her subconscious - - -

Racial Memories - - -

Of - - - Clouds - - -

Icen Glaciers - - -

Orchid Blossoms - - -

As - - -

Soyala stood here - - -

Standing here quietly - - -

Standing - - -

Stretching - - -

Embracing - - -

Reaching out her arms - - - to embrace the golden sun - - -

It were almost as if Soyala were as one with the timid - - - shy - - - gentle faces peeking from the painted forest canopy of the Widow's Walk - - - peering fearlessly upwards at the clear blue sky - - - peering fearlessly into the unknown - - -

Painted Forest Canopy - - -

Painted Forest Faces - - -

Soyala - - -

       Deep in Thought - - -

              Mind - - - floating blissfully in Time and Space - - -

                     Sound and motion - - - jolting her back into the present - - -

Awakened from her dream state - - -

Soyala turned at Gho'a's Joyous shriek - - -

For - - -

Gho'a's second most favorite person in the whole world - - - was headed in her direction - - -

Gho'a let loose another shriek of joy - - - as - - - Kajika rounded the bend - - -

&& THE GOLDEN ORB &&

"Ahhhh - - - – Soyala - - - I've been looking for you.

The Smiling Face of Kajika appeared in Soyala's consciousness - - - even as - - - Soyala wiped her shared tears from her face - - -

Tears - - - of - - - shame - - - or - - - happiness - - -

For - - -

It could be either - - - or - - - both - - -

Across the Rocky River - - - The Weeping Maiden - - - cried silent tears - - -

Icen Tears - - - flowing as glacial melt - - - from - - - the frozen heart of a maiden - - -

The Weeping Maiden - - -

Weeping Stoic Face - - - from across the river - - -

Glacial Melt - - - flooding valley and sea - - -

Gazing lovingly upon the sleeping form of her king - - -

Shared Tears - - -

As if - - - her tears - - - and - - - Soyala's tears were as one - - -

Tears - - - flowing together - - - meeting and joining to form a mighty river - - -

Tears - - - Past - - - and - - - Future - - - flowing together - - - as - - - past loves and future beginnings clashed

Past Loves - - - Future Beginnings - - - Flowing Streams of Love - - -

For - - -

What pain is greater than a sleeping love?

Even - - -

As - - -

Kajika rounded the pathway toward where Soyala was standing - - - he beamed as bright and as genuine a smile as has ever been smiled - - - since - - - man first beheld woman - - -

For - - -

So vain is the race of men - - - that - - - he believes that each and every maiden's tear - - - whether tears of joy or sorrow - - - is shed because of him - - -

Ah - - - you're crying - - - because I'm leaving — - - - somehow - - - you must have heard - - - even though - - - I had instructed all not to tell you - - - until - - - I had told you myself - - -

"Leaving? You're leaving"

"Yes - - -

Yes - - - This very afternoon - - -

I'm leaving - - - this very afternoon - - - all is ready - - - all is packed - - -

Our Father - - - Our Foster Father - - - has - - - ordered that I leave at once - - -

I must go away - - - dear Soyala - - - for some time - - - I'm afraid - - - today - - - I must leave today - - - in fact - - - I - - - must leave - - - this very hour.

Yes - - -

Yes - - - you must have know - - -

You must have known that I was leaving - - -

You are weeping because you had thought that we might spend this whole splendid afternoon together - - -

Together - - - as we once were - - -

But - - -

But - - - my pack horses are already ready - - - and - - - chomping at the proverbial bit!!!

Soyala's questioning eyes - - - betrayed her fear as Kajika continued:

"Yes - - - Our Foster Father has instructed me to make arrangements to celebrate the Sun Festival with the Sun King far to the south.

Strange it is - - - that his Sun Festival is the time of our Winter Homage and the time of your Ascension as Priestess Initiate - - - but none-the-less - - - I must do as ordered although I fear that our sister - - - Chup-Kamui - - - is somehow the intrigue behind all of this!

Yes - - -

Yes - - - I'm afraid - - - dear sister - - - that sad eyes and longing hearts best sum up this moment

As Kajika sought to contain his grief - - - his eyes brightened with a thought:

"But - - -

But - - - I am not gone yet - - -

I am not gone yet - - - dear sister - - - I am not yet gone - - -

Let us steal but a moment for ourselves and revel in an eternal moment of shared joy - - - for - - - we do not need to yield to incessant and merciless duty - - - bending our knee to its each beck and call - - -

But - - -

But - - - enough talk!

Let us try your skill.

I am curious to see whether your skill with bow and arrow has diminished with your imprisonment here - - - within - - - this perfumed cage of rose bramble and briar - -

You used to be a fair shot with a bow and arrow - - - no - - - I am unkind - - - you used to be the best shot with bow and arrow - - - second - - - only - - - to me - - -

But - - -

I suspect that these days - - -

I suspect - - - that - - - your eye has grown dim and your wrist limp - - - for - - - I doubt that you could shoot - - - even that golden fruit hanging from that ancient tree!!!

Yes - - -

Dim of eye and limp of wrist - - -

That is what you've become - - -

Limp of wrist and wild wit - - -

Domesticated - - - that is what you've become - - - domesticated - - -

"Domesticated???!!! - - - Soyala said in mock anger - - -

Limp of wrist and wit???

Give that Bow to me - - - Soyala said - - - grasping at bow and arrow - - -

Show me the target and I will show you - - - who - - - is dim and limp! Soyala said as she notched an arrow in the bow - - -

As - - -

Kajika's eyes brimmed - - - overflowing - - - with a scarcely contained mirth - - - he said:

"Soyala - - - do you see that golden fruit - - - hanging from the top branches of that tree? See if you can strike it.

More ever - - -

Should you be lucky enough to strike it - - - see if you can find it - - - once it has fallen - - -

 With Kajika's words - - - still in his mouth - - - and - - - with a movement almost too swift to follow - - - Soyala aimed and let fly the arrow - - - which - - - struck the fruit squarely in its center - - - breaking it loose from its mother limb.

The fruit had no sooner begun to tumble to the earth when Soyala was up and running - - - jumping over benches and bushes to where she was certain the arrow had brought it to earth.

As Soyala searched through fallen leaves and thick leafy vines - - -

Searching - - -

Searching beneath tangled vines and fallen leaves - - -

Searching through tangled memories and dusty memories - - -

Searching - - -

Finding - - -

Remembering - - -

Remembering - - - how - - - she - - - had - - - pledged fidelity to a Boy-Child - - -

Remembering - - - how - - - a Boy-Child had pledged brotherly love to her - - -

Fidelity and Love - - - pledged - - - solemnly pledged in this very spot - - -

Pledged - - - alongside an oaken sapling - - - now grown straight and tall - - - even as they had now grown straight and tall - - -

Pledged - - - so many years ago - - -

&& The Bowharp &&

As - - -

Soyala searched - - -

Searching amongst distant memories - - - and - - - fallen yellow leaves - - -

Pushing through twisted green vines - - - and - - - doubts and decisions - - -

Soyala saw - - - before - - - buried amongst the leaves and vines of this palace woodland floor - - - an - - - orb - - -

An Orb - - -

Golden Round - - -

Glittering amongst the green mosses and ferns - - -

Fallen Fruit - - - to be picked up and tasted - - -

Nestled in a sweet nest of memories and mosses - - -

An Orb - - -

Too Golden - - -

Too Round - - -

Too Perfect - - -

Too Sweet - - -

A fallen fruit - - -

Golden Fruit - - -

Golden Puzzle - - -

Golden Glitter amongst the yellow leaves - - -

A - - -

Golden Glitter - - -

Gold Glittering - - -

Gold Sparkling - - -

An Orb - - -

Pierced perfectly in its center - - -

Golden Orb pierced perfectly by an arrow - - -

Skewered by an unerring eye and heart - - -

But - - -

Even as - - - Soyala - - - lifted this round egg from its cozy nest of moss - - - her - - - puzzlement grew - - -

Puzzlement - - -

For - - -

She held not one - - - but - - - two nestlings - - - one in each hand - - -

Two proud Nestmates - - -

       One - - - golden orb - - - pierced by an unerring arrow - - -

       Another - - - golden ball - - - tightly wound of spun golden thread - - -

Two Nestmates - - -

     Lying amongst moss and fern - - -

        Snuggled cozily amongst memories and leaf litter - - -

          Joyously basking and blazing in the golden sun - - -

As - - -

Soyala - - -

Gingerly picked up the larger of the golden fruits - - -

     One loose end - - -

      One Carefree End - - -

       One Adventurous End - - -

Golden Ball unraveling - - -

Unraveling - - -

Unwinding - - -

Unknotting - - -

Twisting - - -

Turning - - -

Traveling - - -

As - - -

Soyala followed thread and trail - - -

Running - - -

Twisting - - -

Turning - -

As - - -

Soyala Doggedly Followed the Golden Thread - - - twisting - - - turning - - - its way through briar and branch - - - burrowing - - - disappearing - - - vanishing - - - furtively burying itself under leaves and broken branches - - -

Disappearing - - -

Vanishing - - -

Gone - - -

Forever Gone - - -

Until - - -

Reappearing - - -

Reappearing as a Tangle of Golden Spider Webs - - -

Threading their way through branch and stem and bough - - -

Suddenly - - -

Unexpectedly - - - appearing three meters hence - - -

Then - - -

Disappearing - - -

Again - - - Unexpectedly - - - reappearing - - - three meters hence - - -

Running wildly along the ground - - -

     Dodging rock and tree - - -

       Zigzagging this way and that - - -

Zigzagging - - -

     Burrowing under leaf - - -

       Leaping over bush - - -

         Threading its way through rock and stump - - -

Until - - -

Soyala - - -

Coaxing the wayward thread back into the golden fold from which it was spun - - -

     Doggedly following that elusive thread to wherever it might lead - - -

       Bumped her head solidly against a great grey moss covered thing - - -

A - - -

       Thing - - -

A - - -

       Something - - -

But - - -

       Neither Tree - - -

          Nor Stump - - -

          Nor Rock - - -

But - - -

A sprawling weathered canvas - - - painted - - - in mottled forest green - - and - - - weathered to a dull gray hue - - -

"Ah - - - Soyala" - - - laughed Kajika - - - scarcely concealing his mirth and his merriment: "What - - - have you found there - - - Dear Sister?

It seems to me as if you've discovered our Childhood Shelter - - - which - - - in its gentle folds - - - hid us from the prying eyes of grownups - - - as we traveled through the wilds and wilderness of these palace forests?

What childhood mysteries lie before you at your feet - - - even now?

Perhaps - - -

Perhaps - - - you have before you - - - an as yet unrealized childhood adventure - - - waiting - - - so - - - anxiously waiting - - - to take us briefly back to our time of innocence - - -

As the ancient and weathered cloth gently released its hold of the hidden mystery and fell in soft folds upon the green grass - - - Soyala gasped and clasped her hands with joy. A polished ebony arch - - - tipped in ivory - - - grasped between its outstretched arms one row of gold and one row of silver threads - - - gently nestling between them the finest spun fiery red strings - - - each strung as taut as the tautest of bow strings.

"Kajika - - - Oh – it is beautiful!!! Is this your gift? Is this your secret? It is indeed beautiful - - - for - - - it is exquisitely crafted - - - but - - what sort of object is this?

Does it - - - have a purpose - - - and - - - if so - - - does it have a meaning?

Does it even have a name?"

"Soyala - - - I am most happy to see you pleased.

As for your questions - - - you ask them so quickly - - - that it is difficult for me to remember - - - let alone answer - - - but - - - I'll try:

Does it have a purpose? Yes - - - dear sister - - - Kajika said laughingly - - - "It does have a purpose - - - its purpose is to make you happy.

Does it have a meaning? Yes - - - as you shall soon see.

Does it have a name? Yes - - - I have named it Bowharp.

Little Soyala - - - – can you remember - - - when we as children used to play here - - -

I practiced with my bow and arrows - - - and - - - you played with m bow and arrows - - - plucking on the strings of my bows - - - making up the most beautiful of songs as you plucked wondrous melodies from my bowstrings?

I had long thought about which gift would suit you best - - - so - - - I - - - spoke with a most skilled and ancient crafter of furniture.

So - - - with the promise of my game to fill his table to overflowing - - - for some time to come - - - I bartered - - - bartering game for games - - - if you will.

I brought several of my strung bows to him - - - and - - - with his skill - - - and - - - my tone deaf ear - - - we experimented - - - finding the best combination of all possible sounds - - -

So - - -

Please - - - sit - - - dear sister - - - and - - - let me hear the voice which rivals even the songbird guarding his next - - -

Sing - - - dear sister - - - please - - - sing - - -

Please sing - - - for - - - with affairs of state being such as they are - - - who knows when we will again - - - each have the pleasure of each other's company - - -

With these words - - - both Kajika and Soyala felt a tightening in their throats - - -

As - - -

Soyala seated herself at the Bowharp - - - and - - - began to pluck at the strings - - -

It was not long before wondrous notes and then melodies began to fill the tiny glade of the palace grounds - - -

&& THE STATIONS OF REMEMBRANCE &&

The inside of the grotto was a quarter sphere - - - around which - - - at eye level - - - was a half circle of intricately detailed life sized mosaics - - -

Life Sized Mosaics - - -

Mosaics of places - - - and - - - people - - - and - - - events - - -

Events - - -

Monumental Events - - -

Heroic Events - - -

Defining Events - - -

Events which defined this folk as a people - - -

Events which spanned the course of only one single day - - -

As Soyala marveled at the skilled hand and eye that had crafted these exquisite and detailed forms - - - she - - - approached the first station of remembrance and laid her hand upon it. Slowly - - - almost imperceptibly - - - sweet ethers began to permeate her consciousness. Forms of kinsmen and surroundings begin to meld into a mosaic of colors not much unlike the stations surrounding her.

Even more slowly and imperceptibly - - - cool blue mists coalesced into shapes and then forms - - - that - - - began - - - to - - - move - - - and - - - to - - - speak:

ᛞᛞᛞ THE HUNTER ᛞᛞᛞ

As an infant dawn crept over the hill - - - a small group of men - - - shrouded in the shadows - - - huddled against the cold and waited - - - silently - - - as a crystal clear mountain spring began to gurgle and sing - - - awakened by the first rays of dawn.

A mountain buck - - - nostrils quivering - - - poised erect - - - hesitantly halted and then quickly led his does and their fawns to drink of the cool clear water.

A twang of a bowstring – then several more in rapid succession - - - and - - - the buck and three of his does spotted small red darkening patches - - - mortally wounded.

The hart leapt - - - pawing the air in a futile fight for breath and life - - - and - - - then fell lifeless. A doe - - - still struggling to put herself between her fawn and the barbed death - - - staggered a few steps and crumpled into a lifeless mass. The fawn confused - - - stood - - - motionless - - - for a second too long.

The herd scattered - - - fleeing for its life - - - with - - - archers - - - in hot pursuit of its blood trail.

As the huntsman - - - and - - - his kinsmen - - - gathered round the still warm bodies.

As they stripped the living branches of the mountain laurel from their mother tree - - - the archers - - - laid the laurel wreath reverently upon the still forms at their feet.

As they knelt as one - - - each on bended knee - - - they gave thanks to the spirit of the mountain - - - and - - - the spirits of the deer whose lives that had just taken.

The mountain laurel - - - still fresh with dew - - - cried crystal tears of sorrow - - - which - - - slowly dripped into the still warm blood that was beginning to pool on the cool green forest floor.

Blood and tears embraced - - - as - - - - red hot living pools began their frantic search for mother earth and the father sky.

Small spurts life - - - still desperately clinging to the fawn - - - slowly relinquished their hold - - - to - - - form a red tinged mist - - - which pleadingly rose to beseech its father sky for one more chance at life - - - then faltered - - - to hover above the head of the huntsman and to finally explode into the heat of a roaring fire.

&&& THE MINSTREL &&&

As the fire died down - - - minstrel songs and women's laughter grew and wafted above the din of a boisterous crowd of well wishers gathered round a congenial bonfire - - - for - - - today was prophesized to be the birth of the royal heir of the Turquoise Tower.

Venison - - - which just a few hours before - - - had rejoiced as hart and roe in the woodland glade - - - slowly roasted above red glowing embers - - - which - - - seemed to be gasping a dying breath of their own.

Tower guards - - - drawn by the smell of roasting flesh and promises of draughts of frothing beers - - - had left their watch posts behind - - - and - - - joined as one with dazzling dancing girls.   Swaths of colors - - - swirling - - - reds - - - greens - - - yellows - - - swaying time to the music - - - slowly swept up into a whirlwind of flailing arms and legs - - - as - - - the pace of the music became more frenzied.

A shout – then muffled cries - - and writhing bodies melded with oaken ash and raced toward the sky - - - in a swirl of blackening colors and sounds.

&&& THE WARRIOR &&&

Savage swirling black ash - - - slowed and thickened - - - into a black tar-like pitch - - - as a monstrous warrior - - - torn and bloody - - - bellowed to his foot soldiers to smash open the shipbuilders' vast vats of pitch - - - and - - - flood the river with flaming death.

Men afraid - - - lest they be consumed by their own passions - - - froze then fled - - - abandoning women - - - and - - - children - - - and - - - honor.

Women and children wailed in despair at their abandonment - - - as - - - the giant warrior - - fending off sword and lance - - hewed at the cavernous vats with his obsidian blade - - as the ground became slippery with blood.

Wood splintered - - - then - - - groaned in a futile attempt to contain the life blood of the tree - - - which joyous at its escape - - - joined in a marriage vow with the living waters - - - to wreck vengeance on the ships and the men which had sought to subjugate them both.

A shield maiden - - - noble - - - and - - - strong - - - tore herself lose from the throng of wailing voices - - - and - - - clinging hands - - - and - - - by stealth and might battled her way to the river edge - - - where - - - with flint and nerves of steel - - - she lit the pitch into a ravenous inferno that consumed all in its path.

The massive warrior - - - now with a flaming sea at his back - - - hewed his way toward the Turquoise Tower - - - as - - - columns of red flame sought to devour a blood red sun.

A Flaming Wall of Fire - - -

⅋⅋⅋ THE BUILDER ⅋⅋⅋

As blood red flames continued to challenge his majesty the sun for dominance of the sky - - - earthbound orbs - - - fearful of being outdone by their celestial cousins - - - sought to obliterate all within their reach.

Flaming buckets of pitch - - - swung round on ropes by strong tireless arms - - - and then let fly - - - scattered the advancing throng - - - as - - - pitch laden torches cut searing swaths through walls of human flesh.

With a cry as of one already dead - - - The Builder of Towers and Dreams - - - fighting every higher instinct - - - sought - - - with a single-minded purpose - - - not to create - - - but - - - to - - - destroy all within his path.

As if with one thought with their brother warrior far below - - - his kinsmen hewed at cavernous cisterns filled with the distilled life blood of the pine - - - and - - - lay fire to its very soul - - - as - - - The Builder of Dreams - - - challenged the fiery death to a race - - - as - - - he desperately tore at the mosses and vines covering the rusted sluice gates guarding the canals to the ancient gardens below.

But the gates were stubborn and unyielding. As he hammered first one lock then the other - - - fist sized chunks of granite - - - torn from an unyielding earth - - - exploded into splinters from the sheer force of his blows. With naught but seconds of life remaining he tore at the last remaining - - - and - - - largest - - - gate with his bare hands. Slowly then suddenly flesh and muscle and bone succeeded where cold dead stone had not - - - as he tore open the Fiery Gates to Hell.

As the fiery death - - - now channeled away from the tower gardens - - - and - - - those they sheltered - - - roared past him to passionately embrace her wayward children - - - he could feel her starved passions unleashed - - - as - - - his tattered cloths burned lose from his shivering body.

Men's agonized cries stabbed him to the heart with icy daggers - - - as elite assassins disappeared from the shadows - - - only to become their own funeral pyres. The once stealthful enemy had but one glance and nothing more - - before their cries of terror were burned out of their throats.

As distilled turpentines and spirits poured into the canals and rushed with fiery insolence to greet their sister pitch gorging on the enemy ships below - - - the once powerful enemy fleet - - - obediently waiting in the secret shoals - - - crackled and roared with the wrath of betrayal. .

But - - -

Even as the Fire gorged on wooden ships and human fat - - -

The Crackling Blaze was pierced by the cry of a new-born baby - -

&&& THE TURQUOISE TOWER &&&

As- - -

The red fire walls dissolved into a thick choking curtain of soot and ash - - -

Black soot and then heavier particles of red flaming ash rained down upon the shield wall - - - igniting first the wood shingled roof and finally the massive oaken beams of the Turquoise Tower.

Tower Guards - - - loyally - - - put first their shields and then their mortal bodies between the merciless onslaught of flaming timbers and The Royal Womb.

Hand Maidens - - - bedecked in royal purple - - - lacked no less courage - - - and - - - although mortally wounded - - - thrust again-and-again their bodies between tip of spear and royal mother-with-child.

As a pitiless enemy shredded royal silks - - - implacable flaming timbers indifferently shattered shield and bone alike - - - as - - - The Royal Womb was mercilessly battered to the ground and buried beneath mound-upon-mound of unrelenting ash.

Suddenly - - -

Chilling cries outraced the pace of flame - - - ringing from without - - - ringing - - - with a piercing finality - - - as - - - the oaken supports to the outer stairway were withdrawn - - - and - - - the attackers fell to break their bones on the rock below.

Still - - -

The thick stifling ashes fell unrelentingly - - - to crush shield bearers beneath their weight. Flaming timbers kissed attacker and structure alike - - - with a white hot passion - - - to turn all into a burning hell. Fire balls of flailing arms and legs - - - raced out into the empty space - - - and - - - fell as miniature comets to explode on the rocks below. Swirling ashes - - - grayest of gray - - - whitest of white and blackest of black obscured all else.

Then - - -

All was silent.

For - - -

From deep within the black-white ashen landscape - - - a steel blue grappling hook shot skyward - - - and - - - with a clinking sound locked onto the entrance to the Tower Room. Hand-over-hand - - - a half naked form - - - burned and torn - - - scaled the outside of the Turquoise Tower.

Slowly swirling reds and blacks burst the confines of the tower room - - - as - - - the charred roof of the turquoise tower yielded to the sky.

Ashen cocoons - - - motionless beneath the still smoldering timbers - - - shuddered slightly - - - then gave way to trembling forms beneath them - - - as a grey powdered ash of wood and flesh - - - slowly metamorphosed to human form.

The last of the shields had held.

Slowly - - - gently - - - the first rains came - - -

At first - - -

Teasing their ancient enemy with soft delicate drops of dew - - -

Then - - -

Emboldened - - - and - - - Thirsting for Battle - - -

Raced earthward - - - with a ferocity and determination only matched by the cowardly flight of ash and soot into the sanctity of the sky.

Slowly - - - gently the loving hands of the Minstrel - - - gently wiped the ashes from the mouth, eyes and ears of the newborn king and rejoiced. But the royal womb - - - though bodily whole - - - had found her eternal sanctuary with her hand maidens.

Soft puffs of gray steam - - - swirled around the assembly - - - as those huddled in the catacombs below - - - broke through the rubble to congregate and give thanks to the rains - in the smoldering shell of the tower room - - - as the last wisps of steam gently wafted toward the sky to dance with the clouds.

&&& FESTIVAL &&&

Soft white wisps of swirling steam - - - from giant cast iron cauldrons - - - mischievously slipped away from their mother kettle - - - and - - - streamed into the bright morning sky.

Slowly - - - the gentle sound of great cooking kettles - - - was supplanted by the sound of laughter and merriment as a great assembly of lesser nobles approached - - - bedecked in their finest - - - for today was the day of the royal feast in celebration of the infant king's first birthday.

As the day was hot and with the sun burning brightly – most of the assembly sought shelter under the shade of a carefully erected tent - - - for all of the trees of this place - - - save one struggling oakling - - - were but a memory.

Broiled by the burning sun on their broad backs and the glowing embers before them - - - giant bearded cooks roasted whole oxen - - - as brewers sought to whet the appetite of the guests with great frothing flagons of strong black beer - - - more of a royal liquor than a common beer - - - such as the ones readily found in the local taverns throughout the countryside.

As those of the assembly stout enough to forgo the sheltering shade of the tent moved around in small groups in consensual enjoyment of one-another's company - - - their footsteps and merry making - - - sought out the secret hiding places of the grey ash - - - which hidden from the winds and rains of the past year - - - fled the disturbance as soft grey puffs into the sky.

As the royal astronomer idly fixed his gaze on one of these tiny puffs of ash - - - he followed it skyward and stood transfixed. One after another - - - the assembly followed his gaze to gasp in amazement at what lay above them.

High above - - - in celestial harmony - - - three rings stretched from horizon to horizon - - - and - - - further - - - (if one's imagination would allow) - - - coalesced of the purging fires and departing spirits of a year past.

That - - - which had been - - - as - - - far back - - - as - - - The Collective Memory - - - of - - - this folk could remember - - - One - - - had become - - - Three - - -

One Celestial Icen Ring - - - embracing the earth - - - had - - - now - - - overnight - - - become Three Icen Rings - - -

One of Red - - - as if of fire - - -

One of Blue - - - as if of water - - -

Another of Yellow - - - as if of the sun - - -

Each - - - married to the other - - - in a perfect display of symmetry - - - and - - - understanding.

As the three celestial rings - - - began to move - - - first as three - - - then as a multitude - - - swirling rings of dancing scarves moved aside to reveal the lithe forms of dancing girls - - - as dancers and minstrels - - - well schooled in their craft - - - sought to make the merry - - - all the more merry.

Suddenly - - - as if with one voice - - - the music was made quiet - - - as three great noblemen - - - royal guests - were led to their seats of honor - - - to the right of the infant king - - - each joking and laughing and truly bedecked in his finest raiment - - - raiment fine enough as to make the finery of the assembly seem as rags on a pauper .

First the great lord - - - then his two princes - - - kneeled before the infant king and swore their lives first and then their undying allegiance.

Servant girls with long flowing hair - - - each more beautiful than the other - - - waited on these three lords' beck and call - - - serving first steaming platters of roasted oxen - - - and - - - then bottomless and joyous flagons of rich black beer. They smiled – pleased to have made their lords happy and pleased that all had heartily partaken of the feast - - - for the merriment was great indeed - - - and - - - the banquet was great and joyous.

As the feast was complete - - - and - - - the utensils - - - such as they were - - - were cleared away - - - three of the most beautiful of the dancing women - - - one clad and painted in yellow - - - the next clad and painted in red - - - and - - - the third clad and painted in blue - - - knelt and offered a precious chalice to each of the three lords - - a yellow gold chalice, a red ruby chalice and an blue sapphire chalice. With one voice they as one knelt before their lords and chanted: "My Lords – we offer thee – these precious chalices – as tokens of our obedience to you."

The Lords – likewise and with one voice answered - - - "We thank you for your gift - - - and - - - we heartily accept your offer as a sign of our obedience to our infant lord."

With an almost imperceptible nod from the high priestess - - - six servant girls - - - two clad in yellow - - two clad in blue and two clad in red - - - moved - - - smiling - - - two to each side of each lord - - and bound his wrists and ankles to each chair with ropes made of maidens' hair - - - and - - - spoke: "We bind you lords – with the rope made of the hair of our mothers and our sisters who you have slaughtered."

With these words - - - each - - - of the kneeling women drew a knife: one with a bronze blade; the second with a ruby blade and the third with a sapphire blade – and with one movement – so swift as to be scare followed by human eye - opened a vein on each lord's wrist - - - as each lord - - - unflinching of blade and blood - - - spoke: "We give back to you - - - sisters - - - that blood - - - which we took from you - - - from that very same hand of ours which offended."

As the life blood of each lord slowly dropped into each chalice - - - the merry making continued as if nothing had happened - - - until some minutes later - - - - drop-by-drop - - - each chalice was one-third full.

Then each of the three maidens lifted her chalice and carried it to the High Priestess - - - who - - - made each third chalice whole - - - by pouring living blood into a white silver chalice - - - for white was the union of the three colors: the red, the blue and the yellow.

The High Priestess spoke: "Oh infant king - - - we - - - thus baptize you with the blood of our enemies. May the strength of three - - - become one in you."

With these words - - - she poured the blood of the three lords over the head of the infant - - - baptizing the infant - - - and - - - thus was he made king.

The off-pouring was collected in a bowl - - - and - - - fed to the royal oakling - - - for this was to be the royal tree thereby binding it with the fate and destiny of its people.

In this moment - - - the sight of the infant lord made majestic - - - and - - - the harmony of his people being so joyous and peaceful that the Sky Maidens - - - soft fluffy flights of fantasy - - - born of the union of hot passionate steam and cool celestial clouds - - - tenderly smiled on the assembly below. Likewise - - - as - - - those below gazed skyward they marveled - - - as - - - billowing cumulus clouds - - - framed against the bright blue sky - - - softly wafted from one gentle smile to another - - - as - - - quickly (or as slowly) as one's mind's eye would allow.

Once again the High Priestess spoke: "We are ready for you who have been so patiently waiting - - - mothers who lost sons - - - wives who lost husbands - - - daughters who lost fathers and we are ready for you who have so silently born an injustice - - mothers who lost daughters - - daughters who lost sisters - - daughters who lost brothers. Sink your spear and dagger into the unsundered flesh. What say you my Lords – are you ready?"

The High Lord answered: "We are ready for justice and we are eager to serve our infant king with our lives."

With these words the women slowly and deliberately ended the lives of the great lords as the oakling thirstily drank of its great gift.

&&& BEHIND THE MIRROR &&&

As the High Priestess - - blood - - - bedecked - - - besmeared - - - bemused - - - stood over the crumpled up forms of what had once been great lords - - - she smiled - - - for she too had avenged a fallen father.

As she turned - - - toward the temple - - - and - - - a new beginning for herself - - - and - - - her people - - - we could see the flash of bronze gold beneath her tunic - - - for - - - she was none other than the shield maiden - - - following her destiny.

As she stood - - - silent - - - gazing into the east - - - Seven Golden Pillars of Light - - - pierced the evening sky - - - scorching the charred earth - - - branding it with a golden blaze - - -

Burning the cold grey stone with a fiery golden hue - - - each pillar - - - marked the precise placement of what were to be The Seven Temple Towers - - - each dedicated to one of the Seven Sky Maidens - - - arrayed - - - solemn - - - silent - - - marking the passing of the seasons - - - from - - - summer to winter solstice - - -

As The Shield Maiden stood - - - proud - - - tall - - - silent - - - thoughts piercing the ghostly apparitions of the Temple Towers - - - she could see - - - forming in the east - - - against the backdrop of a kaleidoscopic evening sky - - - a mosaic - - -

From this mosaic - - - shapes formed - - - then - - - gradually faces - - - much as if her children - - - and - - - her - - - children's children - - - were gazing lovingly at her - - - even - - - as - - - she was gazing loving at them - - - across the countless years - - - and - - - lifetimes - - -

Then - - - most wondrously - - - much as if she were gazing into a pristine looking glass - - - one face appeared - - - amongst all others - - - a woman's face - - - a loving face - - - blood spattered - - - slowly being washed clean by tears - - - forty thousand tears - - -

It was she - - - she - - - herself - - - upon whom she was gazing - - -

&&& THE ROYAL OAKLING &&&

As the Royal Oakling thirstily drank of his repast and as the red rivulets slowly sank into the yellow clay the High Priestess spoke:

"You who are not yet born - - - heed your strength - - - for - - - your strength comes not from you alone - - - but - - - from those who have preceded you and from those who will follow you. Just as the clay cannot hold its form in the rain - - - so - - - can the life blood not sustain its form in the drought. You who are formed of the dust and the clay must fortify yourselves with the ashes of those who have passed before you - - - for - - - by doing so our ancestors will live within you and strengthen you. You who are formed from the sky must fortify yourselves with the spirits of those who have not yet been born - - - for by doing so you will live for an eternity."

Long after the guests had departed - - - and - - - long after lifetimes of shadows had deepened - - - strengthening their hold upon the night - - - solemnly spreading their silken sheen across the sleeping countryside - - - the yellow clays upon which the High Priestess had stood - - - awakened - - - and - - - stood up - - - proud and straight - - -

Proud - - - and - - - straight - - - and - - - tall - - - they stood - - - upon - - - the very spot upon which the Three Lords had bled - - - upon the very spot upon which the High Priestess had prayed - - - these - - - yellow clays - - - whetted with rich red living bloods - - - drenched with life itself - - - flowing - - - and - - - mixing with the blue-grey ashes of countless ancestors - - - melding - - - with - - - spirits - - - past - - - present - - - and - - - future - - -

Then - - -

Even As - -

They stood - - - tall - - - straight - - - and - - - proud - - - two forms took shape - - - having awaken of their own free will - - - growing perfect in form - - - and - - - stature - - -

As they opened their eyes - - - and - - - blinked - - - they - - - became - - - aware - - - first - - - of themselves - - - then slowly - - - of each other - - -

Aware of each other - - - they turned - - - and - - - smiled - - - gently embracing - - - kissing each other's smiling lips - - - but - - - ever so slightly - - -

Then - - -

With - - - The hunger of the first born - - - They - - - reached up - - - and - - - plucked the fruit of the tree which was offered to them - - - partaking of the knowledge of their people and of their destiny - - - eating - - - of the bitter fruit - - - knowing full well that not all that is sweet is good - - - and - - - not all that is bitter is bad.

Thus was the race born into peace - - - and - - - serenity - - - and - - - knowledge.

&& The Sleeping Chamber &&

"Now - - - now - - - my sweet Soyala - - - How are you feeling? It seems as if you've had quite an adventure for yourself - - - sneaking into that damp dark grotto in the middle of night - - - and - - - at your age - - - when you should be resting comfortably in bed!

You've taken quite a tumble - - - falling and hurting yourself - - - but - - - you're fine now - - - you'll be up and about any day now."

My goodness - - - what did you think that you were doing anyway?

Soyala's eyelids fluttered - - - then - - - opened - - - her mind - - - struggling to focus.

As the smiling face of the Empress of the Turquoise Palace slowly moved into her view - - - Soyala struggled to remember - - -

"Where am I? Who are you? Why - - -"

The Empress - - - doting over her charge - - - with - - - care and caresses - - - acting more like a maternal grandmother than a royal personage - - -

(Despite her sometimes stern royal admonishments) - - -

All the while - - - choosing to ignore the endless questions and mild protestations of her charge - - - kept on chirping away: "My - - - my - - - whatever on the earth did you think that you were doing? Going on up there - - - all alone - - - and - - - at that time of night."

"You certainly had me worried - - - big sister" - - - chimed in The Builder - - - standing up from the chair in which he had been sitting - - - and - - - stepping into Soyala's view - - - "I thought that that I had lost you. I've never seen so much blood - - - why - - -"

The Minstrel - - - impatiently pushing his mountain of a brother aside - - - squeezed in between him and the bed: "What do you mean - - - 'lost her - - - lost her?' - - - she's fine!"

"Aren't you Soyala - - - you're fine and we're all here and happy to see you" - - - he said half turning to the giant of a brother - - - "she's fine - - - Soyala's fine - - - and - - - all that she needs is a little bit of a rest - - - rest - - - AND - - - quite - - - and - - - turning back to face Soyala - - - "she'll soon be - - - as - - - good as new!!!"

You'll be as good as new - - - won't you - - - Soyala - - -

Soyala - - - still not yet fully comprehending who she was or where she was - - - and - - - having absolutely no idea why everyone was making such a fuss about her - - - looked from one brother to the other - - - trying to remember - - -

The Builder - - - still smarting about the fact that the diminutive minstrel had pushed his way in between Soyala and himself - - - was about to grab The Tiny Minstrel by the scruff of the neck - - - and - - - toss him out of the room - - - when - - - the Empress stepped into the middle of the melee - - -

"Enough! Enough of your squabbling!! OUT!!! Both of You - - - Out of here - - - I say! She needs her rest. She's better now - - - so - - - you don't have any excuse to hang around here anymore - - - OUT - - - OUT - - - NOW!!!" - - - commanded the Empress in her most imperial and threatening tone.

As the small group - - - The Builder - - - The Minstrel - - - The Concerned - - - and - - - The Curious - - - was quickly and unceremoniously ushered out of the door - - - a chamber maiden came in with a steaming bowl of soup."

"Soyala - - - here - - - eat this - - - you need your strength - - - it's your favorite - - - pumpkin soup." Sip it slowly - - - that's it - - - I bet that you feel better all ready."

Soyala - - - the - - - Mists of Forgetfulness slowly rising - - - her mind clearing - - - was gently helped to sit upright - - - as - - - a second chamber maid fluffed her pillow. Leaning gently backward - - - Soyala weakly smiled - - - and - - - then obediently began to sip on the spoonfuls of hot soup offered to her by the first chambermaid - - - gratefully savoring the warmth of the food - - - her first food in five days - - - as it began to course through her weakened body - - - strengthening her body - - - cheering her spirit.

&&& Dreamtime &&&

Sleep.

       Sleep.

              Sleeping.

How - - -

          Unlike - - - unconsciousness - - -

But - - -

          Somehow so strangely familiar - - -

Familiar - - -

          Dream - - -

              Dreams - - -

                   Dreaming - - -

As Soyala's head pressed gently into her pillow - - - her - - - dreams - - - came - - - hesitantly - - - humbly - - - hauntingly - - - then - - - obediently - - - back to her - - -

Haughty horrible dreams - - -

          Sweet seductive dreams - - -

              Languid - - - limpid dreams - - -

Dreams - - -

          Foretelling the future - - -

          Betraying the past - - -

Dreams - - -

Fragments - - -

Broken lifetimes - - -

Mended hearts - - -

A field - - - brown - - - barren - - - lifeless - - - strewn with naught but rocks - - -

Rocks - - - decaying into sand - - -

Sand - - - decaying into dust - - -

Dust - - - the stuff of memories - - - and - - - dreams - - -

Sand - - - blowing - - - blowing - - - sand - - - endless sand - - - unrelenting - - - filling lungs - - - blinding eyes - - - stopping ears - - -

Stone - - - shards - - - slivers - - - half buried - - - half forgotten - - - jagged defiant remnants of some great mountain - - - dancing - - - as if to the tune of some ancient wind pipe - - - plowing deep furrows into the unyielding ground - - - deep into the night - - -

Then - - -

Finally - - -

One-by-one - - -

Growing weary from the dance - - - and - - - of - - - the song - - - and - - - of - - - the companionship of others - - - and - - - most earnestly longing for eternal sleep - - - these great stones quietly lay themselves down as a barrier against flood - - - and - - - beast - - - and - - - memory - - -

Then - - -

Strangely - - -

With the dawn of day - - - it were as if some great green mantel were laid gently upon the barren ground - - -

Green - - - greens - - - dark greens - - - light greens - - - shimmering - - - shining - - - sparkling - - -

Green mats of moss - - - and - - - of - - - fern - - - and - - - of - - - forest - - -

Green shoots - - - green sprouts - - - green stalks - - - growing - - - climbing - - - high into the midnight blue sky - - -

Emerald Greens of mountains and hill tops - - - embracing an indigo sky - - -

Then - - -

Gold - - -

Golden - - - spots - - - dots - - - pocks - - - marring the landscape - - -

Red-Golds - - - Yellow-Golds - - - White-Golds - - - littered across crisp green fields - - -

Then - - -

Grains - - - golden-grains - - - of - - - sands - - - and - - - of - - - dusts - - - and - - -

Red Golden Grains - - - Yellow Golden Grains - - - White Golden Grains - - - sprinkled delicately - - - almost - - - imperceptibly - - - amongst the lush green foliage - - - of the hills - - - and - - - of the valleys - - -

Then - - -

Renegade Child - - -

      Renegade Runaway - - -

      Runaway Child - - -

Carefree Child - - - fleeing from the skies - - - burrowing deep into its earth nest - - - brooding - - - sleeping - - - brooding - - -

Nest egg of the wheat - - - growing - - - growing - - - brooding - - - still - - - growing - - -

Diminutive Grain of the Wheat - - - Egg of the Wheat - - - brooding - - - growing - - - stretching - - -

Cuckoo Egg of the Wheat - - - pushing - - - shoving - - - pounding - - - the turquoise blue hummingbird's egg out of its nest - - -

Sleeping - - -

Stirring - - - stretching - - - striving - - - growing - - -

Dwarfing the white-brown egg of the ostrich - - -

Then - - - finally - - - satisfied - - - wishing to be born - - - let its solitary egg tooth slice open the withered leathery shell of it egg prison - - - and - - - stood - - - blind - - - cold - - - confused - - - alone - - - against the waving fields of golden wheat - - -

As all things must come to pass - - - the hairy - - - fuzzy - - - ball of bird fluff - - - grew - - - until a Majestic Blue Heron stood in its place - - - towering above the wheat - - - surveying all that was his domain - - - and - - - coveting all that was beyond - - -

And - - - too - - - as all great things must come to pass - - - the wheat fields crumbled to dust - - - and - - - The Great Blue Heron - - - withered and wrinkled with age - - - split open to let free a hummingbird from its feathered prison - - -

As - - - The Hummingbird - - - ruby jewel upon its breast - - - newborn - - - and - - - passionate at its newfound freedom - - - wept tears of joy - - - glorious green plants sprung forth where each teardrop had kissed the earth - - -

An emerald forest - - - bedecked with amethyst blossoms - - - gilded golden stamens and pearl white berries - - - poisonous to some perhaps - - - but - - - breathtakingly beautiful to others - - -

Beneath this emerald forest of amethysts - - - and - - - golds - - - and - - - pearls - - - sprang forth a fount - - - showering iridescent plumage with glistening droplets of wisdom - - - and - - - courage - - - and - - - truth - - -

Glistening - - - shimmering droplets - - -

But - - -

It was just the chambermaid - - - sprinkling cooling refreshing rose scented water upon Soyala's forehead - - - to sooth and waken her - - -

Days passed - - - as did weeks and even a month or two - - -

"Soyala - - - Soyala - - - wake up my darling."

A soft voice - - - a woman's voice - - - her grandmother's voice - - - whispered gently in Soyala's ear - - - or - - - so Soyala dreamed - - - but - - - it was only the early morning breeze softly tiptoeing through the bedchamber - - - on its way outside to play with the sweet swaying grasses and the whimsically wandering butterflies in the palace gardens - - -

"Soyala - - - my sweet - - - you must awaken - - - it is time."

Soyala slowly opened one eye - - - and - - - then the other - - - stretching and yawning her way into the morning - - -

Her terrible wounds finally healed - - - Soyala greeted the morning rays with her former joy and exuberance - - - although - - - her sometimes aching joints still reminded her that she was not quite yet ready to dive the one hundred feet into a palace pool!!!

She stretched again - - - subconsciously - - - rubbing some of the lingering purplish scars that had left their mark - - - on her arms and thighs - - -

Purple scars - - - purple memories - - - memories of long thin cuts slashed into her flesh - - - memories of scorched skin - - - memories of searing pain and torment - - - almost as if she had suffered her wounds by running a gauntlet of slashing swords and fiery brands - - - so that another might live - - - rather than having taken an innocent tumble down some child's mountain fortress - - -

"Soyala - - - come to me" - - - coaxed the grandmother's voice - - - "Come to me."

Another time - - - another voice - - - her voice - - - but younger - - - more innocent - - - most sweetly innocent - - - laughing - - - playing - - - dancing in the sun - - - answered: "Yes - - - Grandma - - - I'm coming."

Her grandmother - - - great gentle grandma - - - sitting - - - smiling - - - singing - - - cradling a tiny girl child sitting gently on her lap - - - telling tales of old - - - of - - - heroes - - - heroines - - - battles - - - and - - - of - - - cakes and pies - - - some magical - - - some not - - - and - - - all sorts of delicious long forgotten secrets that no one else but the grandmother could know - - -

Of hidden sweets and hidden treasures - - - of cookie jars and maidens' pleasures

Of secret doors and secret paths - - - of - - - scented jades and bubble baths

Of long haired maids and long faced elders - - - of a lovers' tryst in a copse of elders

Of weeping maids and weeping willows - - - of sleeping queens on great white pillows

Of Jaguar Claw and Jaguars wild - - - of - - - Orchid Blossom and her child - - -

Of sparkling wines and sparkling gems - - - of family trees both branch and stems

Of crystal caves and crystal glass - - - of - - - rugged rock and soft green grass - - -

Of - - -

"Soyala my Sweet - - - it is time - - - come." The voice tugged at Soyala as Soyala - - - almost as if in a trance - - - walked to the far end of the bed chamber and opened the doors of a great and massive wooden Schrank.

Pushing aside all sorts of cloths - - - and - - - shoes - - - and - - - memories - - - Soyala lightly stepped into the past - - - and - - - following her grandmother's voice - - - slide open a secret panel in the back of the Schrank.

Before her in a well lit room - - - lay all sorts of secrets: Secret Knowledge - - - Secret Passions - - - Secret Pleasures - - -

Each calling - - - each yearning to be discovered by a gentle hand and a sweet - - - sweet smile - - - all jealous of the other - - - all calling - - - all pleading - - - all entreating: "Me - - - me first - - - please - - - please - - - Please take me!"

Of all of the secrets - - - the most alluring - - - the most beautiful - - - the most demanding - - - was a dress robe - - - pristine - - - powerful - - - pure - - -

This robe - - - of all robes - - - was neither a simple utilitarian item as the working folk wear - - - nor - - - a fancy frilly useless thing worn by the vain and pompous - - - but - - - well - - - words simply fail me:

> Wool and felt and beaver pelt
>   Conch and coral and forest laurel
> Gold and gems and fur lined hems
>   Broach of jade and gold brocade

But – that is not all - - -

How should we best continue?

> Oyster's jewels strung forty strong
>   Five times five each two feet long

> Silkworm's gift dyed deep dark red
>   Silken sheen from toe to head

Golden clasps with jewels inlaid
  Ruby and Emerald with a touch of Jade

Beaver Cap with a golden peak
  Pearl Pendants dangling past the cheeks

Beaver Wrap for the pigtailed hair
  Sideways bound then flowing fair

Orange sleeve with a silken sheen
  Brocade embroidered emerald green

Secrets - - -

  Yielded - - - and - - - shielded - - -

  Divined - - - and - - - entwined - - -

"Soyala - - - Soyala" - - -

The robe - - - whispering to her - - - embracing her - - - cuddling her - - - had led Soyala to a great freestanding mirror - - - a - - - marvelous - - - miraculous - - - magical mirror - - -

As Soyala coyly peeked into the mirror - - - she saw standing before her - - - a woman - - - beautiful - - - glorious - - - resplendent - - -

Resplendently attired in a magnificent red silken robe decorated with a gold and silver brocade - - - fitted with orange sleeve covers - - - which were themselves also decorated with a brocade - - - but not of silver or gold - - - but - - - of a deep emerald green - - - it seemed as if she were carefully scrutinizing Soyala to ensure that all was perfect and fitting - - -

Although impossible to say who was scrutinizing whom - - - the - - - pristine - - - perfect - - - pure - - - figure behind the mirror - - - smiled - - - and - - - moved her hand slowly - - - slightly - - - ever so softly - - -

Slowly - - - carefully - - - Soyala placed the beaver fur cap upon her head - - - tilting and rotating it this way and that - - - until the cap sat perfectly square upon her head - - - for - - - it must sit perfectly - - - and - - - not sit askew - - - for in the middle of this cap was a ruby and emerald studded golden mount - - - from which hung two pearl pendants - - -

Pearl pendants - - - hanging down alongside her cheeks - - - each perfectly level with the other - - - reaching tantalizing down to brush softly against her breasts - - -

Each pendant consisted of five bundles each - - - each bundle consisting of five strands - - - which in turn consisted of forty pearls to a strand - - -

Two thousand pearls - - - two thousand jewels of the oyster - - - artfully arranged small to large - - - top to bottom - - - each strand beautifully tipped with a single shaped piece of blazing red coral - - -

As if this magnificence were not enough - - - a pearl necklace of three strands of alternating large and small pearls - - - attached to each side of the golden cap - - - perfectly crafted and proportioned - - - looping gracefully to lay gently on the silken red robe - - -

Her hair - - - long - - - lustrous - - - luxurious - - - was carefully bound in a beaver hair sleeve - - - stiffened and played out straight to shoulder width - - - where it was then let to fall freely to her waist - - - as a delicately bundled pigtail - - -

Each beaver hair sleeve was decoratively held in place by four hair clips each - - - each one of gold and studded with rubies and emeralds - - - each of a different size and shape - - - but all perfectly matched - - -

Her feet - - - were warmly nestled in fleecy sheepskin boots - - - the toes of which were coyly turned upward - - -

As Soyala watched - - - the image in the mirror before her - - - stretched out her hand as a diminutive hummingbird gently alighted upon her outstretched finger - - -

Hummingbird - - - as in her dream - - - was it an omen - - - or - - - perhaps a totem?

Perhaps both - - - foreordaining the day when she - - - Soyala - - - would escape from this palace prison - - - and - - - become a woman and then a queen in her own right - - -

So it is - - - with dreams - - - and - - - the flights of hummingbirds - - -

&&& OF QUEENDOMS AND HERALDRY &&&

&&& The Seven Sisters &&&

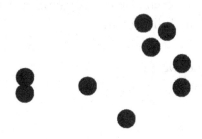

Upon each of these seven hills - - - upon each of these charred and blackened mountain peaks - - - cold grey granite was awakened out of its eternal sleep by the gentle trickle of a silver rain of starlight - - -

Starlight - - -

Seven Pillars of Celestial Starlight - - -

Touching upon each of the seven hilltops - - -

Grain upon grain - - - silver upon silver - - -

Blazoning the hills with a sign - - - a - - - star sign - - - a - - - Totem - - -

Silver Starlight - - - filtered through the red burning flames of watch tower fires - - - tempered by the white hot passions of lovers' hearts - - - quenched in the icy blue waters of the evening mountain skies high above the clouds - - -

Starlight - - - silver - - - silver - - - starlight - - -

Brashly blazoning the hilltops with a star sign - - - a - - - Star Sign of The Pleiades - - - a - - - Star Sign of the Seven Sisters - - - a - - - Star Sign of the Sky Maidens - - -

&&& Moon Glow &&&

As she gently brushed the Moon Glow away from the hilltop - - - The Shield Maiden gently laid her first born upon the golden blaze - - - imbuing her with the totem of the Sky Maidens - - -

Thus - - - was the eldest - - - of - - - Seven Sisters - - - baptized in a Shower of Celestial Starlight - - - emblazoned - - - with the Sign of the Totem - - -

Upon the hilltops - - - seven statues were raised - - -

The First - - -

Cast of red-gold bronze - - -

Her sisters - - -

Carved of precious copper ores - - -

The Seven Sisters of the Pleiades - - -

Polished to a sublime sheen - - -

Emblazoned by the fiery light of the Sky Maidens - - -

Sacred Copper Ores - - - for - - - copper was a holy metal to these folk - - - having freed these people from the eternal labor of stone - - -

Copper Ores - - -

Blue Azurite - - -

Green Malachite - - -

Red Cuprite - - -

Yellow Chalcopyrite - - -

Brown Bornite - - -

Grey Chalcocite - - -

Each sister - - - in her own birthright - - - marked the seasonal passing of the Pleiades through the heavens - - -

From marking the helical rising of the summer solstice - - - and - - - the time of planting - - - to the marking of the winter solstice - - - and - - - the time of festivities - - - these seven maidens stood solemn and dutiful watch over their charge - - -

For never again - - - would - - - an - - - enemy - - - strike unawares - - -

&&& THE SKALD'S CREED &&&

To all whom fear the conquer's bite
  To all whom jeer the peace dove's flight
To all whom hide in deathly fright - - -
  Proudly hear the Sky Maidens' plight - - -

While some might naysay the Star Maid's Light
  While others too the Star Maid's Might
Twas bane and bale throughout the night - - -
  Twas flame and sword which stormed the height —

Twas not powdered tin of a brazier's rite - - -
  Nor an etching scratched into the white - - -
But a shield of she — a conquer's blight - - -
  Beauteously born of celestial light - - -

Admittedly it was the Skald's delight - - -
  Rhythm and rhyme and legend to dight - - -
Shield Maiden Strong — she was hight - - -
  Shield Maiden Troth - she did plight - - -

Shield Maiden!!!

Hear you now what we recite —
  Neath your shield which us unites —
Neath the Pleiades Blaze that doth ignites —
  The Flaming Death and the War Cry Shright

We pledge death!!!

To all whom scorn your sacred sight –
To all whom mock your sacred right –
To all whom doubt this sacred site –
To all whom lour the celestial bright -

This we swear!!!

&&& The Seven Queendoms &&&

While heretics might proclaim - - - that it was some alchemist's trick - - - to use the powders of tin - - - carefully laid - - - into a pleasing pattern of two plus seven spheres - - - gently - - - most - - - gently - - - warmed by an earthly fire - - - rather than the divine luminescence of the Pleiadel Light itself - - - all were unanimous in their love and homage to this Warrior Maid - - - this - - - Maiden of Bronze - - -

In fact - - - so great was their love - - - and - - - so true was their homage - - - that it is told that when the young queen took unto herself a Prince Consort - - - the rejoicing throughout the realm was scarce contained - - -

However - - - even as great as was the love - - - and - - - even as scarce contained as was the rejoicing - - - all was as naught as when compared to the riotous raucous revelry which announced the birth of The Bronze Maiden's first born - - - a girl child - - -

A Girl Child - - - imbued with the Light of the Pleiades - - - destined to become a queen in her own right - - -

Seven Sisters - - - in all - - - imbued with the Light of the Pleiades - - - all queens - - - each taking unto themselves blood-sisterhood with the Seven Sisters of the Pleiades - - -

For - - - was it not natural that the flesh and the spirit should become as one?

And - - -

Was it not true that their mother's mother was not born of the selfsame stuff from which dreams and stardust are born?

So - - - it was done - - -

Seven Sisters - - - Seven Queendoms - - - Seven Blood-Sisterhoods - - -

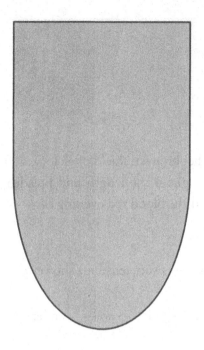

Stardoms - - -

    Pleiadel Sisters - - -

    Blue white light - - - imbuing spirit into the flesh - - -

    Burnishing bronze with a sheen more gentle than moon glow - - -

Queendoms - - -

    Pleiadel Mirror - - -

    Reflecting red-blue flames - - -

    Burning blazons into the bronze - - -

Shield - - -

    Pleiadel Palette - - -

    Plighting Troth and Valor - - -

Blood Sisterhood - - -

Seven Sisters - - -

Seven Queendoms - - -

Seven Shields - - -

As the Bronze Maiden - - - held her bronzen shield of victory aloft - - - the gentle breeze of victory blowing softly but steadily throughout the length and breadth of the valley below her - - - a solitary shaft of blue light pierced the blood red evening sky - - - gently bathing maid and shield with an ethereal glow - - -

Ethereal Glow - - - ethereal flow - - - sweet sensuous shower of starlight - - -

Sweet azure starlight - - - tenderly - - - oh - - - so - - - tenderly bathing maid and shield - - -

Sweet azure shower - - - gently - - - oh - - - so - - - gently - - - washing blood from maid and bronze - - -

Gentle maid - - - imbued with the Pleiadel Spirit - - - basking in starlight - - -

Brazen Shield - - - emblazoned with the plight of troth and valor - - - burning in starfire - - -

And - - -

So it was - - - this - - - Maid of Bronze - - - this - - - Bronze Maiden - - - brought forth her golden shield from the mountain - - - blazoned with an Azure Tower - - - symbol of her plight of troth and valor - - - to her people - - -

Or Field – Azure Tower

With the birth of each girl child - - - each child was lovingly carried to one of the seven mountain peaks - - - to be laid within the Sign of the Pleiades - - - to be bathed in celestial light - - - to be imbued with the Spirit of the Seven Sisters - - -

Later - - - upon the coming of age of each girl child - - - and - - - upon each girl child becoming as Bloodsister to one of the Seven Pleiadel Sisters - - - her mother raised a temple statue upon the sacred spot - - - designating her daughter as Protectress Initiate to the realm - - -

114

Likewise - - - with each initiation of each girl child - - - so too was the shield baptized in the light of the Pleiades - - - with one red (gules) sphere - - - in the pattern of the Pleiades star cluster - - - being added - - - until two plus seven gules spheres stood proud and silent watch over the Azure Tower below - - -

Or Field – Azure Tower – Two plus Seven Gules Spheres

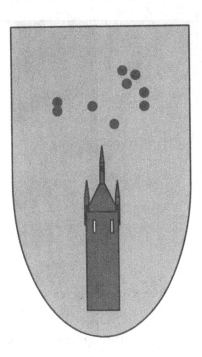

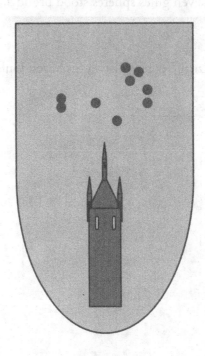

Or Field – Azure Tower – Two plus Seven Gules Spheres - - -

Proud and silent guardians of the realm - - - throughout countless cycles of births - - - and - - - unbirths - - - and - - - rebirths - - -

Until - - -

That day - - - when the clouds of war began to slowly gather over the realm - - - darkening - - - oh - - - so ever slowly - - - but surely - - - darkening - - -

Darkening - - - ever darker still - - - 'till scare could be seen - - - even by the light of day - - -

&&& The Gangrel Ghost &&&

!!! SHE !!!

Clad in a freely flowing gray cloak - - - covered by a great gray floppy hat - - -

Neither young nor old - - - tall nor short - - - thin nor fat - - -

Features - - - neither fine nor course - - - hidden from curious eyes by a long thick mane of gray hair - - - neither kempt nor unkempt - - -

Vagrant - - - homeless - - - gangrel - - -

Wandering like a wraith wafting through the countryside - - - since before the beginning of time - - -

Roving like an avenger - - - challenging king and beggar alike - - - for a share of alms and kingdoms - - -

An ethereal being - - - more real than a shadow - - - less real than a dream - - -

&&& THE LAW STONE &&&

The Seven Stone Sentinels - - - serene - - - stoic - - - somber - - - guardian goddesses of the realm - - - smiling down upon their troubled children - - - comforting - - - consoling - - - caressing them - - - stood stark - - - noble - - - proud - - - against the bright blue early morning sky - - -

Their children - - - troubled - - - terrified - - - tormented - - - stood motionless - - - immobile as the rocks - - - garments of rustic hues becoming as one with the Rockscape - - - compassion - - - hardened and immobile as the painted rocks amongst them - - -

Rockscape - - - great gathering of rock and cliff and sky - - -

Law Stone - - - great gathering of the realm - - - rising above the cliffs - - - bridging earth and sky - - - worn smooth by countless centuries of lawgivers and lawtakers waging eternal battle within the Ring of Doom - - -

Ring of Doom - - - Doom Ring - - - eternal circle - - - never starting - - - never ending - - - all equal - - - none unequal - - - all of equal voice - - - all of one voice - - -

Seven Queens were they - - - and - - - Seven Priests - - -

Seven Chapmen (merchants) were they - - - and - - - Seven of the People - - -

All equal - - - all righteous - - - all foresworn - - - all honor bound - - -

The Queens - - - Bloodsisters of the Pleiades - - - bridging earth and sky - - -

The Priests - - - Bloodbrothers of the Flesh - - - divining all that is wrought of clay - - -

The Chapmen - - - eyes and ears and heart - - - carrying tales far and wide - - -

The People - - - land's blood - - - breathing life and joy and rebirth into the land - - -

The Ring of Doom - - - The Circle of Judgment - - - no beginning - - - no end - - -

Down below this primordial plateau - - - of - - - Queens and Rings and Hope - - - eager - - - hopeful faces turned upward to gaze lovingly - - - pleadingly - - - hopefully upon the calming faces of the brothers and sisters of the ring - - -

Strong and weak - - - rich and poor - - - noble and commoner - - - waited - - -

As each member of the ring spoke his turn and called his allotted witness - - - the sun climbed high into the afternoon sky - - -

But - - -

If one were to tear his gaze away from the sun and the sky and the lawgivers - - - to cast his gaze downward - - - ever downward - - - even further downward - - - far from the glare of the sun - - - and - - - even further from the flare of the passionate and impassioned - - - once could see - - - far - - - far - - - below the great law stone - - - a slender gnarled shadow slowly winding its way past Chapmen and Goodmen - - - past smith and farrier - - - past tinker and falconer - - - past glover and wright and cobbler - - -

Hobbling from the shadows into the light - - - one-eyed - - - gangrel of nature - - - clad in a flowing grey cloak - - - buried beneath a great floppy grey hat - - - long flowing mane of gray hair - - - walking stick - - - even more gnarled and bent than she - - - The Grey Seeress - - - steadily - - - purposefully - - - made her way toward the great circle of doom - - - neither in haste - - - nor of a meandering stride - - - but - - - in a most careful and deliberate manner - - - becoming with each step - - - somehow most purposeful and fearsome - - -

Waving aside the offerings proffered by the nervous trembling hands and timid hearts of the Alms Givers - - - who - - - cowering from her sight lest she fix her one good eye upon their hapless soul -

118

- - thereby dooming it to some indescribable and eternal torment - - - The Grey Seeress - - - moved effortlessly through the throng of the faithful and the curious to the Great Circle - - -

Pushing through the circle of seven times four - - - much as even a shadow might easily pass through the embers of a fire unscathed - - - she waved her hand - - - and - - - the speaker - - - a Priest - - - a diviner of the clay - - - reliving in violent gestures - - - a dark dream he had had just the night before - - - of war and famine and death - - - became suddenly silent - - - mouthing words for which no sound could be heard - - - for which no thought could be told - - -

Then - - -

As all became still - - - The Grey Seeress began to speak - - - with a crackling cackling voice which steadily became stronger - - -

"You" - - - she cackled - - - pointing a bony finger at the circle - - - and - - - turning as she spoke to fix all with her one-eyed gaze - - - "must seek victory - - - for - - - victory will not seek you - - - only - - - death will seek you"

Pointing her bony finger one more time - - - this time at a group of boys standing off in the distance beneath an ancient and massively gnarled oak tree she spoke:

Cast not the acorns from the tree - - -
    Instead - - - bring the two plus seven back to me - - -
Let us place them on the ground - - -
    Trace a line that goes round and round - - -

Now lay that line against the sky - - -
    When the Seven come on nigh - - -
Can you now see that fearsome head?
    Can you now see those eyes so red?

Now call upon your sisters true - - -
    Let them show the path to you - - -
Fear you not the feathered beast - - -
    Let him lead you to the feast - - -

Emblazon upon your shields so bold - - -
    The ruby spheres as you've been told - - -
Form you then this fearsome head - - -
    That lion masters so sorely dread - - -

Two weeks hence you must mount and ride - - -
    Lest you fail and break your stride - - -
Perish naught - - - neither thought nor deed - - -
    Trust your shield and noble steed!

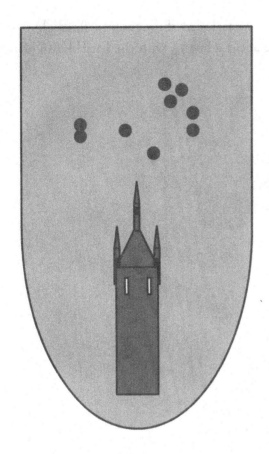 

Her words - - - grating coarsely on the ears of some - - - flowing as gently and as sweetly as a melodic brook on others - - - froze The Ring in time and space - - - as each lawgiver pondered the improbable - - -

The Grey Seeress - - - then turned and left the circle - - - some say as an old grey hag clad in tatters and rags - - - others say as a young blond maiden - - - long flowing hair with garlands in her hair - - - but - - - none-the-less - - - leave she did - - - abandoning a silent and stunned circle behind her - - -

Debate raged throughout the night - - - priests and seers and prophets were summoned - - - bones were read and incantations recited - - - ancient scrolls were studied and scrutinized - - -

Until - - -

It is another story how the bravest of the brave - - - rode out into the night - - - into some far distant valley to capture and tame the lion killers - - -

It too is another story of how the Armorers and Priests toiled throughout a fortnight - - - fashioning shields - - - emblazoned with Sacred Pleiadel Light - - - with the fiery blazon of the Lion Killer - - -

For - - -

As the Doom Ring came to first accept - - - and - - - then to understand - - -

Did not the Pleiades in the midnight sky foreordain the blazon of the Lion Killer?

And justly so - - - for - - - was it not true that the female bird of prey is larger and fiercer than her mate??

Therefore it was the destiny of the sacred powers that each queen bear as her standard as shield of Or Field – Azure Tower – Lion Killer - - -

Thus - - - it was - - - that an even greater story remaining to be told was how this great host rode off to do battle - - - and - - - to win victory - - - on what is now called the Porcelain Plain.

For - - - even today - - - the old women - - - huddled together before the warmth of the hearth - - - tell of the coming and of the prophesy of she who bore the seven sisters - - - and - - - the great victory of the Winged Riders - - -

And - - -

Of how it came to pass that upon the field of victory - - - each of the seven sisters - - - each a queen - - - bore as her standard Or Field – Azure Tower – Lion Killer in the color of her royal house - - -

&& THE ROYAL CELEBRATION &&

&&& Shadow Play &&&

"Your Imperial Majesties" - - -

As the deep booming voice reverberated throughout the massive stone throne room - - - the ruddy faced actor - - - barely contained with the excitement of addressing His Most Imperial Emperor of the Turquoise Tower - - - and - - - his empress consort - - - Empress Feiyan - - - (Flying Swallow) - - - quivered noticeably - - - and - - - flushed even more deeply - - - before continuing - - -

"Your MOST Illustrious Majesties - - - today - - - on this - - - the most festive of your occasions - - - you have standing before you - - - your most humble and obedient servants - - -

We - - - WILL - - - present for your amusement - - - and - - - pleasure - - - a play - - - a - - - Play of Shadows - - - a - - - Shadow Play - - - if you will - - - to honor your Most Imperial Majesties - - - in a most befitting manner for this most momentous occasion - - -

"Shadows – your Most Imperial Majesties - - - shadows (whispered) - - -

"Mere - - - Whispers of Sunlight" - - -

"Whispers - - - Your Imperial Majesties - - - whispers."

Slowly - - - symmetrically - - - torches were extinguished - - - first the great torches ringing the cathedral hall - - - then - - - the lesser torches - - - leaving only the innermost portion of the throne room lit - - - as - - - The Actor's Voice - - - perfectly matching the intensity of the light - - - moved from a deep imperial reverberating boom to a mere whisper - - -

"Shadows - - - Your Most Imperial Majesties - - - shadows (whispered) - - -

Or - - -

Perhaps - - -

Nothing - - -

As the Actor spoke - - - a great sprawling silken sheet was raised from the floor - - - backlit by fiercely burning reflecting torches - - - of - - - reds - - - and - - - blues - - - and - - - greens - - -

"AHHHHHhhhhhh" - - - a most wondrous and audible gasp of amazement escaped from the audience - - - as - - - The Actor continued - - - with - - - yet another grand flourish and a bow - - -

"MY MOST IMPERIAL AND BELOVED MAJESTIES"

"!!!LET THE PLAY BEGIN!!!"

As the remaining torches were dimmed - - -

A Dancer - - - slim and sinuous - - - slow and sensuous - - - silks and locks - - - flowing - - - began to dance before the silken screen - - - mimicked in her every movement by her shadow - - - bowing - - - twirling - - - swirling - - - whirling - - -

Then - - -

Most magically and wondrously - - - the one shadow split into three - - - one - - - to the left - - - another - - - to the right - - - as - - - each followed precisely the movements of the lithe agile dancer in front of the screen - - -

"Shadows - - - shadows" - - - continued The Actor - - - "but who is whom?"

Just as suddenly as they had appeared - - - the two shadow figures disappeared leaving only the one original shadow - - - which suddenly stopped - - - legs spread apart - - - hands on hips - - - standing - - - waiting - - - observing - - - as - - - the young dancer continued her dance - - - twirling - - - round - - - and - - - round - - - and - - - round - - -

Then - - -

The Shadow - - - left hand on her left hip - - - slowly - - - purposefully - - - raised her right hand - - - and - - - with a furious flourish - - - made a swift swirling motion overhead - - -

Swirling hand - - - whirling dancer - - -

Then - - -

Abruptly - - -

The Shadow Hand slowed - - - as did the dancer - - - slower - - - slower - - - ever slower - - -

Until - - -

Both hand and dancer were motionless - - -

The Dancer - - - standing - - - motionless - - - like a limp rag doll - - - hands hanging loosely at her sides - - -

The Shadow - - - poised - - - unmoving - - - stoic - - - proud - - - hands on hips - - -

Then - - -

Throwing back her head - - - The Shadow - - - (silently) - - - roared a raucous laugh - - - disappearing into the aura of the torches - - - as - - - The Dancer - - - quietly faded into the shadows - - -

"Shadows" - - - breathed The Actor - - - "shadows" - - -

The Torches faded - - -

&&& Battle of the Flaming Wall &&&

Quiet - - -

Quieter still - - -

Silence - - -

Silence so powerful and deafening that one could hear hearts beating excitedly in the darkness
- - -

Then - - -

!!!FLAMES!!!

Writhing Flames - - -

      Withering Flames - - -

            Wilting Flames - - -

As - - -

Cymbals clashed - - - and - - - drums pounded - - -

Ninja clad acrobats - - - chased by silken comet tails - - - slid down invisible silken ropes - - - to crash noisily to the ground - - - before rolling silently away into the shadows - - - unharmed - - -

As the smoke and flame from the torches cleared from the air - - - and - - - the great stone walls quieted themselves from the deafening din of the cymbals and of the drums - - - The Actor - - - once again spoke:

"Spirits - - - Your Majesties - - - Spirits" - - -

      Of ancestors past - - -

            And - - -

            Of descendents future - - -

Visions - - -

      Of a future lived - - -

            And - - -

Of a past stillborn - - -

As the comet fire slowly spread - - - via - - - colored lights and blowing silks - - -

The great torches - - - slowly brought to life a gentle green forest - - -

In the midst of this harmony of gentle green mosses - - - softly swaying ferns - - - and - - - stoic pines - - - majestically silhouetted - - - stood - - - a - - - Giant Stag - - -

Majestic - - - Lord of all that Moved - - - Paradise Incarnate - - -

Against this backdrop - - - of - - - green fields - - - and - - - green sky - - - The Actor spoke - - - recounting the story of the day of battle - - - captured in the mosaics of the palace grotto:

"Your Imperial Majesties - - - we now humbly present for your pleasure - - -

"!!! THE BATTLE OF THE FLAMING WALL !!!"

As the Giant Shadow Stag - - - Lord of the Forest - - - stood - - - supreme - - - sublime - - - life's blood pumping proudly through his veins - - - a smaller shadow - - - a shadow of a huntsman - - - bow in hand - - - stealthy - - - silently - - - moved toward him - - -

As the music of a flute - - - gently wafted over and around the great screen - - - and - - - toward the assembly - - - it was punctuated by the shrill of a pipe - - - as - - - the Shadow Bow released its missile of death - - -

As the yew arrow bit deeply into living flesh - - - the Great Stag frantically pawed the air - - - mortally wounded - - -

As the Great Shadow fell - - - the - - - one shadow - - - broke up into several smaller shadows - - - fleeting shadows - - - as - - - the great stag's harem milled about in panic - - - before - - - fleeing into the safety of the green shadows - - -

The Shadow Hunter - - - bow in hand - - - motionless - - - listened - - - as a distant voice - - - a woman's voice - - - melancholy - - - melodic - - - wafted slowly through the forest - - -

> The dawn is awakening
> The Hirsch to the spring
> The yew arrow sings

The laurel leaf cries

Then - - -

As - - -

The green glows of the reflecting torches subsided - - - greens moving toward yellows and yellows towards oranges - - - the mellow greens of the forest reluctantly yielded to the riotous oranges of a roaring bonfire - - - almost as if the living woods of the forest itself were feeding the roaring flames - - -

As the Shadow Minstrel - - - backlit by orange flames - - - Bow-Harp in hand - - - strummed his silent song - - - he strolled lazily across his shadow stage - - - the - - - length and breadth of his known world - - -

Until - - -

Childlike - - - curious - - - hesitating - - - undecided - - - he turned - - - and - - - burst into the world of men - - -

As brightly colored dancers magically appeared from the shadows - - - to challenge their acrobatic skills - - - and - - - each other - - - the great orange-red screen behind them flamed even more brightly - - - as - - - the - - - red - - - orange - - - and - - - blue torch lights playing behind them - - - most convincingly conveyed the image of merrymakers before a great and festive bonfire - - -

> The feasting is merry
> The songs are joyous
> The revelers gay
> The Watch Tower Sleeps

At this magical transformation - - - of - - - sight - - - and - - sound - - -

And - - - Roasted Venison!?!

This small but elite troupe had somehow even managed to conjure up the smell of succulent - - - savory - - - venison - - -

The Royal Pair - - - besides themselves with joy and amazement at the ingenuity and skill - - - of this small troupe - - - their royal demeanor in shambles - - - let the hint of a smile race across their faces - - - to dwarf even the most generous smile ever born - - -

Once more the brightly arrayed dancers disappeared into the shadows - - -

This time - - - betraying their bonds of kinship - - - forsaking all hope for honor - - - abandoning their shadow brethren to the mercy of the raging flames - - -

Shadow bodies - - - screaming - - - writhing - - - falling - - - bathed in the red torch light of infernal flames - - - piled one-upon-the-other - - - as even in death they sought to build a shield wall against the unknown and unforeseen enemy - - -

> The shield wall is breaking
> The maidens are huddled
> The walls are mortared
> The trenches are deep

Against this backdrop of carnage - - - of - - - broken bodies - - - and - - - broken promises - - - a - - - Giant Shadow Warrior rose from the rubble of beastly betrayal and shattered stone - - - ready to do battle with lesser versions of himself - - -

> The fire moat is flooded
> The tide it is broken
> The enemy is burning
> The baby is born

As an ant-like enemy swarmed over the Shadow Giant - - - there appeared in his place a Great Tower - - - as - - - the piercing sound of a flute - - - mimicking a baby's cry - - - echoes hauntingly throughout the hall - - -

Then - - -

As comets flared and cymbals clashed - - - the Great Shadow Tower crumbled - - - leaving - - - standing - - - in its place - - - a - - - King - - - The Turquoise King - - - born of the Royal Womb - - -

> The Royal Womb trembling
> The shields are hoisted
> The maidens are dying
> The host is burning

Then - - -

&&& Getting Pickled &&&

Burp!!!

Slurp!!!

Burilgi sitting comfortably in a corner - - - The Crusher at his side - - - was fiercely gnawing on one of the abandoned "stage props" of the troupe - - - the roasted hindquarter of a deer - - - with which the troupe had been able to create the delicious illusion of the festive bonfire feast.

Burilgi - - - with - - - one eye - - - on the dancing maidens - - - the - - - second- - - on the venison - - - and - - - the - - - third - - - on his thumb - - - lest he lose it - - - was curiously eyeing the strange commotion of actors off to his right - - -

He - - - for the life of him - - - couldn't even begin to fathom their antics - - - let alone their purpose - - - as - - - each scrambled to climb one atop the other - - - only to all come tumbling down into one jumbled heap - - - save one lone actor - - - who was somehow left standing amidst the wreckage of tumbling bodies and flailing arms and legs - - -

"Must be some sort of game" - - - he mumbled to himself - - - tossing the bone to Crusher - - - who - - - totally ignoring the actors and being totally focused on the bone - - - soon made short work of it - - -

"Hmmm - - - That was some tasty treat - - - huh Crusher?" - Queried Burilgi as he searched for something of more substance - - - something - - - that would stick to his ribs - - -

Wiping his mouth with the back of his hand - - - Burilgi continued to eye the dancers - - - shaking his head at the antics of the dancers - - - as - - - if - - - in shocked disbelief - - -

As the dancers - - - disappeared into the wings - - - they - - - of necessity - - - passed by - - - Burilgi - - - who - - - full of amorous affection - - - uncharacteristically forgot his search for food - - - for - - - unlike his brother builder - - - food to him was always infinitely more important to him than was a maiden's smile - - -

As a long-legged beauty passed by - - - Burilgi - - - full of charm and wit - - - winked and said: "Hello my little turtledove" - - - which earned him only a "Humph" from the dancer and a quizzical whine from Crusher.

As Burilgi mulled over this unfortunate turn of events - - - all the while rubbing his chin and mumbling that perhaps she doesn't like birds - - - another dancer - - - this time a long haired beauty passed by: "Hello my little apple blossom" - - - which earned him a somewhat stronger 'HUMPH' - - - the turn of a cold shoulder and a whine and tilt of the head from Crusher.

Undaunted - - - since good things always happen in threes - - - Burilgi persisted yet again - - - figuring that he must be in the company of women who hated birds and loathed flowers. Therefore - - - he thought that he should try something more of his own liking: "Hello my little ham hock" – which resulted in the desired physical contact - - - but - - - not quite of the form which he had envisioned - - - in that he received an swift and rather severe slap across the cheek.

Totally perplexed - - - Burilgi now determined that it was the time for action - - - not words - - - resolving to embrace the next woman whoever she might be - - - and - - - therefore to conquer her with his forthright and irresistible charm.

 Out of the corner of his eye - - - Burilgi spied a lithe female form coming down the corridor. Now was the time for action - - - not words! As he wetted his lips - - - and - - - puckered his lips for the conquering kiss - - - Burilgi turned and grabbed her - - - lifting her off of her feet - - - convinced of the inevitability of first conquering her with a bit of poetry then sealing her fate with a kiss: "Hello my little - - - oh - - - Hi Soyala."

"Burilgi - - - what's gotten into you? Have you gone crazy??" - - - said Soyala pushing and shoving and kicking the giant away from her.

"Uhhh - - - Crazy? Uhhh - - - No Soyala. I was just happy to see you - - - that's all!"

Again Crusher whined - - - not understanding why his lord and master continued to humiliate himself in this way - - - especially - - - since they were both surrounded by mountains of food of each and every delectable description - - -

Hearing the whine - - - Soyala turned and greeted Crusher - - - "Hi – Crushy! Taking good care of your Master? Keep an eye on him - - - because he needs someone to look after him! He's not always as smart as we'd both like for him to be" - - - she said casting a wary eye toward Burilgi.

Crusher whined as if in agreement - - - as Soyala continued her way along the hallway and toward the stairs leading to the lower level.

As Crusher let loose his Hyena Laugh - - - Burilgi turned to him - - - flushed and asked: "Well - - - what are you laughing at? Let's go find some food."

&&& THE STRONG MAN &&&

As The Shadow Play ended - - - there came amidst the swirling dancers - - - and - - - tumbling acrobats - - - The Strong Man - - -

Tall - - - broad shouldered - - - deep chested - - - broad backed - - - tree trunk thighs - - - and - - - traps so deep and thick that his ears disappeared - - -

No sooner had he seated himself upon a stool - - - provided by one of his doting female attendants - - - than two women clad in the scantest of costumes perched upon each of his knees - - - and - - - began to scrape the perspiration from his body - - - into a silver chalice - - - to be sold to the highest bidder as an aphrodisiac to the vain and wanton nobility - - -

As - - - yet - - - two others - - - one at each side - - - were doing their best to massage his massive traps - - - while yet a sixth brought a brimming cup of wine to him for his pleasure - - -

Then - - -

As the torches were once again lighted - - - The Actor - - - now in the garb and demeanor of a showman - - - began to speak - - - as all strained their ears and imaginations to hear what he had to say:

"Your Most Imperial Majesties" - - - spoke The Showman - - - "We have here for your pleasure the strongest man in the seven provinces - - - so strong in fact - - - that he has the strength of ten men - - - as - - - you are about to witness for yourselves."

&&& The Seven Champions &&&

We are about to present to you - - - for your most royal entertainment - - - a contest - - - a contest - - - of - - - strength - - - and - - - skill - - - and - - courage - - -

Here - - - we have before us - - - the champions of the seven realms - - - each of whom will match his strength against The Mighty Khada'an ("Rock") of the North.

With these mighty and most braggadocios words - - - a massive elephant sauntered into the great hall - - - carrying a massive round stone in a sling - - - followed by several lesser versions of himself - - - carrying several smaller stones of decreasingly smaller sizes - - -

As they turned to face the royal majesties - - - they set the stones upon the floor in prepositioned cradles - - - then bowed - - - in the most majestic elephant fashion to the two monarchs - - - trumpeted a salute - - - then turned and sauntered off the stage to an elephant feast of bales of hay and cart loads of turnips and sugar beets - - -

As the torches dimmed - - - the Show Man continued to the sound of drums and trumpets:

YOUR MOST IMPERIAL MAJESTIES

!!! THE SEVEN CHAMPIONS !!!

The Seven Champions - - - astride several brightly decorated horses - - - rode onto the stage - - - and - - - dismounted - - -

As grooms led off the horses - - - torches once again flared - - - and - - - trumpets blared - - - as - - - the seven champions - - - each - - - an impressive specimen of manhood - - - bowed deeply to their Over-Lord and Mistress - - -

Seven Champions - - -

Each - - - muscular and chiseled in features - - - each - - - clothed in the native garb and color of his province - - -

Some bearded - - - others shaven smooth - - -

Some tall and lean - - - others short and squat - - -

All - - - bowing deeply and devoutly to the Emperor and his Consort - - -

Seven Champions - - -

Five Baked Golden Bronze - - -

One Burned and Blackened by the sun - - -

One Albino pure white as mountain snow - - -

Seven Champions - - -

Seven Champions from Seven Provinces - - - clad in provincial colors - - - the origins of which were long lost in the mists of time - - -

Mists of Time - - - having obscured both the origins of this ancient sport and the humble beginnings of the festive colors of the champions - - -

Festive colors - - - whispered to once have been the royal color of each of the seven queendoms - - -

Queendoms - - - once mighty - - - but - - - now - - - relegated to the stuff of colored rags and nursery rhymes - - -

But - - -

Once again The Showman strutted to center stage:

Your Most Imperial Majesties

!!! LET THE GAMES BEGIN !!!

And - - - so they did - - - with each of the Seven Strongmen - - - competing with the lifting of the Seven Stones - - -

The contest itself was most primitive in that all each contestant need do was to lift a stone heavier than his opponent - - - but - - - in all of its primitiveness - - - it offered a most romantic interlude in the dreary life of everyday court in that it harkened back to the days of giants and warrior maids - - - and - - - deeds of valor blunting and thwarting the most ignoble of treacheries - - -

But - - -

Today - - - aside from the court romantics thoroughly enjoying the raw power of the sport - - - it was for many a more base type of entertainment in that wagers were made and money was lent - - -

The contest - - - as mentioned - - - was simple - - - seven stones were to be lifted atop seven stone pillars - - - with - - - he - - - who having lifted the heaviest stone - - - being the winner - - -

135

Simple in plan - - - but - - - most exceedingly difficult in execution - - - for - - - each stone was a perfect sphere - - - thereby - - - making it most difficult to grasp - - - and - - - even more difficult to hold and lift - - -

As far as the strongmen themselves were concerned - - - they were pretty much a varied assortment of shapes and sizes - - - with no one size or shape bestowing any particular advantage to any one contestant - - -

One might think that the shorter man might have an advantage of shorter legs in that he was in more of an upright position at the beginning of the lift - - - whereas - - - on the other hand - - - one might think that the taller man had the advantage of longer arms in that he was better able to grasp and hold onto the stone - - - especially the larger stones - - -

However - - - the truth was that the awkward positioning of hands and feet pretty much negated any natural advantage of size or shape in that the true skill of the lift lay primarily in the technique - - -

The first strongman - - - a short squat bearded fellow from one of the northern provinces - - - succeeded in lifting the first four of the stones - - - but - - - simply did not have the length of arm to hug the larger stones close enough to his chest to keep them from slipping out of his arms - - -

The second strongman - - - taller and leaner - - - did somewhat better - - - but - - - did not have the strength of leg or back to lift the two heavier stones - - -

The third strongman - - - an albino throwback to some ancient tribe of cloud warriors - - - did succeed in lifting the fifth stone - - - but - - - had absolutely no luck in even clearing the sixth stone from the ground - - -

And so it went with the succeeding strongmen - - - with none being able to lift the sixth stone for more than a couple of inches - - -

All stood at the ready as The Showman once again spoke:

Your Most Imperial Majesties - - -

!!! LET THE CONTEST BEGIN !!!

With that - - - and - - - in a giant theatrical move - - - the colossus flung open his arms - - - scattering his female attendants to the far corners of the throne room - - - flailing and falling and tumbling to the floor - - - unhurt - - - with an acrobat's grace - - -

As the Emperor turned to his consort – he whispered: "Ahhhh - - - let's see what amusement we have here - - - my dear!!! This should be most entertaining."

Chup Kaumi - - - daughter of the Empress - - - also by her father's side - - - licked her lips her lips in obvious enjoyment - - - "Mmmmmmmm - - - most delicious - - - you do mean most delicious - - - don't you father? I can't remember ever having seen such a tasty treat!"

Meanwhile - - - Burilgi - - - back in the royal larder - - - focused not on the sensuous women or the strong men - - - but - - - on a tantalizing delicacy that lay just before him - - - but - - - tantalizingly - - - just out of his reach - - -

Just beyond his reach was that which Burilgi believed to be a most rare and royal delicacy - - - hidden from prying eyes and hungry stomachs for so long as to be forgotten - - - forgotten by most - - - but not all - - - for - - - Burilgi most certainly remembered - - - Brandied Beef Tongues!!!

Brandied beef tongues!!!

What a delicate desert with which to finish off the leg of roasted venison - - - of which - - - remained only the scrap of a most distant memory - - -

As The Crusher whined his encouragement - - - Burilgi still far short of being able to reach the top of the storage shelves - - - and - - - his prize - - - even though he had found the highest stool and was acrobatically - - - for Burilgi at least - - - standing on one foot and stretching to his utmost - - -

Meanwhile - - - the distant applause indicated that - - - The Mighty Khada'an - - - Rock of the North - - - had indeed managed to lift all seven stones - - - which - - - huffing and puffing attendants were now struggling to roll off stage - - -

Rolling off stage in Burilgi's general direction - - - whereas - - - the pillars were left to stand in place as keepers went to fetch the elephants - - -

Meanwhile - - - Burilgi - - - exhausted - - - physically and mentally - - - from his physical and mental gymnastics - - - had taken momentary pause to sit down upon the stool upon which he had been standing - - - as Crusher whined his confusion - - - because never before had his master - - - his god - - - failed at anything - - - especially - - - where food was concerned - - -

As Burilgi head in hand - - - elbow on knee - - - assumed his most meditative posture - - - he espied the huge stone spheres - - - which afforded the glimmering of an idea to him - - - why not make steps of these spheres - - - and - - - then stand on the largest - - - so that he could reach his prize?

Not at all a bad idea - - - he thought to himself - - - in fact - - - it was a grand idea - - - most worthy of a warrior - - - he thought - - -

So - - - without much further ado - - - Burilgi busied himself picking up and carrying all seven stones into the pantry - - - carefully placing them in order - - - smallest to largest - - - so that he would have seven steps by which to reach the stoneware crock of pickled treats which had so far eluded him - - - hidden on the uppermost shelf - - -

As Burilgi - - - smiling - - - humming - - - and - - - laughing to himself at his cleverness - - - in a most stately and royal manner - - - walked up his makeshift stairs - - - attendants in the wings of the stage were in the midst of a "dither" - - - wondering who or what might have made off with their stones - - - an elephant perhaps? As they all scurried off in search of the floppy eared thief - - -

Meanwhile - - - Burilgi - - - joyously reaching out to claim his prize - - - stretching as far as he could go - - - reaching out - - - stretching with fingertips - - - was just able to slowly inch a large stoneware crock toward him - - - inch by inch by inch - - -

As he joyously let loose of the shelves with the hand with which he had been steadying his efforts - - - so that he might grasp his precious treasure with both hands - - - the great stone step began to wobble - - - then to roll - - - with Burilgi precariously perched on top - - - doing his best to keep his balance - - -

As the monster seventh stone began to roll - - - Burilgi - - - arms flailing - - - managed to save the brandied beef tongues - - - by placing them on a lower shelf - - - but in doing so - - - he managed to dislodge a metal pot from its resting place - - - which promptly plunked itself atop his head - - - much as a misshaped and misplaced piece of head armor might find a comfortable home on the head of a dazed and befuddled warrior - - -

As the stone began to gain momentum - - - Burilgi - - - much to his horror - - - realized that the great sphere was not only resolute in proceeding toward the throne room - - - but - - - what was much worse - - - that it was headed center stage as if it were fiercely determined that it grant an encore performance to a demanding and appreciative audience!!!

As Burilgi arrived Center Stage - - - arms flailing - - - feet flying - - - grasping for anything and everything with which he might save his life - - - he managed to grab hold of an iron bar from the clenched fist of The Mighty Khada'an - - -

The Mighty Khada'an - - - frozen in his spot - - - unable to move - - - had just finished humbling his opponents one more time by bending the unbendable into a horseshoe shape - - - and - - - had hoisted it aloft in triumph - - - just as Burilgi flew past - - - snatching it from his grasp - - -

As the strongmen - - - finally uprooted from their spots - - - fled for their lives - - - the Royal Pair - - - roared their laughter and approval - - - as the audience followed suit applauding Burilgi's acrobatic antics - - -

Although it would have been some small thing - - - to leap from the stone sphere - - - when one is calm of mind - - - it is an entirely another thing when one is fighting for one's life in front of an applauding and cheering audience - - - so - - - Burilgi did what is natural - - - he panicked - - -

Burilgi - - - arms still flailing - - - mind racing as fast as his feet - - - thought that if he were to straighten the bar - - - he might be able to use it to push against a wall or pillar and at least slow and steady his travels - - - and - - - with luck - - - perhaps even stop his travels - - -

So - - -

With little or no thought - - - Burilgi straightened the bar in an instant - - - straightening the same iron bar which had taken The Mighty Khada'an many minutes and even more facial contortions to bend - - -

Again - - -

Once again - - - both Imperial Highnesses were delirious with delight - - - as the royal assembly went wild with joy - - - stomping their feet and clapping their hands - - -

Amidst this uproar - - - Burilgi - - - finally having finally reached a wall - - - and - - - finally having been able to push off against it with his iron rod - - - his feet momentarily still - - - relaxed and smiled - - - even bowing toward his imperil highnesses - - - until - - - the stone sphere decided to reverse the course of its travels - - - as Burilgi - - - feet still moving furiously - - - chased by riotous laughter - - - managed to roll his way off stage - - -

As Burilgi's movement slowed slightly - - - he relaxed - - - and - - - applauded himself at his dexterity and mastery over this dumb inanimate piece of stone - - - until - - - he looked up and saw the wall of the larder rapidly approaching - - -

Not being able to stop - - - the stone first - - - then Burilgi - - - thunderously crashed into the wall - - - causing all to shake so violently - - - that it appeared as if the whole wall might come crashing down - - -

But - - - much to Burilgi's dazed delight - - - the force of the thunderous impact placed him once more comfortably on his stool as a great stoneware crock of picked beef tongues - - - or - - - perhaps more precisely - - - brandied beef tongues - - - came floating down - - - unharmed - - - right into his lap - - -

Never at a loss to pass up an opportunity - - - Burilgi smiled - - - as he took out a beef tongue and tossed it to The Crusher - - - who swallowed it whole without even so much as a blink - - -

As The Crusher was licking his chops - - - waiting for more - - - Burilgi took a great swallow of the brandy - - - "Not bad Crusher - - - the beef tongues give the brandy a bit of a zip – don't you think?"

As Burilgi pondered the elegance and justice of this moment - - - he tossed another beef tongue to Crusher - - - swirled the brandy around in the crock - - - and - - - as a reward for his good deed - - - took another guzzle of brandy for himself - - -

"AHhhhhhhhh"

Crusher - - - by this time - - - somewhat unsteady on his feet - - - howled his agreement!!!

&& TOWER OF THE SLEEPING BONES &&

The Tower Priestess - - - gliding softly through the night - - - approached the base of the Turquoise Tower - - -

As - - -

The Priestess - - - paused - - - ever so slightly - - - much as daylight pauses slightly before slipping silently into night - - - she gazed upwards - - -

Gazing upwards - - - she recounted how many times she had climbed these ancient wooden stairs - - - and - - - thought forward to a time - - - when she would no longer be able to do so - - -

Wooden Stairway - - -

Standing in sharp contrast to the soft blue stone of this ancient tower - - -

Clinging to its mirrored surface much as a vine clings to its mother tree - - -

Sending its roots deep below the surface to gain purchase to grow - - -

Growing - - - striving ever to reach ever closer to the midnight blue sky - - -

The Stairway - - - reddened wood - - - bending back upon itself twice before ending at a stone portal one hundred feet up the side of the polished blue stone - - -

The Stairway - - - anchored solidly into the hard blue stone - - - had caused many an ancient enemy to smite his bones down hard upon the rocky ground below - - -

As - - -

These very stairs - - -

Having been suddenly withdrawn by defenders within - - -

Having vanished beneath his trembling feet and his echoing terror - - -

Having left nothing before his startled eyes but air and rock - - -

Had ensured the survival of these noble people in their most desperate hour - - -

However - - -

Time changes all - - -

The honor of one generation is mocked by the next - - -

Towers crumble and die - - - escaping the bonds of memory - - - becoming nothing more than the stuff of nursery rhymes - - - and - - - the grains of sand in a child's toy sandbox - - -

There had been a time - - - not that long ago - - - when this had been a holy place - - - as far removed from a warlord's fortress tower as a harp string is removed from a bow string - - - and - - - when - - - a young and beautiful woman - - - had been a Royal Priestess - - - venerated - - - petitioned - - - and - - - loved - - - by all the folk in the land - - -

But - - - now - - - both priestess and the tower were the victims of too many favorable summers and too many gentle winters - - - both - - - having outlived their purpose and loving comrades - - - but - - - neither - - - yet old enough to die - - -

There was a time too - - - when - - - this ancient tower - - - along with her six sister towers - - - had joyously marked the passing of the seasons - - - with - - - she alone - - - proudly marking the arrival of the winter solstice - - -

But - - -

Now - - - she stands alone - - - forgotten by all save an old woman living in a broken down derelict hut at her very feet - - -

As The Priestess slowly wound her way up the eastern face of the tower - - - her torch flickered and danced against the mirrored surface - - - spawning a multitude of miniature star bursts dancing against a turquoise sky - - - starbursts - - - brief flashes of former glory - - -

As she reached the third level - - - she paused briefly to position her torch in its wall sconce and entered.

She entered - - -

     Knowing that the bones had spoken - - -

          Believing all that the bones had promised - - -

               Trusting that tonight she would find her resting place - - -

For - - -

The Bones had

Foretold - - - of - - - The arrival of the Bearer of Bones - - -

Foreknown - - - of - - - The awakening of the Sleeping King - - -

Forewarned - - - of - - - The ascensions of the Sisters of the Pleiades - - -

As - - -

The Priestess - - - ascended the banistered staircase - - - her withered hands - - - caressing the waist-high handrail - - - long since worn to a smooth rich patina by hallowed hands over countless years - - - she reached a flat open platform above - - - leading to an entrance - - - to the flat roof of the tower above - - -

The platform - - - seemingly suspended in space and time - - - with its one wooden stairway - - - wrapping itself around the inside walls of the tower - - - presented a symbolic pausing point - - - halfway between the catacombs below - - - and - - - the next level of earthly departure and celestial embrace - - -

"I wait for you - - - Bearer of the Bones - - -

May your watch over our ancestors sooth their spirits - - - as - - - it sooths ours.

May your spirit become as one with theirs and with their children's children not yet born."

With these words - - - The Old Priestess continued her ascent - - -

Reaching the flat roof of the tower - - - the priestess - - - greeted each of four large stones - - - laying flat upon the roof - - -

Four Flat Stones - - -

    The Four - - -

        The Dorben - - -

        Red Stone on the South - - -

        Black Stone on the West - - -

Yellow Stone on the East - - -

White Stone on the North - - -

As - - -

The Old Priestess laid herself down upon the yellow stone - - -

Laying herself down - - - upon the easternmost stone - - - the old priestess called upon Khangard - - - 'King of the Birds' - - - to - - - free her bones from their mantel of earthly flesh - - -

Thus - - - prepared - - -

She began her death chant:

    Wake ye up my brothers and my sisters!
    Cast off your shrouds of earthly flesh –
    Soar your spirits to distant towers –
    To a time when all men had died –
    And no woman had yet been born.

    As the heavens give birth –
    To spirits past and yet to come -
    Your white glistening bones –
    Having forgotten their own mortality -
    Cry out in anguish at having been forgotten –
    Only to be held captive by the four winds –
    Until they escape as a soft white powder
    To rain down upon the yellow clay
    From whence they sprang.

    Unborn to reborn - - - reborn to unborn - - -
    Endless cycle of time - - -
    Just as all that is living moves - - all that moves is living - - -
    Even Brother Mountain – rumbling and groaning in the night - - -
    Tossing and turning restlessly beneath the silken sheet of Sister Sky - - -
    Passionately pleads for his own immortality - - -
    In mortal fear of the unrelenting winds - - -
    Which work feverishly to reduce his royal visage to naught but a sandy shore.

    Brothers and Sisters - - - seek not immortality in your shroud of mortal flesh - - -

But fight to remember that you have been born of the dust of your forefathers' bones - - -
As will your descendents be born of the dust of your bones.
Remember too that you - - in the guise of your ancestors' bones - - -
Once nurtured the yellow clays and rich brown earths - - -
And thus formed and once bound by the sacred marriage of swirling winds and roiling waters –
Were forthwith fired into near mortal perfection - - -
In the impassioned ovens of eons of blazing suns.

Remember too - - that just as you were once sundered and later rejoined - - -
So too shall the Celestial Three become One.

Therefore - - - trust that as surely as The Three will become One - - -
Tranquility will quickly battle your fear into submission - - -
For - - at the moment tranquility seizes you for her own - - -
The four winds will release their hold on you - - -
And you will finally be able to drift unprotestingly - - -
To earth as one with the silver stardust - - -
To be gently reborn as the Mountain.

Rejoice in awakening - - Oh Sleeping King - - -
For only by living within the spirits of our ancestors - - -
And those generations not yet born - - -
Can we ourselves truly live.

Thus - - -

In peace - - - serenity - - - and - - - dignity - - -

The Old Priestess became as one with the spirits of her ancestors - - - and - - - the spirits of those not yet born - - - while - - - her earthly mantel patiently waited for sun's dawning and Khangard - - -

&&& Day of the Dead &&&

As Soyala wound her way down the winding passages leading to the catacombs deep beneath the Turquoise Palace - - - she confessed that she had no earthly idea why she was here.

Her calling had been anything but a priestess of a pile of dead bones - - - yet here she was - - - torch in hand - - - in pitch darkness - - - winding her way down deep beneath the earth to speak a few silly phrases to a pile of dead crumbling bones!

Who cares?

Really - - - who cares? What if she were to sing a song - - - or explore the depths - - - or simply do nothing at all? Who would know?? Who would care???

In all honesty - - - her being here had more to do with her never having been here before - - - than it had to do with any silly ancient notion of sleeping bones - - - or dead bones - - - or any kind of bone at all.

As she reached the lower level - - - she paused - - - and lit the torches in the wall sconces - - - for at least a bit of light - - - and surveyed her surroundings. It was cool and dank - - - but not as totally unpleasant as she had imagined.

The area - - - within the glow of her torch - - - was level - - - with tables and chairs - - - and chests of cedar which filled the air with a wonderful pungent smell. All was almost cheerful - - for if Soyala were not to know better - - - she would have imagined that she were standing right smack dab in the middle of the warm guestly interior of the Widow's Walk. Seated around the tables - - - were the merriest of guests - - - wearing their finest garments - - - some playing at a game of chance - - - others with a flagon of what was once beer - - - held in a ghostly hand - - - while others just seemed to be seated in the pure enjoyment of one another's company.

Each was beauteously bedecked with the finest of garments he or she had possessed - - - whether it was the rustic supple leathers of a farmer - - - or the softer silks of a lady - - - each wore his and her finest.

Faces were exquisitely molded of the finest clays - - - and - - - painted so lifelike as to entice one into believing that they could at a moment's fancy - - - jump to their feet and dance the most merrious of dances.

As the torch light flicked across their faces - - - these ancient eyes seemed to follow Soyala's each and every movement - - - and at times wink to each other as if all were knowingly sharing in a private joke at Soyala's expense.

As the shadows lengthened - - - then burst apart with tiny sparks of exploding pitch and resin - - it was all Soyala could do to remind herself that these were the dead.

But then again - - - perhaps it was best - - - just to be safe - - - to speak the chant which her position bade her to:

"Oh sleeping bones - - - wake and rejoice at another da__"

Soyala had scarcely the time to get the words out of her mouth when a voice spoke:

"Greetings Granddaughter - - - I have long waited for you - - - even though you mouth your words as if they have no meaning!"

Soyala spun around - - - casting her torch in all of the dark places - - - trying to espy the trickster- - - who - - - would have her screams chasing her running from this place.

Again the voice spoke: "Granddaughter I am here - - - right beside you. You need look no further."

Soyala jumped a good three feet into the air - - - and - - - landed right in the middle of a table top - - - spilling out the dust of ales and porters from long empty beer flagons - - - as she again swept the room with her torch.

"Granddaughter - - - I wish that you would calm yourself - - - for it is a chore for me to follow all of your acrobatics. I am not as nimble as I once was. Come over here where I can better see you."

As Soyala's eyes focused - - - she could see - - - seated alone on what appeared to be more of a throne than a chair - - - the giant form of a great warrior of old - - - his wooden hafted obsidian half moon blade - - black as death - - - resting ready at his side - - - his right hand on the hilt of his red obsidian dagger - - - red as the enemy's blood it had drawn - - - gushing from many a mortal wound.

On his right thumb - - - shinning fangs - - - slashed savagely through the darkness - - - as the deeply carved lines of a green jade thumb ring sprang to life - - - snarling for the chance to once again release a jagged missile - - - to savagely tear into the flesh and pride of many an enemy - - - with the two hundred pounds of slashing force released by the battle bow - - - of wood and horn and sinew - - - laying innocently at his feet.

His headgear was what appeared to be a wolf's pelt - - - such that he peered out from beneath glistening white fangs - - - each not less than four inches each. His armor was simple - - - but - - - effective - - - his upper body sheathed in a maroon leather vest embroidered with a wolf's head of lavender shell beads and glistening white porcupine quills - - - symbol of the wolf clan - - - and his lower body clothed with naught else but a loin cloth. White gold ornaments hung heavily from his muscular clay body: heavy gold wrist and ankle bracelets together equal in weight to the heavy gold collar hanging around his muscular neck - - - gleaming white accenting his bronzed clay skin.

"Come granddaughter - - - we have much to discuss - - - for I have slept for a long time and I have much to say."

Soyala blinked - - - rubbed her eyes - - and blinked again - - - then shook her head vigorously as if to awaken from a dream - - - and - - - cautiously sat down on the edge of the great table - - - still not sure whether the shadows were playing tricks on her.

"Grandfather"? - - - she squeaked - - - then cleared her throat and spoke more clearly: "Grandfather? You're my grandfather?"

"Strictly speaking - - - no - - - but practically speaking - - - yes - - - I'm your grandfather many times removed. You are of my blood."

As the torches flickered and the shadows grew - - - the giant seemed to grow with them: "Enough of questions - - - granddaughter - - - enough of questions - - - for we have little time - - so little time - - - and it required a great effort for me to travel here - - - a very great effort - - - and I have much to say - - - much that is important - - - and as I have said - - - I have so little time."

"As you can see - - - sitting before you - - - I have returned to the clay from which I was born."

Soyala cautiously climbed down from the table - - - upon which she had been standing - - - all the while keeping the table between herself and the clay giant before her - - - her hands blindly groping for a chair - - - and her torch safely placed in a wall sconce - - - not daring to take her eyes off of the giant.

As the flickering torches waxed and waned - - - the shadows breathed life into the clay - - causing the giant figure to appear to move - - - and - - - breathe - - - and - - - sigh with them: "However - - - I was not always as you see me - - - since - - - for a while - - - perhaps too brief of a while - - - I roamed this earthly plane as a carefree being of flesh and blood - - - carefree until the great battle that is - - - at which time my enemy smote me down - - - driving me back into the clay from which I had been born and back into the bosom of my earth mother - - - who eagerly fought to reclaim me as her own."

"However - - - in my death throes - - - I tore myself loose from her motherly embrace and fled to the heavens - - - where - - - my spirit - - - for - - - the first time of my existence - - - found bliss - - - by melding with the spirit of our sacred Sky Maiden - - - who - - - thus - - - became my wife.

All of this may be of no surprise to you - - - for you may have seen this in your dreams - - -

"But alas - - - although with wife and child - - - my bliss was not long to last - - - for my earth mother yearned even more fiercely than before - - - to reclaim her own - - - and not relenting - - - but with her will becoming even more fierce with time - - - she succeeded."

"As my ashes slowly fell once more to mother earth - - - I became as one with the mountain - - - and - - - I once again fell into the loving embrace of my earth mother."

"Overjoyed and secure at the thought of possessing me once again all for her own - - - she nurtured my torn spirit and my first faltering steps - - - and as I grew - - - earth mother slowly relinquished her motherly hold on me and allowed her child to roam free once more. For many eons did I walk this earthly sphere as a mountain - - - always in sight of my earth mother - - - until the aloneness of my spirit sought once again to meld with the spirit of my wife."

"However - - - I was born of this earth and of this earth I remained and could no longer reach the sky - - - although I strove mightily to do so by growing tall and straight as the mountain."

"As my aloneness became more than I could bear - - - and desperate to relieve my torment - - - I laid myself down to eternal sleep - - - between two ancient watch towers - - - as beacons and guardians of my sleeping bones and my slumber."

"But unknown to me and to my later joy - - - my wife had never forsaken my wanderings and had never let me out of her sight."

"As she gazed down upon me - - - and saw my pain - - - her love of me caused her to forsake her freedom and immortality and to race to my side as a great blazing ball of fire - - - bursting asunder the ancient watch tower to the west in a jealous rage - - - for she alone would guard my sleep - - - and no other."

"As we embraced and lay ourselves down - - - side-by-side - - - one last time - - - the gentle rains came and flowed from her eyes as sweet tears of joy - - - and gently washed the pain of longing from her face."

"For many eons we slept - - - until one dark moonless night - - - as she was silently searching for her girl children in the celestial heavens - - - thieves came and stole my sleeping bones - - - and spirited them here - - - to this place - - - where you now see me now."

"I did not miss them at first - - - for I was sleeping. But my wife - - - alarmed - - - sought to awaken me - - - but my sleep was deep - - - for it was the sleep of the dead."

"But my wife was persistent and as I awoke - - - I felt a terrible searing pain tearing at me - - - for my spirit had been sundered - - - and I was no longer whole."

"This is why I have summoned you - - - granddaughter - - - to heal my spirit - - - so that I can aid you during your second coming - - - and so that the one who has been sundered might become whole again."

As the shadows flickered - - - his ancient clay face seemed to soften slightly as with the waning of a great candle's glow - - - "So as you can see - - - granddaughter - - - I had been foolish to think that I could sleep an eternal sleep - - - when all my wife had to do was to prod me in the ribs for a few thousand years to awaken me!"

(Were Soyala not to know better - - - she would have sworn that the giant sitting before her had just smiled and had just shaken mightily with silent laughter.)

"But Grandfather" - - - Soyala began to protest - - -

"Hush - - - Granddaughter - - - for I am growing faint - - - and - - - you are growing distant - - - for it has taken a great effort for me to travel here to speak to you.

I beg of you - - - tonight - - - when the moon is dark - - - take my ancient bones back to the Mountain of the Sleeping King where they once lay - - - so - - - that my torn spirit might once again meld with the Spirit of the Mountain - - - and - - - thereby become whole - - - for - - - only once my spirit is healed will I be able to save you."

"Save me? - - - Save me - - - from - - - what - - - from - - - whom???" - - - asked Soyala.

"Granddaughter - - - I am growing weak - - - faint - - - not much time"

"Lay my bones - - - and - - - the bones of my faithful friend - - - Gray Wolf - - - next to each other - - - so that - - - he and I might go hunting together again" - - -

"I can almost see him now - - - touch him - - - feel him - - - How's it going old boy?

Wish that we could hunt some elk together - - - you and I - - - just like the old times - - - just the two of us - - - one haunch for me - - - and the rest for you!!!"

The ancient warrior seemed to give forth the ghost of a laugh at the thought:

"Remember the last time you and I hunted the mastodon together? Remember when it was so cold that you and I had to crawl inside the carcass just to survive the night - - - and - - - that we found it so cozy and warm that we would have stayed until spring - - - if we hadn't eaten ourselves out of house and home!"

Again the giant laughed at his joke - - - and - - - smiled - - - at the memory of his great faithful friend - - -

Granddaughter - - - Please - - - Do - - - as I bid of you - - - for both of our sakes - - - and - - - for the sake of our people" - - -

"Hurry - - - please hurry - - - for - - - both of us."

As his voice began to fade to a plaintive whisper - - - his voice becoming as one with the shadows - - - the old warrior pleaded: "I beg of you granddaughter - - - take my ancient and weary bones back to the mountain - - - tonight - - - lay me down next to Gray Wolf - - - under the protective gaze of my wife - - - so - - - that - - - I might heal and become whole again - - - please - - - - granddaughter - - - - tonight - - - tonight - - -

With these words - - all was again still - - save for the echoing laughter of the dead.

& Land of the Sun King &

&& Encampment &&

The morning sun rose over a strangely desolate landscape - - - devoid of all life and movement - - - except for one small insignificant speck of what one could best describe as "organized chaos."

Haggard men were shouting and swearing - - - and - - - above all - - - sweltering - - - in a landscape strewn with broken boulders and promises - - - as distraught beasts strenuously brayed and honked their protests at the frenzied race against a rising sun - - - merciless in his fiery fury - - - as exhausted men struggled to load creaking and complaining wagons with provisions and gear - - - and - - - most of all - - - hope at forever leaving this forlorn place - - - before the blazing dawn devoured them.

Soyala stirred restlessly in her tent - - - shaking off the chill of the desert night - - - as the Minstrel and his wife busied themselves with preparing for this last day's journey to the south - - - which was to lead them deep into the realm of the Sun King.

Were this but a scant fortnight ago - - - this encampment would have been a throwback to a more barbarous and joyous time - - - of men and beasts and feasts - - - with naught between them and unknown perils - - - but the warmth of a flickering fire and a warm embrace - - were it not for the gnawing omnipresence of two weeks of desolate dawns and a savage sense of foreboding.

Soyala rose and searched the skies for her Sun Mother - - - but - - - in her place was the Usurper - - - his Majesty the Sun - - - whose fiery rays sent an icy shiver piercing deep into the very marrow of her bones.

As the largest of the dust clouds - - - far in the distance - - - slowly took form - - - the eagle eyes of the watch post could discern fifteen riders - - - each leading two riderless mounts behind him.

As the alarm to "Make Ready" was given - - - the men and animals momentarily froze in time and space - - - and - - - then exploded into redoubled activity.

As Shorty challenged a mule to a test of will power and determination - - - Soyala tore herself from her thoughts as if tearing a fiery arrow from her searing flesh - - - and sprang astride her mare.

As the Sun King's Royal Escort grew nearer - - - the royal party - - - sporting the turquoise banners of their King and Emperor - - - solemnly bid farewell to Soyala and the remaining travelers - - - for - - - although saddened by the parting - - - their faces betrayed the overwhelming joy flooding their hearts at the thought of their return to their home of soft gentle breezes, cool deep waters and sweet fragrant clovers.

These turquoise riders - - - men of birth and not of deed - - - quickly began their ride northward - - - first at a trot - - - than a canter - - - not so much as for a desire to reach the rocky crags and cool springs of the distant mountain sanctuary by nightfall - - - but more-so as an unabashed panicked flight toward home and hearth - - - for their own survival mattered more than their honor - - - (such as it was) - - - and - - - what was most paramount was a burning obsession to leave the memory of this place as far behind - - and as soon as possible.

As the troops of the Royal Escort reached the outside perimeter of Soyala's camp - - - their captain barked a series of orders in a strange tongue - - - as - - - his soldiers practically flew from their mounts to begin to care for their horses - - - for here - - - the horse was paramount - - - in that it was the difference between life and a burning death.

Not until the soldiers began to remove the saddles and packs from their horses - - - and the dust of the hundreds of miles and tens of days - - - from themselves - - - and finally to lead their horses to water and the feed abandoned by Soyala's fleeing Quartermaster - - - did their Captain slowly turn and began to walk toward Soyala - - for it was to she - - unmistakable in her bearing - - - and - - - it was to she and to no other to whom he had been instructed to owe his blind and total obedience upon pain of a slow and exquisite death.

As Soyala's glance carried her beyond the approaching Captain - - - she took note of the Royal Escort: One Captain and fourteen exhausted and starved horsemen - - - clad in the tattered and faded remnants of what were once uniforms of leather scale and leather thong lacing - - - who were just at this moment fervently preparing their preferred drinks of choice - - - whether it be fresh frothing mare's milk drunk from a simple gourd utensil or rich red blood drunk directly from a freshly opened vein on their mares' necks - - - for - - - no matter how fully satiated was the spirit with a cause most noble - - - the gluttony of the ignoble body stubbornly demanded simple sustenance - - - whether - - - as was the case now - - - the drink was that of the white living milk stolen from a mother's larder - - - or - - - the red living blood drunk from the mortal mother herself.

As Soyala carried her glance back to her royal companions - - - sons of the gentry of the Turquoise Palace - - - she mused: "Raw white milk and roiling red blood - - - a repugnant drink for the riders of the Turquoise Banner - - - but a drink wonderfully and eminently practical for these Riders of the Desert Steppes - - - for how else could these beings - - - half horse and half human - - - ride one thousand miles in ten days and ten nights - - - without pause - - - without rest - - - nigh without a single thought - - - save to be at the simple beck and call of their Turquoise Mistress of the Desert Steppes.

As the Captain came alongside Soyala - - - and - - - knelt upon one bended knee before her - - - for a long moment - - - before slowly rising again - - - Soyala studied this captain of the royal escort who was to be her guide and protector for this last leg of her journey into the realm of the Sun King.

This captain was gruff and unaccustomed to finery and politeness - - - for he was a warrior of the steppes - - - who felt more at home on the back of his horse - - - rather than being held captive within the stifling luxury of his tent   Although small of stature - - - we was lithe and fierce - - - scar covered from head to toe - - - riding as one with his horse in such harmony as to make one wonder whether his feet had ever touched the ground at all - - - as one could easily imagine that he had been born in the saddle - - - and had stubbornly refused to ever set foot on this pagan ground - - - but - - - had instead chosen to fly above it - - - hair and spirits streaming unfettered amongst the hallowed clouds. Even his walk was ungainly - - - much reminiscent of a sailor who needs to regain his "land legs" after a months'-long sea voyage.

Soyala - - - as was the custom - - - spoke first - - - using the archaic royal "we" - - - for - - - from this moment on - - - she was this captain's royal mistress and she knew from her advisors that her captain had been instructed to not only obey his mistress - - - but - - - to read her every wish from her eyes: "Hail - - - Captain - - - 'WE' have waited too long for you - - - and until just this very moment - - - 'WE' had doubted your arrival."

"Mistress - - - it is with apology that we have not arrived here sooner. But we are here and now await your command. My men are ready to ride at a moment's notice!"

"Then - - - let's be gone" - - - commanded Soyala - - - "for- - - the day is beginning to burn."

The Captain turned and barked an order to his Lieutenant - - - and - - - as Soyala raised her gaze - - - she was astonished to see a well outfitted troop in formation. Magic had occurred - - - for - - - no longer were the troops clothed in tattered remnants of garments - - - but - - - had somehow transformed themselves into the most royal of a royal escort - - - uniforms were bright and clean and glistening in the sun - - - leather scales stained as red as the burning dawn - - - heads shielded from the omnipresent sun with what appeared to be headgear fashioned from the skins of some giant-toothed reptile.

To show amazement - - - would be to betray weakness - - - so - - - Soyala said nothing - - - as she instructed her companion travelers to make ready and to be underway.

As the morning passed into noon - - and - - - then mid-day - - - Soyala astride her favorite mare - - - a chestnut beauty with a long flowing mane - - - and- - - the Shorty and his wife - - - each astride a stocky roan pony built more for power than endurance - - - making as handsome a couple as one could imagine - - resolutely kept pace with these horsemen of the steppes.

The day - - - as were all days within recent memory - - - was hot and dry - - - made even more miserable by a searing morning wind that burned deep into Soyala's throat. But even as merciless as was the sun and the dust and the winds - - - were these horsemen of the steppes - - - who were even more merciless than all three elements combined.

It was not long before the winds died and shimmering pools began to appear in the distance - - - tempting the unwary traveler to drink of their cool sweet liquid - - - tempting - - - tempting - - seducing as the most practiced maid - - - who - - - once the payment was won - - - would quickly disappear into nothingness - - - for once the riders neared - - - naught shimmered in this desolate place other than the silent shimmering white porcelain bones of those lonely spirits trying to lure a thirsty traveler to his death - - - so that they might invite him to join with them in their eternal company - - - to help ease their loneliness.

Still onward they rode - - - Soyala's mare covered with foam - - - struggled to breathe - - - as each precious life-giving drop of moisture was sucked mercilessly from her parched lungs.

Still onward they road as the merciless sun began to take his toll on rider and mount. The two ponies fared even more badly - - - for they - - - of necessity - - - had to travel twice as far in that they needed to take two steps for each step of the horses.

Worst of all was the desolation of silence - - - for here - - - not even the wind dared speak.

As Shorty's wife leaned over toward her spouse and consort - - - she whispered: "Husband - - - something is wrong here - - very wrong. I feel it more than see it. Can you feel it too?"

"Yes - - - Wife - - - See? Even the great flying clouds of birds veer away from us at a great distance as if we were to have come from the dark places. Everything here is scorched - - - but not as if by the sun - - - but as if by some great fiery demon. The air is quiet - - - no - - dead - - - there is no song - - - no laughter. Even the breeze dares not speak - - - but - - - in the most desperate of whispers - - - and - - - even then remains for the most part silent."

"More of a dying gasp than a whisper - - - husband" - - - echoed his wife.

Then both were silent - - - as they rode steadfastly on.

Dusk was beginning to unfold her nightly blanket - - - as the small troop reached a small outcropping of rock - - - which slowly - - - patiently - - - deliberately had collected the scant runoff of a winter's dusting of snow from its highest peaks - - - and likewise grudgingly afforded some small semblance of a nurturing shelter from the blazing sun for the birth of a small alkaline pool - - - that which the Native Indians called a Tinaja - - - which - - - until this very moment not one of the Turquoise Elite could have possibly mistaken for water.

But - - - now - - - to these riders and their horses - - - this was the sweetest of nectars - - - as first horse - - - and - - - then rider - - - both - - - slowly and deliberately drank their fill.

The Captain spoke: "Mistress - - - here we'll rest - - - until your mounts regain their strength. We each have three horses to each of your one - - - so - - - we could easily continue our pace - - - but - - - your horses" - - - as he cast his disapproving glance toward Soyala's companions meaning not only the horses - - - "need to rest."

Soyala nodded in agreement - - - dismounted - - - and - - - began to loosen the cinch on her mare's saddle.

It was at that moment - - - that the youngest and most reckless of Soyala's companions protested: "But madam - - - we can't be but a few hours from our goal! Look - - - if I'm not mistaken - - - I can see the Temple Mount shining in the distance. If we push forward for but a few hours more - - - we can sleep on silken sheets and soft pillows rather than here amongst the rocks and rubble and - - -" casting his glance toward the Royal Elite - - - "rabble!" As he turned in mock sarcasm toward his companions - - - he laughingly continued: "We can that is - - - if these old men can keep up with me!"

At this challenge - - - his companions - - - first in mock scorn and then laughter - - - responded: "If you can keep up with us you mean!" With these words - - - and - - - a quick sharp dig of the spurs - - - boisterous spirits raced far out into the night - - quickly outpacing the labored march of common sense.

Shorty - - - having thus led his ponies to a quite place - - - muttered to his wife: "Fools! Young Fools!! They race only to their death!!!"

It was not until the next day that Soyala and her royal escort came upon the broken bodies of horses ridden to their death - - - as forlorn footprints stumbled out into the dusty dawn of a rubble strew canyon pass - - - to disappear forever.

No trace of these riders was ever to be seen again.

&& Deer Chasing &&

The baby ground sloth - - - frantic at the loss of its mother - - - wailed plaintively - - - eyes wide in terror - - - as it ran for his life - - - snarling massive hounds - - - trained to chase and run to bay - - - but not kill - - - almost as large as he - - - tearing terrible tuffs of fur from their terrified and helpless prey.

The winding hedges ended abruptly in a circular arena - - - when a tall pale man - - - naked as a soul stripped of all compassion - - - waited with a knife.

Monteria - - - "He who hunts with a knife" - - - Tumseneho - - - "The Man with no Blood" - - - Tona-teootl - - - "The Sun God" - - - stood poised as his hounds surrounded the baby - - - closing the circle always tighter and tighter - - - until Monteria had but to stretch out his hand to plunge his knife deep into the baby's heart.

As the baby's life blood showered Monteria - - - Monteria fell screaming to the ground as if one with the baby - - - writhing in ecstasy - - - even as the baby was writhing in death.

As the Baby Sloth let loose one last plaintive scream and crumpled into one lifeless lump of fur and skin and bone - - - its life force rushed into the waiting arms of its spirit mother and was lovingly cradled to sleep.

As his audience applauded its approval - - - for - - - they knew that were they not to applaud - - they would be the next victim in Monteria's labyrinth - - - Monteria - - - as - - - a beast more ravenous than the hounds themselves - - - fell upon the lifeless body and gorged himself with blood - - - as - - - his audience secretly rejoiced that their blood - - - at least for the moment - - - was still coursing through their veins.

At last - - - finally satiated - - - Monteria stood and strolled leisurely into the great hunting lodge of his complex - - - leaving the small lonely carcass behind - - - for the enjoyment of his hounds.

&& REUNION &&

"Sister!" - - - Cried Kajika for joy - - - as - - - Soyala rode into the walled complex.

Tired - - - but happy - - - and - - - a little stiff and sore from the last two days' ride - - - Soyala dismounted - - - for - - - what her now departed high spirited companions had mistaken for a simple three or four hours' ride - - - had been in fact a torturous two days' ride through winding and treacherous boulder strewn mountain passes.

"Soyala!" Kajika exclaimed again: "Are you a sight for my sore eyes! How was your trip? Are you tired? Hungry?? THIRSTY??? - - - but - - - first - - - let me take your mare - - - for I am sure that she is as tired and hungry as you are. Here - - you sit here - - while I tend to your mare. I'll lead her to fest on oats and hay until her belly is ready to burst! Don't you move - - - now - - - for - - - I'll be right back!"

As Kajika - - - The Hunter - - - turned - - - he almost tripped over his brother Minstrel - - -

 "I never thought that I'd never hear myself saying this - - - but it is a pleasure seeing you too - - - and - - - he lifted Shorty off the ground with a giant of a bear hug - - - and - - - gave him a kiss - - - which Shorty - - - valiantly - - - but - - - in vain - - - fought to avoid.

As Kajika lowered his brother Minstrel to the ground - - - Shorty began to rub - - - rubbing most vigorously - - - Kajika's kiss and some fair amount of skin - - - from his face - - - all the time shuddering and mumbling at the memory of Kajika's embrace - - -

As - - -

Kajika reached for the reins to Soyala's mare to lead her to fodder and water - - - the Captain of the Honor Guard stepped forward: "Lord - - - it is my honor and pleasure to serve my mistress - - - in whatever way she sees fit - - - I'll care for her mount!"

As Kajika turned toward the Captain - - - Shorty - - - quickly snatched at the reins and snorted: "I'll do it - - - Captain - - - you just lead the way and I'll trend to the horses. I've been caring for her (with a wink in his eye and a nod of his head - to imply a double meaning) since she was a foal - - and - - - I'll not abandon her now!"

The matter settled - - - Kajika turned - - - and gently led Soyala by the arm: "Come sister - - - we have a banquet prepared especially for you - - -

As he and Soyala slowly walked toward a great wooden door - - - Soyala smiled - - - contented to once again be with her brother - - -

A massive wooden door - - - carved with a Butterfly motif - - - slowly swung open on well oiled hinges - - - to a cavernous - - - but well lit room.

Before them was the banquet table - - - austere in and of itself - - - but laden with such a delicacy of bouquets - - - as to deride the imagination of its rustic creator - - - who even in his deepest of delightful deliriums could never have conceived of this wild array of colors and scents: lively lilacs and lavenders battling stoic sage and strawberry for the honor of being the centerpiece of this majestic creation - - - towering above the lesser - - - but - - - equally savage - - - skirmishes being fought by garlands of blushing blossoms seeking in vain to subdue merrious mountains of boisterous berries - - - into a more dignified decorum.

This great hall was lighted by a diffuse glow of ethereal light - - - the source of which was indistinguishable - - - which - - - highlighted a great open room - - - of majestic proportions - - - but - - - of simple construction - - - in the center of which stood a massive polished red obsidian boulder - - - perhaps as tall as a medium sized man - - - but - - - an impressive full twenty feet in diameter.

Gently flowing around the soft subtle contours of this red polished mirror - - - was a carved wooden bench. The wood was dark - - - or - - - light - - - dependent upon one's mood - - - and - - - therefore indistinguishable - - - as - - - was all that was in the room - - - and - - - given further thought and subtle contemplation - - - the room itself was strangely soothing and androgynous in its nature.

This vast room lazily stretched high into the rafters - - - to create an atmosphere of unbridled spaciousness - - - with the great unobstructed space above being rimmed only by a second floor balcony which provided a spectacular view of the great boulder in its entirety - - - and - - - likewise afforded several comfortable and private entrances to the second floor sleeping chambers - - - the most noble of which was occupied by the mistress of this great hall - - - while the two adjacent chambers had just recently been emblazoned with a Turquoise Flower Motif in honor of their two royal guests.

Further down the balcony and to each of the sides - - - with doorways scarce to be seen - - - where the lesser quarters of the chamber boys - - - whose sole purpose in life was to be at the constant beck and call of their mistress.

As Soyala allowed her thoughts to slowly drift upward into the rafters - - - so that she might gain a better perspective from which her mind's eye could gaze down into the spacious magnificence of this austere room and the thoughts and loyalties of those around her - - she sensed a slight movement behind her.

Seconds later a soft seductive voice wafted unwaveringly towards her: "Ahhhh - - - there you are - - - my 'Turquoise Flower' - - - your brother did well in describing you - - - for I had my suspicions that out of his love for you - - - he had overstated your beauty - - - but I am most happy to say that this is most definitely not the case. You are assuredly as delicate and beautiful as the Turquoise Flower Standard you bear. Yes - - 'Teoxihuitlxochitl' - - - that shall be your name - - - Teoxihuitlxochitl - - - my Delicate Turquoise Flower."

A tall slender veiled woman - - - strikingly handsome - - - but - - - somehow severe in her beauty and her grace - - - had just entered the room - - - attended by several rather stern - - - and most serious looking young boys.

Her lavender lace veil - - - delicately styled with an azure butterfly motif - - - was of two parts - - - one covering her forehead and the other covering her nose and chin - - - leaving but a slit from which her blazing blue eyes could survey all that was before her - - - for it was rumored that to gaze upon her beauty was to love her - - - and - - - to love her and not to be able to have her - - - caused a pain so unbearable that it was only eased by madness or death.

Her white embroidered dress - - - tied artfully at her slender waist by a dyed maroon hemp cord - - - flowed on the polished stone floor behind her - - - causing the stern looking youngsters to become even more serious and ever more vigilant in that it not become entangled in any of the room's Spartan furniture.

"Ah - - - my little brother Xochipolli - - - my "Flower Prince" - - - it is well that you have found time from your songs of Love and Music and Flowers - - - to bring your sister to us. Yes - - - you have done well - - - for the great lord will be pleased."

Kajika blushed slightly at this familiar use of his blood name before Soyala - - - and - - - somewhat awkwardly strode forward to kiss the hand of Xochiquetzal - - - "Flower Feathers" - - - twin sister of the Sun King and Royal Princess of Love and Flowers and Song.

"It is my pleasure and duty Sister Princess" - - - he said casting a sideways glance toward Soyala - - - who stood uncharacteristically undecided as to whether to be annoyed at Xochiquetzal's over-familiarity with her brother - - - or - - - to be overjoyed that her royal mission from her father had apparently succeeded almost before it had started.

"Soyala" spoke Kajika turning toward his sister - - - "This is Xochiquetzal - - - my sister of my blood oath and twin sister of Tonateootl - - - 'The Sun God' - - - with whom our father has entreated us to make peace and treaty."

"Please" - - - interrupted Xochiquetzal gently pressing upon Kajika's arm - - - "we have time for talk later - - - please eat - - - and then rest - - - tomorrow we can talk - - - for I'm sure that you've had a long and tiring journey behind you. All of what you see here is yours - - - to include these servant boys. They have been tutored in your language - - - and - - - are quick to learn and are especially quick to please" - - - she said as she gently stroked the hair of the youngest boy.

"Come - - - eat - - for you must be hungry" - - - Xochiquetzal said as she took Soyala gently by the arm - - and led her toward the banquet table bedecked with all manners of exotic fruits and flowers - - - long slender purple-maroon banana blossoms - - - bright red and purple berries and sweet slices of sugary sweet melons.

"These are one of my favorites" - - - smiled Xochiquetzal as she expertly arranged Soyala's plate with several thin slices of a delicate white aromatic type of fruit - - - "although they do require some small effort in the preparation. See those purple-maroon blossoms here? These are the white heart meats of those blossoms - - - exquisitely sliced and allowed to steep in cool pure well water until all of the sap blood is gone - - - for if but one drop of sap blood remains - - the whole is unbearably bitter."

"Please - - - try one - - - and - - - you'll see that they are well worth the effort!" - - - she smiled in anticipation as she placed one of the slices in her mouth, chewed, savored and smiled passionately: "I especially love the heart!"

Soyala - - - smiling graciously - - - accepted the offering and nibbled at one of the sweet heart meats and nodded agreeably: "Delicious - - - yes - - - truly delicious!"

As Xochiquetzal smiled in pleasure at her guest's special delight - - - she added slices of sweet melons and small groups of succulent berries to Soyala's plate and then deftly and with no modesty of flair - - dusted this feast with a garnish of sweet peach and maroon colored blossoms - - - as she continued - - - "Yes - - - I find the white heart drained of its sap blood to be so much more delicate and agreeable than that of the barbaric red heart meat drenched with its own blood - - - don't you agree?"

Before Soyala could answer - - - Xochiquetzal gently squeezed Soyala's wrist and led her to a seat on the wooden bench - - - which was slowly - - - lazily - - - doggedly winding its way around the great obsidian boulder - - - trying to determine where to stop once it had completed its journey - - - but - - - being frustrated in not being able to do so - - - for want of being able to remember its starting point.

As Soyala positioned herself comfortably upon a soft wide pillow and fitted her body to one particularly accommodating contour of the great red obsidian boulder - - - she carefully and unobtrusively studied Xochiquetzal - - - for although Soyala was - - - at this point - - - fairly certain that Xochiquetzal was a rival for her brother's attentions - - - she was not yet convinced that she had found an ally by whom she might quickly secure a pledge of alliance and peace from Tonateootl - - - this mighty King of the South.

As Kajika and Xochiquetzal engaged in light-hearted conversation about music and flowers and the upcoming fest - - - Soyala pretended to be weighing the relative merits of a boastful black berry and a reticent red berry - - - but was in reality summing forth every ounce of her woman's skill in distilling the essence of truth from each word and gesture of this Flower Princess - - - for although Soyala's hunger had been satiated - - - her curiosity was quickly growing to ravenous proportions.

As - - -

Soyala's - - - mental forays led her deeper into the hidden places of Xochiquetzal's intents and of the nooks and crannies of this vast room - - - she was delighted to find that all was not as austere as was presumed at first glance - - - tiny little gemstone butterflies were delicately inlaid in table and chair - - - and - - - pillar and post - - - all carefully hidden from sight as if hiding from the ruthless collector's net.

Likewise - - - tablecloth and napkin - - - pillowcase and blanket - - - were delicately embroidered with this same butterfly motif.

As Soyala was about to comment on one wonderfully beautiful and delightful specimen of butterfly embroidery - - - it simply stood up on its spindle thin legs and flitted away to the other side of the room - - - to drink deeply from an artfully crafted silver bell flower chalice - - - filled to the brim with the sweetest of nectars.

Then it was joined by another - - - and another - - - and another - - - as the air itself was soon alive with butterflies - - - soon to be followed by the buzzing and darting sound of hummingbirds.

As Soyala melded with this aura of colors and sounds and aromas of nectars - - - a giant of a hummingbird - - - iridescent in its Turquoise Magnificence - - - appeared - - - hovering above the great red obsidian boulder.

As his lesser cousins prudently gave way to his buzzing presence - - - he exploded into action - - - leaving only a turquoise streak leading to the fluttering remnants of a fiery red butterfly snatched in mid-flight - - - which he had then presumably born away to nest and mate.

It all had happened so fast - - - was it real? Or illusion - - - much as she had experienced so long ago at the Grotto - - - or - - - was it perhaps that the Grotto was real and this was somehow illusion???

As Soyala's focus returned to her surroundings - - - she was aware that Xochiquetzal was coyly inquiring of Kajika as to whether he intended to remain indefinitely in her company - - or return with his sister - - - once her mission was complete.

"...so dear brother - - - now that your royal sister has arrived - - - have you decided upon your plans for the future? Do you intend to afford yourself of OUR company for as long as it pleases US - - - or - - - do you intend to return as soon as possible to the land of your birth?"

Kajika - - - startled slightly at the question - - - in evidence of his having long dreaded this moment - - - but he none-the-less responded: "Dear sister - - - I will be better able to answer your question once my royal sister - - - Soyala - - - has met your lord - - - Tonateootl - - - but - - - if all goes well and if he is agreeable - - - it is most probable that I'll be returning north in a matter of days - - perhaps as soon as one or two days after your Great Sun Feast."

A movement - - - a shadow of a glance - - - an almost imperceptible quiver - - - almost too swift for the eye to follow - - - or even for the brain to register - - - did not escape Soyala - - - as - - - Soyala registered a terrible wave of anger flash over Xochiquetzal's being as if as of a flood washing away the patient patina of countless years - - - to lay the bedrock bare. It was only an instant - - - but unmistakable - - - and - - - savage.

"Ah brother" - - - soothed Xochiquetzal - - - "now is not the time to talk of departures - - - unless we speak of parting company for only one day - - - for the day is about to dawn - - - and I am tired."

Xochiquetzal turned and spoke to both Kajika and Soyala: "Tomorrow - - - we will share out company once again."

Then she turned to Soyala: "Dear Teoxihuitlxochitl - - - My Turquoise Flower - - - I must now leave you - - - for - - - the Sun is about to rise - - - and - - - my brother is as of the sun - - and - - - I as of the moon - - therefore - - I must now leave - - for the moon dares not challenge the sun in the same sky - - - for the day belongs to him.

With that - - - Xochiquetzal turned and headed toward the great stairway leading to the balcony and her sleeping chamber - - - her servant boys obediently following.

As Soyala rested with Kajika - - - seated - - - at her side - - - and - - - as - - - reality slowly melded into the world of dreams - - -

Shorty - - - unannounced - - - burst into the room - - -

Bursting into the room - - - fresh from having tended to the horses - - - and - - - fresh from having exchanged the most juicy of all gossips - - - Shorty - - - half ran - - - half stumbled his way toward Kajika.

This was the last sight or sound - - - that - - - Soyala remembered until late the following day - - - or - - - (perhaps) - - - even - - - the - - - day following thereafter - -

As - - -

Kajika stood - - - and - - - motioned for Shorty to be quiet - - - so - - - that Soyala might rest - - - Shorty began in great whispers - - - and - - - with an even greater flourish of hand gestures - - - to blurt out all he had heard - - -

Blurting out - - - dark rumors of feasts and slaughters and of blood sacrifice - - -

As Kajika bade Shorty - - - to sing a nighttime song for their sister - - - Kajika gently kissed Soyala into a deeper sleep so that she might continue her journey to the land of dreams unimpeded - - - and - - - gently lay her head upon a great soft pillow - - -

As Shorty continued his song - - - Kajika - - - quietly retired to a corner - - - - deep in thought - - - unaware that his every movement - - - if not his every word - - - had been espied upon by Xochiquetzal.

Lying upon her bed - - - with - - - her door slightly ajar - - - Xochiquetzal could see even the slightest of movements of her guests below - - - by - - - a series of cleverly placed magnifying mirrors - - - one on the wall opposite her bed - - - and - - - another in the hallway opposite her chamber door - - - which reflected down into the great space.

As - - -

Xochiquetzal looked and listened - - - her thin lips curled up into a cruel smile - - - for her suspicious had been confirmed - - -

Then - -

Even as the whispers below became more animated and heated - - - she gently closed her chamber door - - - and - - - went to sleep - - - for there was nothing more of interest to be learned - - - until the following day - - -

& Disturbing Dreams &

& & The God Stone & &

(A Nested Dream Sequence)

In a thunderous explosion of fire and smoke - - - a giant flaming meteor slammed into the ground - - - to vaporize what had been but scant moments before - - - bare naked rock - - - spewing forth miles high molten rock - - - to rain down in fiery terror on the sleeping country-side for hundreds of miles around.

Then - - - all was dark - - - and - - - silent.

Eons passed.

Legends were born and died - - - but - - - the legend of the Great Fiery God still lived and breathed.

As the mid-day sun shook itself free of countless millennia of dust and silence - - - a slight breeze parted the smoky veil of soot and ash to reveal a great smoking crater.

Around this crater - - - men came - - - timidly at first - - - and then women - - - as the naked ground lay sleeping beneath its gray blanket of soot and ash.

Then one day - - - unexpectedly - - - a Prophet - - - a Prophet from a far distant land and time - - - came among the people and enjoined the crowd to rejoice - - - for HIS God had answered their prayers - - - and had sent forth his ambassador to them to guide them along the path toward immortality.

And the men listened - - - and the women believed - - - and the children prayed.

As the children prayed - - - and the women wept - - - the men flocked to this holy place - - - bringing their tears - - - and their fears - - - but most importantly - - - their tribute.

Throughout all - - - the High Priest listened - - - and smiled - - - for the word of his god was good.

Then one day - - - the sacred stone spoke to the High Priest - - - demanding that it be freed from its earthen tomb.

So - - -

The High Priest smiled - - - and the women prayed - - - and - - - the men wept - - - for the tribute must be great.

And - - -

It came to pass that the children became as one with the tribute.

But - - - even as the children became as one with the tribute - - - and - - - even as heaving hands and heavy hearts bore the great stone from the smoking womb of its mother mountain - - - wonder-of-wonders - - - a miracle occurred.

As the blood of innocents lavishly poured over the great stone - - - washing away its gray cocoon of ash and soot - - - the great stone began to glow - - - softly at first as a comforting and gentle ember - - - then more brightly - - - until it finally burst into a blazing blue flame as if purging itself of the pent up passions and poisons of eons of entombment - - until its fiery fervor spent - - it lay exhausted and dying in the helpless hands of its bearers.

Still the blood of the innocents flowed.

The naked stone - - - its ashen pallor stripped away - - - now infused with the blood of the innocents - - - became as one with the blood - - - drinking deep draughts of roiling passions and unrequited loves - - - burning deeply with a blood red hue - - - as deep a red and as rich a red as the rich red blood upon which it fed - - - as fiery a red and as blazing a red as the blazing fire of the early morning sun burning its way into the dawn - - - singeing - - searing - - scorching souls and the torn hands and the tattered hearts which bore it.

Then all was quiet - - - as a cool soothing breeze filled the minds and the hearts of the people.

And the people marveled and rejoiced.

And all was silent.

Then a voice spoke - - - the voice of a wise man - - - wise - - - for he had tasted of the blood of the stone: "Hail - - - I will lead you - - - for I have tasted of the blood of the stone."

Then spoke the Stone Bearers - - for their hands were bloody and torn: "Hail - - - we shall teach you - - - for we have become as blood brothers with the stone."

And so it was done - - - as the people once more turned to the Wise Man.

Then spoke the Wise Man - - - ordering the people to erect a shelter for the God Stone - - - even as The Teachers were instructing the people to light torches to bathe the God Stone in eternal light - - - for should his light fade and falter - - - perhaps too would the sun flicker and fail.

And so it was done.

Over time - - - simple tents and flickering torches gave way to stone dwellings as the Red Obsidian Stone - - - five times - - - rose its mountain temple far above the base and Rocken Plain.

And once again - - - all was silent for a long while.

(Soyala - - - sleeping - - - stirred slightly - - - shivered - - - and - - - pulled her sleeping shroud still more tightly around her restless form.)

&&& THE TEMPLE &&&

The Ancient Temple thrust its fiery head into the blood red morning sky.

As a white hot molten orb slowly coalesced from the silver streaked flames - - - it appeared to hang - - - as delicate as a dew drop - - - precariously poised in the early morning sky - - - fearful that the slightest breeze would shake it loose from its fiery vine and cause it to plunge - - - crashing back down to the earth from which it was born.

But the air was silent - - - dead silent - - - silent as death - - - even to the waiting throng of the tens of thousands of anxious upturned faces below.

It was the Eve of the Winter Solstice - - - and for this ancient race - - - the time of rebirth.

Four times had the cosmos been born - - - and - - - four times had it died.

Four times had the cosmos died - - - and - - - four times would it be reborn.

For it was decreed - - - that as flowed the blood of innocents - - - so flowed the ebbs and tides of the cosmos.

As flowed the ebbs and tides of the cosmos - - - so ebbed and flowed the fate of this ancient race - - - for today - - - their temple priests would indeed be busy at their handiwork.

ඊඊඊ 13 Reed Jaguar Claw ඊඊඊ

Tiny rivulets of sweat trickling down the side of his face - - - hemp cords savagely biting into his wrists - - - the young warrior prince - - - forced to his knees by his captors - - - stoic in his pain and his humiliation - - - glared defiantly at the rising sun - - - bane of his being and of his people.

Bane of his being!

Bane of his people!!

Hanging like a living drop of red blood in the early morning sky - - - his blood - - - his people's blood!!!

As he tore his gaze from the fiery carved stone Stela atop the temple - - - pride swelled within his breast - - - for he knew that although his people might suffer the humiliation and degradation of hemp cords and chains - - - their spirits would never be conquered - - - for - - - his people - - - noble and proud - - - were of a heritage even more ancient than that of these people of the stone - - - for - - - they were Children of the Clouds - - - and- - - the clouds were born out of the chaos long before the mountains of stone - - - and - - - should the chaos dare to return - - - the clouds would survive long after the mountains had crumbled into dust.

As the young prince cast his gaze downward - - - tears of pride for his people began to well up in his eyes.

As he listened in the silence - - - he could hear - - - almost as if of one breath - - - the labored breathing of the 40,000 captives bound and forced to kneel behind him - - - for they would be the blood sacrifice to this temple - - - 40,000 captives - - - 40,000 drops of blood - - - 40,000 tears.

Again he turned his head and glared at the temple standing naked in its arrogance before him.

His eyes blurred once more as 40,000 tears of pride were rudely flooded away by 40,000 tears of shame - - - shame at being forced to kneel before his captors - - - shame for his people - - - shame for his sister.

As he continued to stare - - - the one sun - - - the one drop of blood - - - filtered through the prism of 40,000 tears of shame exploded into 40,000 naked burning suns!

As he cast his blinded gaze once more earthwards - - - he could feel his sister close to him - - - her presence comforting him.

&&& 8 FLINT MOUNTAIN ORCHID &&&

The young princess - - - broad of shoulder - - - narrow of waist - - - firm of thigh - - - proud and noble in her bearing - - - child of the sky islands high above the clouds - - stoic in her pain and her shame - - bore her shame and suffering with a dignity that belied her fifteen years - - - for - - - although forced to kneel before these submissive - - - smooth shaven - - - and - - - pompously pampered dwellers of stone - - - she was their mistress - - - virgin - - - pure - - - unplucked - - - unshaven - - - unbowed.

As the young prince - - - gazed once more upon his sister - - - love flowed from his heart - - - for it was she who had sheltered and nourished him from the time of his birth.

As tears of love quietly and gently washed away his burning tears of shame - - - the young prince clenched his teeth and vowed vengeance for his sister - - - himself - - - and most importantly of all - - - vengeance for all of his people.

As the rage against his captors - - - and - - - this temple - - - swelled within his breast - - - he took one deep breath - - - shook his head savagely and the tears were gone.

The young princess - - - Mistress of the House of the Cloud People - - - her rank betrayed - - - not by gems or golden crowns - - - but by the fine spun cotton cloth of her garments - - -

For - - -

If a commoner were to be foolish enough to wear anything but garments of the course maguey or yucca fiber - - - it would be an invitation to an exquisite and excruciating death - - -

For this Daughter of the Clouds - - - who had hardened her body amongst the peaks and crags of the snowy mountain tops - - - and - - - who had tempered her fiery spirit in the clear deep glacial pools of mountain valleys - - - this indeterminable wait was the greatest agony of all.

Her simple tunic - - - although brutally savaged - - - still bore the exquisite embroidery of her clan - - - a great gentle gilded cloud smiling its good fortune upon its children.   Smiling fortune - - - fortuitous fortune - - - Oh - - - were this gentle cloud to smile a felicitous fortune upon her but for one moment more - - - she would exact a swift and terrible vengeance on these barbaric dwellers of stone!!!

For no matter how safe and secure these Dwellers of Stone felt in their fiery mount of carved gods - - - their temple flame would wither and weep before the cold calculating vengeance of this Ice Maiden.

Vengeance - - - cold calculating vengeance - - - cold - - - cold - - - vengeance - - - virgin vengeance - - - cold - - - pure - - - unadulterated - - - merciless in its hate.

As - - -

Visions of battered stone - - - sheathed in an icen shroud - - - - frozen in time and space - - - helplessly suspended beneath a trembling temple flame fearing for its life - - - danced in the Ice Maiden's eyes - - - 40,000 icen darts - - - flew forth from her heart to tear the mantle of arrogance from the sacred flame - - - until it stood naked - - - shivering in the cold for all to see - - - its dull red glow pall in comparison to the blue flamed savagery of the ice.

Icen Shroud - - - Icen Glacier - - - ice - - - ice - - - wondrous ice - - - cool - - - comforting - - - carefree - - - icy sequined sanctuary of the clouds - - - silver blue ice - - - cool carefree freedom - - - streaming - - - shimmering - - - showering - - - majestic miles thick glacial raiment - - - Guardian of the Mountains since time immemorial.

Silver snowflakes - - - gently kissed her blushing cheeks - - - dancing - - - prancing - - - softly melting into a single silver droplet of dew - - - sparkling - - - shimmering - - - in the sunlight.

Then - - -

Searing cinders - - - choking - - - blinding - - - merciless - - - swirling - - - streaming - - - shredding glacial raiments to shards - - - only to disappear - - - screaming - - - screeching into the night.

Searing pain tore through the young girl's shoulders as she was wrenched to her feet and forced to stand - - - naked - - - next to her brother - - - sweat streaming down her flushed cheeks - - - numbed legs screaming in agony from the sudden onslaught of fresh blood surging through her veins.

&&& Last of the Royal House &&&

Reeling from punishing pain - - - the young prince - - - long bereft of his burnished and painted cloak of royalty - - - and - - - his burnished and painted demeanor of sovereignty - - - clad in naught but a breechcloth - - - stared defiantly at his fate - - - as the dried tears of his people still stained his cheek.

Flanked by the plumed elite of the warrior cast - - - the siblings - - - brother and sister - - - last of the Royal House of the Cloud people - - - quietly awaited their fate.

&&& Troodon Warrior &&&

Coal black eyes - - - blacker than night - - - blacker than Death - - - lurking deep within the dark deep recesses of a massive maw savagely sculptured of painted wood - - - darted past razor sharp reptilian teeth - - - into the daylight - - - to transfix their prey with a serpent's stare - - - more terrible than the grip of death itself.

Transfixed - - - frozen in time - - - frozen thoughts - - - frozen heart beats - - - frozen tears.

Taunted by the whispering laughter of Death - - - the Royal Siblings - - - frozen by the feathered serpent's stare - - - shuddered - - - ever so slightly - - - ever so imperceptibly - - - ever so briefly.

Even as the Royal Siblings - - - frozen in place - - - patiently awaited their fate - - - the Troodon Warriors - - - elite of the elite - - - impatiently waited - - - eager to return to battle - - - and to glory.

These warriors of the Troodon Cast - - - clad in the thick blue armored scales of the Troodon - - - adorned with the sculpted orange feathered head of the Troodon - - - - were the elite of the elite. None could - - - or even dared - - - to withstand them.

So ferocious in battle were they - - - that enemies fled at their mere sight.

So fierce in temperament were they - - - that none would dare stand in their presence - - - for fear of becoming one head shorter.

So exalted in esteem were they - - - that each was accorded two wives - - - the younger to tend and to furnish for his body - - - and the older to mend and to burnish his war gear.

Kneeling - - - unflinching - - - at the side of each Troodon Warrior was an Arms Bearer - - - bearing the obsidian hafted weapons of his Lord's trade - - - bare-headed - - - proud - - - clad in the red quilted cotton armor of his cast.

ᙙᙙᙙ THE CAPTAIN ᙙᙙᙙ

Distaining women - - - delighting in few pleasures - - - other than battle - - - the Captain had - - - this very morning - - - allowed himself one small tidbit of a pleasure.

"Thumping" the burnished and painted cape of the young prince - - -

His most valued prize among his latest assortment of war trophies - - -

He had summoned his trembling and terrified house servants to him - - - to do unto him as his whim of the moment commanded.

Now - - - but - - - a scant few hours later - - - he was again "thumping" - - - this time his great and puffed out chest - - - to order his terrified lieutenants to begin their march toward the Great Stepped Pyramid - - -

For - - -

It must be agreed - - - that the ability to command is not so much a matter of intellectual ability - - - as it is the ability to "thump" - - - whether on one's own chest or some poor lieutenant's head - - -

A Natural Born Leader was he - - - for no women had ever given him a fraction of the pleasure he had derived from his being able to order his servants to rush from one side of the room to the other - - - or - - - to command entire armies to race double time up to the summit some obscure pyramid - - - and - - - back on down the other side - - -

Yes - - -

A Natural Born Thumper was he - - - for now - - - to the slow thumping cadence of a drum bearer - - - he thumped the Troodon Guards forward - - - toward the base of the Great Stepped Pyramid.

As the Sacrificial Entourage reached the base of the Great Stepped Pyramid - - - they paused slightly - - - then the Royal Siblings - - - followed by the Forty Thousand Innocents - - began the long ascent toward the morning sun - - - and - - - to the slaughter.

&&& SPAWN OF STONE &&&

Although - - - still but youths - - - both siblings stood easily a head taller than their captors - - - for - - - the mountains stood higher than the valleys - - - did they not?

And their eyes were clear and bright - - - not dark and brooding - - - for the Children of the Clouds lived high among the clouds - - - blanketed in sunlight - - - unlike these Spawn of Stone - - - who lived in the darkened depths amongst the rocks and rubble - - - splintered shards carved from this Great Stone Mountain.

Therefore - - - was it not destiny that ordained that the Children of the Clouds - - - should for all eternity look down upon these Spawn of Stone - - - for no matter how high they raised their stone monstrosity - - - the clouds would still be tragically forever beyond their reach.

&&& THE TEMPLE &&&

At first glance - - - and - - - from a distance - - - a - - - very great distance - - -

She was nothing more than a heap of rock strewn rubble - - - without form - - - without shape - - - without color - - - without meaning - - - kicked together by some giant as his plaything - - - or - - - (perhaps) - - - (just perhaps) - - - a heap of giant pebbles - - - polished round by some serendipitous spirit of the winds or of the rains - - - so - - - that - - - some god child could playfully pile them one upon the other - - - (as god children are wont to do) - - - playing an innocent game of marbles - - - one god child against the other - - - winner take all - - - capturing in all innocence - - - the greatest of all boulders between thumb and forefinger - - - smashing stone upon stone - - - scattering the carefully piled pebble mound outside the magic circle of childhood - - - to be boldly claimed as a price - - - proudly won.

Or - - - (perhaps) - - - (just perhaps) - - - this great pile might have been nothing more than some mischievous trick of light and shadow - - - played upon the weary traveler by some wicked prankster of the gods.

But - - -

Then again - - -

As one drew closer - - -

The Sleights-of-Hand of light and shadow disappeared - - -

That which remained - - - to the sight - - - and - - - to the smell - - - and - - - to the remaining senses - - - was not a passing plaything for some child giant - - - but rather the harsh marks of man - - - polished to a mirror smoothness by the gentle caresses of woman.

Built from monstrous blocks - - - torn from a sleeping mountain tens of millennia ago - - - hewn by tireless hands and burnished to a soft satin sheen by joyous hearts - - - she stood as an eternal monument to some long vanished god's vanity - - - or - - - (as is more often the case) - - - to some ancient mortal's ego.

Silhouetted against the early morning sun - - - she was black - - - but - - - as the nighttime shadows yielded to the day - - - and - - - fell crashing to the earth dead and dying - - - she was a dark brown - - - an earthy brown - - - an earthly brown so dark as to be almost black - - - black as a shadow - - - almost - - - as if she had arisen from the shadows of her own being - - - from - - - the shadowy brown earth herself - - - to stand - - - teetering - - - only to fall under her own weight - - - falling - - - to kneel upon the barren rocky plain - - - striving to rise again - - - only to falter and fall - - - failing to gain that vantage point from which she might see all that passes around her - - - failing to bridge earth and sky - - - leaving the netherworld and the cosmos forever sundered.

Skillfully wrought - - -

Artfully clothed in gradations of color - - -

Physically joining Netherworld with Sky - - -

Physically melding East with West - - - North with South - - -

Center of the Universe - - -

Universal Center - - -

    From - - -

        Her base of Musty Forest Browns - - -

           Rich in iron and manganese oxides - - -

    To - - -

        A level of Deep Russet Reds - - -

           Richer still in iron oxides - - -

    Then - - -

        A level of Ambivalent Ambers - - -

           Richer still in manganese oxides - - -

Center of the Universe - - -

She stood - - -

Proud and tall - - - Defiant - - - a monument to the skillful play of burnt umbers - - - and - - - burnt siennas - - - and - - - raw ochers - - - garnished - - - with an impish willful "dash" of moss green chromium oxides - - - slyly slipped in between the reds and the yellows.

Four tiered levels was she - - -

    Forest Brown - - -

    Russet Red - - -

    Moss Green - - -

Honey Yellow - - -

Striving mightily to bridge earth and sky - - -

&&& THE LONG CLIMB SKYWARD &&&

As the assembly - - - channeled through the closed ranks of Troodon Warriors - - - began the long slow arduous climb - - - they passed the Rendering Pots - - - heated to a dull red glow - - - glowing a dull burnt red - - - mimicking miniature suns on a clear cold crisp morning - - - fueled by the white hot passion of the priests - - - for here - - - in these pots of volcanic stone - - - not only would flesh be rendered from bone - - - but - - - spirit would be sundered from its fleshy mantel.

For - - -

Not only was the human tallow priceless beyond measure - - -

For - - -

Its virgin white purity would fuel and feed the temple flames for the next tens of millennia - - -

But - - -

Its warrior spirits - - - once freed of their fleshy mantels - - - would fuel and feed the armies of the Sun - - - in her daily battles across the heavens - - - against the forces of the god of darkness.

And - - -

Once their time was spent - - - and - - - their valor proven - - -

The Goddess Sun - - - in a moment of benevolence - - - and - - - her desire to beautify her temple - - - would sprinkle their warrior spirits once more upon the earth - - - to be reborn as temple butterflies - - - hummingbirds - - - and - - - orchids.

As - - -

The royal siblings - - - flanked by Troodon Warriors - - - attained the first level of the stepped pyramid - - - the most secret of the Great Creation Myths - - - whispered to them in the smallest and darkest hour of the night - - - by the ancient quivering voices of their grandmothers - - - began to slip silently into their minds:

Four Times had this bloody temple raised itself above the Rocken Plain - - - and with each rising had come an unquenchable thirst for the blood of innocents.

Four Times had this Drinker of Blood - - - this Gorger of Blood - - - drained the blood of an entire race - - - so that it might satiate its thirst.

Four Times had the Wakening Serpent disgorged its prey - - - so that the Great God Stone could walk upon the earth - - - in the wrinkled guise of Four Hands.

AND
(In the deepest whisper of all)

Four Times had the Wakening Goddess of the Sun slain the Sleeping God of the Night - - - to ensure a safe passage for her worshipers and for her temple across the Celestial Plane - - -

&&& TROODON POTS &&&

The Troodon Fires - - - stoked since dawn - - - roared to life - - - flaring nostrils - - - shooting miles high orange-red flame deep into the magenta morning sky.

As the tempestuous tallow began to flow - - - the flickering flame joyfully licked the languid lips of the Troodon Pots into awakening to the delightful anticipation of a feast - - - most royal - - - just begun.

Reptilian heads were they - - - blue scaled and orange feathered - - - with razor sharp teeth.

Whether - - - carved - - - sculpted - - - or - - - cast from the living volcanic stone - - - no one could remember. Even legend and myth offered no hint of a clue.

But - - - whatever the art - - - whatever the means - - - whether subtle or daring - - - it had long since disappeared from the racial memory of these Dwellers of Stone - - - for they had forsaken thought and will and daring - - - in exchange for the more comforting and all embracing ritual of mindless chants - - - and - - - prayers - - - and - - - blood sacrifice.

⅋⅋⅋ Priestly Order of the Tallow Makers ⅋⅋⅋

Much as an earthbound navigator would ply the Mare Liberum - - - the great open sea - - - in his quest for a southern passage - - - warm breezes - - - and - - - gentle waters - - - The Tallow Maker - - - as celestial navigator - - - charted his way through the secret straits and swirling shoals of fickle gods - - - fickle in love - - - fickle in hate - - - and - - - fickle in the rains that fill the ephemeral streams leading to the sprawling and meandering estuaries which feed the great sea beyond.

Laughing riotously at the navigator's frustrations in dodging the ancient wrecks - - - temples to living gods and tombs of dead kings - - - which lay strew and shattered upon the shoals and great barrier reefs of rogue reincarnations - - -

Betting wager upon wager that the riptides of promiscuous transmigrations of virgin maidens to temple butterflies and orchids - - - would tempt the wayward priest from his true course - - - straying - - - little-by-little - - - ever further - - - along the ephemeral stream channels of the gods - - - until - - - with a capricious laugh and a mirthful wave of the hand - - - the rains would stop - - - and - - - still - - - unawares - - - blindly led by a gentle hand - - - and - - - an enticing smile - - - along the ephemeral dry washes of his desires - - - The Strayling would soon find himself stranded in a temple of his own doom - - - grounded upon the dusty floor of some great Kettle Lake - - - like some jaunty juniper berry - - - fallen upon the desert floor - - - to wither and die.

So it was with the gods - - - and - - - their amusements.

As great wooden oar-paddles - - - slowly - - - rhythmically dipped into the great white frothing sea of tallow - - - plying the celestial waters - - - apprentice priests stripped naked to the waist - - - raced against the Near Time when the tallow rains would stop and the ephemeral streams would dry to dust.

As the First Lieutenant to the High Priest - - - The High Priest of the Tallow - - - The Tallow Master - - - "thumped" his underlings to row even more vigorously - - - (for he too was a Thumper) - - - slowly - - - surely - - - the Great Stepped Pyramid gained momentum as it continued its treacherous course across the great galactic equator - - - and - - - toward a safe harbor.

But what remained a most wondrous mystery - - - in the preparation of this sacred tallow - - - and - - - only to be divined by those unfortunate enough to delve too deeply into the mysteries of this ancient sect - - - was how these Dwellers of Stone had managed to keep themselves from becoming as one with their Sun God - - - escaping the shared fate of a super nova - - - slowly roasting itself alive until nothing remained except a lifeless black cinder - - - to be blown away at the slightest hint of a summer breeze.

For nothing short of divine engineering - - - (or) - - - (the intricate workings of a woman's mind) - - - could have sculpted these meters thick stones into such an intricate labyrinth of channels - - - chimneys - - - and - - - chutes.

Channels - - - chimneys - - - and - - - chutes - - - burrowing deep into the sacred stone - - - a most enticing and elaborate labyrinth of causeways and byways leading everywhere and nowhere - - - passive passages - - - twisting - - - turning - - - tumbling into one another - - - confused - - - lost - - - abandoned - - - doubling back upon themselves - - - until - - - in the deepest moment of despair - - - escaping triumphantly in a riotous roiling passion to shoot searing flames deep into the early morning sky.

Sacred shafts scrubbed immaculately clean and polished to a mirror smoothness by tiny desperate hands - - - belched smoke and soot from Troodon nostrils as if from some great awakened and tormented beast - - - as - - - consecrated causeways poured forth golden liquid tallow from the Terrible Troodon's mouth - - - as if he were disgorging some ill-gotten meal.

Golden tallow - - - golden as the sun - - - golden as a harvest moon - - - was of the first rendering - - - silver was of the second - - - and - - - pure virgin white was of the third - - - to be stored as a vast inland sea deep within the bowels of the temple - - - to serve the needs of the temple and its priests for the coming tens of millennia.

The Golden Rendering united the four axes of the compass - - - the Silver Rendering unified the realms of the netherworld with that of the cosmos - - - and - - - the unblemished White Rendering - - - overseen by none other than the Tallow Master himself - - - melded all that was of this earthly plane with the realms of the dead and of the gods - - - thereby ensuring safe passage for this great stone ship across the galactic equator.

Safe passage - - - such was the troth of the Tallow Master.

&&& Rite of Passage &&&

As the sweet smell of boiled human flesh began to permeate the air - - - and - - - fill his nostrils - - - the young prince - - - was awakened to a subliminal memory of his early childhood - - - of a sweet - - - almost sickening sweet scent - - - lingering on the bodies and in the minds of living skeletons - - - hunters - - - lost - - - given up for dead - - - discovered - - - naked - - - half-carried - - - half-dragged - - - from their ice cave - - - to warmth and safety.

Ten they had been - - - all would have perished - - - but for the ultimate sacrifice of their brother.

Such was life - - - and - - - death - - - in the - - - Ice Time.

&&& Preparation Chamber &&&

The young king - - -

Stumbling - - - blindfolded - - - along a passage-way into a vast chamber - - - lit by sacred tallow - - - harvested tens of millennia ago - - - bound - - - standing - - - arms stretched overhead - - - braided rope - - - chained to the dark unfeeling ceiling - - -

Incense - - - powerful - - - overpowering - - - intoxicating - - - senses reeling - - -

Mosaics of precious stones - - - running - - - frantically chasing one-another - - - racing round - - - as if mimicking eternity - - - never beginning - - - never ending - - - recounting the never ending cycle of the rebirth and redeath - - - of the cosmos.

Sacred voices - - - rhythmically - - - chanting - - - remembering - - - worshiping - - - the sacred union of earth and sky - - - the virgin birth - - - the baptismal blood - - -

Perfume - - - perfumes - - - sweet - - - sweet - - - perfumes - - -

Incense - - - burning - - - burning - - - caustic - - - intoxicating - - - overpowering - - -

Delirium - - - Dementia - - - Dreams - - -

Sweet Dreams - - -

In dreams the scent was sweet - - -
But not of orchid meadows bound - - -
But of a bouquet of mortal flesh - - -
Spirits prancing round and round - - -

In mountain fields the dreamers slept - - -
Upon the bare and naked ground –
Unfettered spirits pure and sweet - - -
Upon the lofty summit mound - - -

Chained to the orchid mountain top - - -
Summit solitude there they found - - -
Sweet mountain prison of garland chains - - -
Sweet ivies round them tightly wound - - -

Virgin voices sweetly flowing - - -
Singing melodies of heroic sound - - -
Embracing tightly love and wisdom - - -
With a prose and passion most profound - - -

Rude brash intruder of the senses - - -
Crashing through all defenses - - -
Sparing all but base pretences - - -
At the Chamber Door - - -

Forest palisade is quickly breeched - - -
Rocky mountain crag is easily reached - - -
Halt! Stop!! No!!! They beseech - - -
At the Chamber Door - - -

Summit Solitude under Siege - - -
Bastion Fortress of Lord and Liege - - -
Last quaint vestige of Prestige - - -
At the Chamber Door - - -

Unshackled from garland chains - - -
Unfettered from the loving twain - - -
Unbound from love again - - -
At the Chamber door - - -

The Victor is besotten - - -
The Interloper's gain ill gotten - - -
The Lovers' troth forgotten - - -
At the Chamber Door

No more honorable pretence - - -
No hollow words of recompense - - -
No thing but passions incensed - - -

Incense - - - pungent - - - choking - - - haze - - -

Blue Haze - - -

Burning his eyes - - - -

Blinding his mind - - -

Blurring his thoughts - - -

Swirling in the thick blue black haze - - -

A Voice - - -

Then - - -

A Chorus of Voices - - -

Thousands of Voices - - -

Begging - - -

Beseeching - - -

Bespeaking - - -

Tens of Thousands of Voices - - - New Comers to the Netherworld - - -

Whispering - - -

Wailing - - -

Wandering - - -

Hundreds of Thousands of Voices - - -

Troubled - - -

Tormented - - -

Tortured - - -

Ancient in their suffering - - -

Ancient in their wisdom - - -

ALL - - -

Joining into one voice - - -

Joining into one chorus - - -

Joining into one refrain - - -

AWAKEN YOUNG KING
AVENGE YOUR PEOPLE

&&& THE DARKENING &&&

As female attendants - - -

Or - - -

Perhaps - - -

Young boys - - -

Androgynous in appearance - - -

   For - - -

       It was difficult to tell - - -

           Because - - -

                 The smoke of the incense still clouded his mind - - -

Meticulously - - -

Began - - -

Oiling the Young King's light brown skin to a blue-black color - - -

Oiling the Young King's skin to a blue-black color - - -

As - - -

           Blue-a-Black - - - such as is a midnight on a clear summer's night - - -

As - - -

       Black-a-Blue - - - such as is a vat full of indigo dye on a clear winter's morn - - -

Blue-Black Haze - - -

           Slowly - - - Flooding Jaguar Claw's nostrils and clouding his mind - - -

           Slowly - - - Dissipating from mind and body and memory - - -

Though still groggy and unable to speak - - -

Jaguar Claw was able to discern his surroundings and his captors - - -

The Chamber was spacious - - - and - - - well lighted - - -

Spacious with a mosaic running along the length of the four walls - - -

Spacious with a mosaic running the length of a battle between two giants - - -

Two Giants - - -

One - - - Blue-Black - - - Powerfully built - - -

Another - - - Red-God - - - Slender and Agile - - -

Both - - -

Equally Fearsome Toothed Giants - - -

One - - -

Head adorned - - - with the golden diadem of the sun - - -

Another - - - with the a sparkling hair net - - - a snood - - - with tiny groupings of stars - - - small sparkling gems - - - symmetrically arrayed in a decorated pattern of galaxies and milky ways - - - being devoured by the void.

Each was armed with a fearsome weapon - - - one with a wooded hafted golden obsidian blade - - - massive and razor sharp - - - the other a great flint knife - - - painted with a motif of a dragon devouring a sun - - -

The attendants were - - - themselves - - - clad in simple dark blue tunics - - - embroidered with the golden motif of the Sun - - - and - - - had just finished carefully massaging a blue-black scented oil into the young king's skin.

Just then - - - a mocking voice cut through the last remnants of the swirling blue haze - - -

Ahhh - - - nice to see that you've decided to join us - - - once again - - - BOY!

As the attendants continued to "bedeck" the young king with jewelry - - - rings and amulets - - - accruements of power - - - using the mosaic likeness of the Dark God as their guide - - - the Troodon Captain continued his taunting - - - as he swaggered over to Jaguar Claw:

186

"How are you today – KING Jaguar Claw? It must be difficult to be king over a dead kingdom - - - but have no fear - - - for - - - you will be joining your subjects soon enough."

"Do you know how you will DIE boy? No matter - - - for that too you will find out soon enough!!!"

"And" - - - he said as he poked the Young King in the ribs - - - "once they are through with you here - - - I'll have your heart cut out - - - ROASTED - - - and - - - brought to me for breakfast! I'll have you for breakfast - - - BOY - - - and shit you out in time for dinner. For desert this evening - - - I think that I'll enjoy a tidbit or two of your juicy sweet sister!" - - - he sneered!!!"

At this threat to his sister - - - Jaguar Claw strained against his bonds - - - and - - - strained to shake off the last vestiges of the blue haze.

As the Captain - - - turned to bark an order to his Sergeant - - - he saw hanging from the Captain's belt - - - as yet another one of his many war trophies - - - the head of his old friend and mentor - - - Boar Tusk - - - so named since his two lower canine teeth protruded from his jaw - - - much as a male boar's.

"Sergeant! Post a guard here - - - you go guard the entrance to make sure that we're not disturbed. As for me - - - I'll soon be going home. Too much pomp and ceremony here for me - - - come see me when - - - this business - - - is done. Also" - - - he said half-turning - - - "Bring his heart to me - - - roasted - - - when the priests are through with him!!!"

"Yes – Boy - - - you'll soon be roasting on a spit!"

As his glance - - - followed - - - Jaguar Claw's gaze to his belt - - - the Captain laughed and held his trophy aloft by the hair - - - "Yes – one pretty sight he is too - - - did you know him?" - - - he said - - - holding the severed head close to his own - - - so that he could more closely study it - - - "Yes - - - he'll make a pretty ornament!"

As the swarthy swaggering captain turned to leave - - - he dropped the head - - - still tied by its leather thong to his belt - - - to his side.

As the head fell - - -

It seemed to wink and smile at Jaguar Claw - - - or - - - was it still the effects of the blue haze - - - its tusk - - - biting into the Captain's thigh - - -

Biting - - - slightly - - - ever so slightly - - -

So slight was the pain - - - so slight was the wound - - - so brief was the moment - - - that the Captain did not even notice - - -

As - - -

The Captain left - - - laughing - - - neither - - - he - - - nor Jaguar Claw - - - knew that he would not live out the month - - - for - - - gangrene would soon set it.

He would first lose his leg - - - and - - - soon thereafter - - - his life.

&&& Winter Solstice &&&
(From the Mouth of the Serpent)

Jaguar Claw - - - still bound - - - forced to kneel - - - with - - - his sister's screams still tearing though his mind - - - waited - - - staring - - - straight ahead - - - into the black void into which his sister had disappeared - - -

Waiting - - - Staring - - - Waiting - - -

Fire - - - Burning Fire - - - spewing forth from the void - - - a serpent - - - red and yellow - - - writhing - - - twisting - - - in the flames - - - disgorging its prey - - -

!!!FROM THE MOUTH OF THE SERPENT!!!

A hand coming out of the darkness - - - his sister's hand - - - oh - - - she had come to save him - - - to free him - - - to comfort him - - - to sooth him - - - her hand - - - somehow she was free - - - somehow - - - she had freed herself - - - would - - - free him - - - soon - - - soon - - - everything would be alright - - -

Then - - -

A second hand - - - a - - - larger hand - - - a - - - man's hand - - -

Then - - - another - - - and - - - another - - - and - - -

&!!! FOUR HANDS !!!&

"Embrace me – brother" - - - mocked a falsetto voice - - - "Embrace me!"

"Embrace your sister - - - boy" - - - commanded a man's voice - - - stepping out from the flames - - - "Embrace me - - - as - - - you would embrace your sister" - - -

The voice - - - now - - - backlit by a mosaic serpent - - - masterful illusion - - - brought to life by the summer solstice sun - - - was - - - now - - - awash with a dark and foreboding timbre: "Embrace me - - - boy!"

The Falsetto Voice returned - - - imploring - - - taunting - - - pleading: "Take me Jaguar Claw - - - for - - - I am yours!"

As four hands walked forward - - - he mocked Jaguar Claw even further - - - flinging open his arms - - - throwing back his head in a gesture of total submission: "Take me Jaguar Claw - - - for I am yours!"

The cruel laugh echoed throughout the chamber - - - reverberating - - - growing in intensity - - - reaching deep into the depths of the temple - - - until - - - it burst forth from flaring Troodon Nostrils - - - to shatter sound upon the country side.

"Kiss me brother" - - - again - - - the cruel shrill laugh - - - "Kiss me - - - and - - - I will free you. You do want to be free - - - don't you - - - brother?"

Again - - - the deep menacing voice: "You should feel honored - - - Boy - - - to be a sacrifice to the gods - - - as - - - your sister feels honored" - - -

As Four Hands spoke - - - he turned - - - slowly - - - deftly - - - full circle - - - into the light - - - much as a professional displayer of fashions and garments might coyly - - - teasingly - - - hide her wares - - - in the shadows - - - and - - - then - - - slowly - - - deliberately turn to fully display a richly decorated cape for a wealthy - - - and - - - prospective customer - - -

"Embrace me!" - - - Again the falsetto - - -

As - - -

Jaguar Claw stared in horror - - - the golden painted specter of Four Hands slowly yielded - - - as - - - the face of his sister slowly turned into his view - - - grotesquely contorted in the visage of an agonizing death - - -

!!! Flayed Skin of the Sun Goddess !!!
Sun Goddess Mime

Flayed skin - - -

      Flayed senses - - -

            Flayed being - - -

Chunks of consciousness - - - torn away from spirit - - - crashing into each other - - - annihilating each other - - - cascading - - - into - - - searing starbursts - - - threatening sanity - - - existence - - - being - - -

Cold cruel laughter - - - coursing callously through his veins - - - chilling - - - crushing the warm flicker of life - - - into - - - a - - - sputtering ember - - -

"Embrace me! - - - Boy" - - - cooed the falsetto - - -

      "Embrace me!! - - - Boy" - - - cried the dark timbre - - -

            "Embrace us!!! - - - Boy" - - - commanded both - - -

Tiny flickers - - -

      Voices - - -

            Lights - - -

                Scents - - -

Fading - - - fading - - -

Murmuring - - - whispering - - -

One whisper - - - one voice - - - one thought: "Your Highness" - - -

Forty Thousand Whispers - - - Forty Thousand Voices - - - one thought: "Your Majesty" - - -

Then - - -

      Forty Thousand Whispers - - -

                  Plus - - -

                             One: "Brother"

      Forty Thousand Voices - - -

                  Plus - - -

                             One: "BROTHER"

      Forty Thousand Whispers - - - Lamenting - - - wailing - - - groveling - - -

      One Voice - - - Demanding - - -

      Forty Thousand Voices - - - Beseeching - - - imploring - - - pleading - - -

      One Voice - - - Unbending - - - Unyielding - - - Uncompromising - - -

One Voice: "Brother! Open your eyes!! Look around you!!! Look around this Doom Ring of Skulls. Do you want to be as they - - - mere dusty tokens to a savage end? They once were as you - - - young - - - vibrant - - - alive - - - but - - - now- - - their time spent - - - they spend their hours - - - here rotting - - - crumbling to dust - - -

"Boy - - - prepare yourself for my embrace" - - - enticed the falsetto - - -

"- - - embracing dusty thoughts - - - worn out passions" - - - continued The One - - -

"Passion - - - do you not feel it?" - - - Cooed the dark timbre - - -

"Feel it - - - my brother " - - - continued The One - - - "Feel your power - - - Claim your birthright - - - YOU ARE KING!!!"

"King Boy - - - feel my embrace" - - - taunted Four Hands as he embraced the young king and kissed him lightly on the lips - - -

"Embrace your heritage - - - my brother" - - - Commanded The One - - - "AWAKEN!"

As Four Hands stepped back - - - he held the golden mask of the sun goddess - - - given to him by one of two female attendants - - - and - - - motioned to his assistants - - - to bring the sacred scroll to him.

As the scroll was carefully unrolled - - - and - - - readied for Four Hands' reading - - - Jaguar Claw slowly - - - and - - - with great effort - - - opened his eyes - - - as - - - The One's voice faded into a whisper: "Beware your hair - - - my brother - - - beware your hair."

Four Hands inhaled deeply - - - and - - - powerfully - - - throwing back his head - - - eyes closed - - - completely savoring the moment:

"AHHHH - - - The Power - - - Can you feel it? Mmmmmmmm - - - good - - - Good - - - GOOD!

If only I could stay like this forever - - - but - - - we must hurry - - - yes - - - we must hurry - - - for - - - I have killed her - - - for only a little while - - -

Soon - - - she'll come back - - - come back - - - then - - - she'll be angry - - - no - - - more annoyed than angry - - - because she'll realize that I've saved her temple - - - her priests - - - her prayers - - - (her passions) - - -

Yes - - - she'll be happy - - - once she understands that I've killed the Dark Lord - - - and - - - then - - - she'll be happy - - -

But - - - we must hurry - - - for if she awakens too soon - - - I'll have lost my power - - - and - - - won't be able to kill you - - - my sweet prince - - - and - - - that would be a shame - - - wouldn't it?"

Four Hands smiled gently - - - and - - - then - - - solemnly - - - donned the Golden Mask of the Sun Goddess.

&&& The Doom Ring &&&

"Boy - - - prepare for your doom!"

"Prepare to join this waiting Circle of Skulls!"

"WAIT!"

Jaguar Claw's voice was clear and cold: "I will not be ONE of them - - - I shall rule OVER them!"

"If - - -

I am to be king - - - of - - - the skulls - - - in - - - this - - - Throne Room of Skulls - - - I will not suffer my hair to be cut - - - for - - - I will not enter eternity as a peasant - - - with - - - my hair cropped to my ears - - - but - - - down to beneath my shoulders - - - as my rank demands!

Hold my hair - - - well away from the Death Man's Ax - - - priest - - - well away from my head and my shoulders - - - so - - - that - - - the cut is clean and swift - - - and - - - my hair untouched!"

"Well - - - well" - - - commented Four Hands - - - with a smile - - -

"We've had lords - - and - - - we've had nobles - - - but - - - until now - - - never have we had a true King. Do as he says!"

"Boy - - - you ARE the stuff of Kings" - - - amazed Four Hands. "Tonight I'll drink your blood - - - and - - - spread your tallow upon my bread - - - yes - - - I will most certainly remember you - - - and - - - fondly - - - too - - -"

"Hold him!"

A strapping young apprentice priest - - - clad in a golden yellow tunic - - - hair cropped to his ears - - - stepped forward - - - and - - - grabbed Jaguar Claws hair in both hands - - - as - - - Jaguar Claw obligingly bowed his head low upon the executioner's block.

As - - -

Four Hands slowly raised the Great Ceremonial Axe - - - an axe - - - Golden Obsidian Blade - - - shafted with a black wooden handle - - -

Jaguar Claw - - - stared straight into the wild eyes of the Dark Lord - - - painted smiling - - - upon the blade - - -

As - - -

The Priest raised the blade - - - he paused slightly - - - smiling - - - before bring it savagely down in one swift stroke - - -

The blade bit deeply into the flesh - - - slashing through supple living bone as if it were slicing through naught but air - - - but - - - it was not the young Warrior King who let out a blood curling scream - - - but - - - the strong young apprentice - - - who - - - although- - - standing - - - was blankly staring at the bloody stumps - - - of - - - what had once been his hands - - - not yet comprehending that his hands lay severed - - - and - - - lifeless upon the stone floor.

For - - -

Jaguar Claw - - - at the last possible moment - - - had - - - with the desperation of one facing death - - - pulled his head savagely backwards - - - and - - - had drawn the young apprentice's hands into the swinging arc of the descending blade.

With the one same swift motion - - - born of one - - - who - - - living high above the clouds amidst rock and crag - - - must remain not only supple of body - - - but - - - also of wit - - - Jaguar Claw rolled over onto his back - - - and - - - pulled his feet up and through his tightly bound hands - - - so - - - that - - - his bound hands were now before him.

In a flash - - - he had sprung to his feet - - - pulled a long ceremonial dagger from the belt of the young apprentice priest - - - and - - - had plunged it deep into his body.

With an instinct quicker than thought - - - and - - - with the dagger - - - momentarily - - - frozen in the body of the priest - - - Jaguar Claw slashed through his bonds - - -

As - - -

The young priest - - - already dead on his feet - - - began to crumple to the floor.

As Four Hands raised his Axe to strike - - - Jaguar Claw whirled - - - fending off the axe blow with his left arm - - - while - - - clutching Four Hands by the throat - - - breaking loose the bonds - - - that - - - had bound his sisters flayed skin to the priest's body - - - by - - - the sheer force of his onslaught.

As Four Hands gurgled - - - what most properly should have been his death cry - - - two female attendants rushed toward Jaguar Claw from behind - - - as - - - the Golden Axe clattered to the floor.

Jaguar Claw - - - now beset by two - - - let loose the priest - - - and - - - hurled one of the attendants hard into the wall - - - smashing her skull - - - the other - - - he held by the arm as he reached for the axe.

As he swung down - - - she attempted to shield herself with her free arm - - - but the axe - - - being dumb and made of stone - - - made no notice - - - as - - - it sliced through her arm and clove her skull in two - - - right down her chin.

Four Hands - - - in the meantime - - - had regained his feet - - - and - - - was attempting to flee - - - all the while crying - - - "You'll kill us all - - - fool - - - you'll kill us all! The Temple must pass - - - The Temple must pass."

Jaguar Claw - - - with a bound over the executioner's block - - - suddenly stood between Four Hands and freedom.

As Four Hands reached for his ceremonial dagger - - - Jaguar Claw caught him by the arm - - - and - - - with his right arm free - - - brought the axe down heavily upon Four Hand's shoulder - - - completely severing it from the golden painted body.

Two apprentice priests - - - temporarily frozen by fear - - - and - - - the - - - ferocity of Jaguar Claw's attack - - - realizing that their lives were at stake - - - suddenly sprang into action - - - as - - - they attacked Jaguar Claw from two different directions.

Still grasping the priest's severed arm - - - Jaguar Claw used it to ward off the blows - - - of - - - first one - - - and - - - then - - - the other priest - - - but - - - it was not long before they too were lying lifeless on the floor.

His justice had been both swift and terrible.

Then all was still - - - quiet.

Again - - - the voice of The One: "I shall hide you - - - and - - - protect you - - - brother."

The young King - - - working with the instincts of his totem - - - the Jaguar - - - moved quickly - - - laying the flayed skin of his sister over himself - - - removing the arm ring from Four Hand's severed arm - - - and - - - placing it upon his own - - -

Stripping the golden breast-plate - - - from - - - the still quivering body of Four Hands - - - Jaguar Claw strapped it to his naked chest - - - and - - - then donned the golden mask of the Sun Goddess - - - and - - - stepped out into the daylight - - -

As - - -

The people bowed - - - and - - - gave thanks for the safe passage of the temple - - - Jaguar Claw - - - momentarily dazzled by the daylight - - - paused - - - then - - - imitating the voice of the priest - - - as - - - best as he could - - - gave the people leave to return to their homes - - - and - - - their feasting - - -

"Rejoice - - - for - - - we have lived out this day - - - and - - - the morrow will dawn anew."

"I give you leave - - - to - - - go to your homes and rejoice - - - pray to your gods - - - and - - - pray to your goddesses - - - but most of all - - - give thanks to our Great Goddess of the Sun - - - for it was she who slew the God of Darkness - - - and - - - ensured safe passage for our temple.

"Go now - - - rejoice - - - and - - - and - - - (adding an invention of his own) - - - stay there until morning. Stay in your homes until tomorrow morning."

"Go - - - Now - - - and - - - don't look back."

As the people turned to go to their homes - - - and - - - obeyed his commandment to not look back - - - The Sergeant Major - - - standing at Jaguar Claw's side - - - head bowed with all of the rest - - - turned to leave.

As - - -

The Sergeant Major turned - - - he caught a glimpse of something that set him ill at ease - - -

For - - -

Jaguar Claw's feet - - - were - - - black - - - black as night - - - black as soot - - -

Indeed - - -

Although - - -

His body was well hidden - - - his feet were not - - -

As - - -

The Sergeant Major raised his eyes - - - about to raise the alarm - - - his eyes locked upon Jaguar Claw's - - - and - - - read his doom - - -

Jaguar Claw - - - with the reflexes of his totem - - - struck him - - - a - - - two handed blow - - - cleaving his Troodon Helmet in two - - - and - - - sending his mortal body sprawling down two different sides of the pyramid.

The people heard a cry - - - a - - - scream - - - but - - - obeying the commandment of their priest - - - not to turn and look back - - - quietly went their way - - - toward their homes and celebration.

Jaguar Claw - - -

      Man-Mind Numb - - -

           Cat-Like Instinct - - -

          Slinked off into the shadows - - -

&&& THE LARDER &&&

The Sun - - - the sun - - - the - - - burning - - - blinding - - - blustery - - - sun - - -

Blinded by the sun - - - blind - - - cursed blindness - - - searching - - - stumbling - - - falling - - - lost - - -

Sounds - - - scents - - - long forgotten - - - longing - - -

Buzzing sounds - - - Hummingbird Sounds - - - buzzing - - - darting - - - stopping - - -

Leading him - - - guiding him - - - soothing him - - -

Frosty scents - - - memories of the dark and the dank - - -

Stumbling - - - scratching - - - clawing - - - his way into the deep dark hole - - -

Fleeing the sun - - - fleeing his creation - - - seeking to be unborn - - -

Blinded by the dark - - - blind - - - blissful blindness - - - feel - - - touch - - - move - - -

Pressing - - - deeper - - - pressing ever deeper - - - pressing - - - pressing - - - pressing his naked burning flesh into the frosty stone wall - - - pressing - - - until they became as one - - - sweat - - - simmering sweat - - - mingling with the icy crystals of the sweating stone - - - icy sweat - - - drawing the raging fever from his burning body - - -

Ice crystals - - - freezing the demonic delirium in his mind - - - shivering - - - feverish shivers - - - icy shivers - - - whether - - - from - - - cold - - - or - - - hunger - - - or exhaustion - - - or - - -

Scents - - - faint - - - wafting scents - - - foods - - - fists full - - - indiscriminately torn from cask and shelf - - - draughts of honeys and meads - - -

Tired - - - tired - - - oh - - - so - - - very - - - very - - - tired - - -

Water - - - sweet - - - smooth - - - soothing - - - glacial waters - - - cascading from a mountain fount - - - trickling through the larder trough - - - cooling - - - cooling - - - healing - - -

Tired - - - so - - - very - - - very - - - tired - - -

Sweet glacial waters - - - seeking their lost mountain child - - - tirelessly searching earth and sky - - - seeking - - - searching - - - singing - - -

Lulled by its sweet lullaby - - - the child king stretched out in the watery trough - - - yielding to the gentle rhyme of its weltering waters - - -

Cool waters - - - glacial waters - - - flowing over his beaten and battered body - - - drowning his pain in their merciful embrace - - - extinguishing the fires of the temple - - - stripping his consciousness - - - of all memories - - - of all pain - - - of all emotions - - -

Unforgetfulness slowly yielding to the cleansing waters - - -

Memories - - - pain - - - emotions - - - floating away as one with the oily filth of the temple - - - washed clean from his body - - -

Cool - - - clean - - - cleansing waters - - - drifting thoughts - - - drifting body - - - bliss - - - bliss - - - unyielding bliss - - -

Blissful Bliss - - - ferociously exploding into an aura of starbursts - - - as - - - the heavy wooden door to the cottage crashed open - - - showering a super nova of fiery sparks into the tiny room - - -

ᛥᛥᛥ No Escape ᛥᛥᛥ

As daylight streamed into the larder - - - Jaguar Claw - - - stunned - - - blinded - - - helpless - - - raised himself weakly upon one elbow - - - numbly awaiting his fate - - -

Framed against the door - - - silhouetted against the avenging afternoon sky - - - stood an executioner of the temple - - - a giant - - - spiked feather headdress set upon a massive frame - - - war club in hand - - -

As the dark booming voice raged across the room - - - thunder crashed and echoed throughout the stone cottage: "You won't escape a second time - - - boy. Come out! Show yourself!! I know that you're in there!!! If you don't come out - - - I'll drag you out - - - and - - - then - - - skin you - - - and - - - hang you up to dry!!!!"

With giant strides - - - the massive figure flew across the room and stood blocking Jaguar Claw's only escape - - - "Boy - - - you're mine!!!

A giant hand - - - shot across the shadows - - - grabbed a leg - - - and - - - half-carried - - - half-dragged a whimpering Jaguar Claw across the room - - - as easily as one would carry a limp sack of potatoes - - - lifting him up only to slam him down hard onto a wooden table top - - - scattering a wild assortment of clay pots and wooden bowls: "Now - - - to get a good look at you - - - boy!"

As the giant's left hand held Jaguar Claw firmly by the throat - - - his right hand roughly brushed Jaguar Claw's hair from his face with his right - - - turning the young king's face into the sunlight streaming into the door:

"No - - - no - - - it can't be - - - it can't be - - - "

"Honey Bear? Honey Bear?? Kinkajou is that you!?!"

As a raging supernova - - - cresting inside Kinkajou's brain - - - slowly subsided - - - a great gentle halo - - - slowly began to glow around the silhouetted form standing before him - - - Kinkajou looked up - - - shielding his eyes against the ethereal glow: "Hoatzin? Hoatzin?? Is that you? Sing a song to me Hoatzin - - - then - - - lay me down to sleep - - - for - - - I am so tired."

Hoatzin - - - tears streaming down her cheeks - - - swept up the limp form - - - and turned - - - kicking shut the wooden door - - - locking herself and the child away - - - for an eternal moment - - - from the wearisome world outside - - - as she gently cradled the broken child in her arms - - - rocking him - - - protecting him - - - cooing his favorite lullaby - - - as - - - she had done - - - so many - - - many - - - times before.

ꝯꝯꝯ Hoatzin ꝯꝯꝯ

Hoatzin - - - charged as a foundling - - - whether orphaned - - - or - - - abandoned by raiders - - or - - - squatters - - - or - - - thieves - - - no one knew.

Hoatzin – The Crib Climber – climbing out of her toddler's crib to raid the larder of its sweets - - - sneaking back in - - - when no one was looking - - - all besmeared with honeys - - - never ever comprehending how she would always be discovered - - -

Hoatzin – red hair close cropped and spiked - - - broad smiling face made even more broad by the delicate blue tattooed smile of her people - - -

Hoatzin - - - Crafter of Miracles - - - spirit freely flowing from her fingertips - - - imbuing melancholy metals with the fierce life force of the Jaguar - - - and - - - Coatimundi - - - and - - - wild sage - - -

Hoatzin - - - Caster of Spells - - - and - - - metals - - - casting her net over naked consciousness - - bereft of all memory - - - oblivious of all beginnings - - - and - - - of all ends - - - as precious temple inlays of butterflies - - - and - - - dragonflies - - -

Hoatzin - - - Chaser of Tempests and Pewters - - - plucking fleeting memories - - - from the air - - - much as one would pluck swirling leaves - - - one-by-one - - - from an autumn storm - - -

Hoatzin - - - Weaver of Dreams - - - weaving torn threads of tattered passions into tapestries of mythdoms and kingdoms - - -

Hoatzin - - - great - - - gentle - - - smiling - - - Hoatzin - - - deftly burnishing myth - - - and - - - legend - - - to a pristine shine - - -

Hoatzin - - - sweet - - - sweet - - - Hoatzin - - -

Hoatzin - - -

&&& The Intruders &&&

!!!HOATZIN!!!

!!!WITCH!!!

"Open the door - - - you red headed witch!!!"

"Do you hear us - - - Witch!?!"

Three stern looking figures stood outside the door to Hoatzin's cottage - - - clad in the gray hemp garments of the lowest warrior caste - - - one lieutenant and two soldiers.

The Lieutenant was busy pounding on the door - - - for he was an aspiring thumper - - - while his two soldiers - - - one tall and thin - - - the other short and squat - - - looked nervously around - - - as if waiting to be pounced upon by some great man eating beast.

"Hoatzin!!! - - - Open this door!!!!! - - - NOW!!!!!"

The lieutenant - - - screaming at the top of his lungs - - - appeared determined to thump the massive wooden door to splinters - - - but - - - was only succeeding in thoroughly thumping the eardrums of his squad of two: "Hoatzin – open this door – or - - - we'll break it down!"

The two soldiers - - - cringing with each fist slam into the door - - - slowly gained the courage to speak: "Lieutenant" - spoke the tall thin solder – "I don't think that is such a great idea - - - last time someone messed with this witch - - - first - - - she threatened to skin him alive - - - then - - - she figures that is too quick and merciful - - - so she changes him into a toad she did!"

The Lieutenant half turned his head - - - scowled - - - and - - - continued banging: "Hoatzin – I know that you're in there - - - open up!"

The two soldiers - - - now thoroughly convinced that they were already dead - - - cowed - - - deep in the shadows - - - wishing to be anywhere else but here - - - as their Lieutenant continued to scream: "Open this door - - - NOW - - - or - - - we'll break it down!"

At the word "WE" - - - both soldiers shot glances at each other - - - gulped - - - and began to shake.

Again - - - the thin soldier spoke - - - voice shaking: "Lieutenant - - - this ain't such a hot idea - - - she's a witch you know. Last time someone messed with her - - - she changed him into a toad - - - and - - - an ugly one at that!" – chimed in the short fat soldier.

"Hmmmrumph!" Snorted the Lieutenant - - - as he continued his pounding.

"Hoatzin!!! - - - Open this door!!!!! - - - NOW!!!!!"

As the thin soldier gulped - - - and - - - looked nervously on - - - he whispered to his shorter companion: "Hope that he likes bugs - - - cause that's what he'll be eatin' from now on. Remember old wart nose? Remember what she did to him? Turned him into a toad – she did."

"But that's not the worst of it" he continued.

"No?" – asked the short one.

"No. Old Wart Nose - - - he was a complainer - - - he was - - - always complaining - - - complaining - - - complaining - - - always - - - complaining - - - noon to night."

"And" - - - he continued - - - "on the rare occasion when he wasn't complaining about something - - - he was bragging - - - like about them big roasted nuts he used to brag about - - - too good for the likes of us - - - he used to say - - - then he'd go on complaining about how unfair life was. Well - - - one day he was complaining to Old Hoatzin - - - trying to steal her honey too - - - told him she'd skin him alive – she did - - - if he ever tried to steal her honey - - - well - - - anyways

- - - he - - - not being too smart of a fellow - - - keeps complainin' that she shouldn't hoard it all for herself - - - when - - - well - - - she gives him something to complain about."

"What's that?" Asked the short soldier?

"Bugs" – answered the thin soldier - - - "bugs."

"Yup - - - she gives him somethin' real to complain about - - - bugs - - - eating bugs - - - for the rest of his life - - - bet he wishes he had a mouth full of our chow right about now - - - for - - - I remember how he used to spit at our mess - - - and - - - brag about them big sweet nuts he was always eatin'. So - - she knows this - - - you see - - - so she makes him into something that can't eat nothin' but bugs!!! If she would've turned him into a squirrel - - - he would've been happy for the rest of his life - - - see? Stashing nuts all day long - - - eatin' nuts all night long - - - so she turns him into a toad!"

So then - - - let me get to the worst of it - - - so then - - - he ends up complaining about havin' to eat bugs - - - instead of them big red sweet nuts - - - so he starts complainin' again - - - but he can't talk - - - you see - - - for he ain't got no tongue no more - - - least ways no tongue for talkin' - - - so - - - he starts croaking - - - croaking - - - croakin' - - - croakin' all night long - - - and - - - right under my window - - - and - - - I ain't never done nothin' to deserve anything like that at all - - - "

"No fooling?"

"Nope - - - honest truth - - - that's him - - - right under my window croakin' all night long! Keepin' me and my lady awake all night - - - he does - - - keepin' us awake just for spite - - - because - - - I was too smart to mess with her honey."

"Hey you two - - - quit your gabbin' and get over here - - - give me some shoulder into this door - - - I'm tired of playing games!"

"I'm telling you Lieutenant - - - I'd go slow if I was you - - - in face - - - in fact - - - if I was you - - - I wouldn't go at all.

This Hoatzin ain't no woman - - - (whispering) - - - She ain't not even a witch - - - (lowering his voice even more) - - - She's a Troll!

Maybe even a Troll Witch - - - no woman could be as big and strong as she is!!! They don't come none worser or meaner than a Troll Witch!"

&&& GOLDEN MANE &&&

Hoatzin - - - sat motionless - - - at the head of a long wooden table - - - face buried deeply into her hands - - - as - - - the long stone room thundered and shook from the pounding at the door.

Tugging gently at her hands - - - so that she might - - - once again - - - see her friend's smiling face - - - was Golden Mane - - - a Golden Lion Tamarin - - - constant companion - - - and - - - best of friends.

As Golden Mane - - - persistently tugged at Hoatzin - - - and - - - plied her with her most favorite of fruits - - - (palatable only to a Golden Tamarin) - - - Hoatzin slowly yielded and lowered her hands - - - smiling gently - - - and - - - gazing softly into her friend's worried eyes - - - for - - - although Golden Mane was as small as Hoatzin was large - - - the size of her heart was in no way diminished - - - and - - - if her friend was in trouble - - - she would protect her - - - even at the cost of her own life!

On the roof of Hoatzin's cottage - - - Howler - - - three times as large as Golden Mane - - - and - - - easily more than ten times her body weight at a solid twenty pounds - - - punished the intruders with his cacophonous cries - - - each of which dealt a sledge hammer blow to the minds and bodies of the intruders below.

As Hoatzin looked up - - - she smiled - - - gently stroking the reddish-golden mane of her tiny friend - - - as she took the proffered fruit.

Chewing the bitter fruit slowly and carefully - - - she gently smiled - - - as - - - she lovingly gazed into the worried eyes of her tiny friend - - - reassuring her - - - stroking her golden mane - - - knowing full well that she was well protected.

&&& THE SHRINE &&&

Although the (vast) stone room in which Hoatzin was seated - - - was - - - in-and-of-itself austere - - - it was crammed full of clay pots - - - wooden bowls - - - half smelted ores and delicate 'lost wax' castings - - - piled high against the far wall - - - haphazardly arrayed - - - wherever the slightest hint of an open space afforded itself.

Along the width and breath of the near wall hung - - - all for the making - - - herbs - - - and - - - spices - - - and - - - mints.

And - - - on the wall closest to the hearth - - - hung red roots and black berries - - - patiently waiting their turn to be simmered into a savory soup or a sumptuous stew.

At the foot of the hearth - - - pomaces - - - dried husks - - - squeezed empty of limpid oils and sacred passions - - - were flippantly tossed into the scrap heap of tinders and flints - - - belying their skill in imparting the most delicate of flavors to roasted meats and vegetable stews.

Mortars and pestles - - - silent guardians - - - stoic as stone - - - patiently rested at each far-flung corner of the room - - - obediently awaiting their turn to be called to duty.

Whether it be ore - - - or - - - root - - - or - - - herb - - - awaiting its doom - - - to be pulverized into pigment - - - or - - - potion - - - or - - - poison - - - all was at the ready for the crushing blow of stone against stone.

Stone - - - layer upon layer - - - slabs of stone - - - (perhaps) - - - shards - - - cast off from the temple - - - or - - - (perhaps) - - - splinters cast off from the living mountain - - - afforded a most comfortable dwelling place - - - as unlike the baked clay and straw brick dwellings of the city dwellers - - - as - - - day was unto night.

However - - - that which was the most impressive - - - was the hearth.

The noble hearth - - - this - - - Most Noble and Elegant Hearth - - - warming both heart and home - - - conquering both cold and hunger - - - stood proudly between eating and sleeping chambers - - - raising itself humbly from the ground from which it was born - - - to rise gently through the roof - - - to let waft sweet smelling smokes and perfumes - - - free - - - to dance serenely beneath the bounteous blue sky - - - the canopy under which Hoatzin had built her most comfortable and unassuming home.

However - - - decidedly - - - and - - - certainly most strange - - - to the occasional passerby - - - was this stone chimney - - for - - - to let the smoke escape unimpeded from their dwelling space was a most curious and alien thought - - - for - - - it had been forever the custom of these people to live their lives around their circular fire pits - - - inevitably smoking not only their fish - - - but - - - also their flesh - - - their persons - - - their very beings - - - body - - - and - - - spirit - - - with - - - the pungent perfume of fish oils and hemp.

Along the length of this great room - - - ran a great trough - - - waist high - - - from larder to hearth - - - through which a tiny rivulet trickled - - - last remnant of a mighty glacial stream cascading down the mountain crags - - - affording Hoatzin a cool refreshing drink - - - whenever

205

she wished - - - and - - - showering her tired muscles with cool clear water at the end of a long hot day.

Lastly - - - at the easternmost end of the house - - - at the far end of the sleeping chamber - - - was The Shrine.

It was here that the now washed - - - anointed - - - and - - - clothed body of Jaguar Claw lay in eternal sleep.

&&& Intrusion &&&

!!!MURDERS!!!

"You've killed him!!!"

Hoatzin - - - tears streaming down her cheeks - - - turned defiantly - - - to face the intruders: "Murders! He was just a boy."

"!!! Troll Witch !!!"

"Give him to me!" - - - screamed the Lieutenant.

"NO - - - I'll not give him to you! He's dead!! - - - Don't you understand? DEAD - - - Dead - - - dead" - - - her voice trailing off into a whisper.

"You're lying! Out of the way – Witch!" – With these words the Lieutenant pushed past Hoatzin into the room - - - followed meekly by his two - - - all not that enthusiastic - - - foot soldiers.

"Where is He!?!" – demanded the Lieutenant. "He's hiding here somewhere!"

"You" - - - he said - - - pointing at the tall skinny soldier - - - " you look over there" - - - he said nodding toward far end of the room - - - buried beneath a pile of baskets and other odds and ends - - - "- - - and you" - - - he said - - - pointing with his thumb - - - over the back of his shoulder - - - "you look in there" - - - indicating the Larder – "he must be here somewhere. Dead? Humrmph - - - Not hardly - - - he's hiding and I'm going to find him."

206

"So - - - Hoatzin - - - Hoatzin - - - is it? What over there? Where does that door lead to? Another exit? Is that where he is?"

"Yes" – answered Hoatzin quietly - - - "he's in there."

"Now we're getting somewhere" - - - strutted the Lieutenant. "Hey you two - - - come over here and guard this door. In there - - - huh? Well - - - we'll see - - - if he is - - - 'cause - - - if he is - - - he won't be in there long!"

Without wasting further words - - - for - - - The Lieutenant had practically exhausted his entire vocabulary - - - (for) - - - (he was a Thumper not an Orator) - - - he kicked open the door to Hoatzin's Bed Chamber - - -

There - - - motionless - - - sleeping the eternal sleep - - - lay Kinkajou - - -

"Defilers! Desecrators!! Thieves!!!" Screamed Hoatzin - - -

"Shut up - - - WITCH" - - - screamed the Lieutenant – - - as he strode over to the body - - - prodding and poking at it with the tip of his flint knife - - - to see if some spark of life were still evident - - - so that he could quickly extinguish it - - - as his squad of two - - - backs to the sleeping chamber - - - kept Hoatzin at arm's length.

As the Lieutenant was busy with his poking and prodding - - - and - - - dreams of being elevated to the next level of Thumperdom - - - as reward for having captured the young king - - - he was unawares of a silent - - - sinuous - - - shape - - - slinking past him - - - then - - - leaping to the ledge above the door as quietly and as effortlessly as a ghost - - - (for) - - - the door - - - while of a comfortable size for Hoatzin - - - was - - - easily twice as high as the Lieutenant was tall.

As the Lieutenant continued his prodding and poking - - - interrupted by brief intervals of scratching his head - - - the silent shape above and behind him - - - started a gentle purr - - - which - - - soon became an audible rumble - - -

The Lieutenant - - - still occupied with trying to decide what to de with Kinkajou's corpse - - - barked an order: "Hey - - - wake up - - - you two - - - and - - - quit snoring!"

The two guards - - - startled - - - glanced nervously at each other - - - with the tall skinny one finally saying: "We ain't snoring Lieutenant."

"Yes - - - you are - - - and - - - don't talk back to me - - - I heard you!" - - - said the Lieutenant as he took a step back from the Shrine - - - folded his arms across his chest - - - and - - - began stroking his chin - - - deep in thought.

Again - - - the light rumbling started - - - as - - - the Lieutenant became more and more agitated: "Hey – I told both of you - - - stay awake - - - and - - - don't let Hoatzin in here!" - - - He said - - - half turning and glaring at his two soldiers.

As he slowly moved backwards toward the door - - - still glancing at the sleeping shrine and Kinkajou - - - something brushed against the tip of his ear - - - which he irritably brushed aside. Then it brushed against his other ear - - - again - - - he irritably brushed it away from him.

As he turned - - - full turn - - - to exit the room - - - a long thin furry rope fell full against his nose.

With great irritation - - - he grabbed hold of this rope - - - and - - - gave it one powerful pull - - - to tear it loose from the wall - - - and - - - to be done this annoyance - - - once and for all.

What happened next - - - no one is entirely sure - - - for - - - it ended almost before it began - - - a flurry of motion and the Lieutenant found himself standing - - - in a puddle of his own making - - - and - - - what was once his uniform - - - now hung loosely around his ankles - - - slashed to tatters - - - as - - - he stood face-to-face - - - with - - - an indignant Jaguarondi - - - indignant in having its tail unceremoniously yanked by this vain-glory human.

&&& THE ASCENSION &&&

It was - - - now - - - the third day - - - since - - - Hoatzin had lovingly laid Kinkajou to rest upon the shrine.

At the door - - - or - - - rather - - - at the table - - - before the door - - - eating and drinking - - - were the two guards - - - instructed by the Lieutenant to remain in place until he came back with orders on the disposition of the body - - - until which time Hoatzin was to remain under House Arrest - - - a prisoner in her own home.

However - - - in reality - - - The Lieutenant was nowhere to be found - - - but was instead hidden - - - at home - - - nursing his badly battered and bruised nerves - - - with the magic elixir of his rank - - - Tequila!

Therefore - it is reasonable to assume - - - that - - - the Lieutenant's return on the third day - - - had more to do with his Tequila having run out - - - than his nerves having returned - - - for - - - it was evident - - - that - - - today - - - his Thumping - - - such as it was - - - was somewhat shaky - - - and - - - unsure.

As he nervously walked toward the door to the Sleeping Chamber - - - cursing himself every step of the way - - - that - - - he had not had the foresight to have disposed of the body immediately - - - - so - - - that he would never have had to return to this cursed place - - - he glanced nervously around - - - under tables - - - behind baskets - - - even at the ceiling - - - waiting to be pounced upon at any moment by a grinning - - - laughing - - - devil cat.

As he reached the door - - - he turned to his two guards: "You - - - has the body remained untouched?"

"Yes - - - sir" - - - replied both the short and tall soldiers in unison. He's not been touched - - - and - - - we've stood before the door the whole time - - - took turns we have - - - and" He said shifting his weight from one foot to the other - - - "We've checked on the body every hour - - - just as you've ordered - - - and - - - we've blocked the hole so that that devil cat can't come sneaking back in."

"Good" – answered the Lieutenant - - - let's take the body and burn it - - - for - - - it must be foul by now - - - or - - - maybe we'll just leave it - - - food for the maggots - - - so that we might be done with it!"

"Won't be none too soon for me - - - Lieutenant" - - - spoke the tall thin soldier - - - "this place gives me the jitters - - - ain't natural - - - it ain't!"

Then - - - all three readied themselves - - - and - - - slowly - - - stealthily - - - opened the door - - -

!!!GONE!!!

GONE???!!!

The three warriors - - - pushed past each other - - - crowding through the door jam - - - into the Sleeping Chamber - - - and - - - stared - - - bug eyed at the empty shrine.

GONE!!!

"What? Where?? How???" - - - Raced through each of their minds.

"He's gone" - - - stammered the Lieutenant.

"Sure is" - - - echoed the tall thin soldier.

"Best we be gone too" - - - wished the short squat soldier - - - "should never have come."

As they stood flabbergasted - - - Hoatzin came quietly into the room - - - looked around - - - and - - - smiled - - - smiling - - - as if the weight of the whole world were suddenly lifted from her shoulders: "He has Ascended."

"Ascended? Ascended?? Where??? What???? How?????" stammered the Lieutenant - - - "What do you mean - - - Ascended?"

"Ascended?!" - - - Stammered Hoatzin - - - "Uh - - - Ascended? Uh - - - Yes - - -

He has ascended.

He has ascended to the top of the Mountain - - - returned to his people - - - The People of the Clouds - - - uh - - - I - - - mean - - -

He has ascended - - - to - - - the - - - Clouds - - - Yes - - - To the Clouds - - - high above - - - The Mountain Top - - - home of his forefathers.

He is now a cloud spirit - - - high above the mountain - - -

He is now one of the cloud spirits - - - he is at peace - - - and - - - so am I."

With that - - - she turned - - - walked into the Eating Room - - - and - - - sat down heavily into her chair - - -

For - - - she had neither eaten nor slept for three days - - -

Sagging wearily - - - leaning back into her chair - - - repeating to herself: "At peace - - - at peace - - - finally he's at peace."

As the three soldiers numbly followed her - - - they too sat down on a long bench at the table - - - numb - - - silent - - - confused.

"Ascended? Ascended?? What does this mean??? A miracle."

As Hoatzin glanced up - - - she smiled and said: "This is a time of rejoicing - - - in this time of miracles - - - would you like a drink of my special Mead - - - fresh and bountiful?"

The two soldiers looked nervously at each other - - -

Remembering Old Wart Nose - - - they - - - shook their heads so vigorously - - - that they were in danger of falling off - - - but - - - the Lieutenant - - - young - - - and - - - eager - - - (for) - - - the Tequila had indeed worn off - - - and - - - especially since his nerves were badly in need of calming - - - nodded - - - greedily.

Hoatzin went lithely to her larder and came back with a jug of mead - - - and - - - unknown to the Lieutenant - - - a specially prepared mug - - - carefully dusted with sensuous sweets - - - and - - - the ground powder of a special mushroom.

As Hoatzin poured - - - and - - - the two soldiers looked nervously on - - - the Young Lieutenant drank - - - often - - - and - - - deeply.

&&& Rebirth of a Race &&&

Jaguar Claw - - - having awakened from Hoatzin's Sleeping Potion - - - stirred but slightly - - - conscious - - - but not yet moving - - - surveying his surroundings by scent - - - and - - - by sound - - - and - - - by feel - - - for - - - Hoatzin - - - knowing full well that although the body might heal - - - the mind - - - oftentimes - - - shattered and broken - - - is - - - unable to defend - - - even - - - its own Mind House.

Therefore - - - it was most certainly best to lay that mind of man to sleep - - - and - - - awaken the totem animal instead - - - relying upon the cat - - - cautious - - - camouflaged - - - calculating - - - cunning - - - to survive - - - until - - - the mind had had time to heal - - -

Hoatzin had awakened the cat - - - and - - - had granted Jaguar Claw one slim chance for survival.

Clawing his way out of the Sleeping Chamber - - - with - - - fleshy claws - - - the Young King - - - fingertips bleeding - - - found himself in the lair of his cat sister - - -

Golden Eyes purred a welcome - - - as - - - Jaguar Claw - - - with - - - a cat's cunning and - - - a man's subliminal fear - - - drew the great stone back into place - - - hiding all traces of his spoor - - - from even the best of trackers.

Quickly scaling the sheer rock wall - - - with the speed - - - skill - - - and - - - agility of a monkey cat - - - Jaguar Claw silently made his way upwards - - - along the silver glacial stream - - - guiding him back home to his Mountain Paradise - - - high up in the clouds - - -

Only after a full day's journey - - - and - - - only until he had attained the heights - - - far - - - far - - - from the city - - - and - - - high - - - high - - - above the wafting smokes of Hoatzin's fires - - - did he drink - - - never pausing - - - scooping his hand into the cool stream water - - - as - - - he continued his climb upwards - - - and - - - skywards.

Only after three continuous days of travel was Jaguar Claw able to taste the freedom of the clouds upon his tongue - - - and - - - feel the spirit of the mountain beneath his feet - - - and - - - then - - - and - - - only then - - - did he understand - - - that - - - he was as one with the Spirit of the Mountain - - - and - - - one with all those spirits of the mountain - - - wind - - - and - - - rain - - - and - - - glacier - - -

And - - - one with all of those tens of thousands of spirits - - - past and future - - - which called themselves - - - The Children of the Clouds - - -

It was then - - - and only then - - - that - - - once - - - his feet had rested upon the Sweet Sacred Soil - - - and - - - his spirit had soared into the mountain mists - - - did he dare lay that small leather bundle - - - which had once been his sister - - - to burial - - - praying over her spirit - - - swearing to protect her - - - and - - - finally falling into an exhausted - - - protective - - - sleep over her.

In the depth of his delirium - - - or - - - (perhaps) - - - it was in his dreams - - - there came a maiden - - - lithe of body - - - long flowing dark hair - - - who - - - as he lay sleeping - - - in turn - - - lay - - - her body over him - - - weaving a net of dreams and mists over his sleeping spirit - - - to - - - protect him from witch's eyes and the maws of hungry beasts - - - for - - - just as he had protected his sister - - - so - - - would she protect him.

And - - - so it was - - - over - - - days and nights - - - (perhaps) - - - turned to countless summers and winters - - - did Jaguar Claw truly became as one with the mountain - - - melding spirit with flesh - - - protected nightly - - - by the woven dream nets of the Maid of the Mists - - -

And - - - in time - - - just - - - as - - - The Maid of the Mists - - - would care for his spirit - - - so too did his occasional companion - - - the Lone Wolf - - - care for his body - - - providing warmth - - - when no fire could be lit - - - sharing a naked bone - - - when no food could be found - - -

And - - - as - - - Hoatzin had foreseen - - - slowly - - - oh - - - so very slowly - - - over months of summers - - - did Jaguar Claw's manly senses return to him - - -

It was then - - - as - - - it must be - - - as - - - it always has been - - - that - - - one early summer evening - - - as Jaguar Claw lay sleeping - - - peacefully - - - in a moss covered dell - - - that - - - The Maiden of the Mists appeared at his side - - -

But - - - this night - - - she was not to shelter him from witch's spells or to shield him from the ravenous maws of killer beasts - - - (for) - - - he had come of manhood - - - and - - - he would kill all that he would eat - - - and - - - all that would eat of him - - - but - - - she had come - - - (because) - - - just as he had grown to manhood - - - so - - - too - - - had she come of womanhood - - - and - - - at this moment - - - she had chosen to lay with him.

As they lay - - - together - - - as one - - - throughout that cool summer night - - - warming each other - - - comforting each other - - - they became as one - - - bonded for eternity - - - (or) - - - so they thought - - - for - - - upon awakening - - - they found the mists of dreams and maidens to have disappeared - - - as does the frost on a blade of grass - - - on a warm winter morn.

Then - - - one frosty night - - - when - - - the summer was but a memory - - - warmed only by the presence of The Lone Wolf - - - Jaguar Claw awakened to find a Girl Child by his side - - - an infant - - - for - - - the Maiden of the Mists - - - being ethereal of form - - - and - - - not of the race of men - - - could not nurture a child of flesh and blood - - - even if it be her own - - - so - - - she chose to bestow her gift - - - her Love Gift - - - upon the sleeping Man King - - - for him to love as his own - - - for the child was - - - indeed - - - a child of the flesh - - - and - - - of the spirit - - -

So - - - out of love - - - and - - - longing for his own kind - - - Jaguar Claw took unto himself - - - this Girl Child - - - (knowing not that she was of his blood line) - - - nurturing her - - - sheltering her - - - teaching her - - - loving her - - -

&& THE AWAKENING &&

As Soyala - - - stirred - - - half awake - - - the deep - - - sonorous voice - - - droned on in her dreams - - - "AND - - - thus - - - dearest Soyala - - - here ends the story of the place unto which you have come - - - and - - - of the place from which you must depart."

As Soyala - - - stirred - - - and - - - briefly awakened - - - she saw the glitter of the arm ring on Kinkajou's arm - - - grown tight - - - as - - - his arm fleshed out with muscle - - - white gold flashing on taut bronze skin.

Then - - - a - - - vision of the selfsame arm ring - - - hanging loosely around Jaguar Claw's wrist - - - but - - - then - - - once again - - - grown tight on another's wrist - - - who - - - although his face was hidden - - - had - - - a somewhat familiar demeanor.

The familiar voice continued: "Beware of the seven gifts - - - granddaughter - - - beware. For some - - - it is already too late. Beware."

Soyala's eyes opened wide - - - and - - - smiling before her - - - was the gentle face of the Ancient Warrior - - - her grandfather!!!

The gentle face of her grandfather - - - and - - - the gentle humming sound of a great vermillion hummingbird sitting on his shoulder - - -

&& BREAKING THE FAST &&

Soyala softly groaned - - - still slightly sore from the months of traveling from one prison fortress to another - - - from the turquoise prison of palaces and rose briar bars to the even more stringent prison of royal personages and politically correct politics - - -

As Soyala tightly pulled the sleeping shroud up snuggly beneath her chin - - - she - - - in a most self-evident and contradictory movement - - - rolled onto her back - - - in a subconscious and determined - - - but - - - failing - - - effort to leap to her feet - - -

As she lay there - - - comfortably snuggled beneath pillows - - - and - - - quilts - - - and - - - sweet memories - - - Soyala felt a gentle tickle at her nose - - - as if Gho'a were playfully preening her to wakefulness - - -

Wakefulness - - -

      Long forgotten wakefulness - - -

            Sweet sleep - - -

            Seductive Sleep - - -

            Somnolent Sleep - - -

Gho'a - - -

      Faithful Companion - - -

            Sorely missed - - -

            Forever true - - -

            Faithfully waiting - - -

Gho'a - - - Mischievous Nose Nibbler - - - loyally shepherding her young charge to the lands of red-blue marimo balls and reflecting pools - - -

Gho'a - - - Pristine Preener - - - gently nudging The Child of the Dawn from the over-protective bosom of her goddess mother - - -

Gho'a - - - Guardian Spirit - - - Diviner of Mysteries - - - whose secrets once bestowed become as but faint ripples upon the glass smooth surface of the palace pool - - -

Gho'a - - -

But - - -

It was not Gentle Gho'a - - - nibbling - - - preening - - - enticing her mistress to abandon the embrace of Seductress Sleep - - - but - - - rather a Rambunctious Butterfly - - - Red - - - Rowdy Red - - - Xochiquetzal's favorite - - - perched on the very tip of Soyala's nose - - -

Raucous riotous reds - - - nervous quivering bundle of inquisitive antennae - - - and - - - fluttering wings - - - intently studying with each and every cell of its insect brain - - - Soyala's each and every wakening moment - - -

Fluttering wings - - - fluttering eyelids - - - fleeting streams of wakefulness - - -

Eyes crossed - - - focused on the tip of her nose - - - Soyala slept - - -

The Imperial Brain - - - frustrated that its High Command to waken was being ignored - - - furious that it was being lulled - - - once again - - - back to sleep by the hypnotic rhythm of a butterfly's wings - - - issued a Royal Decree to sneeze - - - and - - - sneeze Soyala did - - - scattering butterfly and dreams to the far corners of the room - - -

As The Great Ruddy Butterfly - - - his game already forgotten - - - drunkenly weaved his way across the room toward a tantalizing assortment of fruity hors d'oeuvres and sugary entrees - - - Soyala stretched once more and with a great sleepy effort - - tossed aside the Sleeping Shroud with which Kajika had covered her - - -

As Soyala's senses slowly began to awaken - - - each - - - stumbling clumsily one after the other - - her sense of sight struggled to follow her now wide awake sense of smell - - - towards the scrumptious aroma of a delicious breakfast which Kajika had ordered prepared especially for her.

As Soyala espied Kajika - - - with - - - his Minstrel brother standing at his side - - - her heart leapt with the joy of recognition: "Dear brothers - - - have I slept long? Is it morning?"

Kajika laughingly replied: "Dear sister - - - yes it is almost dawn - - - but not the dawn you expect - - - for you have slept from the rising of one sun - - - to the rising of the next - - - and - - - then - - - one more for equally good measure!!!"

As Soyala's mouth dropped open - - - in a totally uncharacteristic pose - - - Kajika continued: "Yes dear sister - - - I can most truthfully answer that it is morning!"

Xochiquetzal - - - who had been standing off to one side - - quietly playing with her retinue of butterflies - - serendipitously smiled at this unexpected but most pleasant awakening: "Ah - - - brother Xochipolli" - - - she said - - - touching him lightly on his arm - - - "we see that our sister Teoxihuitlxochitl has awakened from her slumber and has chosen to join with us in breaking our fast."

"This is good - - - no - - - EXCELLENT - - - for - - - she must first break her fast with us and then prepare herself - - - for today she is to meet my Sun Brother - - - Tonateootl."

"Good morning My Turquoise Flower" continued Xochiquetzal turning toward Soyala - - - "it is good to see that you have awakened. I trust that you have had a most pleasant and refreshing sleep?"

Soyala nodded agreeably - - - even as a slight shudder raced through her mind at the memory of that which somehow seemed more real than a dream - - -

"Come – Soyala - Come" - - - greeted Kajika - - - as he walked toward his sister and extended his arm - - " Come - - join with us - - for we have before us a breakfast as delightful in its own way - - - as was our last together - - - when you and I feasted on the roasted meats of mountain Pheasant. While admittedly not of roasted meats - - - for Xochiquetzal abides no meat in her presence - - - what you see before you is of a magnificence as of which you have never before partaken - - - for in honor of our two peoples - - - Xochiquetzal has extended the privilege to us of dining on the cheeses of goats and sheep and the eggs of small birds - - - in addition to our daily fare of fruits and toasted grains."

"She is much privileged" - - - continued Xochiquetzal - - - "for not all who visit with us have the opportunity to "dine" at our table."

"Come – Soyala - - - hurry! Xochiquetzal was just beginning to tell us of the great festivities - - - already underway I might add - - - and - - - and the celebration of the history of her people."

"I sure hope that there is beer" - - - quipped the Minstrel - - - "for I do indeed miss my morning beer!"

As Kajika flashed a stern disapproving look at the Minstrel - - - Xochiquetzal continued: "Yes - - - yes - - - come - - - sit with us - - - and - - - I'll continue with my story."

As Soyala took her seat - - - Kajika carefully poured a large drink - - - of a heavy thick curded milk - - - slightly sweetened with the sweet juices of ripened berries - - - for his sister - - -

Xochiquetzal began her story:

&&& The Legend of The First Sun &&&

It was the beginning of time - - -

There was nothing - - - not even the measure of nothing - - - for time - - - and - - - thus the measures of time had not yet come into being - - -

Then - - -

Something - - - an - - - anomaly - - - or - - - circumstance - - -

Ometeuctli

Ometeuctli - - Lord of Duality - - - Dual Being - - - both male and female - - - was alone - - -

In his/her aloneness - - - and - - - longing for companionship - - - s/he unfolded from him/herself - - - four companions - - - Earth - - - Wind - - - Fire - - - and - - - Water - - - all in perfect balance and harmony - - -

These four were our first Gods - - - Three Male - - - One Female - - -

It was at this exact moment of their creations - - - that - - - time began - - - for - - - time is change - - - and - - - Ometeuctli is unchanging - - -

Now - - -

Let our story begin - - -

At the beginning of time - - - our First Gods: Earth - - - Wind - - - Fire - - - and - - - Water had only themselves for amusement and company - - -

But - - - being Gods - - - they longed for worshipers - - - for - - - what is a god without worshipers?

Longing for Worshipers - - - and - - - bored after eons of perfect balance and harmony - - - each God began vying with the other - - -

Playful - - - at first - - - then - - - in jest - - - and - - - finally in dead earnest - - - THEY - - - discovered buried deep within themselves - - - something - - - a spark - - - a flickering spark of an emotion - - - hidden - - - buried - - - silent - - - during the first few eons of their existence - - -

!!!???WHAT IS A GOD WITHOUT POWER???!!!

It was then - - - that Tezcatlipoca - - - "The Smoking Mirror" - - - more bored than the rest - - - more reckless than the rest - - - more daring than the rest - - - decided to act - - -

Longing for Worshipers - - - and - - - thirsting for power - - - Tezcatlipoca - - - God of Earth - - - devised a plan - - -

In the greatest secrecy - - - he - - - slipped away - - - far from the companionship of others - - - and - - - incarnated himself as the First Sun - - -

As the light of the First Sun dawned - - - Tezcatlipoca - - - created of himself - - - The First Humans - - -

Forming the First Humans from the sweat of his brow and dust - - - dust of the earthy steppes - - - Tezcatlipoca rejoiced - - - for - - - what was a Sun God without worshipers?

However - - - in his great haste - - - and - - - in his even greater fear of being discovered - - - Tezcatlipoca made a monstrous mistake - - -

He - - - had - - - incarnated himself as only half of a sun - - -

By - - -

Incarnating himself as only half of a sun - - - he - - - indifferently doomed the first humans to a miserable and eternal existence of perpetual cold and half-darkness - - -

Cold - - -

Hungry - - -

Half Blind - - -

Barely eking out a miserable existence on a meager diet of bitter acorns and woody roots - - -

Acorns - - - and - - - Roots - - - and - - - nothing else - - - for - - - there was not even a god to smile down upon them - - -

Because - - -

Tezcatlipoca was busy - - - very - - - very busy - - -

Frantically busy - - -

For - - -

Tezcatlipoca was afraid - - - mortally afraid - - - afraid of the vengeance to be wrecked upon him by his two brothers - - - The Gods of Wind and Fire - - - and - - - his sister - - - The Goddess of Waters - - -

So - - - in the depth of fear - - - and - - - in the depth of night - - - he summoned forth his powers and created from himself - - - Wizards - - - Mighty Powerful Bearded Wizards - - - Invisible Wizards - - - Wizards with Four Hands and Feet - - - Wizards with no feet at all - - - riding on air - - - but - - - Wizards All - - - each more powerful than the other - - -

Wizards - - -

> An Army of Wizards - - -

> A Legion of Wizards - - -

> A Swarm of Wizards - - -

But - - -

All is not always as it seems - - - for - - - The Gods were most assuredly doomed - - - were it not for a chance meeting with a dew drop - - -

Chalchiutlicue - - - Goddess of the Waters - - - had - - - some-while-ago - - -

(I must say "some while ago" – for – since we did not yet have a sun – we did not have days or nights – and – could therefore not measure time as we know it)

So - - - and - - - as I was saying: Chalchiutlicue - - - Goddess of the Waters - - - had - - - some-while-ago - - - before the incarnation of the First Sun - - - kissed her brother - - -

A Kiss - - -

A Simple Kiss - - -

A Sister's act of affection - - -

A simple kiss - - - which - - - might have passed unnoticed - - - perhaps - - - even - - - unremembered - - - were it not for a single solitary drop of dew - - - born on the leeward side of some great earthly mountain - - - forlorn - - - forsaken - - - forgotten - - -

As the diminutive dew drop lay shivering in the cold - - - for the First Sun had not yet been born - - - it watched and listened - - - much as would a fragile flake of early morning frost - - - clinging to a blade of icicle grass - - - awaiting the first rays of the early morning dawn - - - watch and listen - - -

By-and-By - - -

The shivers of the cold yielded to the tremors of fright - - - as the Flames of Fervor began to burn hot in Tezcatlipoca's spirit - - -

Trembling - - - the diminutive drop of dew - - - listened to the Rantings and Ravings of The Great Sorcerer God - - - as - - - he plied his magic and might - - - crying forth terrible incantations and spells by which to raise wrathful wizards from the spent earth and clay - - -

So mighty were Tezcatlipoca's exertions - - - that - - - minute beads of sweat began to dot his brow - - -

Minute - - -

Miniature - - -

Diminutive - - -

So - - -

By-and-By - - -

The Lost Child of the Waters was able to slip away unnoticed - - - one - - - among the many - - - along the winding and twisting paths of brook and stream - - -

Until - - -

Safe in warm in the safety of her mother's bosom - - - she was able to betray Tezcatlipoca's dark secret - - -

This is how it came to be that the Gods were forewarned - - -

This is why we have this memory - - -

The fury of the Gods was great - - -

      Thunder and Lighting tore across the skies - - -

      Terrible Gales uprooted trees and mountains - - -

      Floods ground granite mountain tops into sand and tore the very Roots of the Mountain from the protesting earth - - -

The War Banners had been raised!!!

The War Trumpets had been sounded!!!

Now - - - now (whisper) - - - the race was on - - -

      Oath upon oath - - -

      Spell upon spell - - -

Incantation upon incantation - - -

The Gods - - - now fully aware of Tezcatlipoca's guile and guilt - - - swore vengeance - - - and - - - DEATH!!!

They - - - devised a plan - - -

A Plan - - -

A Bold Plan - - -

A Desperate Plan - - -

A plan by which they stripped themselves of memories - - - and - - - powers - - - and - - - rage - - - forming in their place - - -

!!!VENGEANCE!!!

Creating a Race of Giants!!!

Giants - - - Remorseless Assassins of the Night - - -

An Army of Giants by which to not only defeat Tezcatlipoca - - - but - - - to destroy him for all eternity - - -

The Battle raged - - - eon upon eon - - - tipping and tilting this way and that - - -

Until - - -

The victorious giants tore apart the last wizard - - - and - - - devoured him - - - wizard flesh - - - bone - - - and - - - entrails - - -

For - - -

By devouring the Creations of the Earth God - - - the giants would be consuming the body of the Earth God Himself - - - thereby assuming his powers - - -

It was then - - - at this - - - the last possible moment - - - as - - - Tezcatlipoca's powers ebbed to but a flicker - - - even as - - - the last bloody remnants of the last wizard were being slowly sucked into the cavernous mauls of the Giants - - -

That - - -

Quetzalcoatl - - - "The Plumed Serpent" - - - struck - - -

Striking Tezcatlipoca with his staff - - - with a power that would have sundered a mountain - - - Quetzalcoatl - - - stuck Tezcatlipoca from the heavens - - -

The First Sun gone - - -

All reverted to darkness - - -

In the darkness - - -

Tezcatlipoca - - -

     Desperate to rebuild his form and his powers - - -

     Desperately fought with his last remaining strength - - -

     Desperately fighting to change himself into a Jaguar - - -

Changing himself into a Jaguar - - -

Tezcatlipoca - - - killed and devoured the last of the giants - - -

Devouring the last of the giants - - - Tezcatlipoca became mightier than before - - -

     Having devoured all of that which had been himself - - -

     Having consumed parts of that which had been his brother & sister god/desses - - -

Thus ended The First Age - - - The Age of the Four Jaguars - - -

&&& The Legend of The Second Sun &&&

With a void - - - now - - - in the darkness - - - Quetzalcoatl - - - God of Wind - - - flush with triumph and victory - - - renewed with the strength of the gods - - - incarnated himself as the Second Sun.

This was the age of Air - - - and - - - Spirits - - - and - - - Transparent Beings.

"A Second Sun?" asked Shorty.

Yes

Let us pause to consider - - -

What is the God of the Mountain - - - if not the Mountain?

And - - -

What is the Goddess of the Waters - - - if not the river - - - lake - - - and - - - stream?

Likewise - - -

What is the God of the Sun - - - if not the Sun?

Quetzalcoatl WAS the sun incarnate - - - not a half-sun like his brother - - - but - - - the Full Sun in Full Glory - - -

As Sun God - - - Quetzalcoatl brought forth the Second Coming of Humans - - -

Fashioning the second race of humans from the brown and red muds of the earth - - - he imbued them with the golden color and warmth of the sun - - -

Although - - -

Much better off than the first humans - - - being able to warm themselves in the warmth of the full sun - - - thy still knew not the art of cultivation - - - their only recourse being what they could find in the wilderness - - - sustaining themselves on pine nuts and acorns - - -

So it remained for eons - - -

Until - - -

Tezcatlipoca - - -

Humbled - - - humiliated - - - haunted - - -

His smoldering shame unstaunched by the eons - - -

His rage growing unchecked - - -

Until - - -

He struck - - -

Although his strength was greater than any one of the three god/dess - - - by virtue of his - - - as - - - Jaguar - - - having eaten the last of the giants - - - (which in turn had eaten the last of the wizards) - - - his strength could not rival the combined strength of his three siblings - - -

However - - -

Although he could not defeat three gods combined - - - he could defeat one single god - - - and - - - defeat one god he would - - -

     His resolve strengthened - - -

     His resolve growing - - -

     His resolve unbounded - - -

Tezcatlipoca - - - that very night - - - swore an oath - - -

Swearing an oath of vengeance against him - - -

Against "The Plumed Serpent" who had defeated and had humiliated him so many eons ago - - -

So - - -

Tezcatlipoca - - -

     Cat-Like - - -

     Jaguar-Like - - -

          Stalking his prey - - -

Stealthily stretching skyward - - -

Stretching sinew and claw - - -

Slashing - - - Scratching - - - Tearing - - -

Tezcatlipoca - - -

His terrible Jaguar's Claw - - - dripping - - - drenched - - - with God-Blood - - - tore Quetzalcoatl from the sky - - - to come crashing down upon the earth - - -

As - - -

Quetzalcoatl - - -

Screaming - - -

Screeching - - -

Shrieking - - -

Crashed into the earth - - - unseen - - - invisible - - - (for he had reverted to his true form as the God of the Winds) - - -

Great Hurricanes uprooted trees and mountains - - -

Monstrous Gales smashed mountain into mountain - - -

Cataclysmic winds whirled ALL humans into nothingness - - -

All - - -

All - - - except for those few - - - those very few - - - who were able to change themselves into monkeys - - - and - - - save themselves by clinging desperately onto the few trees which remained - - -

Thus ended The Second Age - - - The Age of the Four Winds - - -

&&& The Legend of The Third Sun &&&

Eternally frustrated at the antics of his/her children - - - and - - - craving harmony and balance within the creation and between the four forces - - - Ometeuctli - - - God/dess of Duality - - - father and mother - - - of the four god/desses - - - decreed that the Two Quarreling Gods of Earth and Winds should be banished from the heavens - - -

However - - -

The Quarrelsome Two Resisted - - -

   Earth and Wind - - -

   Fire and Water - - -

The Creation split - - - battling against itself - - -

Until - - -

Ometeuctli - - -

Forced - - - to unite him/herself - - - with - - - his/her two remaining loyal children - - - The God of Fire and The Goddess of Water - - - fought an exceedingly difficult - - - and - - - complex battle - - -

For - - -

Ometeuctli was battling - - - not only against two of his/her children - - -

But - - -

Also - - - against him/herself - - -

For - - -

   Who was Ometeuctli - - - if not The Creation???

   What was The Creation - - - if not Ometeuctli???

228

Once More - - -

       Thunder and Lighting - - -

       Hurricane and Gale - - -

       Floods and Tsunami - - -

       Fire and Ash - - -

Eon upon eon the battle raged - - -

       Without pause - - - the battle raged - - -

       Without quarter - - - the battle raged - - -

Until - - -

!!!VICTORY!!!

The Creation seeking to undo The Creation - - -

       Defeated - - -

       Vanquished - - -

       Banished from the sky - - -

As - - -

       The Gods of Earth and Wind were banished from the sky - - -

       Tlaloc - - - God of Fire - - - stepped into the void and became the third sun - - -

The Third Sun - - -

       In full Magnificence and Glory - - -

Breathing Life and Spirit into splinters of many colored woods - - -

Creating the Third Race of Humans - - -

Once again - - -

Eon upon eon - - -

Peace reigned - - -

This creation - - - although - - - much better for the humans - - - for they no longer had to forage for acorns or mesquite beans - - -

They - - -

Still unlearned and unskilled in the art of cultivating plants - - -

Lived on the bitter seeds of acicintli - - - the tasteless and bitter seed of weeds - - - stolen from the abandoned furrows of some god's garden - - -

(Today we know these seeds as Acecentli – and - to be the seeds of weeds that fill a maize field when it is left uncultivated.)

But - - -

Peace and harmony were doomed - - -

For - - -

Quetzalcoatl - - - jealous - - - and - - - angered - - - at his rejection that Ometeuctli had not come to his aid in his battle against his brother - - - Tezcatlipoca - - - lashed out once more at The Creation - - -

Once again - - - The Creation had to defend Itself - - - against - - - Itself - - -

Quetzalcoatl - - -

Vengeful - - -

Hateful - - -

Wrathful - - -

Rained Fire down upon the earth - - - turning Tlaloc's own powers - - - as God of Fire - - - against him - - -

Rain of Fire - - - to dry up the rivers - - - and - - - to shrivel the seas - - -

Flood of Fire - - - to char and blister all that was once green - - -

Inferno - - -

Torrents of Fire from the skies - - -

Fountains of Fire from the earth - - -

Thus - - -

The Third Race of Humans came to a fiery end - - - except for those few humans who where were able to change themselves into birds and flee the cataclysm of ash and soot - - - flying to the sanctuary of the clear cool air of the mountains - - -

Thus ended the Third Age - - - The Age of the Four Rains - - -

&&& THE LEGEND OF THE FOURTH SUN &&&

Once again - - -

There was a void in the darkness - - -

Chalchiutlicue - - - "She of the Jade-Green Skirt" - - - Goddess of the Waters - - - stepped into this void - - - and - - - incarnated herself - - - as - - - The Fourth Sun - - -

Striving to surpass her brothers in their failed creations - - -

Chalchiuhtlicue fashioned the Fourth Race of Humans from a dough made of the ground seed of the Teocentli - - - (Mother of our Red and Blue Maize) - - - and - - - her goddess-blood - - -

Here - - - for the first time in their creation - - - humans were able to eat of the Teocentli - - -

   Their bellies full - - -

   Their spirits warm - - -

So it remained peacefully for eons - - - until - - - Tezcatlipoca - - - angered that HE was not the sun and jealous that the humans were worshiping his sister and not him - - - unleashed the waters - - -

Sheets of Water - - -

   Pouring down from the Heavens - - -

   Gushing forth from subterranean springs - - -

As - - -

A great deluge destroyed the earth - - -

   Flooding the Land - - -

   Washing all trace of humans from the memory of the world - - -

Some few humans were able to save themselves - - - by changing themselves into fish - - -

But - - -

Still the rains came - - - so great was Tezcatlipoca's wrath - - -

   So great a wrath - - -

   So powerful a hate - - -

   So great was the flood - - -

That - - -

The waters flooded the land - - - drowning the mountains - - - reaching high into the heavens - - - so that even the sky disappeared - - -

Thus ended the Fourth Age - - - The Age of the Four Waters - - -

&&& The Legend of The Fifth Sun &&&

For the fourth time - - - all was darkness - - -

Now - - -

Even though there were now 1,600 god/desses - - - plus - - - Earth - - - Wind - - - Fire and Water - - - no one dared to become the sun - - - so great was their fear - - -

There was not even an earth - - - for - - - it had been flooded until the sky disappeared - - -

And - - -

So it remained until two gods lifted it from the water laden sky - - -

However - - -

Even though the land was now dry - - - all was in perpetual darkness - - - for there was still no sun - - -

Then - - -

Two gods - - - volunteered - - - in incarnate their beings - - -

      One to light the day - - - the other to light the night - - -

      One as the sun - - - the - - - other as the moon - - -

Two gods - - - offered - - - to sacrifice themselves - - -

      Tecuhciztecatl - - - rich - - - powerful - - - handsome - - - great in pride and greed - - - offered to sacrifice himself - - - in order to gain immortality and worshipers - - -

233

Nanahuatl - - - poor and misshaped - - - great in humility and love - - - offered to sacrifice himself - - - for sacred honor and duty - - -

Two gods - - - gave - - - sacrificed their wealth - - -

Tecuhciztecatl - - - rich and handsome - - - sacrificed - - - jewels - - - jades - - - and - - - corals - - -

Nanahuatl - - - poor and humble - - - sacrificed - - - moss and maguey thorns wet with this own blood - - -

Two gods - - -

Tecuhciztecatl - - - offering all that he possessed - - -

Nanahuatl - - - offering all that he owned - - -

Finally - - -

In agreement of the god/desses - - - both gods fasted for four days - - - making sacrifices - - - one of possession - - - the other of self - - -

On the fifth day - - - as a symbol of the Fifth Creation - - - the god/desses kindled a raging fire in a great brazier - - - so that both Tecuhciztecatl and Nanahuatl could purify themselves before illuminating the world - - -

The god/desses chose Tecuhciztecatl to be the next sun - - -

Three times did he run towards the pit containing the raging flames - - - and - - - three times did his courage fail - - -

Nanahuatl seeing this - - - closed his eyes and jumped straight into the heart of the flames - - -

Even as a vast flame shot up into the heavens - - - Tecuhciztecatl - - - being shamed - - - jumped into the dying flames where he was slowly and painfully consumed - - -

Nanahuatl became The Fifth Sun - - -

Tecuhciztecatl - - - following Nanahuatl - - - became a second sun - - - rivaling Nanahuatl in brilliance and radiance - - -

However - - -

The other gods - - - being angered at Tecuhciztecatl's audacity - - threw a rabbit at his face - - - which - - - covered his face - - - blocking the light - - -

Even today - - - we can see the form of a rabbit in the dark spots of the moon - - -

But - - -

Even though there was now a sun in the sky - - - there were still no humans - - -

In order to create a Fifth Race of Humans - - - Quetzalcoatl offered to retrieve the sacred bones of the deceased Fourth Race of Humans from The Land of Death - - - Mictlan - - -

For - - -

It is well known that bones are like seeds - - - everything that dies goes into the earth - - - and - - - from the earth new life is born - - - in the sacred - - - never-ending cycle of death and rebirth - - -

Therefore - - -

Seed the bones into the earth - - - and - - - they shall grow and renew - - -

Accompanied by his Nahual - - - his guardian spirit - - - his twin likeness in every way - - - Quetzalcoatl went deep into the earth - - - passing through secret doors - - - walking winding labyrinths of passages - - - until he reached Mictlan - - -

Approaching the Lord and Lady of Mictlan - - -

Quetzalcoatl asked for the bones of the human dead: "I've come for the bones - - - the precious bones of the humans - - - the jade - - - and - - - coral bones - - - so that I can repopulate the earth with humans."

The Lord of Mictlan - - - sitting on his fiery red obsidian throne - - - surrounded by night creatures - - - spiders - - - and - - - owls - - - and - - - worms - - - glowered at this interloper into his domain - - -

"YOU - - - You may have these bones. Unbury the dead if you must!!! Return the dead to the land of the living. If - - - if - - - and - - - only if - - - you walk around my throne four times - - - four times without faltering - - - to signify the four creations - - - blowing on this conch shell - - - a pleasing melody of my liking. If you falter - - - or - - - fail - - - you will find yourself here - - - as my guest - - - MY guest - - - to share your quarters and my amusement with your precious wo/man bones. How I would loath to lose my pristine white glistening porcelain toys."

Quetzalcoatl - - - suspicious - - - untrusting of the dark lord's true intent - - - none-the-less - - - with the noble unfaltering spirit of a god - - - took hold of the conch shell - - - and - - - placed it to his lips - - -

As he was about to sound the first note - - - and - - - went to place his fingers on the finger-holes of this trumpet - - - he noticed that it had no finger-holes - - - rendering it impossible to sound a note - - -

However - - -

A god was not to be so easily deceived - - - nor - - - defeated - - -

Summing forth his powers - - - Quetzalcoatl commanded worms of the dark places to bore finger holes into the conch shell - - - and - - - for bees to fly into the shell so that it hummed with a beautiful melody - - -

Even so - - - Quetzalcoatl knew that the Dark Lord and Lady would not so easily part with their glistening white porcelain playthings - - -

Calling upon his Nahual - - - his spirit twin - - - Quetzalcoatl commanded his Nahual to impersonate him - - - and - - - in the most hesitantly - - - and - - - stumbling - - - and - - - delaying manner - - - to tell the Dark Lord and Lady that he - - - Quetzalcoatl - - - God of the Winds - - - would leave the bones behind - - -

As the Nahual began speaking to the Dark Lord - - - Quetzalcoatl - - - secretly gathered up the bones and began running - - -

Not deceived long by the Nahual's impersonation - - - The Lord of Mictlan commanded that a pit dug in the fleeing god's path - - - so - - - that - - - he might once again take possession of the bones - - -

Sure enough - - - the way being dark and unknown - - - and - - - Quetzalcoatl running in great haste - - - fell into the deep pit - - - although unhurt - - - scattered bone upon bone - - -

Bone upon bone - - -

That which was not broken - - - was pecked to pieces by a covey of quail - - -

(This is why humans come in different sizes and shapes.)

Quetzalcoatl then turned to his Nahual saying: "This has not turned out well."

His Nahual replied: "What must be – must be. We must make do with what we have."

With that - - - both Quetzalcoatl and his Nahual hastened as fast as they could back out of the realm of the Lord of Mictlan.

Once Quetzalcoatl reached the surface of the earth - - - he took the bones - - - and - - - mixed them with corn dough and his own blood - - - restoring them to life.

Hence was humankind born from the penance of the gods themselves.

But still - - - even though the earth was once again repopulated with humans - - - the sun refused to move - - - parching and burning all of the ground beneath - - -

It was then - - - that the gods realized that they needed to sacrifice themselves so that the humans would survive and flourish - - -

Only by the death of the gods could the humans live - - -

So - - -

Quetzalcoatl - - - took up an obsidian knife - - - and - - - began sacrificing the willing god/desses one-by-one - - - even - - - as others of the god/desses began sacrificing themselves - - -

Then - - -

Once all one thousand six hundred sacrifices had been made - - - Quetzalcoatl - - - with his powerful wind breath - - - blew the sun into motion - - - so that it might move through the sky - - - nourishing the earth - - - rather than scorching it - - -

From that time - - - the gods have lived as spirits - - - in the spirit world - - - and - - - can only see our world through a mirror made of obsidian - - - yet - - - their powers still exist here - - - on earth.

This was the Fifth Age - - - The Age of Movement - - - and - - - The Age in which we find ourselves - - -

&& THE VERMILLION TATTOO &&

"The Fifth Age? We now find ourselves in the Fifth Age?

If we are now in The Fifth Age - - - will this too end - - - and - - - how - - - when?" – Soyala found herself asking Xochiquetzal.

 As - - -

Xochiquetzal was about to answer - - - but - - - before she could being to speak - - - the mischievous dawn began to break - - - silently - - - noiselessly - - - serendipitously - - - unnoticed - - -

"Soyala - - - Yes - - - we are in the fifth age - - - Xochiquetzal - - - began to answer - - - her voice - - - strangely - - - strained - - - and - - - hoarse - - -

Perhaps - - - from the telling of the tale for the last hour or so - - -

"Yes - - - Soyala - - - We are in the Fifth Age - - -"

But - - -

At that very moment - - - when all the guests were most at ease with the telling of the tale and a most scrumptious breakfast - - - a burning red vermillion flame shot across the room - - -

Burning brightly - - - as if - - - a flare of the sun had torn itself loose and hurtled itself to earth - - - hurtled itself to earth in the form and likeness of a humming bird - - -

238

Bright Red Vermillion Humming Bird - - - burning - - - blazing its way through Xochiquetzal's thin veil - - - blistering its tattoo deeply into her pale cheek - - -

Bright Red Vermillion Tattoo - - - burned deeply for all to see - - -

With a shriek and a cry - - - Xochiquetzal tore herself away from the table - - - and - - - fled to the safety of her Sleeping Chambers - - - leaving - - - her stunned and speechless guests behind - - -

& The Pleasure Barge &

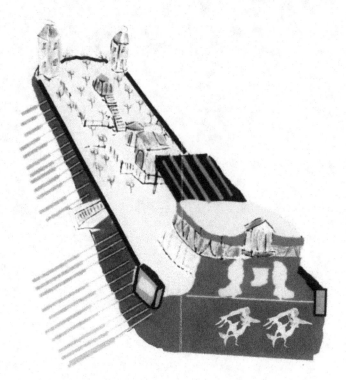

More of a floating palace than a pleasure barge

She measured more than two hundred feet long

Two Hundred Feet Long - - - Sixty Feet Wide

Marble and Palms and Fountains

Knifing through the placid lake waters

Two Hundred Sixteen Oars - - - One Hundred Eight to a Side

Golden Palace

Golden Oarsmen - - - Freemen All

Three Hundred Twenty Four - - - Three Golden Gods to the Oar

Pleasure Palace

Bacchanalian Blackamoors - - - Freemen All

Two Hundred Sixteen - - - Two Beauteous Blackamoors to the Oar

Pleasure Palace
Knifing through the Placid Glacial Waters

It was here - - - that Soyala anxiously waited for Kajika - - - for he had promised to meet her soon after the hunt - - - but - - - although - - - the last of the huntsmen had returned this very morning - - - on this the third - - - and - - - last day of the hunt - - - Kajika had not returned with them.

It was approaching mid-day - - - and - - - still - - - Kajika was nowhere to be seen - - - neither was Shorty - - - for that matter - - - which was doubly strange - - - for - - - not only would Shorty never abandon Soyala in a strange land amongst strange folk - - - but - - - also strange in that he was beyond himself with the excitement of examining every nook and cranny of this strange and wondrous vessel - - -

"Yes - - - yes - - - I can feel it. Something is wrong - - - something is terribly wrong. Something is most definitely wrong - - - I can feel it" - - - thought Soyala - - - as she anxiously scanned the busy port for any sign of Kajika - - -

On any other such occasion - - - Soyala might have flattered herself - - - nay - - - even envied herself - - - for - - - being here. Here she was - - - a lone female - - - among a ship full of men - - -

Men - - -

Bronzed and Blackened from the sun - - -

Festive - - - Pleasant - - - Admiring - - - Adoring - - -

But - - -

Without Kajika at her side - - - she felt ill at ease - - -

Ill at ease - - - uneasy - - -

Uneasy - - - not due to any lack of familiar companionship - - - but - - - rather - - - uneasy due to a lack of irrevocable and undeniable proof that all was well - - -

All was well - - - All was festive - - - All was –

Still - - - a lingering doubt - - - a growing suspicion - - -

Although all seemed relaxed and festive - - - Soyala could not put her worries to rest - - - try as she might - - - even sensing an undercurrent of tension - - - even apprehension from those around her - - - or - - - was it her mind playing tricks???

"Enjoy - - - Enjoyment" - - - she forced herself to relax - - - "Enjoy yourself!" - she practically commanded - - - but - - - to no avail.

"Paradise" - - - Here I am - - - a woman - - - a lone woman - - - adrift amidst a sea of men. This is paradise. This MUST be paradise - - - is it not?"

"For - - - if this is NOT Paradise - - - what could it possibly be?

And - - -

If not paradise - - - how could paradise possibly exceed this golden moment?"

Soyala shook her head - - - in part due to being bemused by her rambling thoughts - - - but - - - more so - - - to tear the troublesome worries free from her mind - - - and - - - so that she might scatter them to the four winds - - - never to return - - - never - - - to return - - -

"Never to return - - - but - - - he must!"

"Men - - - so near - - - but - - - yet - - - so distant" - - -

"Distant - - - where is - - - Kajika???" - - -

&& Eve of Departure &&

"Ahhh - - - There you are my sweet - - - my - - - Delicious!" - - - an oily voice burst through Soyala's sense of foreboding - - - as a short toad of a man - - - warty - - - with a stubble of a beard and spindly legs made his way toward her - - - - "I've been looking for you to make sure that you are comfortable - -- and that all of your needs are attended to" - - - he said as his eyes ravished her body - - - head to toe - - - and - - - back again - - - "for - - - all must be made ready so that we can set forth - - - perhaps - - - in an hour or so - - -"

"Setting forth? In an hour or two?? But - - -" Soyala stammered - - -

"Yes - - - yes - - - my dear - - - my delicious - - - I know - - - your brother - - - but - - - do not fear - - - he'll be with us shortly - - - for others have already sent word to us that although he was slightly delayed - - - he'll arrive shortly - - - safe and sound - - - and - - - hungry - - - no - - - famished - - - I suspect! Best you make yourself ready for him - - - for - - - soon it will be time to dine - - -"

As Soyala forced a weak smile The Toad Man continued – ever hopeful: "Yes - - - yes - - - he's fine - - - and - - - now that you know that he is fine - - - I'm sure that you're fine too - - - should you like - - - I'd be happy to dine with you!" - - - He said as he slowly licked his lips in anticipation - - -

"Yes - - - yes - - - soon it will be time to dine!" - drooled The Toad Man - - - scarcely attempting to hide his double meaning - - -

Seeing naught but the shadow of a smile still lingering on Soyala's lips - - - the Toad Man redoubled his efforts - - - seeking to impress her - - - for - - - today might be his lucky day - - - a - - - maiden so fair - - - so - - - beautiful - - - so - - - Doubly Delicious!

"Soon you'll have the honor of meeting our Emperor - - - Emperor of All Creation - - -

!!! TONA-TEOOTL !!!

Cried - - - The Toad Man - - - arms widespread - - - laughing joyously - - - turning full circle upon full circle - - - "Tona-Teootl - - - our Emperor God!!!"

"Tona-teootl?

Here?

Here tonight??"

But - - -

"No - - - no - - - not - - - tonight - - -

"Not tonight - - - my sweet - - - not tonight - - -

"Tomorrow - - - yes - - - Tomorrow - - - early tomorrow - - -

"Yes - - - yes - - - that's right - - - my delicious - - - tomorrow - - -

"Tomorrow - - - our most beloved Emperor - - -

"Our Most Beloved Emperor - - - The Exalted Tona-teootl - - - will honor us with his presence
- - -

For - - -

King Sun has grown lax in his duties - - - his indolence becoming intolerable - - -

Rising from his slumber later - - - ever - - - later each day - - - until - - - until - - - he has become
insufferable - - -

So - - -

So - - - our - - - Emperor - - - bids us make ready so that he may thrash the insolent sun into
obeying HIS IMPERIAL COMMAND to rise earlier - - - ever earlier - - - for an Indolent Sun
can not be tolerated!!!"

Turning slightly aside - - - The Toad Man smiled - - - and continued to mutter to himself: "And
- - - I do so love to watch a good thrashing!!!"

As The Toad Man's voice trailed off into sputtering - - - sensuous - - - memories of thrashings
past - - - Soyala - - - somewhat aghast - - - stammered: "Thrash the Sun? He means to thrash
the sun?!!!"

Not appearing to have heard the question – The Toad Man continued: "Yes - - - yes - - - my dear - - - you're lucky to be here - - - for - - - Tona-teootl does not abide women in his presence - - - and - - - you are the first he has allowed to be shown in his presence - - -

"Yes - - - yes - - - no female may show herself in his presence - - - not even his own sister - - - for she would then suffer the fate of their mother!"

"Their mother?" asked Soyala - - - somewhere between being curious and apprehensive of hearing the answer: "What happened to their mother?"

"Ah - - - a story - - - a story - - -" croaked The Toad Man - - - "A Story."

"My Delicious wants to hear a story."

"Tona-teootl - - - our most gracious and powerful Emperor - - - abides no female in his presence - - - NO female - - - not even his own sister - - - not even his own mother - - -

"For - - -

The Toad Man continued - - - his eyes widening at the prospect of finally convincing Soyala that he was a force to be reckoned with - - - wise - - - astute - - - learned in the ways of the court - - - in favor - - - with his Lord Emperor - - - and - - - protecting of her - - -

Protecting of her - - - yes - - - protecting of her - - -

Protecting her from the unknown - - - the - - - undesirable - - - so - - - that - - - she might seek the safety of HIS bed chambers this very night!

As his voice dropped to a croaking whisper - - - he - - - continued: "It is rumored that Tona-teootl - - - upon reaching the age of fifteen - - - killed her who had given him birth - - - not quickly or in the dark as might an assassin - - - you understand - - - but - - - first by tearing out her eyes - - - blinding her - - - so that she would not know which way to flee - - - and - - - then - - - by - - - methodically biting off pieces of flesh from her living body - - - until - - - she - - - she who had given him birth - - - drowned in a fountain of her own life's blood - - -

"Yes - - - yes - - - My Delicious - - - a rich red fountain of her own glorious blood!"

A mother's gift to her son - - - for - - - by bathing in her blood he has become immortal - - -

Immortal and invulnerable - - - God-Like!!!

God-Like - - - yes - - - and - - - tomorrow - - - he will become a GOD!!!"

As Soyala blanched and turned away at the thought - - - The Toad Man continued: "Yes - - - yes - - - my delicious - - - as you yourself have already seen - - - with your own eyes - - - it is this knowledge that forces his sister to live as a shadow - - - ever - - - forever - - - hidden in the shadows - - - never to see the light of day - - -

For - - -

Should she step into the daylight - - - she knows and understands that she too would suffer the same fate as that of their mother" - - -

Seeing a black cloud of anxiety sweep across Soyala's face - - - The Toad Man hastened to continue: "But - - - rest assured my dear - - - that - - - he has no such designs for you - - - for - - - you are his guest - - - and - - - Tona-teootl NEVER violates the sanctity of a guest in his presence - - -

But - - -

But - - - then again - - - perhaps" - - - he said with a sideways glance of his toad-like head - - - "this might mean that he intends for you to remain OUR eternal guest!"

"I would like that My Delicious - - - I - - - would like that very much!"

"I would especially like your liking to be our guest - - - yes - - - I would like that!"

"But - - - enough of talking of the future - - - for - - - tomorrow will soon be upon us - - -

"Tomorrow - - - is not only - - - Our Feast of the Winter Equinox - - - which is in and of itself is a royal splendor beyond words - - - but - - - also - - - Our Celebration of the Celestial Crossing - - -

"Yes - - - The Celestial Crossing - - - you have head of it - - - no?" - - - he said with a sideways movement of his massive head - - -

"Yes - - - tomorrow we will cross the celestial plane - - - not - - - as did the heathen kings of old - - - believing that by stirring vast vats of human tallow - - - they could 'row' their way across the tallow as their temple rowed its way across the celestial divide" - - - he said with a chuckle - - -

"But - - - rather through guile - - - for while we are feasting - - - the gods will be feasting with us - - - and - - - drinking - - - yes - - - drinking strong wines - - -

While they are enjoying their wines - - - we - - - we will slip across the great equator unnoticed - - - yes - - - unnoticed - - - invisible - - -

Invisible - - - unnoticed - - - we will slip across unnoticed - - - and - - - Tona-teootl will begin his reign as Supreme Creator for another 25,000 years!!!"

"Yes - - - yes" - - - he said with a genuine smile and a toad-like dance - - - first hopping on one foot - - - then - - - the other: "Tomorrow will be GREAT fun!!!

"Now - - - let's attend to you - - - My Delicious - - -

As he clapped his hands - - - two young servant boys magically appeared at his side - - - anxious to serve - - - beaming at Soyala - - - trying to divine her every wish - - - beside themselves with excitement - - -

Whispering to one another - - - excitedly - - - fervently: "It's a woman - - - a woman - - - a real woman - - - I've heard of them - - - but - - - until now I've never seen a woman before - - -

"Now - - - you two - - - take this Noblewoman down below so that she might ready herself for tonight's feasting - - - for - - - tomorrow will be a full day - - -

As each youngster gently but resolutely took Soyala by the hand - - - leading her to her sleeping chambers - - - The Toad Man continued muttering to himself - - - cocking his head - - - this way and that: "Yes - - - tomorrow - - - tomorrow - - -

"Tomorrow will be a full day - - - My Delicious - - - a Full Day - - -

"King Sun will be thrashed - - - and - - - the days will once again become longer - - - Full glorious days ahead of us - - - yes - - - us - - - us - - - the two of us - - - my delicious - - -

As he turned to go his way - - - The Great Barge was cast loose from its moorings - - -

Five Hundred Forty Oarsmen pulling against the oars

Two Hundred Sixteen Oars slicing through the sea

As Soyala - - - was gently led away from the railing by the two youngsters - - - firmly leading her by the hand - - - their path took them through a small grove of fig trees - - - twelve to a side - - - two tiers of six - - -

Two tiers of six - - - lining a simple - - - but - - - elegant temple - - - built of a stunning blood red marble - - -

Red Marble - - - to better to highlight the dark emerald greens of the fig trees - - -

Blood Marble - - - to better stand stark naked against the Sapphire Blue Sky - - -

Pausing - - - and - - - being taken in by the moment - - - Blood Red Temple - - - highlighted against the kaleidoscopic magenta and turquoise evening sky - - - Soyala's mind's eye was blinded to a rowboat - - - furiously giving chase - - -

Furiously giving chase - - -

As furious a chase as if the rowers' very lives depended upon their reaching the massive barge before she was out of reach - - -

For - - -

Indeed - - -

Their very lives were forfeit were they not to reach the barge with their cargo - - -

Their cargo - - - a rough coarse burlap sack lumped in the bottom of their boat - - -

Furious chase - - - blistered hands - - - and - - - bursting hearts - - -

Where was Kajika?

As Soyala reached the bottom of three flights of stairs - - - ten stairs per flight - - - thirty stairs in all - - - her small charges - - - led her into an enclosed bathing area - - - where the steams and herbal scents from the heated baths magically eased the tension from Soyala's mind and body - - -

As Soyala stood at the foot of a great carved fountain - - -

Rainbowed hues of colors - - - gushed fourth from a Marbled Conch Shell - - - showering all in a majestic Rainbowed Splendor - - -

Marbled Conch Shell - - - clenched in the mighty fist of a Merman King - - -

Merman King - - - resplendent with crown and trident - - - towering twenty feet above the lone woman and the two small boys - - -

Waters - - - cascading - - - mesmerizing - - - hypnotizing - - -

Waters - - - flowing - - - soothing - - - caressing - - -

Waters - - - somehow primeval - - - somehow nurturing - - -

Nurturing - - - nurturing of spirit - - - and - - - mind - - - and - - - body - - -

Beauty - - -

> Unparallel Beauty - - -

> Unfettered Beauty - - -

> Unadulterated Beauty - - -

>> Palace gardens and sweet fountains - - -

>> Marble Statues and tall mountains

>> Ancient Alters and Shrines

>> Sparkling gems and red wines - - -

>> Palm trees and tart figs - - -

>> Golden haired wigs - - -

All for the taking

None for the making

All for the pleasure

Every man's treasure

As Soyala softly descended the stairway leading to her private chamber - - - Goya - - - faithful Goya - - - nestled down for the night - - - standing guard over Soyala's favorite reflecting pool - - - patiently waiting for her mistresses return - - -

&& Twilight Gloaming &&

Long awakened from her slumber by the rattling and clanking of the stowing of oars - - - and - - - the frantic bustle of activity - - - above - - - below - - - and - - - to each side of her - - - Soyala stood on the deck of the great barge - - - facing the sunrise - - - long lustrous hair streaming behind her - - - as the Children of the Winds joyously played with her free flowing tresses - -

It was dawn - - - or - - - to be more precise - - - twilight - - -

Twilight - - - or - - - even more precisely - - - Morning Twilight - - -

Morning Twilight - - - or - - - to be most precise - - - Morning's Twilight Glow - - -

Morning's Twilight Glow - - - that most magical moment - - - softly nestled between dawn and sunrise - - -

Morning's Twilight Glow - - - when passionate pastels chase - - - dusky dreams across the sleepy sky - - -

Morning's Twilight Glow - - - perhaps - - - but - - - still no sign of Tona-teootl - - -

For - - -

As far as the eye could see - - - there was neither ship - - - nor - - - sail - - - nor - - - sign - - - of the mighty emperor - - - nothing - - - save the breeze and the waves - - - and - - - the hint of sunrise - - -

"Humph" – thought Soyala in distain – "The Great Emperor threatens to thrash the sun - - - but - - - he can't even find his own boat!!!"

As the sun - - - lazily broke over the horizon - - - Soyala once again turned her gaze toward the prow of the Royal Barge - - - her view of the waters blocked by the towering canopy in front of her - - -

Towering canopy - - -

Gilded woods and golden threads - - - wood and fabric - - -

Rising a full twenty feet above the main deck - - - and - - - burrowing down another full twenty feet below - - -

Sheltering and shielding the royal personage - - - from - - - the sweltering sun - - - the weltering waters - - - and - - - the - - - starlit sky - - -

A Golden Canopy was she - - - befitting of a Sun King - - - covering a full one third of the barge - - - with her gilded wood and rich gold awning glistening in the sun - - -

Fully one third of the barge did she cover - - - as - - - did the raised temple area and gardens of olive and fig trees to the stern - - -

As Soyala's Mind's Eye - - - again - - - cast her gaze straight ahead - - - piercing straight through the gilded woods - - - and - - - polished marbles - - - and - - - royal fabrics of gold and silver thread - - - she could almost see the prow of this Great Pleasure Barge - - -

Proud Prow - - -

Pleasure Prow - - -

Playfully cleaving the waters in two - - -

Golden Gods - - -

Blue-Green Mermaids - - -

Gently cleaving the waters in two - - -

- - - OR - - -

- - - MIGHT IT BE - - -

- - - SOMETHING DARKER - - -

Drunken Gods - - -

Golden - - - Naked - - -

Mounting Mermaids - - -

Wild Mermaids - - -

Bare-Breasted - - - Bridled and Bucking - - -

Passionately bursting the waters asunder - - -

This vessel - - -

This barge - - -

This floating palace - - -

Was unlike any Soyala had ever seen - - - plying the waters of her Great Glacial Lake - - -

Unlike her cousins - - - the swifter - - - knife shaped three tiered Triremes - - - she was a two tiered Bireme - - -

Joined by mortise - - - and - - - tenon - - - and - - - the fanaticism of a God-King - - -

Blocky - - - heavy - - - slow moving - - - she was sheathed in paper-thin sheets of lead - - - hammered fast with thousands of copper nails - - - and - - - lifetimes of patience - - -

Floating Pleasure Palace - - - resplendent with a Royal Throne Room - - -

Royal Throne Room - - - forty feet tall - - - twenty feet above deck - - - twenty feet below - - - ancient - - - gilded - - - gaudy - - - housing magic - - - and - - - long forgotten secrets - - - ghostly incantations and spells still reverberating fervently throughout its gilded walls - - -

She was indeed a wonder - - - this Floating Pleasure Palace - - -

A wonder indeed - - -

> Marble temples - - - lush gardens of fig and olive trees - - -

> Gushing Fountains and Heated Baths - - - to cool off blistering bodies - - -

> Royal Throne Room - - - forty feet in height - - - housing the spirits and spells - - -

"Yes - - - This was indeed a wonder" - - - mused Soyala - - -

As - - - Soyala straightened up - - - tall and proud - - - her lips coyly curled into a smile of remembrance - - -

If - - -

If - - - Soyala's mind's eye could see Shorty standing before her - - - her mind's ear could hear his all too short and irascible observation:

As Soyala - - - lowered her voice - - - and - - - mimicked his frantic undisciplined gesturing - - - she repeated his very words:

> "Yes - - - she is a wonder - - - a wonder all right!

> ! Mountains of Stone and Rock !

! Oceans of Gold and Silver !

! Heated Pools and Fountains !

! It is a wonder that she can still float !

!! It is a double wonder that she is not sitting on the bottom of this bottomless lake !!

AND

"!!! Us with Her !!!"

As the sun continued to rise - - - now - - - just touching the canopy of the great throne area - - - Soyala began to hear mummers in the crowd: "He is here! The Sun King!! He is here – walking among us!!!"

As Soyala strained her eyes against the glare of His Majesty the Sun - - - she could see a shadow of a man - - - a - - - mighty man - - - a - - - GOD - - - a - - - GOLDEN GOD - - - descending from the sun itself - - - as if - - - a piece of the sun had torn itself away to give birth to a Man-God - - - but - - - how???

&& FLOGGING OF THE DAWN &&

A thin shrill shriek - - - emulated from a - - - tall - - - backlit - - - gaunt form of a man - - - arms straight down at his sides - - - standing - - - defiantly standing - - - face-to-face with the early morning sun - - -

Standing defiantly - - - arms straight down at his side - - - the silhouette slowly raise its arms - - - first to the sides - - - then - - - overhead - - - golden plaited whip in its right hand - - -

Suddenly - - - unexpectedly - - - a voice cried out:

!!! USURPER !!!

!!! PRETENDER !!!

!!! IMPOSTER !!!

Insolent Dawn - - -

Indolent King - - -

Usurper of Creation!!!

I'll flog you within an inch of your life!!!

Wake!

Awaken!!!

WAKE UP!!!

!!! I COMMAND THAT YOU AWAKEN !!!

With these words - - - the emaciated silhouette began thrashing the air - - - the deck - - - the railings - - - violently - - - savagely - - - thrashing the fleeting shadows - - - until - - - none remained - - -

Hour upon hour - - - Tona-teootl - - - flogged the fleeting shadows - - - until - - - none remained - - -

His whip - - - now - - - flayed and shredded - - - lay in tatters - - - alongside his rage - - - its golden plaits seemingly melting as one with the liquid golden sun shine - - -

Tona-teootl - - - exhausted from his wild frenzy- - - head - - - hanging low - - - arms dangling limply at his sides - - - turned - - - paused - - - then - - - raised his arms in a signal of victory - - -

Slowly - - - ever so slowly - - - he raised his head - - -

"I - - - Tona-teootl - - - have beaten the usurper - - -

"I - - - Tona-teootl - - - have humbled the knave sun.

256

"See? Now - - - he dares not cast a shadow in my presence - - -

"I - - - I am weary from my long battle -- - and - - - must rest - - -

With these words - - - Tona-teootl - - - climbed down the golden gilt stairs - - - leading to the marbled deck below him - - - and - - - disappeared - - - The Toad Man - - - hopping dutifully along behind him - - -

As the gathering disappeared - - - some back to the oars - - - others to their heated baths and pools - - - and - - - still few others - - - to hidden nooks and crannies - - - Soyala alone remained - - - trying to make sense of what she had just seen - - - but - - - there was no sense - - - there was no logic - - - or - - - sanity - - -

With these thoughts - - - and - - - now - - - deathly afraid of what might have happened to Kajika - - - Soyala - - - stealthily stole up the stairs - - - leading up to the top of the canopy - - - to see what she might discover from this Grand Theater of the Sun that had just been presented to her - - -

What she saw - - - puzzled her - - - a large basket of sorts - - - buried beneath a crumpled up piece of canvas - - - both - - - dyed and painted golden yellow - - -

Golden yellow - - - golden yellow - - - as if - - - they were fallen pieces of the sun - - -

Curious - - - Curious - - -

Most decidedly curious - - -

How?

Why??

What???

Secrets upon secret - - - but - - - right now - - - events of a much more urgent nature required tending to - - -

The banquet - - -

Tonight was the banquet - - - and - - - she must attend - - - for - - - not to do so - - - would violate her honor - - - and - - - might even cost her – her life.

"Keep your friends close - - - and - - - your enemies even closer" - - - she told herself - - -

"There is many a mystery here" - - - she heard herself whispering - - - "The least of which was Kajika's whereabouts - - -

Where was Kajika? She must save Kajika - - - but - - - first - - - she must save herself!!!

&&& The Arm Ring &&&

Affairs of State must go on - - - smoothly - - - elegantly - - - happily - - - regardless of one's personal turmoil - - - or - - - doubts - - - or - - - grief - - -

Even though:

Kajika still had not returned.

Shorty was still nowhere to be seen.

AND

Soyala was locked up with a madman!!!

A Madman - - - yes - - - mad - - - quite mad - - -

For - - - but for a scant hour ago - - - Soyala might have given him a shadow of a doubt and simply labeled him "eccentric" - - - but - - - no - - - he was mad - - - quite - - - quite - - - mad - - -

It was then - - - in this moment of realization that - - - Kajika's last words came rushing back to her - - - words whispered on that very morning when Xochiquetzal had abruptly rushed from the breakfast table to her room:

"She is as kind as he is ruthless - - -

"It is rumored that he is serviced only by Golden Eunuchs - - - for fear of the temptress who might bear unto him The Usurper to his throne.

"He does not even allow his sister near - - - for fear of incestuous lust - - -

"Either through fear of a son - - - or - - - fear of womanhood itself - - - he shuns all women - - - shunning them so fiercely that even the ground upon which he walks must be swept clean of all footprints for fear that he tread in the footsteps of some ancient and withered grandmother - - -

"It is this fear - - - this overriding numbing fear - - - that has compelled him to walk down the barren path of celibacy - - - compelling even his most trusted warriors to follow in his footsteps - - -

"Dear - - - Dearest Soyala - - - I do not know whether it is the fear of a son which drives him to shun all women - - - or - - - the fear of blessed womanhood itself - - -

"But" - - - he paused as the words choked in his throat - - - as he lowered his voice to a whisper:

"But - - - I do know that I fear for your safety - - - for - - - you are in the greatest of perils" - - -

The Greatest of Perils - - - thought Soyala to herself - - - Yes - - - The Greatest of Perils - - -

A quick nervous know at her door - - - startled Soyala back to reality - - - even as she heard the nervous fumbling at the handle - - - and - - - the short rasping breath on the other side of the door - - -

Bursting in - - - only to fall and stumble - - - then - - - to - quickly raise himself from the floor was The Toad Man - - - bandaged head and all - - -

Turning quickly - - - he sprang at the door - - - with a quickness and nimbleness which belied his great bulk - - -

Glancing nervously outside - - - he quickly closed - - - and - - - latched the door - - - leaning heavily against it - - - before speaking:

"Ah - - - There you are my Delicious! There you are. I see that all is well with you - - - yes - - - yes" - - - he said - - - gingerly touching the head bandage that ran across his left eye - - - "Yes - - - all is well with you."

As Soyala stared - - - The Toad Man answered her unasked question: "Yes - - - my Dearest Soyala - - - all is well with me too - - - for - - - His Emperor - - - Tona-teootl - - - was most kind - - -

259

most kind indeed - - - for - - - he only took my one eye for having offended him - - - and not both eyes - - - as he did his brother - - -

"Most kind - - - our emperor is most kind and generous - - -

"Generous? Kind?!" asked Soyala. "Tona-teootl has treated you most kindly??? He has taken your eye - - - and - - - you believe that he has treated you most kindly?"

"Yes - - - yes - - - most kindly. But - - - you must speak softly for fear that others might be listening and mistaken your love for OUR Beloved Emperor as dislike. Yes - - - yes - - - he has treated me most kindly - - - for - - - as he descended the stairs this morning - - - I was temporarily blinded by the sun - - - yes - - - the sun - - - The Sun - - - Our Emperor Incarnate - - - so I turned my head - - - not thinking - - - I turned my head. Just a little - - - I - - - turned my head - - - without thinking - - - away from our Emperor - - - as - - - if I did not wish to look upon his radiance. This was most unwise for me to turn my head away from my emperor - - - so - - - he was most just and wise in taking my eye - - - so that I wound never again turn my head from his radiance and so that I might forever look upon his magnificence - - - without - - - ever again - - - turning my head. Yes - - - Tona-teootl - - - is most wise and just."

"Wise and just" - - - as The Toad Man's voice trailed off into a whisper.

"But - - - but - - - now for you!" - he said - - - forcing a weak smile. We need to be sure that YOU are ready for this evening's festivities - - - for - - - Tona-teootl is anxious to meet with you. Yes - - - anxious - - - very - - - very - - - anxious.

Dropping his voice to not much more than a whisper – The Toad Man said: "Here - - - here - - - take this - - -

With these words - - - The Toad Man held out a small cast figure of a Jaguar - - - again whispering in the most desperate of tones: "Here - - - take this - - - it will protect you - - - as - - - it has protected many others - - - take it - - -

Soyala - - - at a most profound loss for words - - - reached out her hand - - - taking the small object - - - "But - - - but - - -

"Take it - - - it was made by a Mighty Sorceress - - - long - - - long - - - ago - - - born of precious metals and incantations" - - - as he deepened his whisper: "It is from the Cult of Hoatzin - - - Priestess of he - - - he - - - who - - - died and ascended to the clouds."

"Yes - - - a - - - Totem - - - Sign of the Jaguar - - - Totem of He who died and ascended - - - bane of the Followers of Tona-teootl." - - - dropping his voice even lower - - - "Take it - - - it will protect you - - - I did not have it with me earlier - - - if only I had - - - if only - - - perhaps - - - but - - - I must go now - - - I must go - - - go - - - before I am missed" - - -

"His mask" - - - asked Soyala - - - "His mask - - - Does he always wear his mask?"

"Yes - - - answered the Toad Man - - - Yes - - - Tona-teootl always wears his mask. He was burned - - - horribly burned - - - disfigured - - - burned beyond recognition - - - on the day - - - of his ascension to God-Hood - - - on the day - - - on the day - - - as his voice faded - - - he faltered - - - then - - - turned toward the door - - - "I've said too much already."

With these mysterious words - - - The Toad Man hopped toward the door - - opening it slowly and silently - - - peaking out with his one big round blinking eye - - - to make sure that all was safe for him to leave.

As he half-turned to say one last parting word - - - Soyala - - - gently but firmly pushed him out of the room - - - through the doorway - - - and - - - quickly closed and latched the door behind him - - - breathing - - - what could be best described as one great sigh of relief.

Holding her head in her hands - - - Soyala - - - shook her head - - - as if to once again focus her thoughts - - - and - - - to give herself time to absorb what she had just seen and heard.

Mad - - - Tona-teootl was definitely mad!!!

Mad - - - and - - - definitely mad - - - but worse yet - - - here was Soyala - - - locked up with a madman - - -

Locked up with a madman - - - on a floating prison - - - in the midst of an endless sea - - - confused - - - alone - - - isolated - - -

Alone and confused - - - Soyala - - - was - - - for the first time in her life - - - unsure - - -

Unsure - - -

       Unsure of herself - - -

       Unsure of the whereabouts of Kajika - - -

Unsure as to what she should do next - - -

But - - -

One thing she was sure of:

"Affairs of State must always go on - - - smoothly - - - elegantly - - - happily."

Regardless of one's personal turmoil - - - or - - - doubts - - - or - - - grief - - -

Affairs of State must proceed joyously - - - and - - - with - - - Pomp and Ceremony!"

As Soyala turned to look into the mirror - - - she could heard her Foster Father's words echoing in her mind - - - "Affairs of State - - - Affairs of State" - - - my sweet Soyala - - - "are of the utmost importance!"

"Affairs of State" - - - she whispered to herself - - - shaking her head - - - "Affairs of State."

As Soyala doggedly determined to proceeded with The Affairs of State - - - despite her most desperate State of Affairs - - - she found herself staring - - - once again - - - blankly into a mirror - - - her face - - - her thoughts - - - her hands - - - frozen in time - - -

Frozen in time - - - face - - - thoughts - - - hands - - -

Blank - - - frozen - - - emotionless - - - face staring blankly back at her - - -

Emotionless Face - - - frozen hands - - - frozen in mid-motion - - - frozen fingers - - - clumsily fumbling - - - dropping - - - her Grandmother's Pearl Pendulant to the marbled floor - - -

Pearl Pendulant - - - precious - - - precious pearl pendulant - - - clattering against the marbled floor - - - awakening Soyala from her trance - - -

"Grandmother - - - I'm sorry - - - I'm so very - - - very - - - sorry" - - - Soyala heard herself say - - - as - - - she stooped to pick up the precious heirloom from the floor: "I'm so very sorry - - - that I dropped - - - that I dropped - - - your most wondrous gift - - - your most precious gift - - - (pausing) - - - I'm so sorry - - -

I'm so sorry that I ever came here - - - Kajika - - - I'm so very sorry that I ever let you come here - - - Kajika - - -"

As Soyala rose - - - pendulant in hand - - - she - - - subconsciously - - - expected to see her mirrored reflection rise with her - - - but - - - her reflection had remained motionless - - - stark - - - standing - - - motionless - - - from the instant that the pendulant had slipped from Soyala's fingers - - -

Stark - - - Standing - - - Motionless - - - body rigid - - - hands on hips - - - stern - - - scolding scowl - - - on her face - - -

Scolding scowl - - - etched into an older face - - - a - - - face - - - perhaps - - - in the seventh decade of life - - - stern - - - disapproving - - - frozen in time - - -

Hands on hips - - - rigid - - - frozen - - - standing stark proud - - - forceful in purpose - - -

"Grandmother - - - Grandmother - - - is that you? Is that - - - really - - - you - - - or - - - is this naught but a dream?

Naught but a dream - - -

As Soyala dropped her head - - - despondent - - - hopeless - - - and - - - began to turn away - - - it almost appeared as if the rigid reflection in the mirror had become saddened - - -

Saddened - - - pained - - - stretching out her hands to Soyala as if to entice her back to the mirror - - - eyes misting over with pain and frustration - - -

Again - - -

Soyala paused - - - then - - - turned back toward the mirror - - - expecting to see nothing - - - nothing - - - but - - - her own reflection - - - the - - - dream - - - vanished - - - the - - - hope - - - faded - - - expecting to see - - - nothing - - - nothing - - - save - - - her own reflection - - -

But - - -

As Soyala continued to turn - - - turn - - - back to the mirror - - - anxious - - - fearful - - - alone - - - uncertain - - - she - - - fell into the embrace of an older version of herself - - - older - - - yes - - - much - - - much - - - older - - - but - - - still - - - somehow - - - more - - - beautiful - - - somehow - - - regal - - - in - - - demeanor - - - in - - - temperament - - -

Face-to-Face - - - with a reflection - - -

Face-to-Face - - - with an older version of herself - - - older - - - yes - - - yes - - - much - - - much - - - older - - - but - - - still - - - somehow - - - much - - - more - - - beautiful - - - definitely - - - most - - - regal in demeanor - - -

As Soyala stared - - - still not quite sure whether she was seeing - - - or - - - dreaming - - - or - - - wishing - - - wishing - - - wishing most desperately to the point of hallucinating - - - wishing - - - (perhaps) - - - that she were going mad - - -

Mad - - - mad - - - escape - - -

Escape - - -

Escape - - - Delusions - - - Fantasies - - -

Hallucinations - - - perhaps this was the escape she longed for - - - no more need to wish - - - to wish - - - only to dream - - -

Wishing - - - wishing - - - still wishing - - -

Wishing most desperately for her grandmother - - -

Not caring whether it was reality - - - or - - - fantasy - - - - or - - - insanity - - - for it was not to her grandmother's reflection to which she was speaking - - - but - - - to - - - her Grandmother herself!

Speaking - - - her voice - - - cracking - - - quivering - - - shaking - - - with - - - emotion and exhaustion - - - Soyala poured out her heart: ""Grandmother - - - I wish that you were here - - - here - - - with me - - - now - - - here - - - with me - - - right now - - - you'd tell me what to do - - - where to go - - - what to do" - - -

Then - - - pausing - - - and - - - in a voice a bit less desperate - - - less emotional - - - but - - - still in a voice fully resigned to her fate - - - full of melancholy:

"Grandmother - - - if - - - if - - - only I had know you when you were yet young - - - what adventures might we have shared!"

Pausing - - - wiping a tear from her eye - - - as - - - her grandmother's reflection remained stoic - - - listening - - - hoping - - -

"Grandmother - - - If only I could have known you - - - when - - - you were still young - - - if we could have both been young together - - - then - - - what secrets might we have shared - - - what adventures might we have had - - -

"Grandmother - - -

As - - - Soyala spoke these words - - - she stretched her arms out to the mirror - - - searching for - - - an embrace - - - only - - - only - - - to fall limply - - - helplessly - - - to her sides - - -

An - - - embrace - - - craving - - - an - - - embrace - - - if - - - only for a moment - - - if - - - only for the briefest of moments - - -

"Grandmother - - -

The figure remained standing - - - motionless - - - expressionless - - -

As Soyala - - - once again began to fasten her Grandmother's Pendulant around her neck - - - as - - - thoughts of Duties and Affairs of State once more took hold - - - the - - - mirror's reflection began to move - - - to - - - change - - - to - - - transform - - -

Transform - - - transforming itself into a younger version of itself - - - into - - - a - - - mirror image of Soyala - - -

Face - - - softening - - -

Hair - - - darkening - - - thickening - - -

Body - - growing - - - muscle upon bone - - - muscle upon muscle - - -

Demeanor - - - becoming - - - even more majestic and magnificent - - -

Movements flowing and blending into soft graceful curves and delicate balance - - -

Lithe in movement and grace - - -

Fluid of thought and action - - -

Regal - - -

Regal - - - Queenly - - -

Queenly - - - God-Like - - - in having demiurgically created from thought this separate reality behind the mirror - - - reality - - - reflections of reality - - -

But - - -

Which was which?

Queenly - - beautiful - - - graceful - - - clad in a bronze chainmail tunic - - - emblazoned with a Troodon Head - - - The Sign of the Pleiades - - - The Sign of the Seven Sisters - - -

Bronze chainmail tunic - - - bronze chainmail hauberk - - - burning as brightly as the late afternoon sun streaming into Soyala's Chamber - - - bronze - - - BRONZE - - - Golden Bronze - - -

Golden Bronze Maiden - - -

It was she - - -

THE SHIELD MAIDEN

As Soyala stood - - - mouth agape - - - motionless - - - wordless - - - thoughtless - - - staring - - - attempting to comprehend - - - seeing - - - but - - - not - - - understanding what stood before her - - -

Before her - - -

Standing before her - - - was - - - The Bronze Maiden - - - a - - - mirror image of Soyala herself - - - holding a massive white gold arm ring - - -

&&& BEHIND THE MIRROR &&&

The Giver of Rings - - - gestured - - - nodded with her head and smiled - - -

"Here - - - Soyala - - - take this - - - my gift to you - - - it is yours. It has been a long time since I have given a gift such as this - - - to - - - one - - - as worthy as you."

With these words - - - Two Hands - - - steady - - - patient - - - enduring - - - reached out - - - proffering the gift of gold - - -

With these words - - - Two Hands - - - steady - - - eager - - - accepting - - - reached out - - - graciously accepting that which was offered - - -

An Ancient Rite-of-Passage - - -

Two Hands - - - golden bronze from the sun - - - reached out to the mirror - - -

Two Hands - - - bronze gold - - - reached out to the mirror - - - and - - - beyond - - - grasping - - - possessing - - - as their birthright - - - that which was proffered - - -

For - - -

Indeed - - -

The Giver of Rings - - - had - - - bestowed upon Soyala - - - her - - - sacred birthright - - - a - - - massive - - - white golden arm ring - - - glistening - - - radiant - - - gleaming - - -

Gleaming - - -

Satin sheen - - - glistening in the late afternoon rays of the sun - - - late afternoon rays - - - streaming - - - dancing - - - into Soyala's sleeping chamber - - -

Hands - - - golden bronze - - - touching - - - grasping - - - lifting the massive ring - - - to - - - admire - - - to - - - study - - - to - - - wonder - - - to - - - slide up onto her upper arm - - -

The Ring - - -

Massive in its crafting - - - of - - - Troodon art it was - - -

Troodon Ring it was - - - tear drop jeweled eyes - - - piercing - - - blood red - - - set in the crafted white gold of its massive feathered head - - -

Jeweled Eyes - - - seeing all - - - knowing all - - - betraying nothing - - -

Jeweled Eyes - - - ruby red teardrops - - - burning - - - fiery - - - foreign - - -

Hypnotic in their power - - - mesmerizing - - - paralyzing - - -

As Soyala slowly broke away from the hypnotic gaze of the glistening eyes - - - she - - - raised her head - - - and - - - found herself - - - standing - - - standing - - -

Standing - - - face-to-face - - - with an older version of herself - - -

Standing - - - face-to-face - - - with her reflection - - - Soyala - - - smiled - - - smiling - - - ever so slightly - - - bemused - - - amused - - - playful - - -

For - - -

This was a dream - - - a - - - dream - - - a - - - reflection - - -

A - - - Dream - - -

Face-to-Face - - - with an older version of herself - - - older - - - yes - - - but not so much older as before - - - yes - - - older - - - but - - - still - - - somehow - - - more beautiful - - - somehow - - - most regal in demeanor - - -

Queenly - - - God-Like - - -

Not a Goddess - - - in having demiurgically created from thought this reality behind the mirror - - - but - - - a - - - dream - - -

But - - -

It was not so - - -

For - - -

The Shield Maiden took Soyala - - - gently - - - but - - - firmly by her two shoulders - - - as if to assure her that this was indeed reality - - - gazed upon her - - - and - - - kissed her lovingly on each cheek - - -

"Soyala - - - my - - - daughter - - - it is good to be able to be FINALLY be able to speak with you."

Soyala's mind was a blur - - - awhirl - - - awake - - -

Remembering - - - remembering - - -

Remembering twice before - - - twice before - - - had they met - - -

Twice before - - - had - - - Soyala - - - unknowingly - - - met - - - The Shield Maiden - - -

Twice before - - - once - - - in the Grotto - - -

Once before - - - in the Grotto - - - Soyala had gazed into a mirror - - - and - - - seen her own reflection staring back at her - - - her reflection - - - bloodied - - - besmeared with blood - - - staring back at her - - - calmly - - - serenely - - - staring back at her - - -

Once before - - - in a secret room - - - had Soyala gazed into a mirror - - - and seen her reflection staring back at her - - - her reflection - - - dressed - - - costumed - - - most grandly - - - smiling at her - - - nurturing her - - - loving her - - - teaching her the secret ways of pearl pendulants and ermine robes - - -

Once before - - - in the Grotto - - - had they met - - -

Once before - - - in her Grandmother's Secret Room - - - had they met - - -

Met - - - but - - - never spoken - - -

Met - - - but - - - as fleeting mirror images of one another - - -

Mirror Images - - -

As Soyala raised her hand - - - she - - - caressed the face of The Shield Maiden - - -

Caressed out of love - - - caressed out of wonder - - - for - - - Soyala marveled that the dream was so real - - - so - - - real as to cause all that had come before to be but a reflection of this reality - - -

So real as to - - -

As Soyala half turned - - - she could see - - - as if she were looking through a clear pane of crystal window glass - - - her chamber - - - just as she remembered - - -

Her chamber - - -

269

There! There was her Sleeping Bench - - - and - - - There!! - - - There was her small table and sitting stool - - - and - - - There!!! Over there was her wardrobe - - - austere - - - sturdy - - - faithful traveling companion of many adventures - - -

Many adventures - - - but - - - none such as this one!!!

Smiling - - - it were as if The Shield Maiden could read Soyala's thoughts - - - as she said: "Adventures? You crave adventures? Come - - - my daughter - - - let us see what lies on the path before us!!!"

"But - - - first - - - there is someone I'd like for you to meet!!!"

&&& THE ORANGE MIRROR &&&

Glass - - -

Glass - - -

Orange Glass - - -

Great massive chunk of obsidian glass - - -

Orange as a sunrise - - -

Fiery as a sunburst - - -

Mirrored as an ice pond - - - uncut by wind or skate - - -

Waiting - - -

Patiently waiting - - -

Eternally waiting - - -

Perpetually waiting - - -

Great Obsidian Glass - - - polished - - - flawless - - - ensnaring preening reflections - - - much as its lesser cousin - - - The Tiny Amber Droplet - - - ensnares the butterfly - - - by flattering her beauty and then inviting her to drink - - -

For - - -

      To drink endlessly of one's own beauty - - - is no less deadly a trap - - -

Lest - - -

      The Reality Behind the Mirror - - - take form to ensnare the unwary - - -

& Tableaux &

A Hand - - - A Man's Hand - - - broken - - - gnarled - - - scarred - - - reached out from the darkness - - - stretching - - - grasping - - - touching - - -

A Man's Hand - - - reached out from the darkness - - - touching - - - stretching - - - touching - - - fingertip to fingertip - - - a mirror - - - a mirror image of itself - - - fingertip to fingertip - - -

A Second Hand - - - A Woman's Hand - - - supple - - - strong - - - sensuous - - - reached out from the darkness - - - stretching - - - grasping - - - touching - - -

A Woman's Hand - - - reached out from the darkness - - - touching - - - stretching - - - touching - - - fingertip to fingertip - - - a mirror - - - a mirror image of itself - - - fingertip to fingertip - - -

Two Hands - - - One Body - - -

& Tona-teootl &

Tona-teootl - - -

       Emperor - - -

             Sun Incarnate - - -

                 Divine Celestial Light - - -

Tona-teootl - - -

       Tona-teootl - - -

       Tona-teootl - - -

Tona-teootl - - -

       God Emperor - - -

           Master of Creation - - -

               Lord of Madness - - -

&& Coming of Age &&

As - - - Soyala prepared to enter the throne room - - - The Bronze Maiden's words echoed in her mind:

An Adventure - - - Little Soyala - - - is - - - neither - - - good - - - nor - - - bad - - -

An Adventure - - - is - - - in-and-of-itself - - - simply - - - an - - - adventure - - -

An Adventure - - - is - - - how - - - YOU make it - - - it is - - - how - - - YOU feel it - - - it is - - - how - - - YOU live it!!!"

So - - - Live your Adventure - - - Little Soyala - - - Live your Adventure - - - for - - - like all adventures - - - it starts out with the first small innocent step - - -

Take that first step - - - Little Soyala - - - take that first step - - - and - - - see - - - where the path to adventure leads you - - -

Take that first step - - - Noble Soyala - - -

Seize this Moment - - - and - - - the moment will be yours!!!

It was - - - with these noble words - - - that - - Soyala - - - boldly crossed the threshold - - - crossing the threshold into the realm of untold and unforeseen adventures!

As Soyala paused - - - and - - - viewed the magnificence of the Throne Room - - - it were as if the Bronze Maiden were proudly watching - - - standing and speaking - - - beside her:

Well Done

Shield Maiden

&& The Obsidian Throne &&

Snowflakes - - -

      Snowflakes - - -

            Snowflakes streaming - - -

Streaming - - - falling - - - swirling - - - whirling - - -

Swirling - - - round and round - - - as if - - - held prisoner in some great and wild winter storm - - -

Whirling - - - round and round - - - as if - - - forced to flee in endless circles - - - chasing their own ancient footprints in the freshly fallen snow - - -

Swirling - - - whirling - - - twirling - - - twisting - - -

Snowflakes battered by the winter storm - - -

Attempting to escape the tempest - - - of - - - winds - - - and - - - wiles - - -

Endlessly - - - ebbing and flowing in silent suffering streams - - -

Snowflakes - - -

Silent Snowflakes - - - Trapped within Obsidian Glass - - -

White - - - and - - - Pink - - - and - - - Emerald - - - Snowflakes - - -

Imprisoned within Volcanic Glass - - -

Snowflakes - - - delicate as lace - - - but - - - as - - - jagged as the shattered shards of dreams - - -

Snowflakes - - -

      Tempest of wills and fleeting moments of sanity - - -

275

Swirling - - - whirling - - - snowflakes - - -

Laughing in madness - - - crying with joy - - - and - - - sadness - - -

Snowflake Obsidian Throne - - -

& & Snowflake Obsidian &&

As The Shield Maiden softly strode into the vast Throne Room - - - she saw - - - seated - - - before her - - - in all of his royal magnificence - - - Tona-teootl - - -

Tona-teootl - - - The Mighty God Emperor - - -

Tona-teootl - - - The Sun Incarnate - - -

Tona-teootl - - - The Mad - - -

As Soyala graciously surveyed the grandeur - - - and - - - the - - - splendor - - - of the heavily carved golden obsidian throne - - - Shorty's words flooded into Soyala's consciousness - - - with a special poignancy - - - just realized:

"Yes - - - she is a wonder - - - a wonder all right!

! Mountains of Stone and Rock !

! Oceans of Gold and Silver !

! Heated Pools and Fountains !

! It is a wonder that she can still float !

!! It is a double wonder that she is not sitting on the bottom of this bottomless lake !!

AND

"!!! Us with Her !!!"

"And - - - Us with Her" – quietly thought Soyala to herself.

I sure wish that Shorty were here to see this!" - mused Soyala. "In no time at all he'd have all of us fearing that we'd be sharing our mid-day snack with the fishes!!! I can just hear him now:

!! It is a double wonder that she is not sitting on the bottom of this bottomless lake !!

AND

"!!! Us with Her !!!"

"Us with her" Soyala said quietly - - - as the hint of a smile began to gently tug at the corners of her cheeks.

As Soyala slowly made her way past the lords of the land - - - lining the walls of the great room - - - two deep - - - ornate - - - not so unlike - - - so much decorative wall tapestry - - - Soyala smiled - - - in command of herself - - - and - - - confident of her position - - -

Smiling - - - Graciously smiling - - - Soyala - - - made her way past the lords of the land - - - lords but no ladies - - - for - - - Tona-teootl would abide no women in his presence - - - (no women save Soyala that is) - - -

As - - - Tona-teootl indifferently - - - carelessly - - - motioned to Soyala - - - for her to take the seat to his right - - -

To his right and somewhat lower - - - for - - - he was Creation Supreme and no one who wished to live should dare rise above him.

As Soyala took her seat - - - she noticed The Toad Man - - - all aquiver - - - each and every single wart of him - - - stumbling - - - and - - - fumbling - - - and - - - mumbling - - -

Spilling wine and words - - - with equal abandon - - - and - - - as carelessly and freely as could be imagined - - - without wont or reason - - - The Toad Man carefully poured a beaker of wine for his young charge - - -

As Soyala carefully accepted the beaker of a dark red wine from his trembling hands - - - fearing that more than a drop or two might be spilled - - - she turned - - - facing the assembly - - - taking in all of the spectacle forming before her - - -

As Soyala - - - turned her glance back - - - once again - - - toward Tona-teootl - - - she could not help but notice the magnificence of the natural stone from which the royal throne had been carved - - - marveling not only at the immense innate beauty of the stone - - - but - - - even-more-so - - - marveling at the skilled hands of the craftsman who had freed it from its gravel and lime matrix - - -

Free - - - so that it could breathe the air - - -

Free - - - so that it could chase moon beams through delicate labyrinths of starlight - - -

Free - - - so that it could explode in a bursting radiance of sunlight and solar flares - - -

For - - -

Once freed from its dusty - - - sooty - - - cloak - - - of - - - gravel and stone - - - the - - - Golden Obsidian did indeed glow as if alive - - -

Alive - - -

Living Stone - - -

Glowing - - - Flickering - - - Sparkling - - -

    Glowing with the sheen of one thousand ice crystals - - -

    Flickering with the fires of one thousand dancing fireflies - - -

    Sparkling with the brilliance of one thousand ruby and sapphire gemstones - - -

Glowing - - - alive - - - waiting - - -

&& Seated at the Right Hand of God &&

Gods exploded out of the darkness - - -

Exploding from the shadows - - - as - - - torches lit - - - betrayed dusty funeral shrouds hastily being drawn down by anxious hands - - -

Funeral shrouds - - - withdrawn - - - crumpled - - - discarded - - -

Funeral Shrouds yielding to gods incarnate - - -

Gods - - - incarnate - - -

Standing once again - - - proud - - - commanding - - - supreme - - -

Supreme Beings - - - towering far above the mere mortals of this all too much human assembly - - -

Gods - - - Creation Incarnate - - -

Creation Incarnate - - - Creator Gods - - - one and all - - -

Godlike beautiful - - -

       Godlike proud - - -

         Godlike magnificent - - -

For - - -

That which Soyala had taken to be mere pillars of painted wood - - - were gods incarnate - - - meticulously shaped to magnificent proportions - - -

Living God Giants of a distant past - - -

Six was their number - - - three to a side - - - lining the throne room - - - overlooking the throng of assembled lords - - - with - - - stern overbearing countenances - - -

Six was their number - - - three to a side - - - yielding with rancor and humiliation to the obsidian throne - - - and - - - he - - - who sat upon it - - -

Six was their number - - - Golden Gods all!!!

Golden Gods they were - - - radiant as the sun - - - for - - - were they not made of the self-same stuff as that of the sun? Was it not they - - - who - - had - - - in turn - - - one-after-the-other - - - incarnated themselves as the sun???

Golden gods were they - - - Golden as the Sun - - -

Cast of molten yellow sunshine - - - flowing to earth on endless sunbeams of pure yellow gold - - -

Yellow - - - Yellow - - - Gold - - -

Each - - - in and of himself - - - cast - - - of a shining mountain of - - - yellow - - - yellow - - - gold - - -

Yellow God - - - Golden Gold - - - King supreme of all of the precious metals - - -

Golden they were - - - each a mountain of yellow gold - - -

Pure yellow gold - - -

But - - -

How???

!! It is a double wonder that she is not sitting on the bottom of this bottomless lake !!

AND

"!!! Us with Her !!!"

For - - -

If they were gold - - - solid gold - - - forty feet tall - - - and - - - twenty feet of girth - - - would not the timbers of this floating pleasure palace - - - although groaning and protesting in a most mighty fashion - - - have long ago yielded to their great weight?

Would not the timbers and hull have yielded long ago to this ponderous cargo and sent crashing to the lake bottom these gods of the sun - - - and - - - all of their joyful followers - - - so that all - - - might spend their eternal days dining with the fishes???

No - - - not all was as it seemed to be - - -

There was trickery at work here - - -

As - - -

Soyala - - -

     Queen Surrogate - - -

          Queen - - - to he who would have no woman - - -

     Priestess Initiate - - -

          Priestess - - - of the Turquoise Gardens

     Shield Maiden - - -

          Blood Sister - - - to the Seven Sisters of the Pleiades - - -

Pondered this question - - -

The Toad Man - - - almost as if he could read her thoughts - - - head cocked to one side - - - looking out of his one good eye - - - hopped up behind her - - -

"Mistress" - - -

Soyala - - - startled from her thoughts by the faint warm breath of a nervous whisper racing up her naked neck - - - turned away from her thoughts - - - and - - - turned her head.

"They are not of pure gold - - - as the priests say - - - mistress - - - they are not of gold - - - but - - - of - - - wood - - - yes - - - wood - - - barren naked wood - - - with gold leaf pressed into its curves and contours - - - I know - - - because I was there - - - I was there in the dark of night when they fashioned these mighty forms - - - betraying and tricking the people with the roar of furnaces and flames shooting out into the night - - - I was there - - -

I was there - - -

&& THE SIX GOD/DESSES &&

Towering - - -

              Imposing - - -

                 Majestic - - -

Six Statues - - -

Six Golden Statues - -

Six Golden God/desses - - -

God/desses of the Creation - - -

Lining the length of the Great Throne Room - - - three to a side - - -

Three to a side - - - each equal to the other - - - holding in one hand the fruits of their creation - - - holding in the other a golden globe - - - symbol of the sun incarnate - - -

Fruits of Creation - - - in one hand - - - golden globe in the other - - -

The Toad Man - - - cocking his head - - - looking intently at his mistress with his one good eye - - - again - - - divined her thoughts: "Mistress - - - yes - - - yes - - - these are our god/desses of our creations - - -

You wondered why six - - - and - - - not five - - - did you not? Yes - - - Yes - - - You wondered why six - - - and - - - not five."

"Yes - - - yes - - - I did - - - stammered Soyala - - - still puzzled - - - still - - - not understanding why."

"Six - - - Six - - - is - - - Tona-teootl" - - - whispered the Toad Man - - - "Tona-teootl is the sixth god" - - -

"Six gods - - -

Yes - - - Yes - - - Six - - -

You still do not understand - - - do you not? - - - spoke the Toad Man - - - slowly nodding his head - - - as - - - Soyala - - - slowly - - - subconsciously - - - shook her head - - - whispering: "No - - - no - - - I do not understand."

"Each holds - - - Mistress - - - each God/dess holds in his left hand the fruit of his creation.

"Each holds his special gift of Creation - - -

"See? See??

"There - - - Look closely and see.

"See how:

Tezcatlipoca - - - grasps tightly in his fist - - - the gift of woody roots - - -

Quetzalcoatl - - - gently holds between forefinger and thumb - - - the gift of acorns - - -

Tlaloc - - - carefully cradles in the palm of his hand - - - the bountiful gift of Acecentli - - -

Chalchiutlicue - - - clutches lovingly to her breast - - - the tiny yellow gift of Teocentli - - -

Nanahuatl - - - proudly holds high - - - for all to see - - - the sweet succulent gift of corn - - -

Tona-teootl - - - magnanimously offers the supreme gift of - - -

283

The Toad Man's whispers were abruptly cut short - - - as - - - was all other murmuring in the room - - - by - - - the announcement of the Minister:

"Our Lord Tona-teootl bids you all now to take your place - - - beneath your chosen creator - - -

"Seat yourselves - - -

&& GOD CHILDREN &&

The God Children - - -

The Children of Tona-teootl - - -

The Children of Tona-teootl - - - Twenty Four in all - - -

       Twelve - - - Blackamoor Children - - - with - - - Golden Curly Wigs - - -

       Twelve - - - Albino Children - - - with - - - Raven Hair & Feathered Wigs - - -

Twenty Four God Children - - -

       Twelve Blackamoors to the left side of the God King - - -

       Twelve Albinos to the right side of the Mighty Tona-teootl - - -

Twenty Four Child Servants - - -

       Six Tables to Serve - - -

       Six Tables for Six Gods - - -

Twenty Four God Children - - - serving the bounty of the creation - - -

Twenty Four God Children - - - serving at the whim of the emperor - - -

Twenty Four God Children - - - clearing - - - and - - - setting - - - the royal tables - - - in the blink of an eye - - -

& & I TONA-TEOOTL &&

I - - -

I - - - Tona-teootl - - - have always existed - - -

I - - - Tona-teootl - - - existed - - - long before - - - the first drop of rain fell - - -

I - - - Tona-teootl - - - existed - - - long before - - - the first drop of dew formed beneath the lee of the first barren mountain crag - - -

I - - - Tona-teootl - - - existed - - - BEFORE - - - the creation - - -

FOR - - -

!!! I AM THE CREATION !!!

I - - - Tona-teootl - - - have taken the shape of beasts - - - huge and hideous - - - unimaginable - - - to devour the unwary - - -

I - - - Tona-teootl - - - have assumed the form of gods - - - demure and delightful - - - to beguile the unfaithful - - -

I - - - have been all - - - and - - - I - - - (whispering) - - - have been nothing - - -

I - - -

I - - - Tona-teootl - - - existed before the first drop of dew formed from the firmament - - - and - - - I - - - Tona-teootl - - - will live long after the last star burns out in the heavens - - -

I have transcended the mere shapes and forms of the idols which you see before you - - -

For - - -

As you worship them - - - through them - - - you - - - worship me - - -

They are as I - - - and - - - I am as they - - -

For - - -

I am changing - - - growing - - -

As I grow - - - growing - - - in strength and power - - - my form has changed - - - changed into what you see now before you - - -

I need only to consummate my rebirth - - - and - - - I - - - will be - - - a - - - power - - - a power beyond all powers - - - a - - - thought - - - beyond all thought - - -

Transcendence itself - - -

But - - -

Enough of talk!

Enough of talk - - - and - - - dusty boring history - - -

!!! LET US FEAST !!!

Yes!!!

Let us feast - - - feast - - - upon the bounty laid before you - - -

Let us feast on the bounty - - - as - - - we - - - commemorate our creations - - -

The Assembly - - - sat stunned - - -

Stunned - - - silent - - - not - - - knowing - - - what to do - - - what to say - - -

Stunned - - - silent - - - not - - - knowing - - - fearing - - - even - - - what to think - - -

Looking blankly - - - helplessly - - - hopelessly - - - at each other - - -

Staring in bewilderment and confusion at the - - - tasteless - - - woody roots piled high upon their banquet tables - - -

Woody Roots - - - reds - - - browns - - - indescribable - - - muddy yellows and browns - - -

Wild Woody Roots - - - tasteless - - - piled - - - mound upon mound - - - piled - - - high upon their tables - - -

As - - -

Some of the dutiful began to timidly nibble on the woody fibers - - - Tona-teootl roared:

!!! EAT !!!

Startled - - - the assembly began to tear at the wood fibers with their teeth - - - some - - - losing teeth - - - some - - - more valiant - - - even trying to shave off slivers - - - so that at least they might be able to make them somewhat more palatable - - - as - - - enforcers - - - stern muscular Blackamoors - - - walking behind the tables - - - whipped those who chose to be lax in their devotion - - -

Thus - - - began the first act of the creation play - - -

&& Tezcatlipoca &&

God of Earth

As an acrobat - - - swung across the ceiling - - - flaming torch in hand - - - to light the first fire of creation - - - a - - - celestial halo - - - born of the torch - - - began to burn brightly above Tezcatlipoca's head - - - for - - - He was the First Sun - - -

The First Sun - - -

Fashioning the first humans from earthly dust - - - and - - - the - - - sweat of his brow - - -

Lighting the earthly plane - - - but only in half light - - - for - - - he was too hurried in his creation and had incarnated himself as only half of a sun - - -

Actors - - - laying prone on the throne room floor - - - sprinkled with a fine silvery dust from above - - - lay beneath Tezcatlipoca's brow - - - which drizzled a fine mist of water upon them - - -

Drizzling a fine mist of water upon them - - -

The God smiled - - - as the first humans - - - formed of silver sparkle and the shimmering sweat of his brow - - - arose - - - from the shadows - - - to dance - - -

As the actors - - - arose from the silver sparkle - - - they - - - stretched - - - not yet used to movement - - - or - - - the - - - form or shape of their bodies - - -

Stretching - - - stretching - - - moving - - - stretching - - - dancing to the sound of some hidden melody - - -

Dancing in the half-light - - - feeling their way as much as seeing - - -

Seeing - - - feeling - - -

Seeing - - - feeling - - - sensing - - - in the half light - - - monstrous forms arise from the shadows - - -

Monstrous forms - - - Giants of the half dark - - - arising from the shadows - - -

Giant Actors - - - laying prone on the throne room floor - - - bestrewn with course grained Powders of Pomace from above - - - lay beneath Tezcatlipoca's brow - - - which mizzled a fine rain of water upon them - - -

As the actors arose from the deep - - - dark - - - dank - - - blanket of perfumed pomace - - - they - - - too - - - stretched - - - not yet use to movement - - - or - - - the form or shape of their bodies - - -

Stretching - - - stretching - - - stumbling - - - dancing - - - to the unheard melody of some ancient song - - - ancient - - - long forgotten - - - sung sadly - - - solemnly - - - long before the beginning of time - - -

Stretching - - - stumbling - - - lumbering - - - dancing - - - clumsily - - - to some ancient and long forgotten melody - - -

Dancing in the half-dark - - - smelling their way as much as seeing - - -

Smelling their way to the bounty of woody roots - - - and - - - Man Flesh - - -

As the Giants - - -

Perhaps - - - or - - - Perhaps not - - - Two Actors - - - one sitting upon another's shoulders - - - danced to the sound of the half shadows - - -

As the Humans - - - danced - - - to the sound of the half light - - -

They each took hold of the woody roots - - - presented to them - - - by the god of their creation - - -

Taking hold - - - grasping - - - gasping - - - as - - - each partook of only half his fill - - -

As the giants - - - anguished - - - famished - - - desperate - - - sniffed and snarled - - - they took hold of he who had been created of man flesh - - - and - - - dashed his bones to the ground - - - smiting him mightily and - - - breaking his bones into tiny pieces - - - eating greedily of his brains and entrails - - -

But - - -

Was it an act - - - cleverly feigned - - - or - - - was it real - - -

For - - -

Suddenly - - - there was a most noticeable empty space in one of the royal tables - - - which a particularly fat and boisterous lord had just occupied - - - (perhaps) - - - disappearing into the darkness - - - and - - - belly of some giant - - -

As the giants smacked their lips with joyous delight - - - they - - - disappeared into the darkness - - - disappearing - - - all - - - disappearing - - - save one - - -

One - - - remained - - - the - - - others having disappeared into the shadows - - -

Remaining - - - not moving - - - motionless - - - not able to move - - -

Remaining - - - chained - - - unmoving - - - as - - - a Giant Jaguar approached - - - sensing blood - - - sensing (delicious) fat - - - seeking to flesh out its ribs - - - for it had been starved for several days - - -

Giant Jaguar - - - devouring the last of the giants - - -

So - - - as it had been told - - - in the recounting of the first creation - - -

Now - - - there - - - were two empty seats - - - before Tezcatlipoca - - - God of Creation - - -

Two - - - empty seats - - -

"This - - - is a play" - - - thought - - - Soyala - - - "This MUST be a play!"

"This must be a play - - - as - - - clever as was played six months ago - - - with - - - shadows - - - only - - - here - - - here there is light" - - -

As Tona-teootl - - - leaped to his feet - - - cheering - - - clapping - - - applauding - - - all followed his suit - - - even - - - as the guests at the foot of the Great God Tezcatlipoca - - - breathed a most noticeable sigh of relief - - -

As most noticeable sigh of relief - - - by some - - - but - - - not all - - -

For - - -

Even as the guests - - - at the foot of the Great God Tezcatlipoca - - - were joyously clapping one another on the back - - - those - - - guests - - - seated at the feet of Quetzalcoatl - - - began to look around nervously - - -

&& Clearing of the Tables &&

As - - - the first act - - - of this six act play - - - ended - - - The God Children - - - twenty-four all told - - - scurried out onto the Throne Room Floor - - - four to each table - - -

Twenty-four God Children - - - Twelve Blackamoors to the left of Tona-teootl - - - Twelve Albinos to the right of Tona-teootl - - - scurried out onto the Throne Room Floor - - - to clear and set the tables - - -

Twelve Blackamoors to the left of Tona-teootl - - -

Six to clear the tables - - - entrapping the bits and scraps of the fruits of the First Creation - - - within the folds of the great tablecloth - - -

Six to set the tables - - - spreading the fruits of the second creation upon the freshly exposed forest green tablecloth lying beneath the first - - -

Twelve Albinos to the right of Tona-teootl - - -

Six to clear the tables - - - entrapping the bits and scraps of the fruits of the First Creation - - - within the folds of the great white tablecloth - - -

Six to set the tables - - - spreading the fruits of the second creation upon the freshly exposed forest green tablecloth lying beneath the first - - -

Twelve God Children - - - folding the great table cloth lengthwise - - - entrapping within its folds - - - the scattered bits and scraps of woody fibrous roots - - - gnawed and torn apart as if by some toothed rodent - - -

Twelve God Children - - - bringing forth the bounty of the second creation - - -

As - - -

The bounty of The Second Creation - - - Bitter Acorns - - - was laid upon the tables - - -

All - - - Twenty Four God Children - - - Blackamoor and Albino - - - disappeared from view - - -

With the bounty of bitter acorns - - - laid upon the table - - - Tona-teootl signaled for the second act of creation to begin anew - - -

♅♅♅ Quetzalcoatl ♅♅♅

God of Wind

As an acrobat - - - again - - - swung across the ceiling - - - flaming torch in hand - - - to light the second fire of creation - - - a - - - celestial halo - - - born of the torch - - - began to burn brightly above Quetzalcoatl's head - - - for - - - He was the Second Sun - - -

The Second Sun - - -

Fashioning the first humans from the brown and red muds of the earth - - - a - - - second race of humans raised themselves - - - as - - - great stone vats - - - of - - - liquid muds - - - exploded with red - - - brown - - - and - - - yellow - - - squirming - - - writhing - - - movement - - -

Squirming - - - Sloshing - - - Writhing - - - Life - - -

First - - - one hand - - - then another - - - as - - - one vat after another followed suit - - -

Hand - - - leading hand - - - head following hand - - -

As - - -

The Actors - - - stepped - - - and - - - slid - - - from the vats onto the throne room floor - - - to a wild accompaniment of drums and flutes - - - music as primeval as was the mud - - -

As the actors stepped from the primal ooze - - - into - - - the second coming of humans - - - they danced for joy - - - for - - - Quetzalcoatl had incarnated himself as the sun - - -

Not - - - a half sun - - - as had Tezcatlipoca - - - but - - - a - - - Full Sun - - -

Full Sun - - - blazing glory - - - radiant warmth - - - warm basking glow - - -

As the people feasted - - - fearing neither giant nor famine - - - they rejoiced - - - rejoicing in the bounty of bitter sweet acorns and sweet pine nuts - - -

Sweet acorns and pine nuts - - - delicate sweet meats - - - if - - - one could comfortably crack the tough shells - - -

Tough shells - - - as - - - the sound of cracking filled The Throne Room - -

Sounds of cracking - - - more so of teeth cracking and breaking than of the iron clad maiden yielding her sweet inner meats!

Sweet acorns and pine nuts - - - overflowing forests and valleys - - - as - - - actors joyously rubbed overstuff bellies - - - before - - - bedding down for a warm night's sleep - - -

Sleeping and rejoicing to music and dance - - - music and dance - - -

Until - - -

Tezcatlipoca - - - in a jealous rage - - - transformed himself into a Jaguar - - - stretching his terrible jaguar's claw high into the sky - - - to - - - tear the very sun itself from the firmament - - - so that - - - Quetzalcoatl - - - God of Winds - - - might come crashing down to earth - - - unleashing in his fury terrible hurricanes and gales - - -

Hurricanes - - - and - - - gales - - - then - - -

Actors - - - several actors - - - holding a giant paper mache jaguar's claw - - - scratched and torn at a Piñata Sun - - - as - - - the sun god mime - - - painted golden - - - hanging - - - dangling - - - from the most precarious of perches - - - fought for his life - - -

Fighting for his life - - - clinging on desperately - - - the - - - actor - - - was torn from the (throne room) - - - sky - - - to come crashing down hard - - - upon - - - the - - - (throne room) - - - floor - - - as - - - the second sun fell and died - - -

The Second Sun died - - - and - - - in his place - - - howling - - - wailing - - - mournful - - - winds - - - gale force winds - - - mourned his death - - -

Moaning - - - mournful - - - winds - - -

Fanned by the pain of loss - - - and - - - actors - - - holding giant bird wing fans - - - fanned the winds ever harder - - - gales - - - growing fiercer - - - as - - - human actors - - - fought - - - fought desperately - - - against the ever stronger winds - - -

Actors - - - swaying - - - ever faster - - - to the frenzied beat of the drums - - - and - - - the movement of the fans - - - fought the wind - - - became the wind - - - becoming the hurricane - - -

Hurricanes - - -

Hurricanes born of Gales - - - let loose their furry - - - as actors - - - unable to hold onto the statue of Quetzalcoatl - - - were torn loose - - - to - - - fall to their death - - -

Falling to their death - - - the second race of humans came to an end - - -

Dead - - - gone - - - extinct - - -

Extinct - - -

Blown away as with the dust - - -

Only dust remained - - - an entire race extinct - - -

An entire human race extinct - - - except for those few actors who were able to shed their human skins - - - and - - - assume the guise of monkeys - - -

Monkeys - - - sure of hand and foot - - - single minded in purpose - - - scampering to the safety of the throne room heights - - - even as those one or two remaining actors - - - still wearing the skins of humans - - - unable to maintain their grip - - - fell to their death - - -

Naught remained - - - but - - - a fleeting memory and the gibberish of monkeys - - -

Again - - -

Tona-teootl - - - leaped to his feet - - - cheering - - - clapping - - - applauding - - - as - - - all followed his suit - - - even - - - as those few remaining guests at the foot of the Great God Quetzalcoatl - - - breathed a most noticeable sigh of relief - - -

As most noticeable sigh of relief - - - as - - - those guest at the foot of the Statue of Tlaloc became most exceedingly nervous - - -

"No - - - thought Soyala - - - this is no play - - - but - - - the tortured game of a madman!"

Once again the tables were cleared in the blink of an eye - - - bringing to light the tablecloth of the God of Fire - - - Golden Flame - - - Golden Sun - - - on an orange background - - -

ঙঙঙ TLALOC ঙঙঙ

GOD OF FIRE

Again - - - an acrobat - - - swung across the ceiling - - - flaming torch in hand - - - to light the third fire of creation - - - a - - - celestial halo - - - born of the torch - - - began to burn brightly above Tlaloc's head - - - for - - - He was the Third Sun - - -

The Third Sun - - -

Fashioning the third race of humans from the splinters of many colored woods - - - a - - - third race of humans raised itself - - -

As the Throne Room became littered with pales and spikes of different colored woods - - - actors arose from the floor - - - brushing off splinters of different colored races - - - with as cavalier and carefree an attitude as one could imagine - - -

Even as some races rose - - - others fell backward - - - to hang - - - impaled - - - still living - - - upon the wooden pales and spikes of creation - - -

As - - -

The actors danced and sang - - -

The lifeless and spent splinters were swept away by The God Children - - -

Swept away - - - swept away - - - swept away - - -

Swept away to the soulful rhythm of some strange melancholy verse - - - played to the tune of a single stringed lyre - - -

For - - -

This Third Race of Humans - - - had - - - not only the food of a bountiful creation - - - but - - - also - - - the most wondrous gift of music - - -

Wondrous Gift of Music - - -

Music played - - - most beautifully - - -

Beautifully played - - - but - - - played not by the random and erratic pounding of two sticks together - - -

But - - -

Rather - - -

       Strummed - - - to the rhythmic beat of a heart - - -

Or - - -

Sung to the gentle cadence of a murmuring brook - - -

Sung - - -

Music - - -

Most wondrous sounds - - -

Rivaling even those of nature - - -

Wonderful sounds - - -

Marvelous sounds - - -

Songs and sounds - - - single note symphonies - - - in the making - - -

Until - - -

The gods - - - caused - - - Tlaloc to fall from the sky - - -

God of Fire - - - Flailing across the sky - - -

Flaming Fireball - - - Flaming Sky - - - Flaming Earth - - -

As - - -

Actors screamed in their death agonies - - - and - - - the smell of burned flesh permeated the air
- - - The God of Fire died - - - leaving naught but ashes and embers in his place - - -

Again - - -

Once again - - -

Several seats were empty at the great banquet table - - - as - - - those remaining trembled in silent
relief - - -

Once again Tona-teootl applauded - - -

Once again the tables were cleared - - - and - - - set - - -

And - - -

Once again - - -

Once again - - - without fail - - - or - - - compassion - - - The Play - - - resumed - - -

&& THE TABLECLOTHS &&

Six they were - - -

    Six cloths woven of the finest silks - - -

    Tapestries they were - - - much more than mere tablecloths - - -

    Showing of the Creation Myths of this overly vain and proud folk - - -

Six they were - - -

    Six stories - - - woven by the finest bards - - -

    Tapestries they were - - - much more than mere folklore or legend - - -

    Telling the tale of the Creation Myths of this overly vain and proud folk - - -

Six they were - - -

    One for each of the creations - - -

    Six Stories of Creation - - - spread across each of the tables - - -

    Thirty-Six all told - - - legends layered solemnly one upon the other - - -

Six they were - - -

One pure white - - -

Embroidered with Woody Roots - - - Blue - - - and - - - Red - - - and - - - Brown - - -

Gift of Tezcatlipoca - - - God of Earth - - - to the First Humans - - -

Another - - - Forest Green - - -

Embroidered with the fruits of the oak and the pine - - -

Gift of Quetzalcoatl - - - God of Wind - - - to the Second Race of Humans - - -

Yet another - - - Golden Yellow - - -

Embroidered with the fruits of the wild plants - - -

Gift of Tlaloc - - - God of Fire - - - to the Third Race of Humans - - -

Then yet another - - - Turquoise Sky above an Indigo Blue Sea - - -

Embroidered with clumps of Teosinte Grasses - - - yellow with fruit - - -

Gift of Chalchiutlicue - - - Goddess of Water - - - to the Fourth Race of Humans - - -

Then finally a fifth - - - Fiery Red - - -

Embroidered with a Man Emerging - - - smiling - - - from a Flame - - -

For his gift was that of Maize - - - which sustains us all - - -

Finally - - - buried deep beneath all of the others - - -

For - - - it had not yet been woven into the tapestry of legend - - -

Was the hidden sacred tablecloth of Tona-teootl - - - The Sixth Sun - - -

&&& CHALCHIUTLICUE &&&

GODDESS OF WATER

As an acrobat - - - once more - - - swung across the ceiling - - - flaming torch in hand - - - to light the fourth fire of creation - - - a - - - celestial halo - - - born of the torch - - - began to burn brightly above Chalchiutlicue's head - - - for - - - She was the Fourth Sun - - -

The Fourth Sun - - -

Fashioning the first humans from the Teocentli & God Blood - - -

Fashioned from - - - a - - - vast vat of God Blood - - - the - - - third race of humans raised themselves - - -

Raising themselves from the god blood - - - some - - - except for those few - - - who - - - being too weak - - - slipped back into the blood waters of their baptism - - -

Drowning - - - drowning - - - except for those few - - - who - - - were able to save themselves by changing themselves to fish - - - to escape the terrible flood - - -

Escaping the terrible flood of god blood - - - and - - - escaping the terrible games of Tona-teootl - - - some - - - trusting in their Goddess of the Waters - - - flung themselves into the middle of this vast inland sea - - -

For - - -

Far better to take one's chance with a desperate swim toward land - - - than - - - to face a certain death - - -

As - - -

Actors mocked drowning guests - - - by placing their hands to their ears - - - making the motion of a pair of gills - - - mouth opening and closing - - - to the rhythm of the hands - - -

Yes - - -

The Banquet Table at the feet of Chalchiutlicue was empty - - - save for those un-chosen few - - - who could not swim - - -

&&& Nanahuatl &&&

God of Humility

As an acrobat - - - swung across the ceiling - - - flaming torch in hand - - - once more - - - to light the fifth fire of creation - - - a - - - celestial halo - - - born of the torch - - - began to burn brightly above Nanahuatl's head - - - for - - - He was the Fifth Sun - - -

The Fifth Sun - - -

The Age in which we find ourselves - - -

>   The Age of Plenty - - -

>   The Age of Passion - - -

>   The Age of Pleasure - - -

The Fifth Race of Humans - - -

Born of the charred bones of the banquet guests - - - mixed with the blood of the dying - - -

Actors - - - decorated with the signs and totems of their clans - - - danced a wild dance - - - to the tune of flutes and drums - - - as - - - this fifth race of humans - - - fashioned from the bones of their ancestors - - - forged from the steel wills of their grandfathers - - - bereft of the sympathy of their grandmothers - - - danced - - -

>   Danced - - -

>   Played - - -

>   Sang - - -

Until - - -

&& The Sixth Play &&

&&& Prologue &&&

Tona-teootl waved his hand - - - and - - - all was silent - - - not only silent - - - but - - - motionless - - - for all had frozen in mid-sentence - - - mid-motion - - - mid-thought - - -

"Ah - - - Daughter of the Clouds - - - I'm pleased that you could join us" - - -

Tona-teootl - - - seated upon his Obsidian Throne - - - turned - - - turned slightly - - - to speak to Soyala - - -

For the first time - - - Soyala was able to perceive the full mask of Tona-teootl's godhood - - - golden gold - - - red flames shooting out from the face - - - twisted - - - somehow - - - not symmetrical - - -

Recalling The Toad Man's frantic hushed whisper - - - she thought: "Hideously deformed - - - must he be - - - he must certainly be hideously deformed - - - face burned as bright a red and as twisted by scars - - - as the mask he wears - - - thought Soyala.

Full Mask - - - Golden Mask - - -

Golden Mask of Godhood - - -

Golden Godhood - - -

Golden Godhood - - - golden as the sun - - - golden solar flares rimming the mask as if the sun herself were on fire - - - on fire - - - - being consumed - - - rather than hanging sleepily in the early morning sky - - -

Golden Flaming Mask - - - with - - - hints of fiery red sunbursts - - -

As - - -

The Voice hidden behind the Mask continued to speak - - - speaking in a deep baritone voice - - - strangely not befitting its slender - - - almost - - - gaunt - - - body house - - -

"Ah - - - Soyala - - - Daughter of Jaguar Claw - - - I am pleased that you could dine with us today - - - very much pleased - - - for - - - I knew your father - - - or - - - was he your grandfather? It doesn't matter - - - for - - - they were one and the same - - - were they not? Yes - - - one and the same - - - for - - - I knew them both!"

As Soyala was about to protest ignorance - - - - The Voice behind the Mask - - - waved his hand - - - and - - - continued - - - continuing in that same - - - deep - - - monotonous baritone voice: "You are surprised that I recognize you - - - Soyala - - - Daughter of Orchid Blossom.

"Yes - - - I know of you - - - Soyala - - - and - - - of your family - - - and - - - of your race - - - your ancient race - - - that once overly-proud race which lived high above the clouds - - - so long ago - - - so - - - very - - - very - - - long ago.

You are the last - - - Soyala - - - are you not? You - - - You - - - Who wandered into the realm of the Frost King so long ago - - - You - - - who he took as Foundling and Fosterling - - - You - - - who he adopted as his own daughter - - -

Am I not right – Soyala – Sister of the Pleiades" – he said with a snicker?

"Yes - - - I know you - - - I know you better - - - much better - - - then you think - - - Daughter of the Clouds - - - I know you well!"

"I know you well - - - he said - - - as - - - he began to rub his right arm and shoulder as if in pain - - - "I know all of your family well - - - very - - - very - - - well."

By the way - - - and - - - speaking of family - - - I have someone who I'd like for you to meet - - - I'm sure that you'll be happy to see him!!!

&& THE GOLEMS &&

!!! BEHOLD !!!

!!! MY CHILDREN !!!

??? DO YOU NOT RECOGNIZE YOUR BROTHERS???

??? DAUGHTER OF THE CLOUDS???

As Soyala - - - stared into the shadows - - - sensing movement - - - but seeing none - - - Tona-teootl's lips curled up into a cruel smile - - -

"Do you not recognize your brothers? - Daughter of the Clouds?

Soyala - - - looked - - - from the shadows - - - to - - - Tona-teootl - - - and - - - back again - - - fearing some cruel joke - - -

Sensing Shadows - - - Seeing Shadows - - - Silent Shuffling of Shadowy Feet - - -

Six Shadows - - - slowly slipped out into the light of the Throne Room - - -

Six Stone Statues - - - silently slipped into the light - - - moving slowly - - - stiffly - - - at first - - - as if - - - their stone joints were resisting all thought of movement - - -

Six Stone Statues - - - slowly moving - - - stone mind - - - commanding - - - stone joint - - - to resolutely move forward - - -

Moving forward - - - The Six - - - moved forward - - - and - - - then - - - kneeled before the Great Lord Tona-teootl - - - heads bowed - - - silent - - -

All kneeled - - - save one - - - which stood statue like - - - unmoving - - - before his King - - -

Six Stone Statues - - - save one - - - ground to shape and polished smooth by the workman's hand - - - brought to life by some incantation - - - kneeled silently before Tona-teootl - - -

Soyala - - - frozen in mind and in heart - - - darned not think - - - dared not breathe - - -

Then - - -

Tona-teootl - - - with a gesture so slight as to go unnoticed - - - bid them rise - - -

Rise they did - - - and - - - in uniform movement - - - moved before their Queen - - - and kneeled before her - - -

"Do you not recognize your brothers? - - - Daughter of the Clouds"

The taunt in Tona-teootl's voice was unmistakable - - -

The fiery confusion in Soyala's heart was unquenchable - - -

"What?" "Who??"

Soyala stared intently at the six - - -

Six - - - they were - - -

      Two - - - Fastidiously Crafted of Jade - - -

      Two - - - Meticulously Crafted of Jasper - - -

      Two - - - Painstakingly Crafted of Fossil Corals - - -

As Tona-teootl once again waved his hand - - - the largest of the six - - - a - - - one-armed giant - - - rose - - - and - - - began to speak:

!!! Sister !!!

!!! Save Us !!!

Then one - - - then another - - - rose:

! Save Us !

!! Save Us Sister !!

!!! Please Save Us !!!

Then with one voice:

Please Save Us

- - - For - - -

We are Cursed

A wave of nausea swept over Soyala - - - sweeping up from the depths of her stomach - - - flooding up through the back of her throat - - - turning - - - twisting - - - her - - - every thought - - - her - - every motion - - -

As the room began to spin - - - the sweet sour taste bubbling up in the back of Soyala's throat - - - choked her - - - suffocated her - - -

Soyala fought for air - - - forcing air deep into her lungs - - - only to spit it out again as a sour gagging gasping cough - - -

Swallowing - - - swallowing - - - trying to force the sour taste from her mouth and her throat - - - Soyala fought to slow her breathing - - - forcing rhythm into her breath - - - into her thoughts - - -

Soyala turned to the one armed giant - - - seeking to call his name - - - but - - - the words stuck in her throat - - -

"Burilgi" - - - her eyes pleaded - - - but - - - still no sound would issue forth - - - except for her forced breathing and gasps for air - - -

"Burilgi" - - -

Tona-teootl - - - amused - - - leaned back and laughed - - - gloating over his triumph - - -

"See - - - Daughter of the Clouds - - - I have made them - - - all - - - that they were not - - - the very antithesis of their very being!

But - - - you should not be surprised - - - for - - - one would expect nothing less from a God - - - is that not so?

With a wave of his hand - - - Tona-teootl - - - silenced the Stone Figures - - -

See?

See?? - - - Daughter of the Clouds - - -

See??? - - - Standing before you - - - your brothers - - -

305

All your brothers - - - save - - - your hunter brother - - - for - - - your clumsy hand maiden fell by accident upon his gift - - - and - - - but - - - but - - - all is not lost - - - as you soon shall see - - -

As Tona-teootl motioned with his head - - - Soyala's eyes - - - involuntarily - - - followed his movement - - - to where - - - the shadows lay deepest - - - seeing nothing - - -

Your brothers - - - Daughter of the Clouds - - - are - - - now my servants - - - my - - - playthings - - - for - - - I have created of them - - - the very antithesis of their being - - -

See - - - now - - - Tona-teootl continued - - - his voice alternately dripping with honey and then poison - - -

The Brave Burilgi - - -

Warrior Bold - - -

Whose sword so deftly dealt death to murderers and rapists - - -

He has now become the greatest of them all - - -

The Sweet Poet Bard - - -

Whose songs so sweetly lulled the young to love and the old to sleep - - -

He has now become - - - The Burner of Books - - - The Shredder of Scrolls - - - and - - - The Leveler of Libraries - - -

Your Handmaiden Fair - - -

Whose baskets once overflowed with sweet blossoms - - -

Whose nectar pots overflowed - - - rejoicing - - - with sweet honeys - - -

She has now become - - - The Reaper of Meadows - - - Unflinching - - - Sharpened Scythe in Steady Hand - - -

Slashing sprouting shoots to mere stubble - - - bereft of both blossom and bloom - - -

Your Minstrel most Merrious - - -

Who - - - although dwarfed - - - did sing with a stout heart - - -

Rivaling the Song Bird with his song - - -

Now - - - only sings of death and doom - - -

Draining the joy from the hearts of those who hear him - - -

Tona-teootl continued - - - his voice - - - becoming - - - more-and-more - - - unsteady - - -
becoming - - - more-and-more - - - uncertain - - - stumbling over words - - - shredding sentences
- - - his voice - - - rising to a fevered pitch - - -

Gone was the baritone boom of his gaunt voice house - - - resident - - - in its place - - - was a
shrill voice - - - almost - - - a - - - woman's voice - - - high in pitch - - - shrill - - - painful to the
ears - - - as - - - Tona-teootl - - - began rubbing the hint of an ugly purple mark just showing
from beneath his mask - - -

Your builder brother - - - now - - - The Razer of Cities - - -

Tearing down - - - Towns - - - and - - - Towers - - - and - - - Temples - - -

Charring Cottage and Cot - - - leaving naught but dust and ashes in his wake - - -

But - - -

Now - - -

Now I will create my masterpiece - - -

I'll create from your Forester Brother - - - my masterpiece - - - The Ravager of Forests - - - The
Butcher of all that walks - - -

Bring him here!!!

With these words - - - guards - - - dragged a shredded body - - - painted gold - - - gold as the
sun - - - from the dark shadows - - -

Kajika - - - painted golden as was Nanahuatl - - - The Sun Incarnate - - - for - - - by slaying the Sun Mime - - - Tona-teootl would assume all of the powers of the sun god - - -

Then - - -

Only Then - - -

The words finally tore themselves loose from Soyala's throat:

!!! Kajika !!!

&& The Six Stone Statues &&

Six Stone Statues - - -

Ground to shape and polished smooth by the workman's hand - - -

Brought to life by some incantation - - - stood silently before Soyala - - -

Six Stone Statues - - -

Two - - - Fastidiously Crafted of Jade - - -

Two - - - Meticulously Crafted of Jasper - - -

Two - - - Painstakingly Crafted of Fossil Corals - - -

Six - - - they were - - -

One once was - - - The Warrior Bold - - -

One once was - - - The Sweet Poet Bard - - -

One once was - - - The Handmaiden Fair - - -

One once was - - - The Merrious Minstrel - - -

One once was - - - The Vainglorious Builder - - -

One was to be - - - The Loden Cloaked Ranger - - -

The largest stone - - - that which once was - - - The Warrior Bold - - - was crafted of a giant blood red jasper - - - a - - - brecciated - - - broken - - - chalcedony - - -

Brecciated Red Jasper - - - broken and healed - - - much as an ancient warrior might have been broken - - - again-and-again - - - to - - - struggle - - - again-and-again - - - to - - - knit and heal - - - so that he might return - - - one more time - - - to battle - - -

Healed - - - but - - - jagged and broken - - - from - - - a lifetime of battles - - -

The smallest stone - - - that which once was - - - The Mirthful Minstrel - - - was most delicately crafted of a tiny - - - but - - - most - - - exquisite - - - and - - - most - - - exactingly pure - - - white jade - - -

White Jade - - - Creamy White - - - translucent - - - radiating light - - -

Radiating light - - - exactly as had the being it once was - - - translucent - - - baring - - - spirit - - - and - - - mind - - - and - - - mirth - - - for - - - all to see - - - and - - - enjoy - - -

Now - - -

Twisted from its purpose - - - by - - - Tona-teootl's evil will - - - it seemed - - - rather - - - as if it were pulling in happiness - - - draining happiness from all those around - - - growing darker in the process - - - even now - - - dark grey spots had begun to fleck and stain its pure white surface - - -

!!! SHORTY !!!

A - - - wave of nausea swept over Soyala - - - starting in the pit of her stomach - - - rolling up through the back of her throat - - - sweeping out of her body - - - as - - - she - - - fought to hold onto consciousness - - -

Consciousness - - - fleeting - - - fighting - - - focusing - - - all of her energy into her fingertips - - - clutching - - - clinging - - - desperately - - - to her chair - - -

Room - - - spinning - - - reeling - - - whirling - - - losing consciousness - - - losing focus - - - tearing away the brief veil of composure Soyala had assumed - - - just that short time ago - - - as Kajika - - - had been dragged - - - torn and battered - - - from the shadows - - -

"Kajika - - - Burilgi - - - Shorty - - -

"Shorty - - - my - - - dear - - - dear - - - sweet - - - Shorty" - - - her voice - - - her thoughts - - - trailing off into nothingness - - -

&& REFLECTIONS OF YESTERDAY &&

Tona-teootl - - -

Tona-teootl - - - Lord of Creation - - -

Tona-teootl - - - Lord of Creation - - - and - - - Chaos - - - leaned back and smiled - - - his eyelids heavy - - - his voice languid - - - as if he were - - - resting from the labor of his six creations - - - and - - - as if - - - renewing himself for his seventh and final creation - - -

"Ah - - -

I remember - - -

I remember - - - as if it were just yesterday - - -

It was glorious - - - Full Glorious!

Full Glorious - - - was my Victory - - -

Full Glorious was my Ascension to my Godhood - - -

I killed them!!!

Yes - - - I killed them - - -

Killed - - - All who would oppose me - - -

At first – through stealth - - -

310

Stabbing the men in the back - - - and - - - then - - - as they fell - - - crushing their throats with my knee so that they could not cry out for help - - -

Then - - - as - - - others - - - rushed to their aid - - - disappearing into the shadows - - -

Then - - - as - - - their confusion - - - and - - - desperation - - - grew - - - running amongst them - - blinding them with sand - - - and - - - the gushing of their own blood - - - so - - - that they could not see - - - and - - - as they held up their hands to shield their eyes - - - cutting off their hands - - - so - - - that - - - their swords fell with them - - -

And - - - and - - -

When they were without hands - - - with which to defend themselves - - - I cut off their legs - - - so that they could not run away - - -

As they lay there - - - motionless on the ground - - - begging - - - crying for mercy - - - some - - - propping themselves up on bloody stumps of arms - - - I killed their women before their eyes - - - tearing out their fetuses from their still throbbing wombs - - -

Yes - - - YES!!!

As - - - their warriors lay there on the ground - - - helpless - - - begging for mercy for their women - - - propping up bleeding torsos on bloody stumps of arms - - - I killed their women - - - holding their dead heads - - - in my hands - - - kissing those still warm lips still mouthing words - - -

Yes - - -

Yes - - - YES - - -

Their eyes still rolling - - -

Still seeking child and shelter - - -

I killed them - - - but - - - before they died - - - and - - - before - - - their raving screaming eyes - - - I - - - cut their fetuses out of their still warm bodies - - - tearing out their entrails and dashing them upon the ground - - -

Yes - - - as the Fetuses lay upon the ground - - - lifeless - - - I cut off the heads of their mothers - - - kissing their still warm lips as their bodies fell lifeless to the ground - - -

311

Upon the warm and bloody ground - - - I stood - - - until - - - all was still - - - even the lamentations of the wind - - -

And - - -

And - - -

What of my mother? You might ask - - -

My Mother - - - my mother - - -

Yes - - -

My mother - - - my - - - dear - - - dear - - - sweet mother - - -

Sweet mother - - -

Sweetest of mothers - - -

Her mother's blood - - - far sweeter to me than her mother's milk - - - sweetly kissed my hands - - - my face - - - my parched a dry lips - - - so - - - I drank - - -

I drank as deeply as never before - - -

For - - - she had borne unto herself a GOD!!!

A god - - -

Cannot you see? Cannot you ALL see??

I am that GOD - - - I AM THE SUN!!!

&& THE CRYSTAL SKULLS &&

"Excellent - - - My Lord - - - This is Most Excellent!" - - - Spoke the Toad Man - - - who – much to his shock and surprise - - - had - - - suddenly found of courage for the first time in his life - - -

Placing himself between Tona-teootl and Soyala - - - as if to shield her - - - he boldly spoke: "That is most excellent My Lord - - - for one could expect nothing less from a God!"

Tona-teootl - - - nodded - - - then - - - turned his head - - - looking straight through the Toad Man - - - straight into Soyala's heart - - -

Look! - - - Daughter of the Clouds - - -

Look at your Foster Brothers - - -

Look into the Stones - - -

Look into the Blood Red Stone which was once The Noble Warrior - - - and - - - you will see swimming - - - the tortured spirits of his victims - - - for - - - what more exquisite torture than to be imprisoned with one's screaming wailing victims - - - for an eternity - - -

Look into the Earth Brown Stone which was once The Strutting Peacock - - - and - - - you will see swimming - - - the dusty remnants - - - of - - - his creations - - - Towers - - - and - - - Temples - - - and - - - Tombs - - - for what more exquisite of a torture than to be imprisoned with one's own dead children - - - for an eternity - - -

Look into the Yellow Stone which was once The Divine Poet - - - Yellow-Orange - - - as near to life and blood of color as was his much loved Orange-Yellow Parchment - - -

Gaze into the Orange-Yellow Stone - - - and - - - you will see swimming the shredded and dusty remnants - - - of - - - parchment - - - and - - - papyrus - - - and - - - clay - - -

Parchment - - - and - - - Papyrus - - - and - - - Clay - - - all that remains of that which were once books - - - and - - - scrolls - - - and - - - tablets - - -

Shreds - - - and - - - flakes - - - and - - - dust - - - for what more exquisite torture than to be imprisoned - - - for all eternity - - - with the writings of the greatest poets and thinkers of all the ages - - - and - - - to gain not more than a glimpse of a tantalizing word - - - or - - - a fragment of a shattered thought - - -

And - - -

Look into the Ice Cold Maroon Stone which was once your Passionate Handmaiden - - - and - - - you will see swimming - - - flower stalks slashed at the stem - - - for what greater torment than to wait an eternity - - - gazing upon the lone flower - - - waiting for it to bloom - - - when - - - it is - - - suddenly - - - unexpectedly - - - torn from life - - -

Torn from life - - -

How exquisite the torment - - - to - - - hold - - - cradled in the palm of your hand - - - the gentle flower - - - tender buds swelling with indescribable sweetness and beauty - - - when - - - at that very moment of its birth - - - it is - - - torn - - - from your grasp - - - leaving only the naked dead stalk - - - bereft of blossom and petal - - -

Bereft of blossom and petal - - -

Naked dead stalk - - - never to blossom - - -

Never to blossom - - - never a blossom with which to grace a maiden's hair - - - or - - - one drop of sweet nectar - - - to sweeten one day of one's dreary life - - -

Instead - - -

Living for an eternity amongst the short coarse stubble of a dead field - - - devoid of all beauty - - - devoid of all life - - -

Dead Fields - - - born of the unbending mind - - - guided by the unerring eye - - - and - - - wrought with the steadfast hand - - -

The Steadfast Hand - - - and - - - unbending mind - - - methodically slashing bloom and blossom - - - tireless feet - - - dancing to the indefatigable rhythm of the slashing scythe - - - steadfastly working its destruction - - -

Soyala - - - flush with fever - - - frozen with fear - - - sat motionless - - -

As - - -

Thoughts - - - Flashing - - - Fading - - - Flickering - - - passed her by - - - unheard - - - unnoticed - - - unimagined - - -

Words - - - unheard - - - of - - - Dwarf Minstrels - - - Undone - - - plagued with an eternity of torments beyond imagination - - -

Words - - - unheard - - - forgotten - - -

Thoughts - - - Bursting Anew - - - Racial Memories - - - Awakening - - -

Racial Memories - - -

Thoughts - - - of - - - the burning cold Ice Cold Maroon Stone - - - standing before her - - - yielding - - - to - - - Ancestral Memories - - - of - - - Ice Cold Ice - - - Glacial Ice - - - Ice - - - Ice - - - Glacial Ice - - -

Ice - - - Icen Existence - - - Racial Memories - - - Ancestral Memories - - -

Memories Awakening - - -

Icen World - - - High above the Clouds - - -

Hidden from curious - - - prying - - - eyes - - -

Glaciers - - - Momentous - - - Enduring - - - High - - - High - - - Above the Clouds - - -

Ice - - - Ice - - - cold - - - clear - - - calculating - - - crystal clear - - - ice - - -

Crystal Clear - - - Thoughts - - -

Slowly - - - slowly - - - Soyala's face transformed itself from one of feverish fear - - - to - - - one of icen resolve - - - "Ice - - - ice - - - cool - - - calculating - - - cautious" - - -

Tona-teootl continued - - - not seeing - - - not caring - - - "Such is the torment I - - - Tona-teootl - - - have bestowed upon them! For - - - I am a God!"

Such is the torment of these beings - - -

Such is their torment - - -

And - - -

Of Your People - - -

Do you not wish to learn the fate of your people – Daughter of the Clouds?

Soyala - - - turned her head - - - turning toward the golden visage - - - turning toward the god behind the mask - - - and nodded: "Yes - - - Yes - - - My Lord - - - Tona-teootl - - - with your sufferance - - - I wish to know - - -

The Toad Man - - - upon seeing her change - - - a - - - change unnoticed by Tona-teootl - - - cocked his head sideways - - - as - - - he moved aside - - - askance - - - at her sincerity - - - curious - - - as to her intent - - -

Ah - - - Tona-teootl - - - sighed - - - you know - - - you - - - understand - - - that - - - I am indeed a God! Yes - - - you - - - alone - - - understand - - - when others do not!

Daughter of the Clouds - - - look - - -

Look - - -

Look closely at my throne - - -

Do you not see something strange?

Do you not notice something curious??

Do you not see these "snowflakes" swimming???

Look closely - - - at - - - these - - - 'snowflakes' - - - swimming in stone - - -

Do they not remind you of the torment being suffered by your brothers?

Do they not remind you of spirits imprisoned??

Your People - - - Daughter of the Clouds - - - Your People!!!

Your People - - - Daughter of the Clouds - - - imprisoned for an eternity!!!

Imprisoned in this dark room - - - never again to see a cloud - - - let alone live above one!!!

With a monstrous laugh - - - Tona-teootl - - - turned - - - basking in his glory - - - his - - - God-Hood - - -

&& THE GOLEMS ANSWER &&

Again - - - Tona-teootl - - - became more animate - - - his voice deepening - - -

"Well - - - Daughter of the Clouds - - - do you not wish to greet - - - to speak - - - to your brothers?

I will allow you - - - one question - - - and - - - them - - - one answer - - -

Speak!

The Shield Maiden turned - - - turning toward Burilgi - - - willing - - - through sheer force of will - - - rather than imploring - - - him to speak: "Burilgi - - - How?"

Burilgi - - - his voice heavy - - - heavy as stone - - - spoke:

"Through trickery and Guile - - -

Through False Fanciful Gifts Unknown to Us - - -

The Shield Maiden then turned to the Builder: "Brother Builder – Who?"

"Your False Sister - - -

One born of treachery and deceit - - -

The Shield Maiden continued - - - asking of the Handmaiden: "Dearest Friend – What?"

"There were false gifts born - - - born to each brother - - -

Troodon Feathers - - - Flights of Fancy - - - Unknown to Us - - -

Beautiful - - - and - - - Deadly - - -

Seven Gifts - - - all - - - beautiful - - - all - - - deadly - - -

A Crested Helm - - - born to him who was most boastful - - -

Plumed with the most wondrous of troodon feathers - - -

A Feathered Cloak - - - born to him - - - who was most vain - - -

Layered with the most wondrous of green and red troodon feathers - - -

So that he might strut - - - peacock like - - - preening feather and fancy - - -

Preening - - - all the day long - - -

A Feathered Quill Pen - - - born to him - - - who was most flowery of speech and
manner - - -

Saying so much of everything - - - and - - - making more ado over nothing - - -

So that - - - even when saying nothing - - - it might be done with a flourish!

An Unerring Arrow - - - fletched with the wondrous troodon feathers - - -

Destined for our infallible and indefatigable Forester Brother - - -

Errantly gone astray - - - to prick my finger - - - a finger so fair - - -

Stop!

I will hear no more of this - - -

Brother Minstrel - - - Shorty - - - Is there no return?

The voice - - - small - - - weak - - - confused - - - could not answer - - -

"Shorty - - - Soyala demanded - - - I have purposefully saved you for last - - - because - - - in your way - - - you carry the wisdom - - - combined - - - of all of my other brothers - - - what else do I need to know? Tell me!

Again - - - the voice - - - small - - - weak - - - confused - - - began to cry - - -

"Why am I here - - - What have I done?   I have done nothing wrong.

I don't - - -

As Soyala struggled to absorb all that she had heard - - - she felt a faint tug at the corner of his gown - - - and - - - heard - - - a small voice - - -

Looking down - - - she saw one of the God Children - - - most curious in shape and manner - - - not as well proportioned as the others - - - but - - - a - - - God Child - - - none-the-less:

"Mistress - - - it has become most uncomfortably warm - - - perhaps - - - you'd like a fan with which to cool yourself - - -

As - - - Soyala reached out - - - to accept the proffered fan - - - she thought most strongly:

"Yes - - - a most curiously shaped God Child - - - and - - - a - - - most familiar fan - - -

The thoughts had no sooner formed when Tona-teootl's foot sent the God-Child tumbling back down the stairs - - - "Away!"

Soyala - - - sat - - - puzzled - - - most - - - extremely - - - puzzled - - - so puzzled in fact that she lost all trace of fear and uncertainty - - -

As - - - she stared - - - dumbfounded - - - at Shorty - - - who had never before been at a loss for words - - - and - - - then - - - glanced at her somehow familiar fan - - - then - - - at the small form of the God Child - - - scurrying away as fast as his short legs might carry him - - - she turned her attention once again to Shorty: "Be quiet!"

Then more softly - - - "Please be quite - - - you have done nothing wrong. You have answered my question. Thank you. "

As - - - Soyala slumped back in her chair - - - apparently in defeat - - - Tona-teootl - - - flush with the triumph of a god spoke:

"Ah - - - Daughter of the Clouds - - -

"Yes - - - I trapped their with their greed and my guile - - -

"Trapping them with my gifts - - - then - - - flaying them alive to lay their still warm skins upon the Golems - - - to animate them - - - as - - - I will soon do with your Brother Hunter - - -

But - - -

First - - -

You have one or two more questions to ask - - - before - - - we continue with our Play of Plays - - - our - - - Creation of Creations - - - so-to-speak - - -

Soyala - - - then turned her attention to her brother Poet - - -

Brother Poet - - - you - - - who are versed in flowery and poetic speech - - - you - - - who lull lovers to sleep and entice the old to dance - - - pray tell me - - - in words that are short and vulgar - - - even - - - cutting and cruel - - - if - - - they must be - - - what is our escape?

&& THE POET'S PROPHESY &&

As the Shadow of the Dire Wolf howls in the dark - - -

      Wrapping thick gray fur around sleeping bones - -

The Sleeping King stirs - - - as - - - dreams are shattered.

      Trumpets - - - played by the terrible piercing moans of the howling winds - - -

Blast forth - - - to wake the sleeping king - - - who - - - fitfully tossing and turning - - -

In his death sleep - - - awakens to tear his rock feet loose from the Riverside Cliff - -

To roam the earth once more

Awakened - - - his terrible footsteps - - - race across the barren plains - - -

     To the far end of the world - - - where - - - his savage hands - - -

Tear loose sacred shields and hallowed heirlooms from trembling palace walls - - -

     Hurling them into a raging fire below - - - where - - - they linger - - - briefly - - -

Before becoming as one with the dross - - - and - - - slag - - - and - - - soot - - - of the hearth - - -

     Gone - - - are the last vestiges of a bygone glory - - - dancing on a bronzen shield - - -

For - - - now - - - naught remains - - - save - - - white ghostly ash - - -

As the Flayed Flute celebrates its awakening - - -

     By sweetly kissing the lips of the player - - -

Its mournful notes slowly waft across the Porcelain Plain - - -

     Buried deep beneath the glistening bones of the dead - - -

Playing blithely - - - the leg bone flute - - - dares the dead to forget their sleep - - -

     And - - - to rise and dance - - - far into the night - - - into the dawn of the next day - -

Dancing - - - Dancing - - - Dancing - - - as if there were no tomorrow - - -

Gliding to the rhythmic command of the flayed flute - - -

     The White Canoes silently move away from the safety of the silent shore - - -

Paddles dipping lightly into the deep dark turbulent waters of the vast inland sea - - -

     Canoes - - - cloaked in a thick white fog - - - steadfastly move forward - - -

Chants and Incantations guiding the way though the heavily hanging haze - - -

Hooded Pilgrims - - - cloaked in thick white fleece - - - pierce mist and myth - - -

Seeking the Shrouded Crannog on the Sea - - -

&& THE SIXTH CREATION &&

As an acrobat - - - swung across the ceiling - - - flaming torch in hand - - - to light the sixth fire of creation - - - a - - - celestial halo - - - born of the torch - - - began to burn brightly above the statue of Tona-teootl - - - for - - - He was the Sixth Sun - - -

The Sixth Sun - - -

The Age in which we will soon find ourselves - - -

As the Conch Trumpets blared - - - and - - - as - - - the skin drums roared to life - - - The Toad Man leaned over to whisper in Soyala's ear - - -

Mistress - - - The Play of Plays - - - it - - - is has begun - - - I fear for you - - -

Tona-teootl - - - stroking the rapidly deepening raspberry blotch half hidden beneath his mask - - - half turned - - - half faced - - - Soyala: "Ah - - - Daughter of the Clouds - - - I really am so very pleased that you could join with us" - - -

As - - -

God Children - - -

Twelve on the left of Tona-teootl - - -

Twelve on the right of Tona-teootl - - -

Twelve God Children - - - struggling beneath the weight of the golden platters - - -

Struggling beneath the weight of the golden platters - - - heaped high with mounds of steaming meats - - - began - - - to serve Tona-teootl - - - and - - - Soyala - - -

322

Tona-teootl rejoined:

EAT

PLEASE - - - EAT

Noting Soyala's hesitancy - - - he - - - practically commanded – then – almost immediately softened his voice:

PLEASE

EAT

DAUGHTER OF THE CLOUDS

PLEASE

ACCEPT OUR MOST HUMBLE GIFT TO YOU

ENJOY OUR STEAMING MEATS

AS

YOU ENJOY OUR PLAY OF PLAYS

Also - - -

As you appear to be more than comfortably warm - - -

Please - - -

Please accept our most humble gift to you for this most magnificent fan - - - with which to cool yourself - - -

So saying - - -

A Giant Blackamoor - - - full grown - - - dark and brooding - - - appeared from the blue-black shadows - - - for - - - he - - - and - - - the shadows were as one - - -

A Giant Blackamoor - - - gigantically black and brooding - - - appeared from the blue-black shadows - - - cradling - - - a most beautiful and apparently innocuous gift - - - a great winged fan - - -

Carrying - - -

Carefully Carrying - - - from - - - deep in the shadows - - - a - - - Great Winged Fan - - -

       A Great Winged Fan - - - artfully fashioned from the wing of a troodon - - -

       A Great Winged Fan - - - innocently fashioned from the wing of a male troodon - - -

       A Great Winged Fan - - - maliciously fashioned to trap the innocent and guileless - - -

A Great Winged Fan - - - magically - - - and - - - maliciously crafted to gently take one by the hand and then lead one unawares into the realm of the Golems - - -

Male Troodon - - - Male - - - Full Blooded Male - - -

Full Blooded Male - - - Lord and Master of his Harem - - -

Lord and Master - - - in full majestic breeding plumage - - -

Blood pumping - - - engorging each and every fiber of his being - - -

Full blood pumping - - - Engorging - - - Libido and Plumage - - -

Full blooded Lord and Master - - -

       Wantonly - - - killed for naught but his plumage - - -

       Merciously - - - killed for naught but his feathers - - -

Feathers - - -

Full Passionate Plumage - - -

Refracting white light into an Iridescent Array of Colors - - -

Iridescent colors - - - emerald greens - - - ruby reds - - - golden yellows - - -

Tona-teootl - - - assured of his conquest of the Daughter of the Clouds - - - confident of his godhood - - - smiled - - - most - - - sweetly - - - most - - - serenely:

PLEASE

DAUGHTER OF THE CLOUDS

TAKE THIS MOST HUMBLE GIFT

NO

PLEASE TAKE THIS GIFT AS A TOKEN OF MY ESTEEM

NO – PLEASE – NO

PLEASE ACCEPT THIS HUMBLE GIFT

AS

A MOST HUMBLE TOKEN OF OUR FRIENDSHIP

Please - - -

Please - - - as - - - a - - - symbol - - - of - - - our - - - royalty - - - of - - - our - - - loyalty - - -

Please - - - take this fan - - - and - - - give to me that most small and most pitiful fan given to you by the God Child - - - for - - - it is most certainly insulting to one of your royal and imperial statue - - -

Look - - -

Please look - - -

This - - - This Fan - - - will be - - - most assuredly - - - more to your liking - - -

Look - - -

See? See how it shimmers - - - - See how it glows - - -

Look - - -

See the glow?

See the shimmer?

See how it moves?

Watch it move - - - Daughter of the Clouds - - -

As - - -

Soyala's eyes began to glaze over - - - with - - - the hypnotic suggestion of vibrantly dancing colors - - - Tona-teootl's voice became slower - - - more - - - rhythmic - - - more - - - mechanical - - - more - - - hypnotic - - - even as Soyala struggled to remember - - - seven gifts - - - six golems - - - what was the seventh gift?

Slower - - - rhythmical - - -

Until - - -

"Mistress – would you like for me to serve you now?"

A - - - voice - - - a - - - small voice - - - a - - - God Child's voice - - - broke the spell which had held sway over Soyala - - - "Mistress?" - - -

Soyala - - - started - - - swooning her way to consciousness - - - as - - - Tona-teootl's flying foot sent a God Child tumbling down the stairs: "Fool! Insolent Fool!! Impetuous Fool!!!"

Tiny insolent fool - - - How dare you?! I'll fillet you and serve you as an appetizer!!!

As the God Child scrambled for the safety of the shadows - - - other God Children appeared from the self-same shadows - - - struggling to man-handle - - - golden serving platters - - - heaped high with mounds of steaming meat.

Four God Children - - - to a platter - - - struggling to maintain their balance - - - struggling to climb the stairs to the royal thrones - - - placing platters upon serving tables set before Tona-teootl and Soyala - - - serving platters before the God Emperor and his surrogate Empress - - -

No more - - - tasteless woody roots - - - or - - - jaw breaking acorns - - -

But MEAT!!!

Tender - - - succulent - - - sweet - - - juicy - - - MEAT!!!

But - - - as Soyala wondered - - - "Why were the guests not being served?"

Where - - - were - - - the banquet guests???

Were they not here just a moment or so ago???

Filled with a growing horror - - - Soyala looked up - - - at the Sixth Stone God - - - straining to make out the object he was holding in his hand - - -

Difficult to see - - - difficult to understand - - - certainly not round like an acorn - - - but - - - more elongated like an ear of corn - - - but - - - not an ear of corn - - - not tapered at the ends - - -

Eyes straining - - - mind racing - - - Soyala struggled to accept the obvious - - -

A - - - Bone - - - a glistening white bone - - -

!!! A HUMAN THIGH BONE !!!

Tona-teootl intended for his gift to the next race of humans to been that of human flesh!!!

As a wave horror of horror washed over Soyala's being - - - she fought all impulse to show her feelings - - - striving to hide all emotion - - - as she looked at the plates of steaming meats - - - upon which Tona-teootl was now gorging himself - - -

Steamed - - - slow cooked - - - juicy meats - - -

Steamed sweet meats - - - freshly slaughtered and served piping hot - - -

As - - -

The Dancers Danced - - - and - - - the Singers Sang - - -

Tona-teootl - - - full of food and mirth - - - turned to Soyala - - -

Ah - - -

Daughter of the Clouds - - -

I see that you are not eating - - - come - - - eat - - - for you will need your strength - - -

With these words and a wave of his hand - - - his royal guard - - - lead the last surviving banquet guest before Tona-teootl - - - forcing him to kneel - - -

See?

Am I not brilliant?

Am I not divinely brilliant??

Where the God/desses of old - - - wrought their craft through sheer brute force - - - I - - - who am much more cunning - - - will cause this race of humans to be the vehicle of their own destruction - - - raising the next race of humans in their stead - - -

Raising the next race of humans - - - so that - - - they may raise me to godhood - - -

Yes - - - to godhood - - - for - - - to godhood - - - I must be raised - - - so that - - - all may worship me.

As Soyala begged Tona-teootl to give her pause before she resumed her dinner - - - Tona-teootl motioned to the guards - - - standing before him - - -

Then - - - dear Daughter of the Clouds - - - you must give me leave to enjoy my desert - - - for the meal was heavy - - - and - - - a lighter repast will help the meal to set better - - -

With a nod of his head - - - one of the massive guards - - - with one swing of his obsidian axe - - - sliced off the top of the head of the last banquet guest - - - so that Tona-teootl could scoop out his still warm brains - - - which he did so with great relish - - -

Yes - - -

Yes - - - Divine Inspiration - - - for - - - I divined it myself - - - and - - - since I am a god - - - it is - - - indeed - - - divine inspiration!!!

Yes - - -

First - - - I will instruct the humans to eat - - - all that walks or crawls - - - so that no animal flesh remains - - - not even that of the tiniest insect - - -

Then - - -

I will then instruct the humans to partake of their lesser neighbors - - - for - - - we already spread their lard upon our breads - - - do we not? Therefore - - - is it not logical that we enjoy the sweetest of all earthly flesh - - - that of the humans?

As - - - Tona-teootl stared most intently at Soyala for an answer - - -

The Toad Man spoke: "Yes - - - a - - - most divine plan - - - my Lord Tona-teootl - - - most divinely genius - - - most - - - eminently genius - - -

Soyala - - - listening - - - looking - - - watching - - -

Listening to the twisted logic - - -

Looking upon the god-mask - - - hiding not only a twisted mass of human flesh - - - but - - - also obscuring as twisted a mind - - - she - - - began - - - fanning herself - - - with the small fan given to her by the God Child - - - her mind racing - - - her mind plotting - - -

Fanning herself - - - with the small - - - decorative - - - fan - - - handed to her by the God Child - - - a decorative fan - - - delicately painted with a small - - - but - - - most loyal and comforting figure - - - that of Gho'a - - -

Gho'a - - - faithful companion - - - faithful and tenacious - - - for - - - this was not a fan - - - but - - - her Tessen - - - given to her as a gift by Burilgi in the palace gardens in what seems to have been many a lifetime ago.

Fanning herself - - - as - - - her foot - - - moving - - - betraying her impulse to flee - - - bumped into something - - - something leaning against the side of her chair - - - something - - - metallic - - - a metal serving platter - - - still running red with the meat juices of the feast - - - left behind by the God Child - - -

At that very moment - - - a troop of massive guards appeared from the shadows - - - two subduing and binding the Toad Man - - - and - - - four - - - subduing and binding Soyala - - -

Binding queenly wrists to a prison throne - - - they waited - - - until - - - Tona-teootl - - - with but a slight nod of his head - - - ordered them to move back into the shadows - - -

Soyala - - - queenly wrists bound tightly to the prison throne - - - struggled briefly - - - before remaining motionless - - - apparently accepting her fate - - -

The Toad Man - - - a - - - bound bundle on the floor - - - squirmed like some great legless insect - - - helpless - - -

Tona-teootl - - - flush with triumph - - - leaned over the helpless Soyala - - - gloating - - - basking in his Godhood - - - drooling - - -

"So - - - Daughter of the Clouds - - - you have finally met your maker - - - for - - - I - - - The Creator - - - who have made all things - - - can - - - also - - - unmake all things - - -

With these words - - - Tona-teootl motioned - - - and - - - two albino guards - - - with raven black wigs - - - moved from the shadows carrying a golden bundle - - -

Soyala's eyes widened in horror - - -

!!!KAJIKA!!!

&& LAYING OF THE SKIN &&

"Yes - - -

"Yes - - - Daughter of the Clouds - - -

"Now your will see my finest creation! Make him ready!!!

"Move him - - - HERE - - - where his sister will be better able to see."

"Yes - - - better able to see - - - and - - - enjoy - - - my godhood."

Three huge albinos moved forward - - - two standing behind the Stone Statue - - - leaning it backwards to grasp it by its shoulders - - - while a third - - - lifted at the feet - - -

Calloused hands - - - rubbed raw at the oars - - - and - - - then - - - healed again - - - gripped the slippery stone with an iron grip - - -

Pure White Albino Skin stood stark in contrast to the Forest Green of the stone - - - as - - - with - - - neither a thought nor an effort thought - - - the three giants set the stone - - - not too gently - - - before Soyala - - -

Tona-teootl once again leaned forward - - - lips blowing wet puffs of words into Soyala's ear: "Daughter of the Clouds - - - you should feel privileged - - - for - - - you are about to witness a Demi-God being born."

With that Tona-teootl motioned to yet another albino to unroll the still wet skin of Kajika - - -

Still wet skin - - - hands - - - feet - - - head - - - still grotesquely attached - - - to press it tightly into the deep contours of the moss green stone - - -

Then - - -

With - - - smiles - - - and - - - powders - - - and - - - incantations - - - Tona-teootl fastened the flayed skin of Kajika to the stone - - -

Molding the still wet skin - - - to the polished stone - - -

331

Fastening the still wet skin - - - to the polished stone - - -

Wet Skin - - - God Skin - - - Royal Robe to a Demi-God - - -

Toothed Troodon Clasps - - - fastening the still wet skin - - - to the polished stone - - -

Toothed Troodon Skulls - - - biting deeply into the human skin - - - feasting on the still warm blood - - -

Blood - - -

Blood - - - coursing through the stone - - - skin and stone melding - - - into one - - -

Blood - - - feeding and nourishing the stone - - - spirit and stone melding - - - into one - - -

Stone - - - twisting and bending the gentle spirit trapped within it - - - transforming it into the very antithesis of its very being - - -

Skin upon Stone - - - tight - - - taught - - -

Spirit within Stone - - - twisted - - - trapped - - -

Even as the skin was being laid upon the stone - - - Soyala - - - eyes wide with horror - - - saw a flicker of light in Kajika's eyes - - - pleading - - - mouthing words which Tona-teootl could not hear: "Tear the Troodon Teeth from my skin - - - dear sister - - - Tear the Darkness from my spirit" - - - dead eyes motioning - - - motioning - - - pointing - - - downward - - - ever - - - downward - - - toward the terrible toothed clasps - - -

As the green stone began to glow - - - as the hunter's spirit was infused into the stone - - - Soyala could see - - - almost as if in a vision - - - an image - - - an image of a great cinnamon pelt being laid upon a great table piled high with furs - - - furs - - - wantonly stripped from the still living bodies of great beasts - - - furs - - - for the vain - - - and - - - pompous - - - and - - - decadent lords and ladies of the land - - -

Then - - -

The last flicker of light disappeared from Kajika's eyes - - -

The last flicker of fight disappeared from Kajika's eyes - - -

As the living eyes went dead - - - the - - - Golem - - - moved - - - took a step - - - and - - - smiled.

&& THE TESSEN &&

Soyala - - - apparently resigned to the fate which had befallen her - - -

Had - - - remained silent - - -

Had - - - remained motionless - - -

Had - - - remained resolved - - -

Shield Maiden - - - wrists bound cruelly to the arms of her royal throne - - -

Silent and Stoic Shield Maiden - - - sleeves of her robe - - - flowing over her wrists - - - hiding the cruel cuts to her wrists - - - hiding the quiet cuts through her bonds - - -

Silent - - - stoic - - - resolved - - -

Slicing through her bonds with the fan handed to her by the God Child - - - slicing through her bonds not with a simple fan of paper and wood - - - but - - - with sharpened bronze - - -

Bonze as razor sharp as Gho'a's teeth - - - for - - - it was she who Soyala had painted on the Tessen given to her by Burilgi that day - - - long ago - - - in the garden palace - - - for - - - who better to protect than the innocent Gho'a - - - what better to protect than an innocent fan?

Unseen - - - unheard - - - unnoticed - - -

Even as Kajika's screams sliced through the air - - - the tessen sliced through the cords that bound the Shield Maiden - - -

Agonizingly Sharp Screams - - -

Agonizingly Slow and Shallow Cuts - - -

Slow - - - Steady - - - Slicing - - - through hemp - - -

Slow - - - Steady - - - Slicing - - - through flesh - - -

Until - - -

!!! FREE !!!

Delicate Death - - -

      Delicious Death - - -

        Delightful Death - - -

Silent Death - - - Waiting - - -

Stealthy Death - - - grasped firmly in the Shield Maiden's hand - - -

Waiting - - - waiting - - - waiting - - -

Tona-teootl - - - impatient - - - released the Golems to the safety of the shadows - - -

As - - -

He - - - The Creator of Demi-Gods - - - Impatiently - - - Greedily - - - Gropingly - - -

Lunged for the leather bundle which had once been Kajika - - -

Still - - -

      Soyala waited - - - blood oozing from her wrist - - -

Still - - -

      The Shield Maiden waited - - - blood running down her fingers - - -

Still - - -

The Eighth Sister of The Pleiades waited - - - blood dripping from her fingertips - - -

The Shield Maiden waited - - - firmly grasping the tessen - - - as - - - her life's blood quietly dripped - - - drop upon drop - - - upon the floor - - -

Waiting - - - Oh - - - So patiently waiting - - -

Until - - -

       Blood - - -

          Dripping - - -

            Dropping - - -

              Pooling - - -

       Until - - -

          Drip - - -

            Drip - - -

              Drop - -

!!! SPLAT !!!

One last drop of blood - - - splattering into the crimson pool on the floor - - -

One last drop of blood - - - echoing through the chambers of the vast Throne Room - - -

Tona-teootl - - - Looked - - - Stared - - - and - - - Lunged - - -

But - - -

A moment - - -

       A - - - Slender Moment - - -

A - - - Thread of a Moment - - -

A - - - Wisp of a Moment - - -

Lips upon Lips - - -

Breath upon Breath - - -

Body bent over - - - hands clenched upon wrists - - - close - - - intimately close - - - watching the full rosy lips of Tona-teootl screaming words - - -

A - - - Moment - - - A - - - Slender Moment was all that the Shield Maiden needed - - -

The Tessen slashed across Tona-teootl's arm - - - cutting it off at the elbow - - -

Blood Showering in a Baptismal Fire of Redemption - - -

As - - - Tona-teootl reeled back in agony - - - Soyala slashed through robe and rope - - - freeing her other hand - - -

!!! FREE !!!

Soyala stood - - - facing her enemy - - - tearing the last remnants of cords from her wrists - - -

Finally - - -

On equal ground - - - all - - - pretenses - - - cast violently aside - - - all - - - protocol - - - abandoned - - - left for fools and saints - - -

Naked Truth - - -

Naked Truth - - - Frozen in Time - - -

Naked Truth - - - Frozen in Place - - -

Naked Truth Staring at its own mirror reflection - - -

Staring - - -

Searching - - -

Scrutinizing - - -

Two - - -

Mirror Reflections - - -

Searching - - -

Scrutinizing - - -

Seeking - - -

Two Reflections of each other - - -

Searching - - -

Scrutinizing - - -

Seeking - - -

Much as a child lost - - - might search for life's meaning - - - in the frozen reflection of a looking glass - - - searching for meaning - - - scrutinizing movement and motive - - -

Reflections of a Looking Glass - - -

Naked Truth - - -

Mirrored Reflection - - -

Truth behind the Mirror - - -

Blinding Flash!!!

As had Jaguar Claw before her - - - Soyala slashed flesh from living bone - - - as - - - Mighty Albinos - - - alabaster skin flecked with blood and gore - - - showered in their own baptismal blood - - -

Still - - - Tona-teootl remained - - - standing - - -

Thrusting the raw bloody stump of what had been once his arm - - - deep into the burning incense - - - that very same burning incense - - - which had first breathed life into the Golems - - - Tona-teootl - - - buried the raw stump of his arm - - - ever deeper into the brazier - - - cauterizing the wound - - - burning pain from his mind - - -

As - - - a massive albino - - - lumbered toward Soyala - - - massive club in hand - - - Tona-teootl raised his arm - - - hurling forth flame and rage - - - blistering his alabaster skin to a soft gray soot - - -

"No - - - She is MINE!"

Then - - -

Tona-teootl spoke:

"Daughter of the Clouds - - - your time has come - - - your race is already extinct - - - except for you - - -

"Your Time has come - - -

"You belong to me!

As Tona-teootl raised his hand - - - Soyala - - - reeling - - - saw a shape rush past her - - - thrusting itself between Tona-teootl and herself - - -

"Demon - - -

"Demon God - - - or - - - Demon Spawn - - - I know not which - - - but - - - you will not have her!

"Away - - - Demon - - -

"No harm will come to her - - -

"I will not see harm come to her - - - this I swear!

"Really? - - - Said Tona-teootl - - -

"As you wish - - - you will not see harm come to her - - -

Then - - -

With - - - but a flick of his wrist - - - Tona-teootl slashed The Toad Man across his one good eye - - - blinding him - - -

As - - - The Toad Man sank quivering to his knees - - - bound hands before unseeing eyes - - - Soyala sprang toward Tona-teootl - - - "I will bare your face - - - I will bare your ugliness - - - before - - - I cut your misshapen head from your body!"

&& Mask Changing &&

(The Changing of Masks)

(One after the other in Rapid Succession)

"Bare my Face?

"Is that all that you wish?

"If it is but my mask - - - you want - - - then take it - - -

"Here - - - Here - - - Take it - - - Daughter of the Clouds."

With these words - - - Tona-teootl - - - ripped of his heavy bronze mask - - - flinging it fiercely at Soyala - - - only - - - for it to imbed itself deeply into one of the God Statues - - -

"My Mask - - - Daughter of the Clouds - - - You have my Mask - - - Anything else?"

Soyala - - - startled at the face she saw - - - hideous - - - burnt - - - red and scarred - - -

Hideous - - - burned and scarred - - - not human - - - not - - - even remotely human - - -

Burned and scarred - - - not human - - - but - - - only a mask - - - a - - - silken mask - - - hidden beneath the first - - -

339

"Here I am - - - Daughter of the Clouds - - - Here I am" - - - taunted Tona-teootl - - - as - - - man and woman circled each other - - - Soyala - - - feinting - - - Tona-teootl dancing and dogging the razor sharp tessen - - -

"Recognize me? For - - - I am the Creator - - - The Creator - - - S/HE who existed before the beginning of time - - -

With these words - - - Tona-teootl - - - danced and taunted - - - twisting and turning his way throughout the throne room - - - dancing between pillar and post - - - springing upon table - - - swinging from rope and beam - - - dancing - - - always - - - always - - - naught but a hair's breath away from Soyala and her vengeance - - -

"Come here - - - you - - - monkey - - - come here! Cried Soyala - - - half in frustration - - - half in vexation - - - but - - - always moving forward - - -

Then - - -

Then - - - began the Mask Changing - - -

Tona-teootl changing masks - - - as quickly - - - as - - - a wanton woman - - - or - - - a - - - pompous prince - - - might - - - change friends or clothes - - - at a moment's whim - - -

Taunting - - -

 Daring - - -

  Dancing - - -

   Dodging - - -

Dodging - - -

 Twisting - - -

  Turning - - -

   Tumbling - - -

With each twist and turn - - - his back to Soyala - - - he bore a new mask - - -

One mask after the other - - - each one - - - more fantastic than the one before - - -

Masks - - -

Bold - - - Bright - - - Beautiful - - -

Timid - - - Terrible - - - Tortuous - - -

Sleepy - - - Serene - - - Surreal - - -

Masks - - -

Majestic Mountains - - -

Clashing Clouds - - -

Weltering Waters - - -

Masks - - -

Roaring Rivers - - -

Showering Streams - - -

Babbling Brooks - - -

Masks - - - of - - - The Creator Gods - - -

Ometeotl

The Creator - - - God/dess of Duality - - - Both male and female - - -

Tezcatlipoca

God of God of Judgment - - - Night - - - Deceit - - - Sorcery and Earth

Quetzalcoatl

God of Light - - - Mercy and Wind

Tlaloc

God of Rain & Fertility

Chalchiuhtlicue

Goddess of Lakes - - - Rivers and Oceans

Nanauatzin

God of Humility

Masks of the Created - - - Bird - - - and - - - Beast - - - and - - - Barrow - - -

Masks of the Fantastic - - - Wind - - - and - - - Waves - - - and - - - Whirlpools - - -

Masks of the Familiar - - - Bird - - - and - - - Butterfly - - - and - - - Blossom - - -

Masks of gods & creations - - - and - - - Masks of nightmares & desolations - - -

Masks - - -

"Ah - - - Daughter of the Clouds - - - do you not recognize me?

With these words - - - Creator Suns were stripped away - - - and - - - in their place - - - a - - - boy - - - a - - - young boy - - - a - - - prince - - -

JAGUAR CLAW

Soyala swore under her breath - - - "Jaguar Claw" - - - Grandfather - - - Tona-teootl is goading me - - - taunting me - - - with - - - his victims - - - but - - - I'll not listen - - -

Dancing - - - turning - - - twisting - - - always - - - just out of reach of the slashing blade - - -

Impervious - - -

Invulnerable - - -

Invincible - - -

Then - - -

Another - - -

ORCHID BLOSSOM

Orchid Blossom - - - Tears Streaming down her Silken Face - - -

Eyes thrust wide open with horror - - -

Mouth agape - - -

Her dead face staring back at her - - - Soyala's Fiery Heart - - - suddenly - - - froze into a block of ice - - -

Ice - - - Icen Dam - - - Blood Stopped - - - Blocked - - -

Heart Beats - - - Pounding in her ears - - -

Heart - - - Exploding!!!

Icen Dam broken - - - blood - - - flowing - - - gushing - - - surging - - -

Tessen Slashing - - - Tearing away at priestly robes - - - until only naked skin remained - - -

Until - - -

Tona-teootl - - - dancing - - - prancing - - -

Then - - -

The Golems - - -

       He who once was The Poet - - -

       He who once was The Builder - - -

       He who once was The Warrior - - -

        He who once was The Minstrel - - -

       She who once was The Handmaiden - - -

       And - - -

!!! KAJIKA !!!

The words tore loose from Soyala's throat - - -

Full throaty words - - - raw and bloody - - - burning for vengeance - - -

Then - - -

Tona-teootl removed the last mask - - - the - - - mask of the hunter - - - laying bare his being - - - no more reflections - - - no more mirrors - - - but - - - only self - - -

Soyala - - -

       Tessen Clenched in her knotted fist - - -

       Grasping the Bronzen Shield - - - left behind by the God Child - - -

       Screaming Vengeance - - - Rushed forward - - - for the death blow - - -

As - - -

Tona-teootl - - - back turned toward Soyala - - - turned toward her - - - facing her - - -

Face - - - to - - - Face - - -

Shield Maiden and Creator God - - -

Face - - - to - - - Face - - -

&& Xochiquetzal &&

Xochiquetzal - - -

   Xochiquetzal - - - Sister of Tona-teootl - - -

   Xochiquetzal - - - Blood Sister of Kajika - - -

Xochiquetzal - - -

  Face behind the Veil - - -

    Face emblazoned with a Hummingbird Tattoo - - -

  Limb Slashed from Living Body - -

    Bloody stump cauterized with fiery powder - - -

Xochiquetzal - - -

Even as Soyala stared at the lithe - - - full fleshed woman's form - - - before her - - - Shorty's Words echoed in her mind - - -

    What sort of being is she?

Shorty's Words - - - truer than ever - - -

"What sort of being is she?

"For - - -

"Even though she bears the namesake of a Goddess - - -

"There are two sides - - - two faces - - - to this deity - - -

"Which of the two is she?

THE NOBLE

OR

THE IGNOBLE

"Is she the noble goddess - - -

Blessed with Fertility - - - Beauty - - - and - - - Female Sexual Power - - -

"Or - - -

"Is she the ignoble goddess - - -

Cursed with Human Desire - - - Pleasure - - - and - - - Human Excesses

"Which of these two faces does she wear?

"With which face will she chose to show to us?

As Soyala stared - - - she - - - slowly lowered her hand - - -

"Xochiquetzal - - -

"But - - -

"Ah - - - Daughter of the Clouds - - - you - - - are - - - perplexed - - - are you not?

"You - - - are - - - confused - - - are you not?

"You are - - - perplexed - - - and - - - confused - - -

"Yes - - - I can see that - - -

"But - - -

"This is not - - - unexpected - - - is it not?

"For - - -

One the one hand - - - you know who I am - - -

"But - - -

"On the other hand - - - you do not know who you are - - -

"Yes - - - I can understand your confusion - - - my dear Soyala - - -

"Yes - - -

"Yes - - - You are perplexed and confused - - -

"For - - -

"You understand who I am - - - just - - - as little as you understand who you are - - -

"Who are you - - - Daughter of the Clouds - - - Who are you?

"I know who I am - - - Murderess - - - hissed Soyala - - -

"I know who I am - - -

"Ah - - - but you don't - - -

"For - - -

"If you did - - - you would embrace me - - - Sister!

"Sister" - - - mocked Soyala - - -

"Embrace you? I will kill you and feed your rotting corpse to the worms for a most royal feast
- - -

"Worms?

"Wouldn't you rather feed your curiosity - - - before - - - feeding the worms?

"Don't you yearn to know - - - who - - - I am - - - who - - - you are?

"Don't you thirst to know - - - how - - - I killed my brother - - - and - - - my mother - - - finding
both in an incestuous embrace???

"Don't you want to know each exquisite moment of their deaths - - -

For - - -

They did not greet death swiftly - - - oh - - - no - - - they embraced death - - - slowly - - - oh
- - - so very slowly - - -

"Don't you lust to know - - - how - - - each - - - betrayed me - - - one - - - as a mother - - - one
- - - as a brother - - - how - - - both - - - forsake me - - - to live not as mother and brother - - -
but - - - as loving husband and wife?

"You too were born of brother and sister - - - Daughter of the Mists - - - were you not?

"Are we - - - therefore - - - not both sisters born of incest?

"You - - - born of brother and sister - - - and - - - I - - - born of mother and brother - - -

"Come - - - Sister - - - let us embrace - - -

"Let us embrace at last - - -

&& Ashes to Ashes &&

Soyala - - - mesmerized - - - hypnotized - - - motionless - - -

Tessen - - - hanging limply at her side - - -

Bronzen Shield - - - clasped tightly to her chest - - -

Whether her mind was still absorbing all that had been said - - - or - - - whether her mind had been numbed and drugged by Xochiquetzal's words - - - we cannot know - - -

Soyala - - -

Unmoving - - -

Unspeaking - - -

Unfeeling - - -

Motionless - - - standing - - - obediently silent - - - as if a stone statue - - - waiting to be awakened to life - - - or - - - dispatched speedily to death - - -

Standing - - -

Waiting - - -

Silent - - -

Silent and Motionless - - - as if - - - she too - - - were - - - one of the golems - - - crafted not of carved and polished stone - - - but - - - of woman-flesh - - -

Waiting - - -

"Now - - - Daughter of the Clouds - - - You are MINE!

As - - -

349

Xochiquetzal raised her arms - - - one - - - of human flesh - - - and - - - the other - - - grown full formed - - - of - - - golem stone - - - she smiled - - -

She smiled - - - bringing forth fire and flame - - - from - - - painted fingertips - - -

Soyala - - -

Stunned - - - Silent - - -

Moved - - -

Moved - - - but - - - a fraction of a movement - - -

Moving ever so slightly - - - as - - - she raised her shield to deflect Xochiquetzal's flaming death - - -

Again - - -

Xochiquetzal shot forth flaming death - - - and - - - again the Shield Maiden with force of will and desperation - - - blocked the flame - - -

Soyala - - - staggering - - - desperately fought to raise her shield for a third time - - -

Raising her shield for a third time - - - Soyala succeeded in deflecting Xochiquetzal's attack for but moments - - - before - - - her shield was torn forcibly from her hand - - -

As - - -

Soyala stood defenseless - - - defiant - - - an evil gleam danced in Xochiquetzal's eyes - - -

"You cannot save yourself - - - Daughter of the Clouds - - - let alone save your people - - -

Die - - - Daughter of the Clouds - - - Die - -

As - - -

Xochiquetzal raised her arms for a forth time - - - Soyala raised her head - - - staring defiantly - - - expecting her doom - - -

&& Charm of Hummingbirds &&

The Throne Room exploded into a shower of blazing corpuscles of human flesh - - -

Globules of human fat - - - exploded in their fury - - - spraying the Throne Room with white hot balls of fire - - - splattering into walls - - - and - - - columns - - - and - - - ceiling - - -

The Great Obsidian Throne - - - showered - - - with - - - miniature balls of fire - - - began to crackle - - - and - - - crack - - -

Exploding into a thousand shards - - - as - - - captured spirits - - - frozen in time - - - and - - - space - - - and - - - rock - - - streamed skyward - - - seeking their long lost freedom - - -

Flowing forth from the shattered rock - - - even as - - - a fiery red hummingbird - - - tore itself loose from Xochiquetzal's Cheek - - - ranging free once again - - -

Spirits - - - reincarnated as a charm of hummingbirds - - - streamed forth from the throne room - - - streaming forth - - - through - - - crack - - - crevice - - - and - - - cranny - - - to regain a life above the clouds - - -

Soyala - - - still standing - - - for - - - it was not she who had been struck by god fire - - - but - - - the shattered corpses of alabaster albinos - - - rushing forward for one last desperate attack - - - incinerated into ghostly white ash - - -

Xochiquetzal's rage and fury blocked by a shield - - - a - - - bronzen shield - - - emblazoned with the Sign of the Pleiades - - -

Sign of the Pleiades - - -

Shield of the Bronzen Maid - - -

Golden Bronze blunting the rage and fury of Xochiquetzal - - - reflecting - - - god fire onto the charred corpses of alabaster albinos - - - incinerating all to a ghostly white ash - - -

Ghostly White Ash - - - raining down upon the throne room - - - down upon Soyala - - - making her seem as if she were a ghost of herself - - - come to life - - - raining down upon a diminutive god child - - - god child holding the Shield of the Bronze Maiden before his mistress - - -

God Child - - - tall and strong - - - waist high to Soyala - - -

God Child - - - unwavering - - - fearless - - - tearing off his golden wig - - -

!!! SHORTY !!!

Once again Xochiquetzal raised her arm to cast forth god fire - - - as - - - a Fiery Red Hummingbird - - - dived - - - to strike her in her bloody eye - - -

As a massive thigh bone - - - torn from Tona-teootl - - - The Sixth God of Creation - - - fell from the ceiling - - - Shorty - - - raised his shield over his head - - - even as it crushed him to the floor - - -

For a fifth time - - - Xochiquetzal - - - raised her arm to summon forth god fire - - - to strike her enemy - - - the last of the cloud people - - -

Xochiquetzal - - -

       Hurling forth flame and venom - - -

Soyala - - -

       Standing upon her own funeral pyre - - -

As - - -

Soyala crumbled to ash - - -

&& HOMAGE &&

Even as that which once was Soyala - - - crumbled to ash - - -

A hummingbird - - -

A fiery red hummingbird - - - hovered above her - - -

Honoring Her - - -

Thanking Her - - -

Paying Homage to Her - - -

As - - -

He rallied the fleeing spirits of the Cloud People - - -

Leading them up into the clear blue sky - - -

Shepherding them back to their ancestral home high above the clouds - - -

He - - - turned and paused - - - pausing briefly - - - as if to say goodbye - - - before continuing his journey - - -

Blithe Spirits - - - streaming toward their ancestral home among the rugged mountain peaks high above the clouds - - -

&& Flotsam and Jetsam &&

Even as the flaming barge played out her final moments - - - and - - - even as the last of the Beauteous Blackamoors had sunk deep beneath the waves of this ancient glacial sea - - - a lone form - - - could be seen - - - clinging to a piece of wreckage - - -

A - - -

Lone Form - - -

Clinging - - -

Then - - -

Clambering - - -

Clinging to a scorched and seared wooden timber - - -

Clambering astride a smoking and smoldering wooden timber - - -

A - - -

Lone Form - - -

Painfully pulling itself atop a still smoldering wooden timber - - -

Laying gasping upon the charred remains of golden godhood - - -

Charred Timber - - -

Smoldering - - -

Scorched - - -

Shattered - - -

Rocking and cradling the tiny exhausted form laying curled up within its arms - - -

Lone Form - - -

Reaching - - -

Stretching - - -

Straining - - -

As - - -

The Tiny Form - - - pulled a large floating wicker basket up alongside himself - - -

Untying a cord from his wrist - - -

Tying it fast to the ancient floating timber - - -

He tore loose a splintered piece of golden godhood - - - and - - - began to paddle wearily toward shore - - -

Lone Diminutive Form - - -

    Golden Basket in Tow - - - glistening in the early morning sun - - -

      Silver Streaked Sweat - - - glistening in the early morning sun - - -

        Clear Crystal Tears - - - glistening on his moistened cheeks - - -

Stout Heart Swelling - - - Above Waves and Sea and Heartbreak - - -

Shorty - - -

    Loving devout Shorty - - -

      Stout of Heart Shorty - - -

        Fearless and Unwavering Shorty - - -

As - - -

Shorty - - -

Slowly paddled his way toward shore - - -

He was joined by ancient friends - - -

    Released from servitude - - -

      Reincarnated - - - as - - - hummingbirds and butterflies - - -

        Rejoicing - - - in - - - their redemption and salvation - - -

Streaming from Shore - - -

Charms of Hummingbirds - - -

Kaleidoscopes of Butterflies - - -

Ancient Friends - - -

Embracing the brave Shorty - - -

Shorty - - -

Lovingly cradled in the arms of the great and loving god Nanauatl - - -

Steadfastly paddled his way toward shore - - - Golden Wicker Basket - - - in tow - - -

Golden Basket - - -

Golden Cradle - - -

Gently Rocking a Maiden most noble to sleep - - -

Noble Maiden - - -

Emblazoned on a Shield of Bronze - - -

Maiden most Noble - - -

Bronze Tessen resting quietly in her lap - - -

Faithful Gho'a resting contently at her side - - -

& Epilogue &

Brown - - - browns - - - dusty browns - - -

Withered and torn like the pages of some old great book - - -

Parchment yellows - - - and - - - oily oranges - - -

Sheepskins laid flat - - - stretched taut beneath two great ancient candles - - -

Ancient Candles - - -

Waxing and waning warriors - - -

Fending off cold - - - and - - - darkness - - - and - - - the heavy burden of too much fellowship - - -

Thoughts - - -

      Thoughts - - -

           Random thoughts - - -

Dripping randomly onto the parchment - - - much as drops of yellow candle wax might randomly drip - - - drop-upon-drop - - - upon some great empty yellowed tabletop - - -

Dripping - - -

357

Dripping - - -

Silently dripping - - -

Drop upon drop - - -

Thought upon thought - - -

Swirl upon swirl - - -

Swirls - - -

Coy delicate swirls mercilessly teasing long bold flourishes from the red and blue inks - - - and - - - the candle wax - - -

Until - - -

The ancient yellow parchment - - - heavy - - - with - - - ink - - - and - - - pigments - - - and - - - candle wax - - - softly slips to the floor - - - to bury itself snugly beneath some great cozy comforter of orange and red bird feathers - - - to - - - sleep soundly throughout the long and countless cold winter nights - - -

&&& Glossary &&&

First Stanza:

PLIGHT: to put or give in pledge: ENGAGE *<plight* his troth>

Second Stanza:

BALE: great evil

BANE: death – destruction

Third Stanza:

BRAZIER: 14th Century - One who works in brass - - -

Technically speaking - the correct term would have been "Brownsmith" (one who works in bronze) rather than "Brazier" (one who works in brass).

Note: Although – both – brass and bronze - are an alloy of copper – brass is soft – whereas - bronze is hard – and – can be used for swords and bells.

Brass: 60% Copper & 40% Zinc

Bronze: 80% Copper & 20% Tin

Reference to Powdered Tin (Alloy): An allegorical allusion to the classical confrontations of proponents of a belief with non-believers – e.g. the Pleiadel design of the shield maiden's shield was "etched" by:

Divine Means: The power of the Pleiadel Light itself.

Mechanical Means: The "scratching" through one layer of metal to another.

Thermo-Chemical Means: A thermal diffusion of alloys – by which a powder of the stannum-group (tin) was applied to the surface of the bronze shield and then heated causing the elements of this alloy to permeate the body of the sword – causing - the powder-covered area to become white while the rest of the shield remained bronze yellow.

Forth Stanza:

SKALD: 1780; an ancient Scandinavian poet; broadly: bard
Often went into battle with the warriors – to record events –
Much as would a modern day combat photographer or historian

DIGHT: 13th century; Middle English
From Old English *dihtan* to arrange, compose
From Latin *dictare* to dictate, compose

HIGHT: 15th century; *archaic* : being called : named

TROTH: 12th century; loyal or pledged faithfulness
fidelity <pledged my troth> - or – plight my troth

Fifth Stanza:

SHRIGHT: Obsolete – a shriek – past participle of shriek

Sixth Stanza:

LOUR: 13th Century –
To look sullen: frown
To be or become dark, gloomy, and threatening <an overcast sky lowered over the village>

Notes of Interest: The term "smith" refers broadly to a worker of metals.

Brownsmith: Works in copper or bronze
Blacksmith: Works in iron
Brazier: Works in Brass
Goldsmith: Fabricates articles from gold
Greensmith: Works in Lead or Latten (Yellow Alloy similar to brass)
Redsmith: Works in Gold
Tinsmith: Works in Tin
Whitesmite: Works to finish/polish iron